Andie Newton is the *USA Toda
Girls from the Beach*, *The Girl from Vichy*, and *The Girl I Left Behind*. She lives in the beautiful Pacific Northwest with her family. When she's not writing gritty war stories about women, you can usually find her trail running in the desert and stopping to pet every Yellow Lab or Golden Retriever that crosses her path. Andie is actively involved with the reading and writing community on social media. You can follow her on Twitter and Instagram or check out her author page on Facebook.

> 🐦 twitter.com/AndieNewton
> f facebook.com/AndieNewtonAuthorPage
> 📷 instagram.com/andienewtonauthor
> BB bookbub.com/authors/Andie-Newton

A CHILD FOR THE REICH

ANDIE NEWTON

One More Chapter
a division of HarperCollins*Publishers* Ltd
1 London Bridge Street
London SE1 9GF
www.harpercollins.co.uk
HarperCollins Publishers
Macken House,
39/40 Mayor Street Upper,
Dublin 1
D01 C9W8

This paperback edition 2023

2

First published in Great Britain in ebook format
by HarperCollins*Publishers* 2022
Copyright © Andie Newton 2022
Andie Newton asserts the moral right to be identified
as the author of this work

A catalogue record of this book is available from the British Library

ISBN: 978-0-00-854197-2

Printed and bound in the U.S.A.
by Lake Book Manufacturing, LLC

For Matt, Zane, and Drew

Humankind will be like the mothers it has… and the Czech country already had, and has had even today, its mother heroines.
—Pavla Moudrá, 1932

Prologue

Nazi Germany, October 1944

The clock above the mantle ticked, ticked, ticked. Greta Strohm never thought this day would come. She pressed her forehead to the warm window glass in her parlor, closing her eyes, trying to calm herself and have faith in the plan by thinking about her new baby's soft and shiny blonde hair.

Greta had spent weeks preparing the nursery, needling the baby quilts herself using the finest German wool available. She had made so many, more than one child could ever use. Soft cottony jumpers had been set out only to be refolded and tucked inside vanilla-scented drawers. Paintings of traditionally dressed children dancing in meadows had been hung with the most meticulous of hands. Glass canisters of talc, sponges for the bath, and baby rattles that had arrived just that morning were placed perfectly on the shelf.

1

It was, she had told herself, a nursery to die for.

Her eyes sprung open with her chiming clock, announcing the top of the hour. She blindly adjusted her wristwatch. *They should be here.* She paced her carpets, rolling her hands nervously while thinking about all the lies she'd told, when she heard the pop and grind of tires creeping up the gravel road to her estate.

Greta yanked the curtains aside—there was no going back now. The car had parked, and she watched with anticipation as the driver opened his door. She saw the nurse's shadowy silhouette in the back seat, holding her new baby in her arms.

Greta took a moment to collect herself at the front door, padding her perspiring forehead and fanning her neck. She had a reputation to uphold, after all. She was the wife of Ludwig Strohm, a known member of the Party, and nobody should ever see her unkempt. She placed her hand on the doorknob, fingers curling, taking a deep breath through her nose before opening the door.

The nurse breezed into her home, face aglow and smiling with the baby bundled in her arms. "Frau Strohm, your new son."

Greta scooped him into her arms, breath lumped in her chest, which she wasn't prepared for, though she should have expected it. The nurse carried on talking about how she should care for him, setting down the bag she'd brought with all his baby things, but Greta didn't have any use for such talk. She kissed the baby's tiny fingers and all her nerves dissolved.

The nurse pulled a baby bottle from the bag along with

a few small towels for burping, before pulling out a book, which she placed on the side table. "We ask all our adoptive parents to follow Johanna Haarer's guide to mothering…" She reached for the baby with grabbing hands.

"I'm quite all right," Greta said, waving the nurse away. "You can leave."

The nurse seemed caught off guard with this abrupt dismissal, looking at Frau Strohm with a furrowed brow before scanning the parlor and asking about her husband, but Greta ignored her, kissing the air above her baby's face as he cooed.

The nurse's lips pursed. "Very well." She clicked her heels once and left out the front door.

Greta buried her nose into the crook of the baby's neck, breathing deeply, getting lost in the feel of his incredibly soft skin, when she felt something crackle in her hand, something tucked in with the baby.

This wasn't part of her plan, the one she had so carefully worked over and over in her mind a thousand times. The car outside had started up and was now circling the fountain to leave the estate, stirring up a plume of caramel-colored dust and rock, and although Greta couldn't be sure, she thought the nurse was staring at her, studying her through the fog.

Greta laid the baby down on the divan and unwrapped him from the blanket. He fussed once she'd completely uncovered him, throwing his chubby legs out in her parlor, stiff as boards, just as she pulled a note out from behind his back. She stared at the crumpled piece of paper in her hand, trying to ignore the sickening feeling of dread before unfolding it.

"No…" she said as she read, glancing at the nurse driving away and then to the note. "Lord, no—" Her legs gave out, and the baby wailed beside her as she collapsed to the divan.

The message was clear, distinct, and meant only for her.

I know your secret.

German Protectorate of Bohemia and Moravia, June 1944

Chapter One

I plunged my spade into the garden dirt and Ema scooted closer on her knees, dragging her bottom-heavy seed bag. The sun shone brightly for the first time in many days, and somewhere between the third hole and the last, with a honey breeze lisping through the linden trees and the sun warm on our backs, I'd slipped away into another world, thoughts and breath like sands sliding through an hourglass. I swept a lock of Ema's golden hair behind her ear as she laughed from playing with a wiggly worm.

"Did I ever tell you the story about the actress? She was from Prague," I said, and Ema shook her head, rubbing dirt from her hands. "Would you like to hear it?"

"Does it happen before *they* came?" She would never talk about the Reich in a bad light outside our home, even if we were in the garden. It was our rule.

"Oh, yes," I said. "It happens before." I patted her knee and we moved on to the next patch of dirt. I dug some more, and Ema dropped seeds as I talked. "The story starts

7

when the woman was a girl, eighteen if she was a day. All the local theaters wanted her to star in their plays. She had tawny hair that looked warm and golden in the setting sun." Ema touched her hair, picking a lock of it up and looking at the blonde color. "It was an important day for her because she was getting her photo taken by a famous photographer. She spent her morning setting her hair just so, checking her makeup, applying real lipstick," I said, and Ema's eyes twinkled. She loved the idea of lipstick.

"Was she famous?" Ema asked.

"No, but people told her she was beautiful. Very beautiful," I said, and Ema's mouth gaped open.

"What was her name?" Ema asked, but I would never tell her the truth.

"Imogene," I said, and Ema crinkled her nose. "Ema?" I said, questioning. "You want her to have the same name as you?" She nodded, and I patted her warm back, feeling the thin fabric of her dress against her skin. "Her name was Ema, and she had thick and lush eyelashes that fanned over her eyes."

"Like you, Mama," she said, and I smiled.

"Like me," I said, motioning for her to drop another seed, and I went on about the woman from Prague, who had no idea she'd meet the man of her dreams that day at the photographer's, when my sister's panicked voice cut through the air on the other side of the hill.

The spade slipped from my hand.

"Mama?" Ema called, reaching for my skirts, and in an instant, I'd been pulled back into the secrecy that had become the whole of our daily lives, not a life of stories or of lost moments in the sun, but one of dirt, warm and gritty, sticking to my skin.

"Yes, Ema?" I said, eyes closing briefly, knowing there was only one reason my sister would yell my name out in the open where all our neighbors could hear her.

"It's news about Papa, isn't it?"

Ema's eyes looked like blue glass in the sunlight, innocent, scared. "I don't know," I said, trying not to alarm her as tears spilled off my cheeks and dripped into the dirt. In a desperate attempt to turn back time and reclaim the moment, I dug another hole in the dirt, face tense, wiping the tears away with the back of my hand. "Drop the seed," I said, eyes fixed on the hole, but Ema had frozen. "Drop it, Ema," I said as my sister yelled for me again.

Ema plucked a seed from the ones she'd spilled, and reluctantly, with her little fingers shaking, planted it.

I pushed a pile of dirt over the seed with my palms.

"But, Mama," Ema said as I patted the dirt down. "Aunt Dasa…"

I looked over my shoulder to our house, at the rickety porch, its broken flower baskets and peeling paint, and savored the trailing vapor of hope that our husbands would return one day, alive. We'd heard rumors they were arrested. We'd heard rumors they escaped. Three years had passed since they joined the Resistance. Three anniversaries, three birthdays, and three summers we'd spent living on our own in occupied Bohemia.

I tapped Ema's arm for her to stand. "Come on, sweet girl," I said, and she hid behind my skirt.

"Dasa," I shouted back, bracing for what was to come,

feeling the seconds slip away, still living in a world where my husband breathed. "Over here." I knew Ema could hear the quiver in my voice, and I looked down to tell her it was all right, smoothing her hair away from her forehead, even though I knew it wasn't, and that our lives were about to change once again, for the worse. I wondered how much more we could take. The Germans had sent my father to the mines and executed him for stealing Reich coal, leaving my mother a ghost of what she used to be, spending her days in bed and praying for her own death. "Be strong," I said, but at the same time, I felt myself weaken.

Dasa ran over the hill, arms flailing, only to fiercely grip the sides of her skirt when she realized the neighbors could see her. My heart thrashed in my chest, waiting for her to come close enough to tell me the fate that had been handed down to our husbands.

I'd thought about this moment so many times, but not one of those thoughts included me and Ema in the garden. I always imagined I'd find out about my husband's death while selling vegetables in the square at our stand. Ema would be behind me, gathering carrots in a sack, when a stranger would slip me a note instead of money with my husband's last words.

It was more than most widows received.

Dasa hurried through the garden rows, shaking her head and wiping her running nose. Just when I thought she was about to tell me those fatal words, she latched onto me with both hands, gripping my sleeves. "Anna..." She hung her head, taking gulping breaths.

"Say it." *He's dead. They're dead.* I swallowed, feeling the lump in my throat, arms shaking, with my daughter tugging on my apron. I closed my eyes tightly. "Say it!" I was mad at Dasa for drawing out the pain. As if the knife that had been in my heart wasn't bad enough, now the news would be like pulling it slowly from my chest. "For God's sake—"

"I need your help," Dasa said, and my eyes popped open.

"What?" She pulled me to walk, but I yanked her back by the hand. "Dasa, tell me now. Is this about our husbands?"

She paused before shaking her head, and I doubled over in a pool of breathy moans and sobs.

"We must hurry." She tried to lead me away again.

"Dasa, wait…" My body still shook from the news that this wasn't about our husbands, and I needed a second to warm back up, breathe life back into my limbs. A hand flew to my pounding chest.

Dasa pulled the kerchief from her head and her chestnut hair fell loosely to both sides, eyes shifting, looking over my shoulder to the road and over my property. That's when I realized her children weren't with her. I grabbed her arm. "Where are your children?" Not once had I seen her outside without at least one of her three girls trailing behind her. I shook her shoulder after she didn't answer. "Dasa—"

"Safe," she said. "In the house. With the baby." She whispered the word *baby*. Another secret of ours.

People on the street had stopped to stare, some getting off their bicycles. Shutters opened from our echoing voices. "Come on," Dasa said, again pulling me to walk, and we headed up the hill, through the chamomiles that had yet to be picked, and down the other side to her derelict farm.

She grabbed my elbow when I wasn't moving fast enough, rushing me through the tangle of flowering weeds that had replaced her green pasture, when I caught a glimpse of her hands. A smear of red streaked on her skin, which she immediately tried to hide behind her back.

"Sister," I said. "What have you done?" I stood still in the weeds, covering my mouth, waiting for an answer with her eyes roving over my head to her field, unable to look at me directly.

Ema tugged on my skirt from behind, and I turned around as if nothing in the world was wrong. "Ema, darling," I said, fixing her dress collar and smoothing her hair bunches. "We're going to play a game."

Her face fell. It was something we'd practiced. A command without any questions. A secret language. *Play a game.*

"Hide and seek, all right? Go inside Aunt Dasa's house and lock the door. Your cousins are in there. Don't come outside, no matter what. Do you understand me?" She nodded. "I'll come and find you after a while."

"Your grandmother's in there too," Dasa said.

"Go, baby," I said, patting her bottom, and Ema ran off through the brown grass toward Dasa's house. I waited for her to slip inside before turning back around to my sister, who was breathing so heavily she couldn't cross her arms.

"I did what I had to do," Dasa said. "I couldn't... I wouldn't..."

"Tell me exactly what's going on or I'll—"

"The Germans came for my children," Dasa blurted, and I gasped, spinning around, looking at her farmland, her house, and the street, but nothing had changed in the last few seconds.

I grabbed her forcefully by the forearm, getting her to look at me in the eyes. "Your house? Our road? Were they in a truck?" I would have heard a truck rumble past my house to get to hers.

Dasa's eyes flitted all over the place. "It wasn't like that," she said.

"What was it like?" I demanded to know.

"There was this woman, you see? And I asked Brigita to pick a tomato for our lunch because she's the oldest, and my littlest one followed, because she always follows..." Dasa twisted her kerchief in her hands as she talked. "They're so red—so delicious—and I wanted the children to taste something delicious. I turned my back for a moment." She held up one finger, inhaling deeply after holding her breath. "One. Moment."

"Dasa, what are you saying?" I asked, but she'd withered into my arms like a dying plant. "Dasa!" I gave her a shake. "Look at me," I said, and she pointed to her crumbling barn.

"There," was all she said, and my eyes trailed to her barn and the closed door. The last time I saw that door closed was when she had cows, but it had been years since the Germans took all her livestock.

She followed me through the weeds, rubbing her hands together, turning them over and over, mumbling about how she didn't have a choice.

"Open the door, Dasa." I stood in front of the door, staring into the dark space where the door was cracked and all seemed quiet.

She put her hand on the handle, pausing. "I rang the bell frantically—" she rang an imaginary bell in the air "—and the children came running in, and I... I..."

I took a deep breath, trying to prepare myself, but there was no way a person could really prepare. "Dasa," I said, arms flat to my sides. "Open it!"

She closed her eyes briefly, then rolled open the squealing barn door.

Chapter Two

We stepped inside clutching each other. I saw her shoes first, between the long, dark shadows of me and my sister on the sunlit floor, followed by black stockings on thick legs, then the unmistakable Reich-issued skirt and apron on a motionless body.

"I think I killed her," Dasa said, and I covered my mouth, knowing that no matter how many hourglasses I could escape into, our lives *would* be changed forever, just as I thought. "She came here to steal my babies. Brigita said she asked how many brothers and sisters she had and if there were other children that looked like her on the same road."

"The rumors are true," I breathed. "The Brown Sisters…" I leaned forward, getting a better look. Her flaxen hair, once tied up in a bun, lay in a ratted knot next to her head, only slightly covering her blood-splattered ear where Dasa had clubbed her. A bee buzzed in through the open barn door and landed on her hand.

"Why us?" Dasa asked. "How'd she know to come to my farm? We've been so private."

"I don't know."

Rumors of the Reich's dreaded Brown Sisters coming for our children were like the warning at the end of a fairy tale. We weren't sure what to believe, or when to believe it, with the stories often sweeping through the village like a breeze through the trees. But regardless of the rumors, the story was always the same. The Reich wanted our Aryan-looking children to raise as their own.

Dasa let go of my hand to walk around the body, rubbing her arms as if she felt chilled, looking at the Brown Sister's half-open eyes and her drawn lips. "Anna…" she said. "What am I going to do? She's dead. Isn't she? I killed her?"

I nudged her with my toe, but I couldn't be sure. I'd never touched a dead person before. I bent down to see if she was breathing. "I think so," I said, and Dasa's entire body trembled. "Does Matka know?"

"I dragged her through the field after I…" She gulped. "Matka didn't say anything when I asked her to watch the children." She glanced out the barn door where it was still and quiet, normal, with birds flying over her field. "What if one of the neighbors saw?"

"If someone did see, we'll know soon enough," I said.

We had to be careful. From this moment on, we had to act as if we were being watched even more than we already were, as if someone did know. Secrets like this were worth a fortune. All the food we had in our cellar was at risk, our homes, what was left of our jewels, the ones the Germans didn't steal. Our bodies.

"Josef Danek," I said into the air, "look what's happened to us."

It was my husband Josef who'd talked Dasa's husband into abandoning us all in the name of the country. He thought with his heart, and in war sometimes you must think with your head. Leaving your wife and child to fend for themselves seemed like a cruel and unusual torture at times. I blamed him for our misfortune. I blamed him when only Dasa's husband visited last year for one night, leaving her another baby to remember him by. I blamed him when my father died and left us without an income. I blamed him for leaving me to wonder every single morning if he was waking up alive somewhere or had closed his eyes forever.

"What do we do, Anna?" Dasa asked, and I paced, hand to my forehead, breathing in the warming daytime air.

"The Resistance—our cousin Tomas," I said. "We can ask him for help."

"We don't know where he is," she said, though I thought we should try to find out. Tomas and his rebels hid in the Tabor Tunnels. Trying to locate one of their secret entrances would be a challenge, and risky, but if ever there was a reason to look, I thought this would be it.

Dasa whipped around. "We'll bury her, somewhere in the garden," she said, hands twisting, but I shook my head, unsure. We'd have to wait until the dead of night and there were so many hours between now and then.

"Please, Anna. Please," she said, her voice shrill. "I don't know what else to do and my children—"

I reached for her, immediately taking her in my arms and squeezing tightly. "All right. We'll bury her. Sometime around midnight."

We dragged the Brown Sister into a dampened shady spot behind the moldy hay bales to keep her hidden. The flies followed us, swarming over the body, with some landing in the dead woman's hair as we sprinkled hay over her limbs. When she was almost covered, when the last of her fingers were about to disappear under the hay, Dasa folded her arms. "Now what?"

I closed my eyes, my stomach swirling. "Pray the hours pass quickly, sister. Voices carry, and the Reich has a way of getting neighbors to talk."

We walked to Dasa's house without a word between us, watching the road, looking left and right for more Brown Sisters. The distance had never seemed so long, much longer than a barn should ever be from a house. We walked past the chicken coop to her front door, where Dasa picked up a rock that seemed out of place on the smooth dirt path.

"And then there's this," she said, pushing it at me, and I gasped. A pitted old rock covered in blood.

"Is that the…" I covered my mouth when she nodded. Chickens ruffled their feathers, clucking from hearing our voices. "Find a place for it," I said, looking to see if someone was watching.

She struggled to conceal the rock in her hands without touching the bloody wet spot. "What do we tell Matka?"

"Nothing," I said. "She'll say you've brought bad luck to your doorstep, and what if she's right? What she doesn't know won't hurt her."

"But the rock," she said, pulling away. "What do I—"

The front door flew open, and Dasa hid the rock behind her back using the folds of her skirt.

Matka squinted in the doorway. "What are you two doing?" Chickens flew out of the coop behind us, feathers tossing up in the breeze. "You roused me from my bed to care for your children, and I was doing quite fine all alone, wishing I was dead and with your father. You two look suspicious." She looked us up and down from our feet to the tops of our heads. "What have you done?"

Our mother grew up a trusting woman, but after the Third Reich marched into Prague, she thought everyone was after her, hiding something or lying to her in one way or another. She'd made of list of her German friends, lifelong friends she'd had since childhood, checking them off one by one as they turned their backs on her, until she had no friends left at all.

"We're only standing here, Matka," I said, and she squinted again. Dasa stared at her shoes with the rock still behind her back as a chicken pecked at some seed near her toe. "What do you think we're doing?"

Ema peeped out from behind Matka's skirt, thumb in her mouth. "Mama?"

I put my arms out and Ema ran toward me, giving me a kiss. "Let's get inside," I said, shooing Dasa's girls inside after they'd tried to come outside too, but Matka remained steadfast at the door, looking at us, her eyes beady.

Dasa squeezed past her, and much to my dismay, she still had the bloody rock clutched behind her back. She'd brought it into the house.

Dasa's children ran about the room in circles, playing chase, cooped up from being inside on a warm day, while Matka tried to settle them. I turned to Dasa, whispering below the children's squeals and still holding Ema in my arms. "What are you doing with that?"

"What am I supposed to do with it?"

"Not bring it inside!" I said.

"Shh!" she said, forcefully, and her children thought she was talking to them and got quiet. "You're scaring my girls." She smiled, nodding at her children as if everything was all right. "Carry on, girls."

Matka watched us from her chair, arms crossed, before finally picking up her book of fairy tales and calling the children to sit on the floor. She bent the cover all the way back, cracking the spine. "Now," she said, glancing up once to Dasa and me, clearing her throat. "Let's pick up where I left off…" She licked her finger and slowly turned the page. "The Czech maiden searched the villages for a way to trick the devil, but she only had to listen to the whispers of her heart and trust herself. She had the answers all along…"

"You need to hide that rock," I said. "It has German blood on it, and if Matka sees it—"

"Where?" Dasa cradled the rock in front of her now, careful not to touch the bloody wet spot and also trying to hide it from Matka by turning away. "I thought German blood turned black when spilled."

"You've been listening to too many of Matka's stories." I

grabbed a tea towel from the kitchen and wrapped the rock up before shoving it into a pot. "We'll bury it with her," I whispered, glancing at Matka as she read. "Hold yourself together, sister. You'll get us arrested with just one look of your face."

Dasa ran her hands over her face, drawing her cheeks down, before straightening up and quelling her blubbering lips.

"And clean your hand," I hissed, looking at the smear of blood still on her skin, and she tried rubbing it away with the tail of her apron.

"Use some water," I said.

"I can't. The pipe's busted—"

"Mama! Mama!" Ema yelped from Matka's feet, and I went to sit with her, moving her into my lap on the floor while Dasa got the baby, who'd woken up from his nap. We huddled in close on the floor, sitting around Matka as she read, listening to tales of kings and devils and maidens while a dead Brown Sister lay in the barn, and the rock Dasa used to kill her with sat in a pot in the kitchen.

I closed my eyes, now realizing we'd have to tell Matka sooner or later what happened. I felt an urgency to get rid of the body as fast as we could, but also nervousness for knowing we'd have to wait until it was dark. The flies had probably collected above her body by now like a black blanket, trying to get at her while the sun rose and warmed.

Matka stopped reading, and my eyes popped open to see her staring at me. I looked at Dasa, who I thought was thinking the same thing—we'd have to tell Matka—and then all the children turned to stare at us.

I hid my eyes in Ema's hair bunches, giving her a squeeze, waiting for Matka to start reading again.

Matka cleared her throat, cracking back the book spine. "And the maiden crept through the dark house, feeling the devil's eyes laid upon her…" she continued, before a knock at the door startled us all.

I looked once over my shoulder. "Dasa, are you expecting someone?" I asked, but she shook her head. Dasa's daughter, Brigita, jumped up to answer it, and I yanked her back by the elbow.

"Stop!" I said in a shouted whisper, and after waiting for another knock, I snapped my fingers at all the children to hide in the back bedroom. Brigita took the baby from Dasa, and they snuck down the hallway. Then it was just us three in the parlor, Matka still in her chair, while Dasa moved to peek out the curtains. I held my breath.

"Ah, thank goodness," Dasa said, lowering her head and following up with a sigh.

"Who is it?" I asked.

"It's Mr. Ott." Dasa paused as if that should have been enough. "From down the road." She reached for the door to let him in. "I asked him—"

"What are you doing?" I moved to stop her, and she pulled her hand back.

"It's Mr. Ott," she said, again. "I asked him to come by a while ago to help with my busted water pipe."

"Mr. Ott is German, Dasa," I said, and he knocked again, slow and hard.

Knock. Knock.

Matka stood up, sending the book flopping to the floor

and closing on itself. "Dirty Germans, can't trust the lot of them," she said, pointing her bony finger at the door. "Don't let him in. His wife's an evil woman. And he's no better while he's married to her. Nazis, Germans—Germans, Nazis. All the same."

"But he is different," Dasa said.

Mr. Ott and my parents were friends when we first moved to Tabor, but things changed quickly between them. My father opened a watch repair shop in the village, and when he refused to stop doing business with the Jews, the authorities sent him to the coal mines. But when he stole coal to give to his Jewish friends who were prohibited from buying their own, he was arrested, and it was rumored that Mrs. Ott was paid for the tip, which is why I couldn't believe it when Dasa said she'd asked Mr. Ott to help her with her pipes.

He knocked again, and I pulled Dasa in close, whispering, "You wondered how the Reich knew to come to *your* farm? Maybe he's why."

Dasa shook her head, eyes shifting between the door and Mr. Ott's shadow through the closed curtains, where he caught a glimpse of her through an upturned fold in the fabric.

"*Hallo*," he said with another knock, and I closed my eyes. "Do you still need me to fix your water pipe?"

"I have to answer it," Dasa said. "He knows I'm here." She straightened her apron and tightened the tie. "Be right there," she said to him.

"Something isn't right," Matka said, sneering. "I don't know what it is."

"God, Matka. When was the last time something was right?" I asked, and that seemed to quiet her. I smoothed my hair back, looking at the door, trying to appear settled and calm. "Now," I said, "answer it."

Dasa went to answer the door as Matka sat back down in her chair, her book squarely on her lap, watching, listening, studying Dasa and me.

Mr. Ott shimmied through the door with his equipment, apparently ready for a big job, when he noticed she wasn't alone. "Oh, hallo," he said, surprised.

"My sister and mother are here," Dasa said, one finger pointing briefly, and a very uncomfortable silence followed, with him and Matka locking eyes.

Matka stood up again, but this time she folded her arms. "How's your wife?" she asked through her teeth.

"Fine… fine…" he said, looking down where he'd set his tools, but the tension was unmistakable, thick and heavy with Matka unblinking.

"Matka," Dasa said, "I don't think now is the time."

"It's quite all right," he said to my sister, but then turned to Matka and addressed her by her first name, causing her mouth to hang open.

"Mrs. Novakova!" she said. "That's my name to you. My husband might be dead, but I'm still his wife."

He apologized. "What happened between you and my wife is unfortunate, but it also has nothing to do with me. I was friends with your husband. I liked him." He hung his head momentarily, and that acknowledgment seemed to be enough to satisfy my mother. At least for the time being, while he was here to help Dasa with her pipes.

Dasa flipped back the curtain under the sink to expose the broken pipe, and Mr. Ott set out his tools on the floor. He assessed the work that had to be done while I covered the day-old bread squares and gathered up the peppercorns Dasa had set on the counter for that evening's bread soup.

We quietly watched Mr. Ott as he worked, arms folded and standing close. He mumbled to himself in German, and we three exchanged glances. Being fluent in that language was another of our secrets, one we held close to our chests, like most smart Czechs.

"I'm sorry, what did you say, Mr. Ott?" I asked.

"Nothing, ma'am," he said, "I didn't want you to hear me curse, so I spoke in German. Does it bother you?"

"Not at all," I said. "We don't understand anyway." I chuckled—ignorant Czech women—and when he continued to mumble, Matka, Dasa, and I leaned in to hear every last German word he spoke.

"Fix this, husband," he said in German, apparently reliving an earlier conversation, "fix this and that"—he looked at the wrench in his hand—"not bad tools, though. Expensive." He glanced up at us, and we acted confused as if we had no idea what he said.

"Would you like a glass of milk?" Dasa asked, and after he said yes, she walked to the ice-box. "Oh," she said, grimacing, without even opening it up. "We're all out. Sorry. I just remembered." She smiled awkwardly. "You could stay for some bread soup."

"Thank you, but I can't," he said, and inside I sighed with relief. He wasn't staying, though it was customary to ask and if Dasa hadn't, it would have appeared suspicious.

He looked down the hallway as if he heard a noise while fiddling with his wrench. "Are the children home?"

"No!" Dasa yelped, then tried to look relaxed. "What I mean is…"

Matka stepped forward. "They went to visit my sister, Mr. Ott," Matka said. "In Prague."

Dasa and I looked at each other before looking at Matka. Her sister didn't live in Prague.

"Is that right?" he asked, his head now under my sister's sink where he couldn't see us.

"Yes. That is right." Matka turned around, motioning for us to move in closer, and when we did, she pointed to one of Mr. Ott's tools lying on the kitchen floor, and the inscription etched on the handle. I covered my mouth. *Mr. Bilek.* A fine man, a kind man. Owned a mechanic shop not long ago, until one day he disappeared and was replaced by a German. I was both disgusted and sad to see his name. Dasa looked visibly sick and turned toward the wall.

Mr. Ott scooted out from under the sink to test the tap. "All fixed!" He smiled, proud of himself, and began cleaning up his tools, when a burst of water erupted from the pipe, drenching his trousers. "Ack!" He dove under the sink, using a towel to stop the leak, then suddenly he reached for the pot on Dasa's counter. Before I could react, he'd pulled the rock out and handed it to Dasa, who looked like she wanted to toss it up into the air with a scream.

"There," he said, followed by some curse words he thought only he knew, wrenching on the pipe a few times and placing the pot underneath. "I got it. Keep the pot there for a few days, in case." He breathed heavily from the frantic activity.

Dasa nodded, barely able to squeak out her words. "Yes, sir," she said, eyes shifting to mine. She lost her grip on the rock and struggled to keep it covered with the tea towel. Matka rescued her, taking the rock herself.

"Yes, yes…" Matka said, glaring at me while also rushing to get Mr. Ott cleaned up and out of the house. "Well, you've been such a help. Nice to see you. Don't say hallo to your wife though, because I know she had something to do with my husband's arrest and death." She smiled, and Mr. Ott looked very confused. Matka had a way of slitting your throat and leaving you to wonder why you were bleeding. "Off you go, now." She handed him a basket with a few eggs Dasa had collected for him as payment. "Go! Go!" And just like that, she shooed Mr. Ott out of the door while holding the rock under one arm.

Matka turned around once she'd closed the door, eyes thinned into slits.

"Now," she said. "You two better tell me what's going on."

Chapter Three

Matka held the rock in her hand, patting it like a sack of flour and gripping the tea towel that covered it. "You tell her," Dasa said.

My mouth hung open, trying to figure out a good way to break the news, but there wasn't one. I took a deep breath through my nose, back straightening. "Dasa killed a woman," I said, and Dasa gasped.

"Why'd you have to say it like that?" she cried, but Matka had already stumbled backward into the door with a bang.

"Who?" Matka demanded. "And how?"

Dasa pointed to the rock. "There."

Matka immediately set the rock on the table, her eyes round as an owl's, studying Dasa's murder weapon. She flipped back the points of the tea towel, slowly uncovering the blood spot.

"She was a Brown Sister," Dasa said, and Matka closed her eyes. "She came for my children. I had to do it—"

"So, the rumors are true," Matka breathed. "We should have known as much." She held her hands to her face as if she was about to weep, but quickly ripped them away. "Where is the dirty bitch?"

Dasa and I turned to each other.

"Well?" Matka looked at the both of us, but settled on Dasa.

"You're not angry about the bad luck I've brought to our doorstep?" Dasa asked.

"I'd only be angry if someone saw you," Matka said.

"Am I going to hell?" Dasa clawed at her cheeks. "I feel like I killed a villain from one of your fairy tales, and you know what happens in those fairy tales, Matka—"

"On the contrary, my darling girl," she said. "The Reich killed your father. It's only fair we take one of theirs. Now, where's the body?"

Dasa looked relieved—she wasn't going to hell. "In the barn," she said. "I dragged her into the barn…"

As Dasa told Matka the story, I worried about what to do next. Mr. Ott, if he was the one who had informed on Dasa's children, probably had a good payment coming to him for each of their heads. He wouldn't, or at least his wife wouldn't, let that pass without an inquiry and making sure the girls really had left for their great-aunt's house.

"We're going to bury her in the garden after the children go to sleep," Dasa said. "There's a full moon tonight. We shouldn't have to use torches."

"Yes, yes," Matka said. "If the flies and heat don't get to her first." She covered the rock back up, one point of the tea

30

towel at a time. "But what about the children? If there's one Brown Sister, there's more."

"We haven't thought about that," I said. "This just happened."

"Well, you sure as hell better start thinking about it," Matka said. "The moon tonight is a sign. All things planted will grow. And when that body sprouts suspicion, you need a plan for your next steps. It's bad enough you brought the rock into this house. It is bad luck. But where you bury her is just as important."

I moaned, hands to my face. I wanted to tell Matka she was wrong, but deep down I knew she was probably right. Having a dead woman in the barn was bad enough, but bringing the bloody rock inside and passing it between us… We were all connected it to it now, whether we liked it or not.

The baby cried in the next room where the children were hiding, and I called them in. Ema seemed the most concerned, grabbing onto my skirts and holding on. I scooped her up, and she locked her legs around my waist. "Everything's all right," I said, touching my forehead to hers.

Brigita handed her mother the fussy baby. "What's going on?"

"Germans," Matka said, not one to hide things from the children. "It's what's always going on now, isn't it?" She waved the children over to her chair and picked up her book of fairy tales. I set Ema down with her legs crisscrossed on the rug.

"Now," Matka said, "let's see what that devil is up to

and how the good Czech maiden is going to"—she pointed her bony finger at them, causing them to jolt—"beat him at his own game." Matka sat back with the book in hand, cracking its spine with what little crack there was left, and read on while Dasa and I talked in the corner.

"I think you should come and stay with me," I said. "The children shouldn't stay here. Not now." I reached for the jar of chamomile oil Dasa liked to use on the baby, dipping my finger into the jar to smooth the oil over the baby's gums. "There you go, little one…" He stopped fussing once the oil met his lips.

"But what about my farm? The chickens, the eggs!" Dasa said, chewing her nails. "It's the only thing keeping me from the mines." Dasa ripped her fingers from her teeth, spitting out the nails, when she realized she still hadn't wiped her hands of the Brown Sister's blood. She handed me the baby so she could scrub herself clean in the sink.

"At least for tonight," I said.

"And the night after that? My children, their fair hair. And Ema's—"

I closed my eyes. "I don't know."

We waited until dusk before sneaking over to my house, through Dasa's brown pasture where nobody from the road would see us with the children. Matka didn't like having to change beds, but she wasn't about to stay at Dasa's now that the Reich had visited it.

"There will be more dead Germans by daybreak if I stay

at that house," Matka said. "And as for you, Dasa. You'll confess to God. We can go to a church and make it official in the sanctuary," Matka said. "He'll understand because she was a devil. When the signs are right."

"You can't have it both ways, Matka," I said. "You can't be religious yet lead your life by signs and omens and fairy tales."

"Yes," she said. "I can. It's who we are, Anna."

"I'll tell you who we are, Matka. We're a family of secrets, and this is just another secret we'll have to keep." I reached out to pet the baby's head in Dasa's arms. "There's so many now…"

Knowing German was the mildest secret we kept, and the baby so far was relatively easy to hide from the villagers. Our husbands' fates were our biggest lies. Matka had taken her wedding band off, thinking someone would kill her for it, but I kept my wedding band on. Rumor had spread that my husband was working in Prague, when in fact he'd fled for the Czech Resistance. It was the lucky break I needed to keep the German men away from my land, but things were harder for Dasa. To qualify for assistance, she'd told the New Town Hall her husband had died, and it was to her detriment. Ever since, more and more of her pasture had been eaten up by German landowners, taking what they wanted.

We led the children into my cellar, walking down the rickety wooden stairs with Ema half asleep in my arms.

She roused when I went to lay her down. "Where are you going?" Ema asked.

"Aunt Dasa and I are going to sow some seeds tonight. The moon is right for planting, all the signs are there."

"That's right," Dasa said as she made up beds for her girls with blankets and hay we used for insulation—Brigita with the biggest blanket, and her two other girls sharing one. "You know how the best planting happens during the night."

"Yes," Ema said, sweetly.

These were stories we told ourselves. Stories we'd been brought up on. All good Czech families had their stories.

"But how come I can't sleep in my own bed?" Ema asked.

"Ah, sweet girl," I said, "you ask too many questions." I tucked her into her new bed. "It's just for tonight." Ema sucked her thumb, looking up at me from the floor. "Kisses," I said, and she pulled her thumb away so I could kiss her cheek.

"But you didn't finish the story," she said, reaching for me, and I kissed her once more.

Matka brought down Ema's old baby basket, and we placed Dasa's young son into it, blankets wrapped around him, unknowing what despicable deed his mama and I were about to go off and do. I lit a few candles in jars and placed them on the shelf. Brigita watched us looking at the baby, and Dasa snapped for her to roll over and go to sleep.

"I'm scared," Brigita said after she pulled the blanket over her head. "Something isn't right. Both of you, Aunt Anna, Mama…"

Dasa kissed her daughter's head through the blanket,

giving her a squeeze, before following Matka up the stairs without another word.

"Mama," Ema said from the covers, hands grabbing at the air between us. "The story. Lay down…"

Candlelight flickered between us. "Scoot over," I said, and she made room for me on the floor. Dasa waved impatiently for me at the top of the stairs, but Dasa would have to wait. The Brown Sister would have to wait. Right now, Ema needed me.

I lay down.

Ema played with my fingers, the candlelight dancing over her little cheeks and glistening in her eyes. "Now, what story did you want to hear?" I asked, and she swiftly answered.

"The one about the actress in Prague."

"Oh yes, the woman from Prague."

I brushed a wisp of hair from her eyes.

"Tell me how pretty she was. Tell me about the prince."

I kissed her hand, thinking up ways I could tell her about her father and me, ways a child would understand. "When her prince first saw her, it wasn't the makeup he noticed, the fancy dress, or the jewelry that glittered around her wrists and neck."

"It wasn't?" she asked.

"He noticed her eyes. Looked right through them as if he could see her soul—as if he knew her soul—but how could he? He'd never met her before. And that's what it's like when love strikes. There's a connection. Like me and you." I snuggled her close. "We didn't know each other before you were born, but we loved each other instantly."

"I love you, Mama," she said, and I kissed her cheek when she threw her arms around my neck for a hug. "Did they get married?"

"They did," I said. "And it was the most beautiful wedding in all of Prague. An evening wedding under the stars. And they danced and danced and danced, and he told her he'd never leave her side, and she believed him because he was her love."

I stared off into the gloomy cellar, remembering the champagne, the cheers, and the toasts from our families. Everything in the world seemed possible that night—a fairy-tale start.

"Was the devil there?" Ema asked.

"The devil?"

"Every story has a devil in it," she said, and my eyes welled with tears, remembering all that had gone wrong since.

"The devil showed up after the wedding." I pressed her fingers to my lips. "But that part of the story will have to wait for another night."

She rolled over and sucked her thumb. Josef would have hated her sucking her thumb at five years old, but it was a comfort to her, and I let her do it.

I took hold of the light string, pausing, looking at our children sleeping on the cellar floor, in that dank and dark place where no children should ever sleep. "Damn you, Josef, for leaving me," I whispered into the air, and I pulled on the light string.

Dasa rubbed her arms nervously by the door. "What do

you think she looks like now?". She gulped. "Will she smell?"

I scoffed. "How would I know?"

"All Germans smell," Matka said. "Rotten. Rancid. Take your pick. Death doesn't change anything, not even their looks."

I stole a peek outside from the front windows. All seemed quiet with the moon hiding behind a smattering of clouds. I turned to Matka. "Don't answer the door." I swapped my house apron for a garden one and took a torch, just in case more clouds rolled in.

"I don't want to do this," Dasa said.

"We have to," I said.

"I know... I know..." Dasa said. "It's the story of our lives."

Matka pulled us to the floor by our sleeves near the door. "We must pray."

We clasped our hands together and prayed silently on our knees, eyes closed tightly, listening to the kitchen clock tick.

Please... don't let anyone see us... My mind drifted, and I thought of Josef, his face, his smell, all foggy and lost to me now. I'd hidden all our photographs; it was easier that way, making the walls seem cool and sterile. But his voice, his last words to me before he left for the Resistance, had haunted me ever since.

We said our goodbyes under my portraits near the stairs, the ones he saw me posing for the day we met in Prague. He held me tightly, and I rested my head in the hollow of his neck where it was warm.

"Why now?" I asked as he petted me. "The war will end soon. You don't have to do this—"

"Nobody knows when it will end, Anna, and I can't sit by any longer. Think about what the Germans have done to us, our friends, our people—where did they all go? Where is our country?"

Tears spilled over my cheeks as he held me. "I can feel it," I said. "What if there's a two-front war? My father always said no nation can win a two-front war."

Josef sighed. "My darling, this is for us. For our daughter. When the war does end and she's asked what her papa did in the war, she will lift her head high and say, 'My papa didn't work in the mines for the Germans, he fought in the Czech Resistance.'" I shook my head, but he only pleaded with me some more. "Anna, what kind of man am I if I don't fight the injustices?"

"A living one," I said, sniffling. "This doesn't feel right, Josef. Please, don't leave. You never listen to me. You never hear what I have to say. Ema's so young. She won't remember you." I swallowed painfully. "You said we'd be safe here, that you'd take care of us."

He paused, looking longingly into my eyes as I cried. "War comes to us all, Anna. One way or another, it will come to you too whether I stay or not, and I'm not talking about what you see in the villages, the rationing, and the curfews. This is bigger than the both of us." He hugged me, squeezing tightly before pulling away. "I'm sorry, my darling, one day I hope you'll understand. In the end, we're measured by our choices. It's what makes us who we are."

He kissed me passionately as if it was the last time he ever *would, then he grabbed his coat and hat and left out the front door, leaving me stunned and still, standing in our home. Alone.*

War comes to us all. If only I knew the depth of those words back then—the weight of it—I might have held onto his leg instead of standing in place, unmoving.

Matka stood up after praying, but instead of hugging us, she wished us luck. "Oh, and Anna, Dasa," she said, clasping her hands together. "Don't say any prayers for the Nazi. She's going straight to hell and the last thing you want to do is give her a recommendation to someplace better. All right? But do thank her for me, will you?"

"Why, Matka?" Dasa asked.

"Because she got me out of bed." Matka laughed, looking at her folded hands, smiling slyly.

Dasa took a noisy breath. "All right, Anna," she said. "I'm ready. Shouldn't take long."

I didn't say anything. I spent my days digging in the dirt. Holes weren't easy or quick. Much less one big enough for a body. This was going to take all night.

I cracked open the front door, listening. "Do you hear something?" Dasa asked.

I shook my head. "Only the crickets."

"Good," she said. "That means no people."

We snuck out my front door to the potting shed for tools. I picked through the spades, feeling them with my hands in the sheltered moonlight of the shed, until I found the shovel, pulling it up from a jumble of garden tools with metal skimming off metal.

"Be quiet!" Dasa hissed. "Someone will hear."

"I'm trying to be quiet." I threw a pair of gloves against her chest. "I can barely see."

We walked through my garden, up the hill and through Dasa's pasture to her barn, which looked gray in the dimming moonlight. Our footsteps bristled through the weeds. "I wish my husband was here," Dasa said. "I'm scared."

"Well, he's not here," I said, "now, is he?"

"You don't have to say it like that."

"They left both of us, Dasa," I said, stopping, looking at her under the moon. "They *left* their wives. Now, look what has become of us." I shook the shovel in the air. "Look what we have to do." I started walking again. "At least yours visited you. Left you another baby to remember him by."

She reached for my arm, turning me by the elbow. "It's not our men that did this to us, Anna. It's the Reich. They made us this way." She flipped up her apron. "They're the reason we became country maids."

I pulled my elbow away and we continued walking, taking big steps through the tangling weeds buzzing with night flies. Thoughts of what our lives used to be like flitted dangerously through my mind. Our apartment in the city square. Saturday-night performances at the theater. The lights, the glamour. Then the day I was told we were moving to the country, casting aside our professions in the city to buy a big farm, big enough for the whole family. It would be safer for us, Josef had told me. Together.

"I miss my life in Prague too," Dasa said. "You're not the only one."

Dasa had a nice apartment with many rooms for her

growing family. She was never in need of money or companionship. She had all she ever wanted—the clothes, the sophistication, the pride of a newly created First Republic amidst the rubble of the first war—like so many of us.

"I know," I said.

She rolled open the barn door, and we walked inside where it was a total black-out. I felt blindly for Dasa's shoulder in the air, still holding the shovel as we walked around the hay bales where we'd left the body. She stopped suddenly, and I bumped into her from behind, knocking her forward. "No…"

"What is it?" I asked, but when she didn't answer right away, my stomach sank.

"She's… She's…" Dasa searched the ground with her hands while I felt with my feet, expecting to feel a lump of flesh somewhere, something soft against my shoe. "But it can't be. It just can't be! Anna, the torch," she said, and I fumbled for it in my apron pocket. "The torch!"

I flipped on the torch, lighting up the space near our feet, the mound of hay, and the…

"My God, Dasa," I breathed, staring at the floor. "She's gone!"

The tiny hairs on my arms stood up from the eerie sensation of eyes on my back in the dark. I dropped the shovel, leaving it to clang on the floor. "Go, go, go!" I said, pushing her to run, and we ran out of the barn and around the side in the itchy grass, grabbing for each other and holding on.

"Someone moved her!" Dasa cried. Chirping crickets

from the weeds made us jerk breathlessly. We gripped each other tighter.

"Or she's still alive," I said.

Dasa gasped. "The children!"

We ran back to my house, shutting the door with a bang, which startled Matka in her sitting chair, bolting her to a stand. We raced to cut the lights.

"Where are the children?" I asked.

"Where you left them," Matka said, and both Dasa and I held our chests. "What happened? What's going—"

"She's gone, Matka," I said. "The barn was empty."

"What do you mean, the barn was empty?"

"Dasa didn't kill her," I said. "It's the only explanation."

"Well, she couldn't have gotten very far," Matka said. "Get back out there, find the bitch and kill her once and for all."

We heard footsteps outside the window. "Shh…" We moved in close together, hands holding onto each other in the dark, when the doorknob twisted in place.

"It's the SS," Dasa whispered. "They've come for us."

"They don't twist doorknobs," Matka whispered back. "They knock down doors. It's someone else."

I held my breath.

"It's Tomas," we heard from the other side of the door, and while I exhaled in relief that it was our cousin, Dasa folded to the floor.

"Hurry in," Matka said, opening the door. His eyes fell to Dasa lying on the floor, and he helped her up.

I lit a candle that flickered warmly between us. "Why—" My voice got caught in my throat, afraid of what he'd say. It must be serious if he'd left the safety of the Tabor Tunnels, and I braced myself for his dreadful message. "You have news about Josef? Is that why you're here?"

Dasa gripped my arm.

"Nothing new," he said. "I'm sorry. The last I heard, he was in the forest with a detachment of rebels."

I closed my eyes briefly with this, patting my chest.

"And my husband?" Dasa asked.

Tomas took her by the shoulders. "He sends his love," he said, and I turned away. "I'm here because there's talk of a German transport truck and some disappearances. I wanted to warn you. Be careful who you trust—"

"We already know," I interrupted. "There was a Brown Sister here asking about Dasa's girls."

His eyes popped from their sockets. "Where are your children now?"

"Safe," Dasa said, fingers twisting. "But that's not all." She held her breath before blurting, "I killed her."

Tomas gripped the back of a kitchen chair before falling into it.

"I had no choice, cousin." Dasa paced, shaking from head to toe, telling him the whole story, beginning with the tomatoes she wanted her children to taste. "Anna and I went to bury her, only now she's gone. We just came from the barn where we'd hidden her body."

"What do you mean, gone?" Tomas blinked once.

Dasa groaned, hands flying into the air, looking exasperated from having to relive the story again. "Exactly what I said."

Tomas pulled his hair back with both hands, face

stretched. "This isn't good," he said as Matka shook her head, agreeing. "This isn't good at all."

"What are we going to do, Tomas?" Dasa gripped the front of his shirt with both hands. "She could be out there somewhere—"

"She could still be in the barn," I said at the same time, realizing that was exactly where she was, remembering the feeling of eyes on us in the dark. "Dasa, that's it. She's still there, probably recovering and not even sure what happened to her."

Tomas dashed for the door. "If she's in the barn, I'll find her."

"What are you going to do?" Dasa asked, and he turned to Matka, who nodded once.

"Make it final," Matka said. "God forgives the brave. You know that." She folded her arms. "But also, nobody says you have to show mercy."

Tomas rushed out the door with the promise to return with news. Dasa sat on the divan the moment the door had closed, hands twisting in her lap.

"What if she isn't a Brown Sister?" Dasa asked as I sat next to her. "Maybe I was mistaken, and because of the rock, she doesn't remember anything and has already wandered back to her home, none the wiser."

Matka scoffed. "We don't have that kind of luck."

Chapter Four

Ema tapped my forehead as I lay out on the divan between Dasa and Matka, who'd also fallen asleep. She tapped again after my eyes cracked open halfway, only instead of waking up gently, I jumped up from the divan and stood in the middle of the room, scaring both her and me.

Dasa bolted upright from the cushions.

"It's morning," Ema said, thumb between her teeth.

"Let me think!" I said, hand to my forehead. "Let me…" I remembered Tomas leaving, but he never came back. The window curtains were still drawn, but I felt like the sun was out and it had been many hours. I moved toward the window, but Dasa beat me to it, throwing aside the curtain and letting in a stream of light that beamed into Matka's eyes.

"Close that!" Matka squinted from the divan. "What time is it?"

Dasa looked over her shoulder. "Anna, what are we to do now?" She let go of the curtain to chew on her nails.

Ema dragged her yellow baby blanket behind her on the floor. "Ema," I said, arms open. "Come here, sweet girl." I picked her up and rocked her in my arms.

"I don't like sleeping down there," she said, wadding her blanket into a ball between us.

"I know... I know..." I brushed the hair from her forehead, kissing her once, but my mind was on all that must have gone wrong with Tomas and the missing Brown Sister. My head throbbed.

Dasa's three daughters shuffled out of the dark cellar one by one in a daze, adjusting their eyes to the dull morning glow in the parlor. "Can we go home now?" Brigita asked, handing her mother the baby. "I want my own bed."

Dasa gathered her children in a circle. "I'm sorry you had to sleep..." She bent to her knees and touched each of her three girls' cheeks before hanging her head, unable to finish her sentence.

Matka stood sharply from the divan, clapping once. "All right, children. Let the adults deal with this." She pointed down the hallway. "Hide in the back bedroom until we can think."

Ema watched her cousins walk away. "I want to stay with you," she said to me, head resting on my shoulder. "Please, Mama."

I closed my eyes briefly from her pleading voice. "I know you do." I set her down, knowing I had to be strong even though I wanted her to stay. "But I need you to hide

46

with your cousins. No questions." I smoothed her hair back as she sucked on her thumb. "I love you, Ema." I pressed my forehead to hers, closing my eyes again. "I love you." I watched her walk away, dragging her blanket behind her on the floor, her blonde bunches pulled loose from their ribbons after sleeping on them. I held my face in my hands.

"Tomas killed her," Matka blurted. "He was successful. We must believe it. The signs were right. The moon, the night, the still air… He'll come and tell us. We just have to wait."

"He won't come here now. The sun's out," Dasa said.

"He'll send a messenger, a note," Matka said. "He won't leave us to guess."

Dasa turned in circles, patting her baby's bottom in her arms. "And what if he wasn't successful, Matka? What if…" She gasped. "What if the SS are on their way to my house right now?" She dashed to the window again, throwing up the curtain and searching the road. "They'll put me on the evening train to Pankrác Prison. And then the children…"

"You'll hide here with your children," I said, but honestly, I didn't know what to do. If the Brown Sister survived and came looking for Dasa's children, the Reich would find all their little blonde heads after a quick search.

"Hiding won't change their looks." Dasa let go of the curtain and slices of light shone on the floor as the fabric swayed.

"I know what to do!" Matka whipped around, smiling wildly. "Could we pull it off?" She chewed her thumbnail, pacing. "Could we? I think we can…"

"Pull what off?" I asked, but she continued to talk to

herself. I held Dasa's hand, thinking Matka must have thought of something promising. "Tell us!"

Matka pointed in the air, and Dasa and I held our breaths. "Coal, girls. That's what!" she said, and while I shook my head, Dasa threw hers back. "We can make a paste out of coal and dye the children's hair. Nobody would take a second glance."

"You're mad, Matka," I said. "We'd have to steal the coal first. I barely have enough to heat today's soup."

"Did you forget our father died because he stole coal?" Dasa said. "We're on a watch list as it is."

"No, girls. You're wrong," Matka said. She threw her shawl over her shoulders. "I'll be back."

Dasa paced with the baby after Matka left, stopping only to take peeks out the window with every voice that carried in the breeze, every laugh, every bicycle that rode by. The baby had started to fuss from hunger.

"You'll have to feed him," I said, but I knew she probably didn't have enough milk to satisfy him, as nervous as she was. "Let me help you."

I took the baby while she sat in one of the kitchen chairs, taking deep breaths through her mouth to calm herself. I gave him a dab of the chamomile oil, rubbing it along his gums, though it only held him so long. He let out a hungry cry and Dasa reached for him. "Come back to me," she said, and the baby nestled against her bare breast, blissfully unaware of the world he was born into. He fell asleep after sucking her dry, and I brought up the baby basket from the cellar so he could hide in the back bedroom with the others.

We waited for word about the Brown Sister, and we

waited for Matka, listening to the kitchen clock tick. "When is she coming back?" Dasa asked. "Where'd she go?"

"I don't know…" I rubbed my aching neck, leaning against the kitchen counter, glancing at the clock then glancing at Dasa. Thirty minutes had passed, and I was getting worried. "I can't wait anymore," I said, and I set out to find Matka, throwing open the door to leave, but I ran into Tomas. "My God!" I clutched my chest and he ducked inside.

He took three labored steps into the parlor and faced a stricken Dasa, who had her fingers clenched between her teeth. "Did you find her? Did you kill—"

"She's dead," he said, and Dasa fell to her knees to pray. "I started a rumor that she joined the Resistance. The Reich won't be looking for her."

"Thank you, Tomas," Dasa said tearfully from the floor. "Thank you…" We embraced after she stood up, relieved that was the end of it.

Tomas went to the sink to wash his hands as if he'd been digging all night. The water turned maroon and then pink as it ran into the drain. I didn't want to see her blood in my house. He turned off the faucet when he caught me peering into the basin, and that's when I saw the bloody scratches on his arm.

I wasn't sure what to say. *Thank you for killing her* came to mind. I settled for just a thank-you. I reached for my jar of calendula oil, pointing with my head to an empty chair for him to sit.

I swirled the jar in the air, watching the flowers float up to the top then sink slowly to the bottom. "This will keep an infection from starting and help it heal." I cleaned the scratches with a wet rag, then spread a thin layer of the oil over his wounds.

"I'll start the soup," Dasa said, but she was still recovering from Tomas's news, and I insisted she have a sit too.

I reached for the carrots I'd grown in my garden and gave them a wash. I was always missing a few ingredients for a proper soup, but still had my herbs to make it taste decent. I held the jar of marjoram to my nose, inhaling deeply.

"I don't have any liver for dumplings. But I do have plenty of vegetables, and enough broth to make a fine pot of something hot," I said, but I only had enough coal to make it warm and only one day's ration of meat to share between eight people.

"Sounds wonderful," Tomas said. "Thank you."

I opened up a jar of coriander, giving Tomas and Dasa a smell, when Matka burst through the door, scaring all three of us.

She stood in the parlor, grinning. "Matka?" I set the jar down, walking toward her and searching for an explanation, when she shoved a dirty fist at us, opening it palm side up.

"Coal," she said, showing us the three hunks of coal.

I gasped, hurrying to close the door as if someone from the road could see it. "Where did you get that coal?" I asked, but Matka's hand was as dirty as her apron, and it was clear she'd dug it up.

"I have coal hidden here and there," Matka said. "Always have. A last resort in case we ran out or needed money to pay someone off. We can make dye with this. All the children will be dark-haired in no time." She set the coal on the table so she could dust off her hands. She finally noticed Tomas. "You're back!" Matka lowered her voice. "Were you... victorious?"

He nodded, and Matka clapped once. "Good, one less thing we have to worry about. I do hope you made the bitch pay. Killed her slowly, perhaps?" She smiled.

"Matka," I breathed. "She's dead. Isn't that enough?"

She turned to me. "Killing her slowly is the reward, Anna. The Reich has been killing me slowly for years. It's only fair." Matka turned back to Tomas. "Where did you bury her?" she asked, but Tomas didn't say. "Well, I suppose it doesn't make a difference. The dead don't like secrets. One way or the other, she'll make her presence known." Matka paused, studying his clean clothes, his scratched arm, and his hands where the slightest traces of blood could be seen on his cuticles. "You did bury her, didn't you?"

"What else would he do with her, Matka?" Dasa asked.

"I'm glad you came back, nephew," Matka said.

"We all are," Dasa said, but then she stood up, suddenly alarmed. "But why'd you come in the daytime?"

We hadn't thought to ask. The Brown Sister was the only thing on our minds when he walked into the house. He could have passed us a note or waited until the night to tell us, when it was safe. Dasa walked closer to him, rubbing her arms as if she felt chilled.

"There's something else, isn't there? Something more important than telling us about the woman from the barn."

He took a deep breath, nodding, and I closed my eyes. "I'm sorry," he said. "I didn't know how to tell you. The woman from the barn was a scout. There will be more, and they'll be looking for your children specifically, Dasa, as they work from lists. Be prepared."

Dasa stumbled backward. "This is terrible news."

"How do you know this?" I asked, but when Tomas refused to answer, I gulped. The Resistance had their methods, ways that were just as brutal as the Germans'. He had killed her slowly after all.

"Who put us on a list?" Dasa asked. "Who?"

"An informant. Someone who knows you, I suspect." He paused, almost regretful he had to explain. "Dasa, you are without a husband and your children are blonde with blue eyes. The Reich will be calling again. Your little ones are the perfect pick. The easy choice."

Dasa covered her mouth. "Have strength," Matka said, but it was more of a demand.

Ema padded down the hallway when she heard Tomas's voice. "Tomas!" she squealed, and all the children ran in from the back bedroom. They loved Tomas and hung on him like monkeys on a tree, and of course, he didn't mention his shoulder. He would never spoil the children's joy, but I could tell it hurt.

"Matka..." Dasa said. "An informant."

"It was Mr. Ott," Matka said. "Bastard, that one. I told you he was no good."

"I didn't want to believe it," Dasa said. "I feel like such a fool."

"Ema, come here," I said, fingers motioning, but she was too busy giggling from Tomas holding her upside down, her eyes delightfully wide. "Ema, come here, sweet girl," I said, and Tomas set her down. I smoothed the hair away from her forehead, bending to my knees.

"Yes, Mama," she said, but her body and her attention leaned toward the other children and to Tomas where she had been having so much fun.

"This is serious!" I said, and a hush fell over the girls, but more so over Ema who'd stood still from my commanding voice. I swung my head to Matka. "Get the coal."

Matka snapped at the children to sit, and they each pulled out a chair and sat down dutifully. I reached for the mortar and pestle I used to grind my herbs, and Matka handed me a hunk of her coal. "This had better work," I said.

"It's good Czech coal from the north," Matka said. "It will work. Luck is on your side this time. If it wasn't, I would have forgotten where I'd hidden it."

"What are you going to do to us?" Brigita asked.

"It's going in your hair," Dasa said, and her children's eyes grew wide.

I mashed the coal into a pasty powder with my pestle, dribbling oil and some water into it to form the right consistency—not too runny, oily, or chalky. All eyes watched me from the table. I scooped up a glob of the coal mixture with my hand. "Who's first?" I asked, and all the children shook their heads.

Dasa reached over and took a glob of the coal mixture herself. "You're all doing it," she said. "Even the baby after he wakes up. It doesn't matter who's first." She motioned with her head to Matka. "Get the brush."

Matka got the brush from the back bedroom and went down the line, brushing each of the girls' hair out, getting rid of the tangles, before Dasa and I came by with the paste, smoothing it into their hair, turning their sandy locks into gray ones. Ema was last.

She sniffled, watching with disgust as her cousins felt their hair where it had turned sticky and matted.

"Tip your head back, sweet girl," I said, but Ema shook her head.

"I don't want to." Her eyes puffed with tears. "I want Papa. Where's Papa?"

I hung my head, not able to answer, but Tomas was. "One day he will come back, Ema. He'll drive right up to your house and take you for a drive. One day." He reached over the table to wipe a tear from her cheek. "When the war ends. You wait and see."

"Don't say those things to her, Tomas. It's not fair." I bent down to Ema's eye level. "You have to do it." I paused, searching for the right words, something she'd understand without telling her the scary truth.

"But why?" she asked, and I took a deep breath.

"You should tell them," Tomas said, and Dasa threw her hands out.

"Tell them?" Dasa asked. "They don't need to know. It's bad enough, what they have to deal with—"

"I agree with Tomas," Matka said. "Let's tell them."

We were quiet, looking at the children mope at the table with their pasty gray hair, and I thought maybe we should tell. Not the absolute truth, but enough for them to know the dangers we were facing.

"You're scaring me," Brigita said. "Tell us what?"

"Dasa?" I looked to my sister. I wasn't going to tell them if she said no.

Dasa placed a hand on Brigita's shoulder, closing her eyes. "Fine, tell them," she said.

I pulled out my chair and sat with the children. "You know we love you," I said, and they nodded. "You know the Nazis don't like us because we're Czech. They've taken most of our liberties away. Your mother," I said, motioning with my head to Dasa, "and your grandmother, and I want to do everything we can to make sure we stay together. Part of that means we have to come up with a disguise."

The children looked lost. "You don't want us to be us?" one of them said.

I shook my head. "We don't want the Nazis to accidentally think you're one of them. German. Because of your blonde hair and blue eyes," I said, and that seemed to make sense to them. "The hair dye is so that you can blend in. Not be so noticeable. In case a German comes to visit." I turned to Ema. "It's like we're playing dress-up."

Her eyes lit up. "Can we wear makeup like the woman in the story?"

Dasa looked confused. "What story?" she asked.

"The actress," Ema pipped, and Dasa's eyes shifted to mine. "The one who got married in Prague under the stars. Then the devil came and ruined everything."

"There were a lot of women in Prague," Dasa said above a whisper, then she looked at her hands where her nails were stained, and all the feathery lines in her hands had turned gray with coal.

I scooped out the last bit of coal paste from the mortar. "Tip back your head, baby," I said, and Ema tipped her head back and looked at me upside down. She closed her eyes tightly when I smeared the paste into her hair, moaning and squirming from the feel of it until she'd completely slipped out of her chair, giving me the most repulsed look on such a sweet face. "Don't touch it," I said when she reached for her hair. "It needs to dry."

Dasa's children sat at the table, hands in their laps, not saying a word as I wiped the paste from my fingers with a rag. Matka held her head in her hands. I wiped and wiped and wiped, but the coal had stained my skin just like Dasa's, and I threw the towel into the sink.

The soup I'd started earlier was ready and we ate around the table, slurping it slowly to make it last. Tomas told jokes to the children, making them forget for a few moments about the paste in their hair. "You know the best way to ward off the devil?" Tomas asked, and the girls all shook their heads. "Throw a pinch of black pepper on your neighbor."

The girls giggled, all reaching for the coarsely ground pepper I had on the table and tossing a pinch in each other's faces. Matka and Dasa sneezed, which made the girls giggle even more, but nobody giggled like Ema, who sat with her blanket bunched up with black pepper sprinkled on yellow. "My dolly!" she said, trotting to the back bedroom to get the small doll that fit in her pocket, to throw some pepper in her face too.

"We'll keep the curtains closed," I said. "And the girls can play outside at night."

"That won't work forever," Matka said. "Another visit from Mr. Ott or anyone else and it could be all over. Especially since I already said the girls are with my sister. What if the Brown Sisters come back with a transport truck?"

We talked about the possibility of the girls going into hiding, but Tomas had concerns about sneaking them away. I thought I heard a car drive up outside. I turned to listen, quieting the girls, telling them to shush, but it wasn't enough. "Be quiet!" I hissed, and then there it was, the unmistakable pop and crack of gravel being driven on.

I stood up at the same time Dasa did. Only Germans were permitted to drive.

The engine revved once before turning off.

"Someone's here," Dasa breathed.

"And it's a car," I said.

Tomas grabbed a long knife from the counter and Matka took the pan.

"Nobody move," I said, and we froze, not a word between us, just as Ema tore out of the bedroom shouting with joy.

"It's Papa, it's Papa!" she said, hand reaching for the door.

"No—" I yelled, but the door had already swung wide open, welcoming the person inside.

Chapter Five

Ema stood in the doorway, squinting in the face of the sun as I raced to shut the door. "Ema!" I threw my back up against it, and she immediately burst into tears. My chest pounded.

"Papa..." she bellowed.

"It's not Papa," I said, firmly, and she ran off to Dasa, bunching her blanket between her arms. I peeked underneath the window curtain, holding my breath, and nearly collapsed into a heap of sobs with relief when I saw it wasn't the Brown Sisters coming to check off their list, but it was Mrs. Lange. "Oh, thank God," I said, holding my chest. "It's all right."

"Who is it?" Matka asked.

"It's Mrs. Lange," I said, still breathing heavily. We had nothing to fear. Mrs. Lange was a Czech like us, but because she married a German, she was still able to drive.

Matka walked closer. "But *why* is she here?" She touched

my arm, and I paused, because I didn't know the answer to her question. "Anna, why is she—"

"I don't know," I said, and Matka put her hands on her hips. Mrs. Lange wasn't known to make social calls.

"What if she's here to steal your sister's children?" Matka asked, and Dasa gasped, hand flying to her mouth.

I shook my head. "She's not that kind of person. I've known her since Prague, from the theater." I looked at Dasa. "You know her, Dasa. She wouldn't—"

"Or would she?" Matka interrupted.

I looked out the window once more, only this time Mrs. Lange had stepped out of the car and walked around the back, one hand shielding the sun, looking at my house and at the vegetables I planned to sell in the square. I put my head to the glass. "Of course," I breathed, thankfully remembering. "She's here to help me transport my vegetables to the market."

"She's never helped you before," Matka said. "I'd remember it if she had."

"She mentioned helping me last week, after she saw me struggling with my cart. I forgot." I moved away from the window and reached for the door. "But I'll tell her I can't go today."

"No." Matka stepped in between me and the door. "You have to go," she said.

"Why?" I asked.

"You've never missed a day," Matka said. "People will wonder why today, of all days, you are gone."

"She's right," Dasa said. "You have to go."

"But not with that Lange woman," Matka said. "Ride your bicycle into the village."

"I can't turn her down after I've already accepted her invitation for help," I said.

I lifted the window curtain, taking another peek at Mrs. Lange and *her* car—the car that used to be ours until the Reich decreed that Czechs weren't permitted to own motor vehicles.

Matka peeped over my shoulder. "Another bitch. A muttonhead that stole your car. The Reich thinks they're clever by taking our things away, but who are the smart ones now? We've killed us a fine Nazi bitch—"

"Matka!" I said. "Mrs. Lange did me a favor. She promised to sell it back to me one day. She's Czech, I told you that. She just wants to help." I looked at the door, thinking about what to do.

"Like how Mr. Ott helped Dasa?" Matka squinted.

"I'm not going to the market today. It's too much with—"

"You are going!" Matka snapped. "Think about what your empty stand will look like in a crowded market! Everyone knows Anna and her herbs. There will be rumors and questions, and they will travel all the way to your doorstep, and Dasa's. Besides, you leave your stand empty today, and a German will be in it tomorrow. You know how it works."

"If I'm going to the square, then that means I'm going with Mrs. Lange," I said. "I can't turn her down, that would look even more suspicious—"

"Hallo…" Mrs. Lange said from the other side of the door, followed by two knocks.

Dasa gasped, pulling her children in close and huddling in the kitchen.

"Why are you hiding? It's Mrs. Lange," I said. "You've met her a hundred times."

"I'm hiding because my children are in Prague, remember?" Dasa rasped.

"We are?" Brigita asked, and Dasa clamped her hand over her daughter's mouth.

"Be quiet, children," Dasa whispered.

I cleared my throat, hand on the door. She'd wonder why I wasn't ready, and I had no idea what I was going to say. *I slept in?* She'd never believe it. Matka rushed up behind me and whispered in my ear.

"Tell her I'm sick, that's why you're late."

"What would you be sick with?" I asked.

"You don't have time to worry about that. Open it before she becomes suspicious."

Matka ducked around the corner, and I opened the door.

"There you are!" Mrs. Lange said. "I thought you'd be outside waiting." Her eyes skirted over my unkempt hair before gently drifting over my shoulder and in the direction of my kitchen. "Is everything all right?"

I took a step outside, barely opening the door and squeezing myself through the narrow crack. "My mother has a cough." Matka coughed loudly from the parlor, which sounded slightly muffled through the closed door. "Hear that? I'll just be a minute. Taking care of her while she's sick has set me back."

"Do you need help with her?" she asked, making a move toward the door, and the image of Dasa and her children cowering under the kitchen table flashed through my head.

"No—" I reached for her arm and she looked surprised I'd touched her. "I mean…" I glanced over my shoulder to where Matka was watching us through a split in the curtain. *Suspicious. Act normal.* I pulled my hand back, smiling. "She'll be fine. It was a late night and an early morning. That's all," I said, cringing behind my smile, remembering the blood that got washed down my sink.

"I see," Mrs. Lange said, but she had a look on her face that said she didn't quite believe me, which brought on a swirl of nervousness in my stomach, something I'd never felt around her before.

"I'll go gather up my things," I said, and she followed me to the car where I loaded my vegetables into wooden crates. She spit-shined her headlamp where a drop of dirty water had discolored it.

"I do love this vehicle," she said as she shined, stopping suddenly, eyes sliding to mine as I bent over, a handful of carrots in each fist. "Sorry, Anna, I didn't mean to…"

"It's quite all right," I said. "I'd rather you have our car and not someone else."

"I don't agree with the laws. You know this, don't you?"

I picked up a crate. "I know," I said, but she was still looking at me. "Shall we load up?"

"Pardon me." She opened her car boot, and we loaded the carrots and the cucumbers, all ripened by the June sun.

63

"I also have some herbs in the house," I said. "If you wouldn't mind another minute, I'll be right back."

Mrs. Lange looked up from the boot. "Not a problem, Anna." She slid the crates together side by side as I turned to walk into the house. Matka closed the door behind me.

"Good luck," Matka said, handing Ema off to me.

"What are you doing?" I asked, but she only pressed her lips together. Dasa looked to the ground, holding her own daughters' hands. "I'm not bringing Ema!"

"It's not any safer here than it is there," Matka said. "Besides, if you don't take her people will wonder why. You always take Ema to the market."

I smoothed a matted lock of gray hair from Ema's forehead, tears welling in my eyes. It was one thing to go into the market by myself, but to take Ema while the Brown Sisters were in Tabor? I felt like I was bringing my little lamb to the slaughter.

"It's me on the list," Dasa said. "Not you. Remember?"

"I'm sorry, Anna," Matka said. "You must know I don't like it either. But Dasa is right. You're not on the list." She folded her arms tightly like she normally did when she expected me to obey, and I wanted to cry.

"You should go," Tomas said. "Act like it's another day."

"Here, use this. Just to be safe." Matka took off her kerchief and wrapped it over Ema's pasty gray hair, tying it under her chin. Ema pulled at it near her ears while Matka tugged it back into place.

"I don't like it," Ema whined.

I squeezed Ema's hand as Matka pushed me gently

toward the door, and I felt pulled in two different directions.

Matka gasped from the window. "She's coming back!" She snapped her fingers for everyone to get into the back bedroom. Ema hung onto my skirts, looking up at me with her big eyes as the rest of our family scrambled to hide.

"It's all right," I said to her, feeling nauseous at having the choice made for me. "It's just Mrs. Lange." I bent to my knees for a moment, touching my forehead to Ema's.

Mrs. Lange knocked on the door, and I opened it wide up this time, showing off my empty house. "Are you ready to go?" she asked.

"Be right out," I said, but she stepped into the house as I turned around to gather my herb jars, and I wondered why, since I didn't invite her in. No Czech woman would ever walk into a home uninvited. "It's a nice day today, isn't it?" I threw my voice so Matka and the others could hear me in the back bedroom.

"It is, yes." Mrs. Lange bent down to pull a coin out from behind Ema's ear, making her laugh, then examined Matka's kerchief on her head, lifting it slightly near Ema's ear and getting a glimpse of her hair. I closed my eyes briefly, hands on the jars, praying she wouldn't ask me about it.

"Are you playing dress-up?" she asked Ema, and Ema's shaking head turned into a nod when I nodded.

Mrs. Lange stood, quietly looking over my kitchen, and eyeing the mortar and pestle I had on the counter smeared with a thin layer of coal paste, when she took a sudden heaving intake of air. "I can smell your herbs. The marjoram especially. Did you make soup?"

I was glad the soup bowls had been put away. I wasn't sure how I'd explain eight empty bowls around the table, but I did explain my rough and calloused hands as a consequence of gardening when she looked at them, dampening any thoughts she might have had about the coal stains.

"Life was different before, when we knew each other at the Prague theater," she said. "Wasn't it?" She rubbed her wedding band, looking at her finger. "The plays we starred in, the late nights, the parties..." Her smile faded after a second or two, and I carried the crate of herbs to the front door. "Where's your mother?" she asked, and I froze, holding the crate in both hands.

"She probably went to go lay down," I said. "She's not well, remember? I told you outside."

"And Dasa, will she be in the village today?" Mrs. Lange glanced down the hallway as if she expected Dasa to come out from one of my bedrooms when she had a house of her own, and I looked at her, blinking, with the jars clinking from the shake in my hands.

"I don't know," I said. Ema watched us both, studying, trying to figure out what new secret we had to keep, while a strange silence passed between me and Mrs. Lange, and suddenly I felt I *should* worry about her.

"I thought I'd buy some eggs from your sister," she finally said, breaking the awkwardness.

"Egg day was yesterday at the market for Czechs," I said. "Only German eggs allowed the rest of the week."

"Oh yes, I suppose you're right. I ask because I haven't seen her in a while, and who could forget those adorable children she has?"

She took Ema by the hand and walked her out to the car, and it felt as if she'd taken my heart along with her. I turned, looking down the hallway where Matka had poked her head out from the bedroom door, jabbing the air with her finger and mouthing pinched words to act normal and avoid suspicion.

"Go!" she said just as Mrs. Lange honked, motioning for me with a pat of the passenger seat.

Chapter Six

Mrs. Lange drove onto the main road. Ema played with the doll she'd brought with her, pretend-walking the doll over the back seat. "Stay down," I said to Ema, and she moved to her knees on the floorboards. Mrs. Lange's gaze shifted once, and I covered my eyes, smelling her strong floral cologne, too strong for the daytime.

"I have some bad news," she said, and I pulled my hand away from my eyes.

"What is it?" I asked, and when she paused, my heart sank, thinking Matka was right—she was going to turn my daughter in, drive Ema right up to the Brown Sisters for a reward. "What—" My voice got caught in my throat, looking straight out the windshield as we drove into the village with no way to stop her.

"My husband wants to sell the car," she said.

"Oh…" My heart thumped wildly from the scare.

"I'm sorry, Anna," she said. "I'll try my best to hold onto

it, but I must obey my husband. I know I promised to sell it back to you one day."

I managed a shaky nod. "I understand." I grasped the leather seat, feeling dizzy as we approached the village. I caught another whiff of her cologne, a nose-tingling tang, something that probably had turned dark yellow in the bottle. I rolled the window down.

When the car was mine, all I smelled was leather.

Josef picked me up in the city after rehearsal, rolling up to the curb outside the theater, one hand on the steering wheel and the other slung over the seat, grinning. We talked about buying a new car, but not a Praga Alfa with its regal headlamps and swanky interior. Exhaust fumes poured from the tailpipe. "Do you love it, darling?"

"Josef, I…" He jumped from his seat to run around the side of the car and open my door. "Let's go for a ride," he said, then he kissed my cheek and I couldn't resist.

People stared as they walked by, and I pretended it was normal for me to be picked up in a brand-new car in the middle of the day. I fixed my lipstick in the side mirror. "People are staring as us, Josef."

"They're wondering what you're doing with a frog like me," he said, and I patted his leg as he started up the engine.

We drove off through the city, hitting a pothole, and I clutched frantically onto the side door. After I recovered, we both had a good laugh. "I like it," I said. "It's fancy and beautiful."

"Not as beautiful as my wife." He smiled. "This will be our family car," he said, glancing at my stomach.

"Oh, Josef. We just got married," I said.

"I know," he said. "But it could happen any day. I want us to

be prepared. Soon enough we'll have several children in the back seat jumping around."

"Hopefully not jumping," I said. "Are you sure we can afford a car like this?" I felt the smooth seat, taking my gloves off to feel the leather against my bare skin. "Leather. Smells heavenly. Smells… expensive."

"I have my own accounting business now," he said. "We can afford it, darling." We drove out of the city and into the country. I held onto my hat from a whirl of wind through the open windows. "Do you want me to slow down?" he asked, but I shook my head, utterly excited by a kick of speed on the open road. I threw a hand out of the window to feel the wind between my fingers. "Let's see how fast she goes!"

We sped off down a long country road with a sharp turn, the tires drifting and skidding, both of us laughing, hearts thumping, coming to a stop in a meadow blooming with white wildflowers. He cut the engine, reaching for my hand and we sat for a while in the quiet, listening to the rush of a stream flowing nearby, and an occasional bird chirping in the trees.

"I love you, Anna." He brought my hand up to his lips for a soft kiss before sliding closer to me on the leather seat. "Feels like yesterday I spotted you getting your photograph taken. Fate brought us together. I wasn't supposed to be in the city that day." He brushed a lock of hair from my eyes. "I won't buy the car if you don't want me to. But I think you deserve it. We deserve it. Please say yes."

I looked into his eyes, thinking what a wonderful man I married. "But it's your money," I said, and he shook his head.

"We're in this together," he said. "Always."

He moved in for a kiss, and I wrapped my arms around him,

sinking into the soft leather seat, his hand slipping under my skirt and up my netted stocking as the car engine ticked warmly under the bonnet.

Mrs. Lange turned off the engine and my eyes cracked open. "Anna?" she said, and the memory of that day was replaced by a Nazi Party banner flapping off a lamppost outside my door. Wehrmacht soldiers walked by casually, smoking, peering into the car, looking at me looking at them as I sat rigidly in the seat. "Anna?" she said, again.

"Yes, thank you." I broke away from the window to look at Ema who was still sitting on her knees in the back. "Stay down," I said, and Ema nodded. I felt Mrs. Lange watching me as I got out of the car.

Czechs rode by on their bicycles, while others stopped at merchant tables and negotiated a fair price for goods. I loaded the vegetables and herbs onto a cart with wheels that Mrs. Lange had in the car boot, before going back for Ema in the back seat, but Mrs. Lange insisted on getting my daughter herself, bringing her out by her little hand.

Ema hopped out of the car holding her doll, and continued hopping as I rolled the cart into the square, saying she was a bunny while holding onto Mrs. Lange's hand. I worried her hopping was causing too much attention. "Ema," I whispered, "stop."

Mrs. Lange patted Ema's hand. "Mama says stop."

I shared a stand with Mrs. Dolakova, a Czech woman who mainly sold cherries and handcrafted leather goods the Germans had yet to prohibit. I said hallo to her but she refused to acknowledge me with Mrs. Lange by my side, rearranging her leather display, drawing the strings on all her bags with sharp yanks.

I wheeled the cart around the stand and pointed under the table, lifting the striped tablecloth. "Ema," I said, glancing up to the crowd. Germans who had once been our friends passed by the Czech merchants for German ones, a typical day. "I want you to stay under here."

"Why?" She tugged on her kerchief, pulling it off her head, and I tied it back on, looping it tightly under her chin.

"Ouch," she said. "Mama, it's too tight."

I got on my knees and touched her, forehead to forehead. "Give me strength," I whispered, and Ema looked up.

"Mama?"

"Ema, sweet girl," I said, "We're going to play a game."

Her face fell when I said our secret phrase; she knew not to ask any questions. "I need you to be invisible today." I pointed under the table again, and she crawled under the tablecloth. I took a deep breath, standing straight to collect myself, only Mrs. Lange had been watching me the whole time. I smiled, slipping on my merchant apron before unloading my herbs and setting my jars out. I unscrewed the lid off the black pepper, smelling its biting freshness, while Mrs. Lange looked toward the square when she should have walked away. She'd only offered to drop me off, but instead, she asked if she could help.

"That isn't necessary, Mrs. Lange," I said. "You've done so much already, giving me a ride when you didn't have to."

"I don't have any plans today, Anna," Mrs. Lange said.

"You'd be helping me out." She smiled, and a strangeness passed between us, then I watched helplessly as she slipped on a spare apron from one of the crates.

Mrs. Dolakova pulled me to the side by the elbow. "What is that woman doing here? She's taking over your stand!"

"Mrs. Lange wants to help," I said, swallowing, trying to hide the unsettled look on my face. Germans had taken over our shops, our homes, and even our market stands.

Mrs. Dolakova didn't look convinced. "I don't trust her," she said, looking over my shoulder to Mrs. Lange.

"She won't be a bother—"

"She drives your car, Anna," she said. "Don't forget why. They've taken our livelihood, our homes... I had Jewish friends. Where are they? You wait." She looked over my shoulder again to Mrs. Lange who was whispering to Ema under the tablecloth. "They'll take our children next if they don't wipe us out completely. One by one."

"Do you know something?"

Her eyes thinned. "Do you?"

"Anna?" Mrs. Lange called, and Mrs. Dolakova walked away.

"Wait—" I said, reaching for her shoulder, but Mrs. Lange called for me again, and I closed my eyes. The entire exchange happened so quickly.

Mrs. Lange waved me toward her. "Did I do this right?"

"Oh, ahh..." Mrs. Lange had arranged my vegetables out as if they were her own, and even hung up some of the herbs I had wrapped in bunches with twine. "Yes, you did. Thank you." Ema's hand reached for my ankle, her little fingers brushing against my skin. I tucked her hand back under the tablecloth and she went for my shoes, walking her doll over my toes.

Mrs. Lange sat down on my stool, which sent Mrs. Dolakova into a state, slamming her money box on the table behind me. "Everything all right?" Mrs. Lange asked, studying her nails, but I was too stunned to answer—she did look like she was taking over my stand. "Anna?"

"Of course," I said. Mrs. Dolakova slid a finger across her neck when Mrs. Lange wasn't looking, and I wanted to die.

God help us, Josef Danek, I thought, feeling for my wedding band with Ema's doll walking up my leg.

My herb jars brought a few lowly customers to my table. "Can I interest you in a cucumber?" I asked, and they were plump and dark green, exactly what a cucumber should look like, but I couldn't push a cucumber into anyone's hands. Not one customer came to buy Mrs. Dolakova's cherries.

She gave me an elbow. "Here's a sale…" She waved one of her regular customers over, who shuddered upon seeing Mrs. Lange at our stand. "She's not with me," Mrs. Dolakova said.

"Does she know that?" the woman asked.

"That's a very good question." Mrs. Dolakova looked at me. "I don't think she does."

Together they picked through the cherries that had split

from the rain, gathering them in a sack. "I have some news for you," the woman whispered over the table. "Beware of the tax collector. There's a German stand selling cherries too."

Mrs. Dolakova gasped. "I'm being replaced?"

The woman paid for her meager sack of cherries. "Watch out," she said as she left.

"The tax collector." Mrs. Dolakova retired to her chair. "It's only a matter of time before he tells me to leave." I placed my hand on her back, but there was nothing I could say to make it better. German merchants had preference over Czech merchants.

"Do you have something for pain in those jars?" She dug her palms into her eyes. "My head is pounding all of a sudden."

I sorted through my jars until I found the mint oil. "This will help…" I dabbed some on my fingertips and massaged her temples, working my way deep into her scalp. She moaned, feeling some relief.

"Do you have anything that'll give the Germans the trots? You know, a good bout of diarrhea?" Mrs. Dolakova whispered. "We can tell them it'll blue up their eyes."

I smirked, wanting to laugh, but wouldn't dare, not with so many Germans around or with Mrs. Lange sitting so close. She pointed to my jar of chamomile flowers, perking up. "Is that hemlock?"

"It's chamomile," I said.

She smiled, snidely. "I found some hemlock growing near my cherry trees. You know it's poisonous, Anna. I bet the Germans wouldn't know the difference between chamomile and hemlock if it was given to them in a cake or steeped in their tea."

"But that would kill—"

"I know," Mrs. Dolakova said. "I bet you have some growing around your property too."

We did have some. I'd made up a jar of crushed flowers when we had a vermin problem, but I hadn't thought about that for months. "Would you really be able to go through with it?" I whispered, and her gaze trailed off into the distance before shooting back to me.

"Would you?" she asked.

Moments later, Mrs. Dolakova's nightmare came walking through the square. The tax collector. We both stiffened, watching him as he made his rounds, passing by the German stands to collect from the Czech ones, who immediately boxed up their things afterward.

"Maybe they're leaving because of the change in weather?" The clouds had rolled in and a sweep of coolness blew over my skin and over my vegetables. I put my hand out, feeling for a raindrop, when the tax collector pivoted, walking straight toward us.

"We're about to find out," Mrs. Dolakova said.

"Mama?" Ema said from under the table, and I bent down to make sure the tablecloth hid every inch of her body from the collector's peeping eyes.

"Shh, shh…" I said through the fabric, hoping he couldn't hear me or see what I was doing. Mrs. Dolakova yanked once on my sleeve.

"Mrs.—" he said directly over the top of me, and I stood

up tall, throwing my hands behind my back. Mrs. Dolakova smiled.

"Yes?" I asked.

He pushed his glasses up his nose, inspecting my stand and Mrs. Dolakova's cherries for many seconds, not saying a word, his petite mouth pinching at times. Mrs. Lange got up from her stool and stood next to me, hands on her hips. "Is this your stand?" he asked.

"I'm helping today," Mrs. Lange said.

"I see." He looked at Mrs. Dolakova next, and she straightened, smiling nervously as he marked something off on his clipboard. "You can't sell cherries."

"Why not?" she asked, but of course we already knew.

"Pack them up," he said, and before she could protest, he flicked his chin at me. "And you. No cucumbers."

My hands fell to my jars. "What about the herbs?" I asked, and in a moment of desperation, I asked about the carrots too. "I planted some yesterday, but in a month they should be ready."

"Herbs? Yes. Carrots? No." He folded up his arms with his clipboard close to his chest. "There's a German merchant already selling carrots on the other side of the square."

"That man there?" Mrs. Lange scoffed, pointing across the square. "His carrots are big and dirty, grown for burrows and rabbits, not the kind you cook with. Anna's here won't compete," she said. "Surely you can—"

"Are you running this stand?" he snapped.

"Well, no," she said. "I already told you—"

"Then no carrots." He turned to me and Mrs. Dolakova. "Now, time to pay your taxes." He pointed to our money boxes. "Forty percent of what you made today."

"Forty percent?" I asked. "It's never been that high."

"Open them up," he said, and Mrs. Dolakova and I opened our paltry money boxes.

"I'll pay it!" Mrs. Lange said, and we watched in astonishment as she dug into her handbag and pulled out a few coins from her coin purse.

"Mrs. Lange," I said, "you don't have to—"

"It's not a problem." She turned to the tax collector. "Hope this is enough."

He took the money, dropping the coins into his money belt and I thought that would be it, he'd leave us alone, but he shot a look to Mrs. Dolakova after she'd only packed up her cherries. "Pack your entire stand up for the day," he said.

"Why?" Mrs. Dolakova said. "I still have leather goods to sell."

"Do it." He turned to walk away as if he was finished with us, but then reconsidered, lowering his clipboard. "No daughter today?"

"Daughter?" Ema's fingers danced up and down my leg.

"Yes," he said. "The young blonde girl. You usually bring her, do you not?" He put his hand out when a raindrop fell on his head, looking into the sky where the clouds had rolled in, shrouding the square in grayness.

"It might rain soon," Mrs. Lange said, and the tax collector turned on his heel and left, not waiting for an answer so he could collect from the others before the rain came.

I let out a breath, feeling the shake in my hands, and rubbing them steady while Mrs. Dolakova packed up her stand, throwing her leather goods into baskets and mumbling about the Germans and how they were going to kill her one way or another. She looked sharply up at me. "I'll be getting my health card soon enough, Anna. You too if the Reich decides you can't assimilate."

"What do you mean?"

"The woman from the stand behind," she said, and I looked over her shoulder, only the stand was bare. "The Reich ordered her to go to a health screening. She thought it had something to do with assistance for the poor, only she hasn't been seen since. That was five days ago." A squadron of German fighter planes buzzed overhead, high in the clouds, coming back from a fight in the east. "The day those planes stop coming back is the day we have a prayer of surviving. Until then, be careful, Anna." She patted my back, then rolled her cart away.

"Anna," Mrs. Lange said, but my thoughts were scattered, first from the tax collector and now the news from Mrs. Dolakova. I felt Ema's doll walking over my toes.

"Not now, Mrs. Lange." I held my head. "I… I have a headache." An SS officer walked into the market, taking in every sight and smell of the square. "My God," I breathed. I couldn't move—every muscle tightened, with fear coursing through my veins, seizing my heart and my head.

"Anna…" Mrs. Lange said again, reaching for my arm, but my eyes were only on the officer who had started to walk toward us, moving from stand to stand, boots clicking against the cobblestones and hands clasped behind his back.

"Smells wonderful over here." A smile had lifted the officer's face before he scowled, eyeing my tattered dress, dingy apron and kerchief, and my coal-stained hands. "On second thought, I smell black pepper." He looked Mrs. Lange over. "Is this your stand?"

"No," she said at the same time she popped open the umbrella over my table. "But I'm always looking for a good business venture."

"Mmm." He walked off to the fountain where a small gathering had formed, more SS in uniforms, and I thought they might be formulating a plan—which Czech mother they should rob.

I blindly reached for Ema's hand under the table. "I'll meet you in the car, Mrs. Lange," I said, but before she could reply, I'd pulled Ema out from under the table and dragged her away.

"Where are we going?" Ema asked.

"Not a word, Ema," I said as she yanked and scratched at her kerchief. Another raindrop fell, and then another, as I walked faster, trying not to look suspicious, only to stop suddenly in the middle of the pavement with an audible gasp.

A Brown Sister.

She had flaxen hair just like the one from Dasa's barn. She ambled through the street handing out candy to little children. Ema stepped on my heels, and I frantically looked for another way to walk, causing people to watch and talk. I spun around, pulling Ema the opposite way.

"Mama, the car's over there…" Scattered raindrops turned into a hard sprinkle. "Eww…" Ema said, and I looked down, horrified at the sight of gray streaks running down her cheeks. She swiped at her forehead, making it worse as the coaly-water ran into her eyes. A hand grabbed me forcibly.

"Don't take my—" I shrieked, pulling Ema defensively toward me.

The tax collector. He slowly drew his hand back under his umbrella, looking at me as if he thought I'd gone mad. "What are you—" His gaze fell to Ema where a dribble of gray snuck past her blue eyes and down her cheek as she blinked up at him.

His eyes bulged from their sockets.

"Get out of my way," I said, and I pushed past him, tugging on Ema's hand, when I heard the tax collector shout to someone behind me.

"Hurry, Ema. Hurry…" I went to scoop her up, but there was no time.

"You there!" I heard. A uniformed member of the Reich —looked like the SS—but they were a blur. "Stop!"

The crowd thinned immediately from the rain. A pair of hands caught me by the shoulders. "Let go of me!" I wriggled and thrashed, trying to get away as he called for the Brown Sister.

"Come here, child," the Brown Sister said. "Want some candy?" She snatched Ema's kerchief from her head and Ema's hands flew to her hair. "We got one!" She pulled Ema by the arm.

"No!" I shouted, and we fought over her, tugging Ema back and forth between us. "Leave my daughter alone!"

Passersby watched us in horror, protecting their own children and not offering to help.

She threw my child over her shoulder in a final act of thievery and hauled her away while I was held back. "Mama!" Ema cried over the woman's shoulder, nose scrunched up and eyes watery slits, disappearing into the rainy streets. "Mama—"

A truncheon flew up in the air for my head. "Ema—" I screamed, bloodcurdling and cold, before folding to the pavement.

Chapter Seven

S he was born on a Sunday. My parents were in the parlor, waiting for word, and Dasa helped the midwife. Josef paced the hallway, watching the clock. Dasa said I'd fall madly in love with my baby, and I didn't fully understand what she meant until I heard her first wailing breath and looked into her eyes. Josef ran into the room while I was still breathless and sweaty, throwing open the door and kneeling by my side. The midwife shouted at him to get back, but it was too late, he was already looking at our daughter with the same wide eyes, and he was not going to leave.

Everything turned hazy after that, people coming and going and saying things to me I don't remember, taking peeks of the baby in the midwife's arms. I was suddenly an observer myself, detached and cow-heavy, lying in my bed. Josef swept my hair back and looked into my eyes. "Bring her here," I said, and he called for the midwife after the baby had been cleaned and swaddled.

"Maybe you should rest," Matka said, and my father agreed, but I shook my head.

The baby fussed in the midwife's arms and I reached out for her.

"Come back to me," I said to my baby girl, and the midwife placed her in my arms. One hand reached out, wrinkly fingers grasping, and I melted into a pool of warm tears of love.

Josef shooed everyone out of the room and then it was just us. Her skin was so soft, much softer than I imagined. She cooed, snuggling in the blanket, and Josef sat on the bed next to me, one arm wrapped around me. "What should we name her?" I asked, but I wondered if there was a name good enough. "There's Helga, and Alice and…"

"Ema?" he said, and I smiled.

"Yes." It was the most beautiful name. "Ema."

We watched her in my arms. "Look what we created, Josef," I said, and I felt her warmth through the blanket, her little face pinching and relaxing subtly. We'd painted the walls pale yellow in the spare bedroom to go with the blanket I'd sewn and filled it with the best furniture Josef could buy. How silly we were. "She has to sleep with us. In our room."

"Whatever you like, darling," Josef said.

I placed her between my legs on the bed and she looked like a tiny bean all wrapped up. "Ema," I whispered, and she moved. "Maybe I'll rock her again."

"You don't have to—"

I picked her up, tucking her in close. "There, there, now," I said. She smelled of talc and something else, something I could only describe as heaven—powdery, floral, and warm. She cooed again. "Everything is all right. You're safe." I kissed her forehead as her fingers curled around my thumb. "And I'll never let go…"

"Anna!" Mrs. Lange said over my face, and I sat bolt

upright from the ground, holding my head. "What are you doing on the pavement?" She leaned over me with her umbrella as passersby walked around me. "It's late. I've been looking all over for you!"

"Where is she?" I scrambled to get up, but wasn't sure where to go, and realized some time had passed while I was out on the ground, which immediately made me retch in the gutter. "Did you see?" I asked, but Mrs. Lange looked lost and confused. I yanked her toward me by the lapels, my heart pounding and body shaking. "Where's my daughter?"

Mrs. Lange covered her gaping mouth, and I stumbled away, clutching my stomach and screaming Ema's name in the street, but most people kept their heads down and scurried away as if I was a sight to be seen—a madwoman. "Someone saw something!" I said, darting after people. "You there"—I pointed—"did you see what happened?" I grabbed one man's arm, then another's, but nobody would stop, nobody would answer. Shutters closed above Nazi flags waving from dowels, with the spit of rain dripping heavily off the seams. I heard Ema's voice calling for me in my head. I saw her crying face.

I looked to the gray sky, pleading with fists punching the air. "Give me back my daughter!"

And then I was alone. Not one soul walked the small enclosure where they took her from me—not even Mrs. Lange. The rain had dissipated into a mist, and I saw Ema's doll lying in a puddle between the cobblestones.

The market, I thought, wiping my eyes. *The Nazis.*

I snatched Ema's doll from the ground, tripping and stumbling my way back to the square. The market had closed, and my vegetables and herbs were gone. The fountain area was near empty too, cleared of all the Nazis that had been there earlier. Only a solitary man looking into the water, gazing at his reflection with the fountain spray breezing over his face and arms. A ghost of a person, if I'd ever seen one. I shuffled toward him.

"They took my son," he said, falling to his knees. He clasped a toy soldier in his hand, squeezing and squeezing, and my gaze drifted to the water, taking his place, drowning in the thought that I might never see Ema again, not wanting to leave the spot I'd last seen her, yet also wanting to run. I clutched her doll tightly.

Matka came up behind me. "There you are! What's going on with you? I was worried after you didn't come home." She reached for my chin to pull my face up, only she'd just noticed the others who'd gathered around the fountain like me—the man, and two women I didn't remember wandering up, all sharing the same blank stare, the lost stare, the childless stare.

"Where's Ema?" she asked, pulling her hand back.

"They took her," I said.

Matka's hand clamped over her mouth. "The... the..." she muffled into her palm, and I nodded. "Brown Sisters," she said, and the others looked up.

"Do you know something?" one woman asked. "Tell me..." She cried openly among the shadows that had surrounded us, reaching for me and then Matka, who stepped back, unsure what to say, except the truth.

"We only know what you know," Matka said. "That the Germans are filthy bastards."

A shout came from a window. "New Town Hall!" we heard.

I grabbed the man next to me by the shirt sleeve, and he came back to life. "Our children!" I said, and all of us ran the few short streets to the New Town Hall, where it was dark, the administrators long since gone home, except for a strange flicker of light way up high in one of the large windows on the second floor. I covered my mouth, watching from the street in silence, looking for signs of our children, when Matka yelled up.

"Give me back my granddaughter—"

"Ema!" I yelled, and the others repeatedly shouted their children's names in frantic, desperate voices. A gray silhouette passed by one of the windows, and we quieted, each grabbing the other, thinking we might have some news. The curtains flew up, and we all gasped. The woman who took Ema.

"Ema!" I shrieked. "Mama's here!" I pounded on the double front doors with my fists, demanding they open them up, but nobody came. That's when we heard the revving of a lorry from behind the building. The man grabbed a brick and one woman had her handbag to throw, and we ran after the lorry, screaming and shouting our children's names so they could hear us, but Tabor's mayor was there to stop us, rolling closed a gate that had never been there before.

"Let us through!" I said, but he put his hands up as the lorry drove away from us. The man who'd lost his son threw a punch at the mayor's face and guards poured out of the building, pinning him to the ground.

"Traitor!" Matka shouted at the mayor, waving a closed fist in the air. "You're a traitor to the Czechs!" Her voice echoed through the streets as I dropped to the ground with the other women, begging for him to give us our children back, grasping at his feet and pulling on his legs.

The mayor commanded the guards to take the man inside, and they dragged him kicking and fighting into the dark building where all turned quiet. He turned back around to find Matka's finger in his face.

"You will *pay* for this," Matka said.

The mayor sneered. "What did you say?"

"I said you will pay—"

He pushed Matka and she fell on her hip, crying out. "Watch what you say," he warned, eyes cast down, "all of you." He left with a turn of his heel, leaving us mothers crumpled in agony on the cobblestones.

Matka whispered in my ear, "Tomas. He'll find out where they took her, but we must hurry home."

"Yes, Tomas," I said, and with that, I felt some measure of hope, something to cling onto. We raced home as fast as we could, Matka holding her hip and me holding my head where the truncheon had clubbed me, but I lost Matka several paces back once we reached our neighborhood.

I threw open the front door, expecting to see Tomas sitting at the table waiting for us with Dasa and her children, but the house was quiet and dark.

"Ah! It's you." Dasa had walked out of the kitchen with the baby in her arms. "Tomas took the girls," she said, but I pounded through the house, searching for him anyway. "They went into hiding. He thought it was safer that way in the end. But I couldn't let the baby go, not while he's still feeding." I staggered out of the hallway to see Dasa kissing the baby's forehead and smoothing back his hair where the coal had already rubbed off.

"Ema—" My voice cracked, and with that, my sister's face changed—she knew something terrible had happened. "The Brown Sisters took her," I said, and Dasa shrieked.

Matka had just walked in and hung her head.

"Where?" Dasa asked, but my mind was on Tomas, and how I was supposed to find him. I held onto the wall, feeling faint and weak but trying to find strength.

"They left in a lorry," Matka said. "And not just with Ema. They took others too."

Dasa clenched her baby tightly. "What are we going to do?"

"Wait and see if Tomas comes back tomorrow morning," Matka said.

Dasa shook her head. "Tomas said he'd send a message once the girls were safe. He had no plans to come back."

I pushed myself away from the wall. "Then I'll go to the tunnels," I said. "I'll search until I find an entrance." Matka forced me to sit on the divan.

"You can't go in this state," Matka said. "You're exhausted. You'll get caught. You need your wits about you for this one, Anna, and right now you're a scattered no-good."

"I can't wait until tomorrow." I pushed myself off the divan to grab a bag. "My daughter needs me." I hastily gathered up some things, fresh shoes, and a jacket for an evening search, but Dasa blocked the door.

"She's right, Anna. You can't go tonight. What if the Germans find you out past curfew, walking the village streets? You won't find Ema if you're arrested."

I stood for a moment with my things in my hands before letting out a little cry and backing away. In my cloudy mind, I knew there was some sense in waiting, regardless of the pain. I stumbled down the hallway to Ema's room, pushing open her door with one hand and peeking into her dark room. A tower of blocks only half stacked sat on the rug. An open book tented over a stuffed bear on the floor where she last played. Her bed, cold and black with shadow.

I collapsed to my knees, curling up with Ema's baby blanket on the rug. "Josef—" I sobbed into the cotton "—look what's happened to us." A debilitating pain ripped through my body, a loss, an unimaginable loss, and a horrific moan erupted from my mouth that brought Matka to the floor where I lay. Dasa rushed in with the sedative we used for childbirth, holding a soaked rag over my nose until I went limp and rested somewhere in between dead and alive.

"Bastard Germans," I remember Matka saying as I faded away. "They will pay…"

My daughter's smell woke me up with a jolting shiver. "Ema!" I called out, looking at her bedroom door, expecting her to walk through it even though I knew she wouldn't. I lumbered down the hallway into the parlor, fists catching on the walls, shouting for Matka to get up and for Dasa to come out of the cellar, but they were already sitting on the divan, thinking up a plan as the day broke.

Dasa looked up, eyes heavy. "I'm sorry," she said. "You didn't want to go to the market, and it was your daughter they took…"

I held my head where it throbbed, and she got up to put her arms around me. I resisted at first but fell into her embrace, and we wept onto each other's shoulders. "We were too busy thinking about my children and the list," she said. "We didn't think of yours."

Matka wiped her eyes of tears, nodding.

"How much more can we endure?" Dasa asked. "The Reich has taken everything."

I broke away, wiping away my tears too. "We're Czech, Dasa," I said, and she looked at me. "This isn't where the story ends. It's where it begins."

Dasa sniffed her running nose. "How did it happen?" She shook her head. "I'm sorry… you don't have to—"

"The SS were at the market." Dasa put her hand over her mouth as I talked. "I made Ema hide under the table the whole day. But one stopped to look at my herbs."

"What was an SS officer doing at a Czech table?" Matka asked, but I was too ashamed to tell her how Mrs. Lange appeared to have taken over my stand. "Don't tell me…" she said. "It was that Lange woman?"

I dipped my eyes for a *Yes*, and Matka grabbed her hip, shaking her head.

"A Brown Sister yanked her from me, Dasa. Right there

in the street." Pain gripped my heart, feeling Ema's hand slip from mine all over again. "I tried to hold on…"

"That woman—traitor! She will pay too, after this war," Matka said, sneering. "People can hide now, but one day…"

Dasa squeezed Matka's hand. "Now's not the time for a rant."

Matka took a few deep breaths, looking toward the floor. "You're right," she said. "We need to focus now. Find Tomas. Find a tunnel entrance. I wonder…" She went to the bookcase and dug through the old books. "Where's that one book your father kept?" she asked, tossing books over her shoulder.

Dasa stepped toward her. "What are you doing?"

"Found it!" She blew dust from the cover. "Hussite history," she said, opening the book and flipping through the pages, before lighting up with a gasp. "Girls, look! I don't know why I didn't think of this before." She moved to the divan and pointed to a hand-drawn map in the back of the book. "Your father took notes. All the stories he'd heard at the mines about the tunnels, he matched them with the information in this book." She looked up, and we leaned in.

There was one tunnel clearly noted in the south near a big meadow, as if he'd seen it himself, while other possible locations were noted with a question mark throughout the village square and seemed very unlikely, places I couldn't imagine a tunnel existing—the New Town Hall, for one. "This one in the south by the meadow seems like the clear choice. It has the most notes, but getting there would be a problem. We'd have to pass through the German neighborhood and that's too far and risky." She moved her finger up and pointed to a location in the village center after musing over all the other possible spots. "This is where I think Tomas's rebels are hiding. Where he's hiding."

"But that's the butcher shop," I said. "He's German."

Matka shook her head. "Only on paper. Did it for business. Now look at him. He's thriving. I know a Czech heart when I see one." She pointed at the map. "There was a tunnel there before the war, there will be one now, and I've been wracking my brain, wondering where Tomas buried that Nazi bitch—if you noticed, he never answered my question about where she was buried—and there's only one place that's truly plausible. One place where he'd be able to get rid of a body for good, with no chance of her popping back up. A butcher."

I was too stunned to say anything. The thought of Tomas taking the dead woman to a butcher.

"Think about it," Matka said, suddenly wincing and holding her hip.

"The butcher's a Nazi," Dasa said. "He butchered my cows and fed all the Germans."

"Trust me," Matka said. "He could get rid of a body and nobody would know. It makes sense. Right where the Hussites built a tunnel all those years ago. It's still there." She pointed at the map again. "I'd bet my life on it."

"There has to be more than trust to go on, Matka," I said. "More than your intuition and talk of Czech hearts. If we go there and he's not who you think he is…"

"I was a customer in his shop not long ago. I watched him pick over a prime cut of beef for scraps, gave them to a fancy German woman wearing nice shoes and a hat. He told her it was the best he had that day. I saw it with my own eyes." She nodded once. "He is German only in name."

I looked at Dasa, and she at me. Matka was a person of signs, a woman of language. She held onto mere mentions, inferences, and brought them up years later as fact. Only now it was different. If we were wrong about the butcher, he'd call for our arrest, like any other German in Tabor.

"No," I said. "We'll go south of the village near the meadow, try to find the tunnel and enter there."

"We can't do that!" Matka said, wincing again from her hip. "We'll have to walk right past Mr. Ott's place and we all know his wife will report us for suspicious behavior." She shook her head. "Absolutely not."

"Then what about the tunnel near the bank of the Lužnice River? Josef thought there was one there once."

"We'll be wasting our time when we don't have time to waste," Matka said. "It's in the country and they'll suspect us of fishing and you know Czechs aren't allowed to fish. The butcher shop is where we'll go. I'm listening to my heart, Anna."

"I know you are," I said. Matka had got up from the divan, rubbing her hip, and I wondered how she was going to make the ride into the village with me. "But how can you possibly—"

"I'll manage," she said, but she was hobbling.

"Matka, you can't go," I said. "Last night…"

"I'm going with you, Anna. I walked home, didn't I? Don't worry." She limped on, but then stumbled painfully forward.

"Matka!" I said, grabbing onto her. "Look at you." We both hung our heads. "You can't go."

Our foreheads touched, and she smoothed back my hair, sniffling. "I want to go, my daughter," she whispered.

"I know you do," I breathed, and Matka turned to Dasa, who sat up straight with Matka's eyes on her. She held the baby closer, her eyes large and frightened.

"You'll have to go in my place, Dasa," she said, but I knew Dasa would rather die than leave her baby. "It's too dangerous for a Czech woman to walk the village streets alone after what happened yesterday."

"It's all right, Dasa," I said. "You don't have to."

Dasa shook her head after taking a moment. "I'll go. You shouldn't go alone." She kissed her baby repeatedly, burying her face into the hollow between his neck and shoulder, where she muffled her cry. "I love you," she said to him, kissing his cheek, and petting him before putting him down for a morning nap. "Mama loves you…"

"He opens at nine o'clock, but like all good butchers he'll be there earlier," Matka said. "And you'll need a plan. You can't walk in there and expect him to offer up all his secrets."

I closed my eyes. "What do you think I should say?" I still had my eyes closed when Matka said I should turn into the actress I once was, take on a character. "What do you mean?"

"Like in one of your plays," Matka said. "Didn't you play a spy?"

My mouth hung open. I had played a spy, once. "Yes," I said. "A cabaret dancer turned spy during the Great War."

Josef bought me roses for playing the lead. It was a beautiful night. Standing ovation. "But that was ages ago…"

"But you remember the character, don't you?" Matka asked. "You could be her again, Anna. He's either going to open up the vault or call for your arrest. The trick is when to let him know which side you're on. Timing is an actress's greatest skill, isn't that what you always said?"

"Yes," I said, "but Matka, there are so many other tunnels to choose from." I unfolded my arms to point at the map.

"And all of them are uncertain. We already went through this, Anna," she said. "I believe this is your best option." She felt her chest. "I feel it in here."

Matka kissed us goodbye. I kept waiting for her to say something about killing a bitch or making someone pay, but instead, she looked at her hands. "Come back to me, all right?" She wiped a gush of tears from her cheeks that had fallen so fast, even she couldn't stop them from dripping on the floor, and I thought of Ema, feeling the weight of what would happen to all of us if we failed with the butcher.

"We will, Matka," I said, followed by Dasa.

Chapter Eight

We took our bicycles by the handlebars and walked them off my property to the road. "Do you think anyone's watching?" Dasa asked, and shutters clacked in the distance.

"Yes."

We got on our bicycles and pedaled down the road as the roosters crowed. Any earlier would have looked suspicious, and any later would have been futile with the crowds arriving for their rations.

"Promise me, Dasa," I said as we approached the village. "That one day the traitors will make themselves known, and they'll pay for what they've done to us." I caught a glimpse of my neighbor peeping out of her upstairs window, which was just high enough to see into Dasa's garden and watch our children when they played.

"I promise," she said.

We got off our bicycles once we reached the village, astonished by the swelling rush of morning foot traffic, as if all the Germans in Tabor had been invited to come out of their homes at the exact same time and make friends with the Czechs who'd assimilated.

"Come on," I said, and we rode another way, down a cobbled backstreet with laundry hanging window to window on strings, only instead of people, we ran into parked cars. Cars with Nazi flags—cars from the Reich—crowding the already narrow street.

The SS were still here. Which meant so were the Brown Sisters.

"I'm nervous." Dasa straddled the bicycle between her legs.

"Me too." We placed our bicycles in the rack outside the butcher shop. A man smoked from a window one floor up, watching us, close enough to hear us, close enough to talk to us. I'd glanced up casually, but what had started as a casual glance became an intense stare, our silence becoming more like words by the time I'd made it to the striped overhang.

We stood against the building. "What if this doesn't work?" I asked.

Dasa hugged me while my eyes were closed. "You will succeed, sister," she said. "You're the best actress I've ever seen, one with charms. You'll get him to talk." Germans pushed past us while the Czechs looked at the ground, trying to get by unnoticed. "You can do it."

I opened the door to the ting of bells. "We're closed!" the butcher immediately yelled from the back.

"Hallo?" I said anyway.

We stood next to his blood-stained meat counter with

strips of white paper all about the floor, the clammy sweetness of days-old meat in a warming space settling all around. I gagged, thinking of him quartering the Brown Sister's body. Dasa plugged her nose.

He poked his head out from the back. "I said—"

Dasa and I straightened, and he walked slowly toward us, studying us, wiping his hands on his apron and leaving pink smears on white. "We don't open up for two hours. Come back then." He glanced at my hands, my ratty dress, and my scuffed pumps. "And today is German day."

I cleared my throat. "Good morning," I said. "Sorry to intrude. You are closed, are you?" I asked, but he continued studying me, looking me up and down, and Dasa too. My eyes ached from a night of tears on Ema's floor and I was sure they were still swollen. I took a deep breath before continuing. "I hear you offer a service no other butcher can offer."

He walked behind his counter and folded his arms. "Maybe," he said after a pause, eyes still skirting over the both of us. "Who's asking?"

I recited the lines I had memorized years before as if I'd just read them off the script. "We've heard about you," I said. "Through a friend. I'm sure you know the one…"

"Me?" His eyelids lowered. "What have you heard?"

I felt Dasa trembling as she stood next to me. "Things…" I walked the length of his counter, my fingers skipping over the top. "You are a good German, no?"

His eyes swung to Dasa, but she looked to me.

"Who are you? What do you want?"

I laughed a girly giggle, eyes dancing over his corkboard

where ration and shopping times were pinned and noted. I leaned backward on my heels as if I had time to spare. "What does anyone want from a butcher?"

I still had a smile on my face when I noticed the man who'd stared at us outside was now in the street talking to a German policeman on patrol. He pointed his cigarette at the butcher shop. I felt my insides shrink, and the character I'd been playing evaporated from my grasp like water on a hot pavement.

I turned around to face the butcher, my mouth hanging open, and he reached for one of his sharp knives, curling his fingers around the handle and setting the blade on the counter.

"Sir, I..." My eyes shifted, catching sight of the policeman again who was now walking across the street toward the shop.

"Anna," Dasa breathed, grasping for my hand.

The policeman looked through the window, cupping his hands around his eyes.

"What do you want?" the butcher asked, and I gulped, feeling the private seconds we had with him disappearing, hands sweating, heart thrumming.

"I need to find the Resistance—Tomas. Please," I blurted just as the door swung open with a frenzied clang of bells.

The butcher's gaze lifted over my head to the policeman standing behind me, the bells tinging softly from a closed door.

"Fräulein," the policeman said. "Turn around."

He spoke in German, but all Czechs were expected to know simple commands—I couldn't pretend I didn't understand. I swallowed, composing myself the best I could before turning around, gripping my handbag.

"It's German day for butcher rations," he said in sloppy Czech, and I focused on his gray uniform pocket, too afraid to look into his eyes. "Where are your documents?"

I opened my handbag and dug around, but my documents were the only thing inside. Dasa scooted even closer to me.

"And yours," he said to Dasa, and she looked like she was about to be sick.

"Mine too?" she asked, thumb to her chest.

"Dasa, your documents," I said, but she wouldn't move. The last thing she wanted was for the police to know who she was, but what else could she do? "In your handbag." I reached for Dasa's handbag. "Dasa—"

The door opened again. "Hallo, ladies!" It was Mrs. Lange, and she panted as if she'd just run from across the street. "I made it after all, thank you kindly." She took one deep breath that turned into a sigh. "I hope it's all right that I sent a Czech in to get my rations," she said to the butcher, fluttering her fingers in the air, and he nodded, hesitantly.

Mrs. Lange smiled, looking satisfied, then looking confused, as if suddenly realizing the police were in the same room with us. "Is something wrong?" she asked me, and the officer folded his arms. I caught myself with my mouth hanging open, looking at Mrs. Lange, wondering what in God's name she was thinking.

"Are these Czech women with you?" The policeman pointed.

"Officer Richter," Mrs. Lange said, blushing. "Do you

remember me? So nice to see you. Please forgive me." She giggled, and I didn't know it was possible to giggle in front of the police. "Yes, they are with me."

Mrs. Lange turned to me. "Tell him, Anna," she said. "Go ahead. Tell him how I was such a ninny this morning and asked you to fetch my rations in my stead." She sighed, trying to look exhausted by clasping her hands together. "I have so much going on, you see?"

I stared at her as she blinked her big blue eyes. She'd become another person. She'd become… an actress again, like in Prague.

An actress.

"Oh, yes," I said, coming to life. "That's it. That's why I'm here." I smiled.

The policeman snapped for my documents anyway, taking a discerning look at my photo, comparing what I looked like to the black-and-white image pasted inside. "There's policy to follow. Don't let it happen again." He handed my documents back, and to Dasa's relief, skipped over hers.

"Sorry, officer," Mrs. Lange said. "She was doing me a favor. You know how simple-minded they can be." She cleared her throat with that comment. "I'm here now, so I'll be getting my meat today."

He turned on his heel and left. Then it was just the three of us standing in front of the butcher, the question I'd asked about Tomas still wedged between us, unanswered.

"Sir, I—"

He ripped a piece of white butcher paper from the roll and slapped a cut of fatty meat onto it to be wrapped.

"Anything else?" he asked Mrs. Lange, and she handed him a coupon she pulled from her dress pocket for that day's ration.

"No." A smile flashed on her face. "Thank you for understanding."

He groaned before walking to the back of his shop. Mrs. Lange waited until he was out of earshot before grabbing me urgently by the shoulders. "I know where Ema is!"

"You do?" I breathed, and Dasa caught me from collapsing. "But how?"

Mrs. Lange's eyes shifted across the street where the policeman was walking away. "Not in here," she said, now taking a guarded look at the butcher in the back, who'd taken a rack of ribs off a hook and threw it on the counter, reaching for his cleaver. "He wants us to leave, I can tell."

"Then where?" Dasa asked, still holding onto me.

"Meet me at your house," she whispered. "I told my husband I had to return the things you left in the market yesterday. It won't look suspicious." She motioned with her head to the window where a line of Germans had started to form for that day's rations, not yet knowing Mrs. Lange had received hers early. "Staying here will."

She tucked her meat under her arm, and we followed her outside where she disappeared into the foot traffic. "Dasa," I said, taking her hand, wanting to rejoice in our luck, but the man who'd alerted the police looked down at us from his window. "Come on," I said, and after we'd walked far enough away, we embraced on the pavement.

Mrs. Lange had already parked and unloaded my things from the car boot by the time we'd made it to my house, but she was nowhere in sight. Dasa and I got off our bicycles in the dirt, looking at each other, knowing that if Mrs. Lange wasn't outside, then she was inside.

With Matka.

We dumped our bicycles, bursting through the front door to find Matka waving a kitchen knife at Mrs. Lange as she backed up to the divan, begging for mercy.

"Put the knife down!" I demanded.

Matka sliced at the air, her eyes wild, stepping ever so close to Mrs. Lange, who looked like she was about to wet herself with her heels scraping the floor. The baby screamed from where Matka had set him down, making it hard to hear.

"She's helping us," Dasa said, picking the baby up and trying to soothe him as Matka pressed on with the knife.

"She knows where Ema is!" I shouted, and Matka snapped out of her chaotic state, pulling her shoulders back along with the knife.

"And we're supposed to trust this traitor?" Matka asked.

Mrs. Lange took several shallow breaths with one hand held out between them, as if that would stop Matka from coming at her again with the knife. "My husband," she said, looking at me and then to Matka. "He has friends. Nazi friends. I sometimes listen in on what they say. I may be legally German, but I'm Czech, just like you."

Matka scoffed, throwing her hands up.

"Where's Ema?" I asked.

"Yes, where is Ema?" Matka pointed her knife this time instead of waving it. "Talk fast."

Mrs. Lange sat on the divan, holding her chest. "They took her to a facility in Warsaw."

"Poland!" Matka yelped. "Ema… in Poland?" She turned away, mumbling to herself about Nazis and devils.

"Why Warsaw?" I asked. "And what kind of facility?"

"It's where they test the children, make sure they can pass as German. Doctors will do their inspections then the Reich will place her in a special nursery for—" Mrs. Lange covered her mouth. "Do you really want to know?"

"I must know what's happening to her."

She took a strained breath, looking down at her folded hands before continuing. "She will be indoctrinated into the Nazi way and adopted by a German family. And Ema…" She paused. "Ema will forget her Czech roots at this age. She will believe her new mother is her real mother."

I burst into a sobbing cry, and Mrs. Lange looked horrified by my reaction, covering her ears. "I'm sorry…" she kept saying as I cried. "They'll move her to one of their German nurseries. I hope to find out more tomorrow, possibly the location."

"Why tomorrow?" Dasa asked, and Mrs. Lange took a deliberate look at the baby in her arms, which made Dasa scoot backward and attempt to hide him with his baby blanket—she was the first outsider to know we had a baby.

"There's a garden party my husband and I were invited to. The same people who know about the adoption program will be there. It's why there's so many officers from the Reich in Tabor. I'll overhear things at the party."

I looked at my shaking hands, the ones that were supposed to protect my daughter, but had failed. I couldn't sit at home and wait.

I crawled up off the floor, taking Mrs. Lange's hand. "Take me with you." I swallowed dryly, croaking my words, knowing only that I had to get as close as possible to the people who knew where Ema was, otherwise I was dead already.

"And what would you do?" Mrs. Lange asked. Her eyes flicked to Dasa and Matka as if she expected their help, but Matka stepped closer.

"Yes…" Matka breathed. "Take her with you so we can kill more bastards—more German bitches to plant in the garden. And maybe your husband."

Dasa gasped after Matka trod too closely to revealing our secret. "Matka!" She pulled her into the corner where she wasn't shy about telling her to be quiet.

"My husband," Mrs. Lang said, and Matka looked over, "is not—"

"He's German!" Matka shouted. "A Nazi. A devil." She broke away from Dasa and folded up her arms.

"Not every German is a Nazi, Mrs. Novakova," Mrs. Lange said, but Matka raised her eyebrows as if she wasn't convinced. "He loves his country, yes. But he isn't a very good German, as it turns out."

"He isn't?" I asked.

"You know what that means, don't you, Anna? When I say he's not a good German," she said, and I nodded, turning to Matka.

"He's not a good German, Matka. Hear that?"

"There are others, too," Mrs. Lange said.

"The butcher?" I asked.

"He's fickle," Mrs. Lange said. "I wouldn't go there again. Not after the police followed you inside."

Matka put her hands on her hips. "Police?" she bellowed. "What police? What are you talking about?"

"It's not what you think, Matka," I said. "Someone turned us in for being at the butcher shop on German day. Mrs. Lange saved us from being questioned."

"Oh?" Matka took her hands off her hips, and we were quiet, but Mrs. Lange still hadn't addressed my request.

"Mrs. Lange," I said, sitting next to her. "I've known you for a long time. Please"—I folded my hands into a praying position—"take me to the party."

"And I'll ask again, Anna. What would you do? Ask them what nursery they're planning to take your daughter to? They're not going to tell you."

"She's right, Anna," Matka said. "You can't show up there as yourself and ask questions. You'll never see Ema again if you do." Matka put her finger to her chin, thinking, mumbling, talking to herself before turning around with a shout that should have rattled the windows. "I know!"

"Keep it down, Matka," Dasa hissed.

"I don't have to keep it down. I know how to get her back!" Matka smiled, and it was the sly kind, lips curling on her face with delicious deception. "Anyone could look plain and homely if they want, and you know German fluently. They would never know!"

"What are you talking about?" I'd stood up and reached for Matka's hands, waiting for her to tell me her great idea.

Matka nodded once. "You'll solicit for a nurse position."

I was immediately disappointed, falling onto the divan and holding my head.

"This is it, Anna," Matka said. "The answer to our prayers!"

I scoffed. "A nurse? That's your idea?"

"Think about it," she said. "You could pass as a German, and you're great with children. You go there, to this nursery, solicit for employment and become one of them. Then you—"

"What, Matka?" I asked.

"Steal her back," Matka said, and I moved my hands away from my head. Dasa stopped petting her baby, and Mrs. Lange shifted once in her seat. "Beat them at their own game!" Matka raised a clenched fist in the air, but we continued to stare at her.

"Anna, pretend to be a German nurse?" Dasa said, breaking the silence. "She can't—"

"My God," I said, standing up, and Matka looked crushed, probably thinking I was going to reject the idea, but I'd played a German once at the theater. It wasn't a big part, but I was very good. "That's it. I'll be a German." I turned to Mrs. Lange. "Will you help me?" I asked. "Can you introduce me to the people who know about the program? If they think I want to be a nurse, who knows what can happen!"

"I…" Mrs. Lange stood from the divan, twisting and pulling on her fingers. "Anna, I don't—"

"All you have to do is make an introduction," I said. "I'm not afraid to mingle with the Germans, like the old days in Prague, or when I was a child. I can remember how to do it, and I'll play the part of a German woman." I waited for a response but she only looked at me. "For Ema, Mrs. Lange," I said. "Please…"

Mrs. Lange closed her eyes for an incredible amount of time. "An introduction?"

I threw my arms around her neck while her eyes were still closed. "Thank you, Mrs. Lange," I said, tearfully. "When will we leave—what time, and where will you pick me up?"

She pulled away sharply. "Now wait a minute, Anna. I haven't said yes yet. I'll have to convince my husband. He might think the risks are too great for us, he might not agree…" She pulled and twisted her fingers again, thinking. "There might be a way, now that I think of it," she said, and I held my chest, looking at Matka and Dasa for a brief second. "If I can make him think that bringing you to the party is his idea, maybe say something about payment for taking over your stand for the day. That might work, but he's smart and will probably see through it. I don't know…"

"That's it!" I nodded excessively. "He'll believe that. Will you do it?"

She looked me up and down. "You'll need to clean up. Wear a nice dress. Look lovely, but no cosmetics aside from a little powder. A good German woman, especially one who wants to work for the Reich, would be natural."

I threw my arms around her again, but this time she hugged me back. "Thank you," I said. "Thank you, thank you."

"Your neighbors will be suspicious if I drive out here for a third day in a row," she said. "I think the best thing would be for you to ride your bicycle into the village. Meet me on the corner where we parked yesterday. If my husband agrees, we'll be there at one o'clock."

I took a deep breath, and for the first time since Ema was taken, I felt like I had a real chance at getting her back.

She went on to tell me some of the party details. The host was named Fischer, an SS officer living on a country estate that used to belong to a rich Czech doctor, and he was celebrating his new wine library with a special dedication to the Party. I'd have to play the part of not only a German woman, but one that was important enough to be invited. It would be the performance of my life.

"But Anna," Mrs. Lange said. "Dear girl, you need to rest." She pulled back a clump of oily hair dangling in my eyes. "You won't gain employment with the Reich looking this way, no matter what you wear. You look like a mother worried sick over her daughter, and you must look like a fresh-eyed German girl whose heart belongs to the Führer. You must also be unmarried, Anna."

I instantly felt for my ring.

"She'll be rested," Matka said. "I'll make sure of it. Even if she has to digest some of her homemade herbal medicines."

"I'm sorry this happened to you, Anna," Mrs. Lange said. "It's why I insisted on staying at your stand yesterday. I'd heard things and was worried, but I didn't know enough, and I was too much of a coward to mention it. I thought I could protect her." Mrs. Lange pulled her handbag strap over her shoulder and went for the door. "I've always liked you, Anna," she said. "From the first time I met you at the theater." She looked down momentarily. "I'm Czech too."

She left, and after I closed the door, I reached for my sister and mother for an embrace.

"God help you," Matka said, pulling away to cross her chest. "And if this doesn't work, I'll be digging a hole in the garden for her husband."

She turned on her heel, leaving Dasa and me still holding onto each other.

Chapter Nine

The next morning Dasa helped me get ready. Matka pulled something from her apron pocket wrapped in a swatch of lace. She pulled the edges back, showing us a bar of expensive pink soap.

"I hid it in the potting shed." Matka held it to her nose for a sniff, looking up. "I'd been saving it for a special occasion."

Dasa leaned down to smell the soap herself. "Matka..." She grimaced. "Not this soap. It smells awful."

"This is lovely soap!" she said, smelling it again. "Fine Czech soap."

"Let me smell it," I said, and I turned away after getting a hefty whiff. "Ugh, Dasa's right. Out of all the soap to save, why this one?"

Matka's face fell, looking down at the bar of soap between her hands, pausing, rubbing her thumb over the smooth side of the bar. That's when I realized the soap must have been a gift from our father. "It was part of a set," she said. "Perfume and lotion…" She wrapped it back up in the lace. "You don't have to use it."

I reached for it but caught her hand instead. "Wait," I said. "It's all right."

"No, Anna," she said. "Dasa's right. It's too strong. I want to help, give you your best chance, and I thought by using this expensive soap…"

"I'll add some herbs to it." I reached for my lavender jar but decided on the lemon balm instead to cool the floral tones in the soap. I ground the dried leaves into a powder using my mortar and pestle.

Matka drew my bath and even from down the hallway I could feel the humidity of the warm water as it glugged into the tub. "Make it cold water," I said, walking into the room.

"It's worth the little bit of coal to get you the hot water," she said, holding her hand in the running water. "German skin isn't plump and white from bathing in cold water."

Dasa sprinkled a handful of lemon balm powder over the bathwater before they both left me to bathe.

I slipped into the tub with Matka's expensive soap. The water enveloped my limbs and warmed up my bones, and I tried focusing on the task at hand to keep from crying and puffing up my eyes, scooping warm water in my hands and holding it to my face as it ran through my fingers, the water turning milky and murky from the soap.

My head throbbed and my neck ached. Dasa came back in to scrub out my fingernails with a brush and wash my hair as I soaked in the water, silently, with thoughts of failure creeping in like spiny barbs on ivy. Back and forth the brush went over my nails, foaming gray. Back and forth.

Dasa's eyes flicked to mine, and I knew what she was thinking. I felt it. I always had, as we were so close.

"Don't ask, Dasa," I said.

Dasa slipped my hand back into the warm water and a ring of sudsy dirt dissolved into the soapy water. "Have you thought of—"

"I said don't ask."

"What if they catch you, find out who you are?" She hung her head before reaching for my other hand, holding the brush to my nails. "If you're caught, then all of us are. The baby…"

"Listen to me right now," I said, trying to sound sure, but I was far from it. I sat up slightly in the tub. "Only Mrs. Lange and her husband know who I am. There's no reason for anyone from the Reich to suspect I'm not one of them."

"One look at your documents and they'll know who you are," Dasa said. "Even before you get to the party, while you wait for Mrs. Lange, what if you get asked? We were asked at the butcher shop."

"If a German questions me, it's because he suspects I'm Czech. That won't happen, not with the way I'm going to look today. I'll play the part. And also, I'll only speak German."

She shook her head. "Pray you don't get asked, Anna," she said, scrubbing my nails vigorously one last time before dropping my hand into the water. "Pray."

I thought about what it would be like if I got caught impersonating a German while she built up a lather in my hair. They would come here, arrest Matka, Dasa, and take her baby boy, just like she said. I had no reason to doubt this. I closed my eyes under Dasa's hands on my head, her fingers on my scalp, pulling and rubbing, with soap running down my forehead and over my closed eyes.

I wiped my face. "Maybe we should prepare," I said, having a change of thought, and her hands froze in my hair. "In case I don't come back."

"What has happened to us, Anna? Our family. This world. When will it end?"

Matka passed by the door with the baby, and Dasa's hands slipped from my hair to rest on the lip of the tub. "I think it's time to name your baby," I said, and she buried her head in her sleeve.

"I can't," she said. "I'm waiting for my husband to return home."

"We're all that's left, Dasa. Your baby needs a name," I said as she shook her head. "And this might be the last time we see each other. I want to know my nephew's name." I slipped underwater so I couldn't hear her reply, watching her leave in a blur from under a cloud of suds.

After my bath, I padded down the cellar stairs to find my cosmetics case, pulling on the light string and spying it on a shelf covered in dust. "Look natural," Mrs. Lange had said. I picked through compacts of shadows and rouge until I found the powder, opting for a brush over my moistened cheeks and closed eyes. I resisted using the rest of it, the eye pencils, and old tubes of lipstick, now dry and brittle, fragments of my old life.

Ema had begged me to let her wear my makeup. She only wanted to pretend to be a princess from one of Matka's fairy tales. I shut the case before I could tear up—nobody would hire me if I had red eyes—and ran upstairs fully powdered. Dasa stood in the parlor with her favorite dress, pressed and cleaned and hung on a padded hanger, untouched for years.

"I snuck over last night and got it," she said. "Don't worry, the neighbors didn't see me." I felt the maroon fabric in my fingers. So soft, a forgotten softness, like a lost memory, and the embroidery along the neckline, a tiny vine of roses on a cream-colored collar. It was a dress of sophistication, something she had probably worn many times in Prague before we had to leave, a demure statement of wealth. "My husband wouldn't like knowing I held it back when the Germans came and asked for our valuables. We could have been fined, withholding something so expensive, but I couldn't let a German girl wear it, not after they took our cows. Nobody will think you are Czech in this dress." She pushed it at me. "Take it."

After I slipped on the dress, Matka brushed out my hair and styled it in a plain style. Young. "You don't look a day over twenty," she said, but I didn't believe her until she handed me her mirror and I saw how moist and supple my skin looked. "Definitely not the skin of someone who works in the garden all day either. See, the warm water was worth the coal."

The fabric against my thighs felt even better than it did

between my fingers, and there was a realization of how far the Reich had gone to strip us of our humanity, down to the smallest of luxuries like clean fabrics and modern dresses.

I fastened on a shoe.

"Nothing with a strap," Matka said, disappearing into my bedroom to find the pumps I wore to funerals. "These are the most expensive and people will think you have money," she said, and I put them on. "You should walk to the square, Anna. You know a walking German woman wouldn't raise a flick of suspicion, but one on a tattered bicycle would."

"Yes, Matka."

We ate lunch with a fork and with our children's empty chairs beside us, four eggs each from Dasa's chickens, more than we'd ever allowed ourselves to eat before, and a handful of roasted carrots. Dasa kissed her baby's forehead as he sucked on his hand, pushing her eggs around on her plate while Matka nibbled at hers.

"I wonder what the weather will be like today," Matka said, and I scoffed.

"Now is not the time to talk about the weather," I said.

"Well, what should we talk about? The Nazi bitch we killed? What do you think her name was?" Matka asked. "I bet it was something awful like Hedwig. Nobody good is ever named Hedwig."

"Nobody, Matka?" Dasa shifted in her seat. "In the entire world, not one good person is named Hedwig?"

"Do you know a good one?" Matka sat back. "I knew a Hedwig once. God, she was an ugly thing. Had a Pinocchio nose."

"That doesn't make her a bad person," Dasa said.

"You didn't see the nose! It jutted out between her eyes like a finger, even when she was telling the truth. What a cold black heart she had." Matka went back to her eggs, forking up a full bite. "Which would be good fertilizer, now that I think of it."

I hung my head momentarily, taking a breath, then we all went back to our eggs, tines scraping our plates.

"We should talk about what you'll do in case I don't come home," I said, and Matka dropped her fork, pushing her plate across the table. "We can't ignore the possibility."

I reached for the baby in Dasa's arms. "And the baby…" I said, smoothing a blond curl from his forehead where the coal had rubbed off. I nestled my nose into the gap between his shoulder and neck, smelling deeply to remember him, but it was his eyes I'd remember the most, which sparkled like Dasa's—the eyes that had looked up at me after I'd delivered him. "Put a kerchief over his head and find the tunnel south of the village. It's your only option."

"But the informants," Matka said. "Mrs. Ott. She'll see us on the road."

"Any walk into the village with the baby is suicide. You'll have to find a way to make it there unnoticed. Pray for some luck, Matka." I kissed the baby's cheek. "I don't like it any more than you do."

"Adam," Dasa said, and I closed my eyes. "The baby's name is Adam. It's a good name for a good person." She walked into the parlor and stood with her thoughts.

"Adam," I said, and I kissed him again as he cooed. "You are Adam."

Matka looked away with a quivering chin, and I scooted out from my seat. "It can't be time yet," Matka said, but it was time, and in the heavy pause that followed, the kitchen clock seemed to tick just a fraction louder. She brought a hand to her chest when it chimed the top of the hour.

Dasa handed me a pair of white driving gloves she'd worn in Prague, when we could drive, when we were allowed to own cars. I went to slip them on and Matka stopped me. "Aren't you forgetting something?" She glanced at my wedding band. "I'll keep it safe for you."

I gazed at my hand, fingers opening in a flit of sunlight shining scantly through the open window, so gold and yellow and warm, and my thoughts stretched back many years to the day Josef slipped it on my hand. He said it had no beginning and no end, an infinity. *Forever.*

I pulled the ring from my finger and immediately closed my eyes, holding it tightly in my fist after I'd taken it off, feeling as if I'd pulled an organ from my body and not just a ring from my finger.

I handed Matka the ring and she dropped it into her apron pocket, but I asked for it back—I wasn't ready to part with it. "I'll keep it in my undergarments," I said, tucking it down the front of my dress.

"Now," she said, pulling Dasa and me to the floor on our knees. "Let's pray."

"Dear God…" Matka said, but she dissolved into tears before she could finish.

I got up to leave, pausing with my hand on the doorknob and with them still kneeling on the floor. "Don't,"

Dasa said. "Don't say goodbye." The baby fussed in her arms. "We'll see you after."

I nodded once, walking out of my house and shutting the door between us. The baby wailed as if he knew I'd left, sending a shudder through my body. *See you after.* I squeezed my handbag, feeling my documents inside and Ema's doll.

Chapter Ten

I stood on the street corner as Mrs. Lange had instructed, gripping my handbag tightly, when I realized I looked nervous and changed my stance. A German would enjoy the sunshine, and she'd have a full stomach from that morning's bread and meat rations. A *good* German would look down at the people just slightly even before knowing who they were, a pretentious gaze shifting always.

Minutes felt like ten and then fifteen, and that terrible thought I hadn't allowed myself to think about ran through my mind like a howling wind.

He might not agree, Mrs. Lange had said, but I couldn't bring myself to believe it before.

I checked my watch again, and in a single breath all my Czechness came pouring out in the form of a frantic breath and a trickle of tears when I saw it was past one o'clock.

Across the street, the butcher walked out of his shop to shoo Czechs away from his door, saying he was out of scraps. "Closed for the rest of the day," he barked, and my spine straightened just as the Czechs in line slumped forward from his news. *The butcher.*

I wiped my lashes dry before tapping my way across the road as any German lady would do, and slid effortlessly into the butcher shop. The bells clanged sharply despite my soft hand, and the butcher whipped around from behind the counter. "We're closed—"

"Hallo," I said, after a short pause with both of us looking at each other. "Do you remember me?"

He'd wadded up a bloody rag in his hands and lobbed it on the counter. I wondered if he was thinking about calling the police from down the road, which made my pulse quicken. He smoothed a clump of greasy hair away from his eyes.

"Do you?" I repeated.

"I do," he finally said, only he walked closer and looked me up and down from my toes to the top of my freshly washed head. "What do you want?" He folded his arms.

"You know," I said, but I wasn't sure what I wanted. A contact in the Resistance? A message passed to Tomas? I lifted my chin.

He chewed something unseen in his mouth. "No. I don't." His eyes shifted toward the window and he looked alarmed, which made me look. More people had lined up outside, waiting to be let inside the shop. He angrily flipped the closed sign over in the window before reaching for my arm to throw me out.

"Tomas!" I blurted. "I need to find Tomas. You know him." It wasn't a question; it was a statement.

He watched the line of Czechs dissolve through the window. "Maybe."

"I would appreciate any—"

"Are you trying to get yourself arrested?" he asked. "The German police passed by a few minutes ago, the same officer that was in here yesterday." He leaned in. "The one who asked you for your documents." I shook my head vigorously—I wasn't trying to get arrested. He pointed at my dress and shoes. "You're not yourself today. You're pretending to be German. Clearly. And you want to bring me down with you?"

He grabbed me by the elbow, shoving me toward the door. "Please," I said, digging my heels in, but the floor was slick and I was sliding. "I'll do anything!"

He stopped, one hand on the doorknob and the other with his meat-hook fingers digging into my arm. I could smell the sweetened sweat on his neck and all but feel the scratch of his beard stubble against my cheek, he was so close.

"Anything?" he questioned, and my stomach sank when I realized what I had offered. I held my head up, lips pinched.

He rolled the shades down over his windows with great force, robbing the store of all its light. "Come with me," he said, gritting his teeth, and he grabbed me by the stomach, pulling me by my dress into the back where it was warm and smelled of blood from the butchered animals and chopped-up meat.

I braced for the moment when he'd toss up my skirt and thrust himself inside of me, sizing up his girth, his large shoulders, and thick hands, but instead he moved a giant carving table away from the wall and pointed to the metal drain underneath.

"Go," he said, but when I didn't move, he pointed again.

"Where?" I shook my head. "I don't understand…"

He jammed a mop handle into the slats and lifted up the drain cover. "If I see you in my shop again, I'll turn you in." He reached under another table and detached a hidden ladder strapped underneath, lowering it into the hole.

I stepped forward, peering down below. "Is that—"

"Lord, woman," he said. "Isn't this what you wanted? To find Tomas?"

I looked back and forth between him and the drain, managing a shaky nod before climbing down the ladder where it was musty and dank as autumn nightfall. I stood at the bottom of the ladder, folding my arms for warmth.

He chucked a torch down from above. "Head that way," he said. "No turns, walk straight." He pointed. "You'll find who you're looking for. But remember, if you show up in my shop again uninvited, I'll turn you in."

"Thank you," I said, and he groaned, lifting the ladder away and clamping the metal grate back into place. I flipped on the torch and watched him through the drain slats above as he slid the table back overhead, and the tunnel turned gray even with the torch, which was more of a glow.

I pointed the torch to the ground, illuminating my shoes and the dirt, then up the brick and stone walls. "Hallo?" I said, and my voice echoed down the long and dark tunnel, followed by piercing quietness. "Hallo—"

Whispers and a phantom's footsteps from behind made me turn in circles. "Who's there?" I asked, pointing the torch in all different directions, breathlessly tripping and catching myself on the wall. Cobwebs wisped over my face. "Who's there—" I stumbled into a fork in the tunnel. I could only go left or right. Then to my horror, my torch grew dimmer, yellowy.

The whispers turned into laughter with the accelerated pace of footsteps coming up from behind in the dark. "No, no, no, no…" I said just as my light faded into a pinpoint and vanished completely.

A hand clamped over my mouth in the pitch-black. "Who are you?" a man's voice whispered into my ear. Warm, and smelling of cigarette smoke. I mumbled my answer under the compression of his roughened fingers before he peeled his palm away.

"I'm a…" My pulse glugged in my ears, and a woman mocked me in the dark.

"She doesn't know her name!" she said. "Let's kill her."

"Anna," I said, swallowing. "I'm Czech."

A torch flipped on, and I saw their faces. Both were smeared with cinder and dressed in black. Hands wrapped in bandages, hiding the scars and wounds that told their stories. The woman tugged on my dress hem. "You don't dress like a Czech," she said, and the man pinched me.

I slapped him across the face, which shocked him as much as me. His mouth drew open. "I'm Czech. Don't insult me." He rubbed his face where I'd hit him and I dug out my documents. "See."

"Documents can be faked," he said, pushing them away.

"And you're dressed like a fancy German." I heard more voices down the way, followed by a woman crying.

"I'm here to find Tomas," I said, and they both looked at each other.

"How do you know about him?" the woman said.

"I told you, I'm Czech." I adjusted my handbag over my shoulder, standing tall. "And he's my cousin." Their expressions changed from curious to concern. "What's the matter?" I asked, but they walked away to talk privately, leaving me alone in the dark, with their torch glowing between their faces. "Excuse me," I said. "What are you whispering about?"

Finally, the man turned around. "Anna." He paused. "Dankova?"

"How do you know my surname?" I reached for him. "Do you know my husband—Josef?" I swallowed. "He's with a band of rebels, but I haven't seen him in—"

"Come." He motioned for me to follow. "This way."

We walked left at the fork, through switchbacks toward the voices and the crying, but soon I realized the voices and the crying were coming from above in the shops, and in the homes. I tried to place where in the village we were walking, but it was near impossible. Large spacious openings that were more like long corridors turned into crude narrow passageways with cobwebbed candle sconces.

We stopped next to a hidden staircase made of stone slabs. "Go," the woman said, flicking her head, and I followed the man down. I heard more voices.

"Don't speak," the woman said from behind as we took our last steps into a dimly lit room crammed with people, all cinder-smeared and ragged and dirty. They led me to a man wearing a wooly black hat. Hushed voices followed, talking about my dress and my hair.

"This is Anna…" The woman pointed her torch in my face, and I shielded my eyes. "Dankova."

"Oh?" the man said, looking suspicious. The woman snapped for me to give him my documents. He used the torch to read my details. "Josef's wife?"

"You know my husband?" I felt blindly for my handbag for something to hold onto, thinking he only knew my husband because he was dead, a martyr, and this was how they greeted martyrs' wives. I held my breath.

"Yes," he said. "I know him." And I took that to mean he wasn't dead, which was a relief, and I felt myself breathing again.

"What if she's a spy? Look at her!" someone said from behind, and I closed my eyes.

"I need help. That's why I'm here. Mister…"

"Call me Radek." He handed my documents back. "But your husband isn't here."

"That's not why I came," I said. "I need to find an SS officer's estate. I know it's on the outskirts of the village. I thought my cousin could help me. I know he hides out in the tunnels, and I saw him recently…" I looked around the room as I talked, taking in all the faces looking back at me, studying me, listening. "I can see my cousin isn't here, but I promise you I wouldn't have come if it wasn't important. I would never risk the whereabouts of the Tabor rebels if it wasn't a life-or-death situation."

He continued looking me up and down, studying my

dress and my shoes, which had turned dusty from the walk, before motioning for me to follow him to the back of the room where some people had maps laid out on tables. A woman with blonde matted hair pulled her hands from her trouser pockets to fold her arms, watching me, learning more about me than I about her. "There are many estates the SS have taken over," Radek said. "Take your pick." He pointed to the map. "Every mark is an estate."

I leaned forward to get a better look, but there were handfuls of marks all over it. "There's so many…"

"Do you have a name for this officer?" he asked.

"Fischer," I said. "His name is Fischer. Has a wine collection."

Radek called for someone else across the room to come help, and while they looked at the map together, I noticed the woman who'd been eyeing me was now much closer. Her shirt had been unbuttoned down to the vee of her breasts, which were as perky and taut as any woman's before she'd had children.

I looked at her pointedly to let her know I felt her gaze, and she reached for another woman, this one with dark hair and wearing a gardening apron that looked remarkably similar to the one I had at home.

She pointed at me. "Anna Dankova," she said as if the other woman didn't know who I was, but how could she not? Everyone had been staring at me in utter silence just a few seconds ago. "You're different than I thought you'd be." She unfolded her arms to casually slip her hands back into her trouser pockets.

"Do you have an issue with me?"

The blonde reached for my face, tucking a lock of hair behind my ear and tickling me with her touch. A shiver prickled up my spine. "You're so beautiful... Josef didn't mention how beautiful you were."

I became very still. "You know my husband?" I was the one eyeing them now, and it wasn't hard to notice that underneath all the tunnel grime, they were striking, with piercing blue eyes and figures that were curvier than mine despite a resister's diet.

The blonde smiled. "I do." She had a sparkle in her eyes I didn't want her to explain. I turned away when they giggled, but my mind was now firmly entrenched in the mud, and I didn't think I could feel any sicker than I already had with Ema gone.

"Anna?" Radek touched my arm.

I cleared my throat and tried to look strong, as if the woman's words hadn't touched a nerve, but they had soaked into my skin and into my memory where I could count on them haunting me later when I wondered what else could be taken from me. "Yes?"

"We found it," he said, finger pointing, and I leaned in to get a better look, the torchlight shining yellowy on their faces and dimly on the map. "It's about seven kilometers away. Jordan Pond," he said, but I was already shaking my head.

"That's barely out of the village," I said. "It can't be the place."

They continued to whisper about other locations they thought it might be, and I realized they were taking a guess. "It's the best we can predict." He paused, and I felt him looking at me while I studied the map. "Where did you think it would be?"

"West of the village, in the country," I said, "rolling meadows and garden parties. Not a home near the reservoir, and the cemetery."

"Our best guess is almost certain," Radek said.

"I don't know..." I said, and my eyes immediately felt heavy—so much uncertainty and doubt. I turned around, not wanting him to see me so weak. It was, however, more information than I had before I climbed into the tunnel. "All right," I said as if making myself believe, and I turned back around, hand to my forehead, thinking of what to do next, how I was going to get there before the day was over and I missed the party. "Thank you for this."

"Why are you going there?" Radek asked. "It can't be for the company."

I pulled my hand from my forehead to fold my arms, pausing.

"You can trust us," he said.

"That's not it." I looked at the ground briefly. Saying the words aloud made it all that more real. "The Brown Sisters took my daughter," I said. "I'm going to find her. You know what they are doing... stealing our children and turning them into Germans?"

"I know about it, but how are you going to find her?"

"I speak German," I said, reaching up to feel the rose embroidery on my collar, "and with my clothes..."

"What's your *plan*?" he asked. "You do have one, don't you? The Germans will see through any kind of—"

"I do," I said. "I do have a plan." His head tilted in

me company. I covered my face in my hands, thinking I'd certainly miss the party now, when suddenly there was light cracking through the darkness. A little girl not more than six or seven years old waved me through the door, and I walked right into someone's cellar filled with many jars of food. She watched me dust myself off, as if she was used to helping the rebels and I was just another person that passed through her cellar door.

"You're crying," she said quietly in Czech, and I realized that my cries had scared her. I bent down to meet her eyes, swiping my tears away.

"I'll be all right," I said. "Thank you for letting me through." She smiled, playing with the blue ribbons dangling from her braids. "You saved me."

She lit up with these words, but I was startled by a man thumping down the cellar stairs. "Papa," the girl said, and I held my breath, but decided he must be part of the Resistance in some way and would be all right with the sudden appearance of a woman in his cellar.

"Thank you, sir," I said, and he seemed alarmed by my dress, looking me over with his eyes lingering on my embroidered collar. "I'm Czech."

He nodded when he understood. "Me too," he said, motioning for me to follow him upstairs into a daylit sitting room with sweet-smelling gardenias in a vase by the window. I was struck by the neighborhood I could see from the window. A German neighborhood. This man was one of the lucky ones who'd changed their papers before the occupation. He was… acting. Just like me.

"Do you have a car?"

"My wife was a Jew," he said, smiling at the couple. "She was taken a year ago."

The couple waved to me next. "My daughter was taken two days ago."

We drove the rest of the way in silence.

Chapter Eleven

He dropped me off at the cemetery, in a quiet spot near some trees. I scrunched the sack of food in my fists, looking at the grieving widows who'd gathered around their husbands' graves, sharing a meal with their memories, and being thankful they had a grave to visit. I set the hat on the front seat when I stepped outside. "Thank you," I said, and the man's last words came not through his mouth, but through his eyes, quietly wishing me luck. The girl peeped up over the back seat, and we waved goodbye to each other through the dust.

Leafy green tree branches cracked and moaned overhead with a sweeping wind scraping against the raised tombstones. I pulled the apple from the sack, eating it slowly as I passed by the widows. They'd pulled their kerchiefs down low to keep their sobbing to themselves but looked up one by one as I got closer, scrutinizing my dress, my shoes, and the deliberate way I walked through the cemetery.

The end of the path opened to the reservoir and a beach on the far side with sunbathers, which I didn't expect, but no homes. Nothing that said garden party or afternoon social. For all I knew, I was on the wrong side of the village, and the officer I needed to talk to was kilometers away with Mrs. Lange and her husband, chatting about Party business, while I was here, in the sun, and in a cemetery with the dead and their heartsick wives.

I lost my appetite, dropping the sack and the food. *This isn't the place.* I wasn't sure if I'd be able to hold my sorrow or my anger in for being so trusting, first with Mrs. Lange and then with Radek; I felt it brewing up inside me and rising to the surface like one of my herbal teas, strong, unruly, and sickening.

I was about to burst out, shriek, curse, maybe even both in desperation, when I heard chatting and music carrying in the breeze. I listened with a keen ear, eyes shifting, looking into the air.

I heard what I thought was the clink of plates and glasses. I thought I'd imagined it, a dream, but when I walked to the edge of the reservoir, I found a road—not a path, but an actual road—and a chimney barely visible through the leaves. "My God," I breathed.

I waved air at my eyes, collecting myself, praying *this* was the place. I walked around the first bend in the road and saw a parked car. I skidded to a stop amidst the pebbles, before taking a few more steps, cautiously hopeful, and finding another car, followed by another, and a uniformed attendant up ahead, standing in front of garden stairs that led up to a large estate.

Then I saw *my* old car—Mrs. Lange's car—parked fourth from the front.

I turned around, clamping my hand over my mouth as my heart raced. I'd found it. *This is the place.* I wanted to rush in there, feeling I'd already lost so much time, but also knowing I needed a second to think. I went over a few impromptu lines I'd thought up.

Anna, the good German from Prague, visiting her aunt. Mrs. Lange, if I have to say who she is. I curtsied, pretending to meet this SS officer in charge of the Reich nurseries, smiling my hallo and thinking that was ridiculous—I'd been to parties with Germans before the occupation. This would be no different, I told myself.

My hands trembled at the wrists, which was normal for me before a big performance. I shook them out in front of me, exhaling all the breath from my lungs. *I can do this,* I thought, and I felt the character I'd created wash over me like a slow, soaking shower. *I can.* I pulled my handbag strap over my shoulder, about to walk up, but a hand grabbed my arm from behind.

"Anna!"

It was Mrs. Lange and she'd dragged me from the road to talk near the bushes, her eyes like daggers: pointy, and sharp, but also scared. The initial shock on my face took a sour turn and all the anger I'd felt at having trusted her finally reached the surface. I felt it red in my face, and white hot in my clenched fists.

"You left me," I hissed, pulling my arm away to walk toward the party, but she pulled me back.

"No—" Her voice rose sharply before quieting. "Don't, Anna," she said. "You'll cause trouble."

"Trouble for you." My mouth hung open, searching for words. "My daughter was stolen from me. Ripped from my arms." I got an inch from her face. "You should be ashamed of yourself. I waited for you." I tried to walk away again, but she fought me.

"Anna," she said, only this time her fingers dug into my arm to the point of pain. "I'm sorry. It's not me, it's my husband. He thought it would look suspicious if we brought you. I told you he might not agree. I tried my best."

"I had more faith in you," I said. "I never thought you wouldn't come." I pulled my arm away to walk up the road.

"Wait! You can't go in there like that."

I turned around. "What do you mean?"

"You're angry," she said. "And your shoes!"

I looked down, and she was right about one thing. My shoes were dirty. No German would go to a garden party with dust on their toes. I spit-shined them and Mrs. Lange nearly fell over. "Not like that! Someone will see you!" We scooted behind one of the cars. "Anna. This isn't something you can jump into. You must play the part. Be demure, subtle, yet proud." She paused. "And clean. You wiped the dirt from your shoes, but how do your palms look?"

I turned my hands over and looked for a place to wipe them—my stockings, my dress, my arms—but there wasn't a place to clean them without transferring the dirt someplace else. I opened my handbag and rubbed them against the liner, licking them to get them wet, leaving the smell of my saliva on my hands.

"Anna," she said, and I took a shuddering breath, wishing she'd leave me alone, but also thinking I needed her. I looked up.

"Are you going to help me?" My lips pinched, waiting for her to tell me I was on my own, but to my surprise, she touched my hand gently.

"I already have." A couple walked down the road, stealing a kiss behind one of the cars, only they saw us and walked on toward the cemetery. Mrs. Lange leaned in once they were gone. "I've been listening and talking." She whispered into my ear. "We didn't pick you up, but I was still going to find out as much information as I could for you."

I closed my eyes briefly, glad to hear this from Mrs. Lange, and took a long deep breath through my nose, but my eyes had turned heavy, and I didn't want to cry again, not with the garden party within earshot and guests in sight up above in the courtyard.

"But I was telling you the truth about causing trouble. If my husband sees you, he'll be furious. I'm not sure what he'll do. He was very adamant—"

"I'm going to the party," I said.

"I beg you," she said. "I'm talking to people, getting information. Trust me." She looked over her shoulder toward the attendant, who couldn't see us. "Archibald Minz is his name. He's in charge of the program. I've worked up quite the conversation with him."

"Mrs. Lange," I said. "I don't—"

Her husband called for her from the courtyard, and she gasped, looking frantically over her shoulder before grabbing me by mine. "Please, Anna." She gave me a shake. "Wait here. My husband, he's looking for me. I'll be back," she said, and she walked off, leaving me by the boot of someone's car.

I wasn't sure how long I'd waited. Long enough to sweat in the sun, and feel my feet ache. I paced, hands to my waist, waiting, and waiting, and thinking, with laughter and the clink of glasses rising like a cloud over the estate, beckoning me. I'd come so far, made it to the garden party against all odds, only to find myself waiting on Mrs. Lange as I had done just hours ago on the street corner. Matka had probably already dug holes for the Langes, and I didn't blame her for it, and honestly, she might as well dig a hole for me too for waiting on Mrs. Lange again after I'd come so far.

I reached into my handbag for Ema's doll, closing my eyes, and remembering the sound of her voice when she giggled, dancing the doll over the back seat in the car, her shining eyes when she looked up at me. Her sweet kisses. Her innocence. The thought of never seeing her again seemed unfathomable, and the pain so great. I couldn't wait —I couldn't do it!

My eyes popped open. I was going to the party.

The attendant turned around as I walked up, standing proudly with his clipboard, but all the guests had already arrived and their cars were parked, and he had nothing to do. He tipped back on his heels, smiling. I ran my hands over my hair, brushing back the strays.

"Hallo," I said, nodding once, and he looked like he was going to let me pass without so much as a question, his smile growing wider, but just as I walked up the steps to the courtyard, he cleared his throat.

"Pardon me, Fräulein," he said, and he flipped through the pages on his clipboard. "Did you arrive in a car?"

"You don't remember me?" I questioned, buying some time, and he groaned, glancing at his papers once more, looking for something, but for what I didn't know because he hadn't asked for my name. I fingered my collar, smiling bashfully. "I arrived not that long ago and you complimented my rose embroidery."

His face turned to butter. "Sorry, Fräulein," he said. "I don't remember. Maybe you're thinking of the other attendant? I took over his shift not long ago."

"Oh?" I said, face lifting. "Yes, I suppose you are right." I walked away, waving goodbye with my palm to my cheek. "Good afternoon."

"Good afternoon."

I exhaled from my mouth once my back was turned, having fooled him, and confidently walked up the stairs to the courtyard, not wanting to give the attendant a chance to reconsider my intentions.

My heart raced once I'd made it to the top. Another set of stairs on the far side of the courtyard led to the gardens below, where at least twenty people moved slowly through the grass, elderly men with canes, and women with fox stoles over their shoulders even in the warm June sun. I watched the guests with my hands on the railing, looking for anyone who looked like a uniformed SS or Mr. Lange. There were plenty dressed in day suits.

A piano played behind me in the ballroom. That was where the real party was, with the din of many people and the smell of salty meat. I slipped through the open French doors, thinking I'd find a small assortment of savory canapés, but was stunned to see it was a long and crowded buffet, steaming with more food than what was available in all the Tabor market. My tongue instantly tingled, and I swallowed desperately.

I took a moment to inspect the guests. Most of them looked my age—younger than thirty—smartly dressed, elegant for a day party, yet casual. I guessed that these people were the new Reich—the generation that had been indoctrinated from their early days, whereas the older generation outside had been converted.

"Excuse me," I said, squeezing through the crowd. "Pardon me—" I gasped. Three Brown Sisters stood in the corner near the mirrors, which I hadn't prepared myself for. I slowly looked back over, taking a flute of champagne from a waiter's tray. They looked the same as the one from Dasa's barn—dull and Aryan, but much younger, probably eighteen at best. They talked among themselves while eating cakes from a shared plate.

An SS officer in a black uniform, old, gray, stiff as a pole, pointed for them to follow him outside to the gardens, and they unquestioningly obeyed, scooting off in their soft-soled shoes and Reich-issued aprons. *Archibald Minz.* It had to be him.

I made up my mind right then to follow them but was

jostled to the side by a woman pushing me toward the buffet table. "Your turn," she said, and suddenly I was in line. "Go," the woman said, nudging me to move, and I did, caught up in the food buffet with no recourse but to join in. "Get a plate!" She elbowed me, and I reached for a plate, when another hand reached at the same time from the opposite side of the buffet table.

Mr. Lange.

His eyes looked cold and bulging, and we both stood frozen, looking at each other and holding the same plate. A lock of peppery hair fell in front of his eyes. Mrs. Lange appeared out of nowhere with a plateful of salad and patted him on his shoulder to move along, but he wouldn't budge, not even enough to let go of the plate between our hands. She looked at me and froze herself.

"Move on," someone said from their side of the line, and Mrs. Lange patted him again, only this time he looked at her, and they argued with their eyes before abandoning the buffet altogether and walking outside. I followed them out.

I stood next to Mr. Lange, all three of us with our backs to the party and our eyes over the garden. "I had to come," I finally said. "You don't know what I've—"

"We could get arrested," Mr. Lange growled, and I shot him a look. His face turned red as a stalk of rhubarb blistered from the wind.

"Ema was ripped from my arms. I don't care if—"

"Enough!" Mrs. Lange said through her teeth, smiling, pretending everything was all right. She even waved to someone in the garden. "Husband," she said, still waving,

"I will handle this." She paused. "Anna, you will wait in the car."

I turned toward her, and Mr. Lange turned toward me, blocking me from seeing his wife's face. "I can't," I said, trying to see around him. "I won't."

A couple had walked out of the ballroom to the courtyard, mindlessly chatting, talking about the warm weather. "And then the reservoir…" the man said, and we three straightened, looking into the garden, waiting for them to leave, but the man pointed with his wine glass at the view, talking to the woman who'd been entranced by his charms. "One drop of poison to finish them all," he said, followed by a laugh.

"Poison them?" she questioned.

"The whole village," the man said.

"But don't we drink from the same water source?" she asked, and Mr. Lange's eyes shifted to catch a glimpse of how close they were to us on my left side. They walked away giggling, arm and arm, enjoying the party, the garden, and the wine. Mrs. Lange reached across her husband, tapping my arm.

"Meet us by the car," she said.

I twisted and pulled at my hands. "Mrs. Lange, I…" The Brown Sisters had walked up behind and stood not that far away, finishing the cakes from their shared plate.

"Anna." Mr. Lange looked down, his voice raspy and deep. "Go." He took his wife's hand and the last thing I saw of Mrs. Lange was her mouthing for me to trust her.

They walked back into the ballroom, but I was still standing in the courtyard, watching the Brown Sisters pick the last nibbles of cake from their plate, their whispering giggles carrying in the breeze.

I thought of how a conversation might go. I could compliment them on their shoes, and they would compliment my dress. From there, I'd ask them about nursing, and where they were from. But of course, the conversation could go differently. They could become suspicious. What if they had been in the market? They might recognize me, even with my hair nice and clean.

I adjusted the handbag hanging from my shoulder, about to walk over and talk to them, six steps, maybe even eight was all it would take. I looked at the stairs that led to the road, and to the French doors where I'd last seen Mrs. Lange. I felt pulled in two different directions. My stomach ached, a gut-wrenching squeeze from not knowing who to trust or what direction to follow—my heart or my head.

I closed my eyes briefly, reminding myself that it was me who'd found my way here. I felt sick and fragile and weak over the decision, and for drawing it out, then one of the Brown Sisters laughed uncontrollably over something whispered in her ear, and before I could talk myself out of it, I ran down the stairs and past the attendant to the car where I burst into tears.

The sun had set and the air turned cool, and I waited, head in my hands with awful thoughts running through my mind. Thoughts about dying from the pain. Worse, thoughts about living without my daughter for making the wrong choice. Then Mr. and Mrs. Lange came out of the party and walked down the road without a word passing between them, their bodies stiff like strangers.

I pushed myself away from the car, trying to read Mrs. Lange's face, look for any kind of sign that she'd been successful in getting the information I needed.

Mr. Lange got in the car and started up the engine with haste while Mrs. Lange walked straight toward me.

"Did you—"

She shoved a crumpled piece of paper in my palm as she made her way to the passenger-side door. "Get in," she said.

"Is this…"

Mr. Lange rolled down the window. "Get in or it will look suspicious."

I got in the car, and once in the back seat, I unraveled the note in my hand.

Edelhaus Nursery. Dresden.

I sank down and crossed my heart, and I'd never done that before, but it felt right and fitting. The knot in my stomach relaxed enough for me to know I wasn't going to get sick all over the seats. Mrs. Lange glanced at me over her shoulder while Mr. Lange turned the car around in the gravel to drive me home.

"Thank you," I mouthed, and she nodded so delicately her husband missed it.

Mr. Lange stopped the car several yards away from my house in the dark to avoid peeping neighbors, many of whom had moved their suppers outside to enjoy the night air under garden lanterns.

"Stay away from us," were Mr. Lange's last words to me before he drove away, and they sped off in a speckled, evening dust.

I couldn't wait to tell Matka and Dasa the news. Ema

was within my grasp. I had an address, and my German documents would arrive any day. I was successful. We had a plan. My God, we had a plan! I ran up from my road and bolted through the front door, out of breath and panting, bursting at the seams to tell them the good news, only the house was even darker than it was outside. I stood in the doorway.

"Matka?" I gulped. "Dasa?" I called, but nobody was home.

Chapter Twelve

J osef carried me through the front door of the farmhouse in Tabor as if it were the day after our wedding in Prague, throwing the door open and whisking me inside. I held onto my hat, giggling from a twist of his tickling fingers in my side.

"All right," he said, setting me down. "Open your eyes."

I opened my eyes slowly, not sure what to expect after a long drive with a scarf around my eyes. "Josef," I breathed.

He rushed around the house throwing open the curtains, letting all the afternoon light spill in through the windows. I searched the brim of my hat nervously with my fingers. "Don't tell me you're thinking of buying a house." The furniture looked stiff and new as if it had never been sat in, and the kitchen was sparkling clean with pots and pans hanging from a rack on the ceiling. Josef opened the kitchen window and something citrusy floated in with the breeze.

"You have to see this." He took me by the hand, leading me down the hallway into the bedrooms, each one larger than the last. Three bedrooms on the ground floor and an upstairs loft.

I took it all in with not so much as a comment. I couldn't imagine how we could afford a house, much less a fully furnished one.

"But this isn't all!" He smiled, taking me back into the kitchen and showing me a door I thought might be a closet. "Look at this..." He opened the door, and at first, I didn't know what the fuss was about, all I saw were stairs that disappeared into the dark. He walked down first, the wooden steps creaking and cracking, and found a light string.

My mouth drew open. "Josef," I said, walking down, step after step, gazing at the canned food jars stacked nicely on shelves. By the time I had made my way to the last step, I'd covered my mouth. "Who left this food?"

"A client of mine."

In the corner was another set of jars, only these had herbs, and some were filled with oils. Dried lavender and linden leaves hung from strings. I held one of the jars up to the light, giving it a spin, and bits of chamomile swirled up inside with the oil. Josef watched me. On the table next to the jars was a set of papers, handwritten recipes for ointments and cures for all sorts of maladies. I flipped through them. "Stomach aches, headaches... Josef, I... I..."

"One of my clients left for England and sold me this house and the one next door for your sister and her family. Fully furnished. Your parents can live here too, I already talked with Dasa's husband."

I set the jar down, shaking my head, eyes closed, wondering if I'd heard him right. "You already bought it?" I asked, and his silence said he did. "But I don't want to move. We've made a life for ourselves, Josef. In Prague. What about your accounting business?"

"We'll be safer here," he said. "In the country."

"But... you said we'd be safe in Prague, too, not long ago." I reached out. "Do you know something I don't... about the Reich?"

Josef had told me not to fear a German invasion, even after we'd visited Berlin and seen what the Reich had done to the Jews, with their restrictive laws and humiliation. The League of Nations would protect us from Germany, he had told me. He was sure of it.

He turned away to walk upstairs, and I could tell he was disappointed that I didn't like the house. I chased after him.

"I didn't mean to—"

"It's me that's sorry," he said, shutting the cellar door behind us. "You don't like the house."

"It's not that," I said, reaching for his hand. "Josef, I have ideas too," I said. "We stay in Prague and register as German on our papers. We both speak German. Our landlord already said he'd list us as German tenants. Years ago, nobody cared who was who, my parents told me all about it, how people had to choose whether they were German or Czech after the first war, no documents needed. I'm sure we can still declare. It's only a ruse, of course, we would never be German in our hearts." My eyes trailed to the floor. "Or..." I looked up slowly. "We move to England, like your client—I'm sure there's a way."

Josef shook his head. "And run?" He scoffed. "No. We are not running. This is our country." He took me in his arms. "Darling, trust me. I don't think we have anything to be worried about, but if we do, I think we will be the safest here."

"Safe? The Reich has annexed much of the country already. How is it safer to be here, in the middle of Bohemia living as

Czechs, than in Prague as Germans? I'm a woman from Prague, Josef. I don't know anything about living in the country."

He held me tightly after kissing me on the forehead, and I eyed the kitchen and parlor from his chest as he smoothed my hair back. "You will learn, we all will," he said, yet I was torn between what I felt was right and trusting my husband. "Trust me." He placed a hand on my stomach. "I will take care of you and our child."

It was hard to resist him when he talked that way, his eyes cool blue, wavy dark hair, and those kissable lips. He brushed an eyelash from my cheek, moving in for a proper kiss with his arms wrapped around me.

"Damn you, husband…" I said, giggling from the tickle of his kisses moving from my lips to my neck. He twirled me around into a slow dance near the front door.

"Welcome home, my darling."

I shut the door, listening to the silence crackle. "Matka…" I felt the tears coming, a puffy well in my eyes, thinking they weren't just out, but gone. "Dasa…" The kitchen curtains fluttered on the dowel from an unfelt breeze. My mortar and pestle sat on the kitchen counter, washed but with a wadded-up rag inside as if only half-washed and rushed. My glass jars had been opened and the herbs gone through, some of the contents spilling into the sink. I counted the jars still left on the rack. *One, two, three…* I stopped, fingers between the thyme and the basil where a jar was missing.

The chamomile oil for the baby.

They'd left, as we discussed. I shouldn't have been surprised. We'd talked about what to do if I was unsuccessful, and it was late enough for them to believe I wouldn't come back.

I dried my eyes with a few rough swipes of my hand, trying to be strong, as Matka would command me to be. I slid to the floor with my back against the wall, pulling the address of the nursery from my pocket, and studied the bend of every letter, praying Radek would keep his promise and deliver my German documents in a matter of days.

But as the days passed, the painful realization that I shouldn't have counted on the Resistance echoed in my bones. Weeks had gone by since, and still, there was no sign of Radek. The youthful German woman I'd portrayed at the party had been replaced with the Czech I'd been since occupation: in need of a bath and tired. Each day felt like an eternity with my mind churning endlessly in thought, consumed with worry, regret, and what-ifs.

I ventured into the garden as I did every morning, to put on a show for the neighbors and pretend it was an ordinary day, sowing my seeds, and picking vegetables. I waved from afar, cursing them silently, followed by a reach into my apron pocket to feel Ema's doll. "I love you, Ema," I breathed into the air, and when I spoke her name aloud, a little weep always followed. I noticed yellowing in the trees and acknowledged how much time had passed with the approach of autumn.

I hauled a crate of carrots from the garden to the front where I'd normally put it before market day, looking up to see a car I didn't recognize turn down my road. I stood like a statue with my crate as the car drove past at an alarmingly slow rate of speed. *The Resistance wouldn't send a car*, I thought, and I waited to catch a glimpse of who it could be when I saw Mr. and Mrs. Ott's stone-cold faces through the windshield.

They watched me watch them, gravel popping under their tires. There was nothing else to take from me, but still, my stomach knotted up with worry.

They drove around the bend toward Dasa's house, and I dropped the crate, running inside and up the stairs to watch them from the loft window where it was stuffy and warm.

I braced the window ledge, eyes wide.

Black exhaust fumes pooled from their car's tailpipe and I wondered if they were going to turn around. And as I watched and wondered, another car rolled up to Dasa's house. I gasped audibly, shockingly. Car doors opened and closed. Another couple shook hands with the Otts, a woman in a fancy hat and a man in a suit. They looked at the house and the pasture before pointing to the barn in the back and sizing up her available property. Both hands flew to my mouth. "Bastards," I said, sinking to the floor, shaking, where more terrifying thoughts curdled my mind, thinking Matka and Dasa might have been caught, or at least the Otts had seen them on the way to the south tunnel.

I held my stomach, moaning loud enough for someone to hear me if they were standing under the window. "God —" I moaned again, but a knock at my door silenced me. I crawled across the floor and peeked cautiously down the stairs into the parlor where I could see a sliver of blue sky out my front window. A man's hat passed through the glass, and I scooted back so as not to be seen.

I thought carefully of what to do, but then got up off the

floor, thinking it was the Resistance. My documents had arrived! Another knock on my door, only this time I ran downstairs to throw the door open. But it wasn't the Resistance. It wasn't even Mr. and Mrs. Ott. It was a man in a uniform, one I'd never seen. He wasn't SS or Wehrmacht, but something else. Something sinister. German.

"Hallo," he said. "Do you understand German?"

We stared at each other for what seemed like an ungodly amount of time, before he smiled cynically, and for himself. "Dirty Czechs," he mumbled in German, patting his front pockets before opening a black leather briefcase and pulling out a card. "Be prompt," he said, handing me the card, but I never moved. "Be…" he pointed to both corners of his mouth, stressing the words, "prompt!"

He turned on his heel and left. No German had ever delivered good news on a card. I pulled back the curtains when I heard his car start up and immediately covered my mouth. Miniature Nazi flags near the headlamps. Not just a German. *The Reich.*

I ran about the house in a flurry looking through every window, checking to see if I was being watched. I dragged the bookcase across the parlor, wedging it under the doorknob. The German drove away, and I found myself in the kitchen, where I felt the safest, with my jars scattered around me on the floor and where the memories of Ema, Matka, and Dasa were the strongest.

I read the card.

Meet at the New Town Hall tomorrow at seven o'clock in the morning for a health screening. Attendance is mandatory.

I sank to the floor and lay curled among the jars until the sun dipped below my window and the house turned shadowy and dark. Another day alone, but how long until there were no days left at all? Mrs. Dolakova was right, they would get us one by one eventually. "Josef," I said, tears pooling on the kitchen tiles where I lay, "look what's come of us."

My eyes skirted over the jars, full of herbs I'd picked with Ema—the day we picked the parsley for soup, and that morning we dried the mint for tea. The ointment for wounds I'd made for Ema's scraped knees... Chamomile for headaches, lavender for sleep. The jars clinked and clanged as my fingers brushed over them, only for me to draw my hand back, fingers to my lips, when I saw one jar tucked way back behind the sink. "And a sprig of poisonous hemlock," I whispered to myself.

I wiped my eyes, blinking to see clearly in the darkened space. A gnarled twig, dried and brittle among a bed of crispy white flowers. I'd intended to use it as rat poison, but there it was, waiting for me all along—a way out.

I scrambled to reach for it, unscrewing the lid and shoving the twig into my mouth. The taste of death hit me immediately, rank and musty. Chewing, chewing, chewing, flaky bits sprinkling through my finger gaps onto the floor. Thoughts of failure coursed through my veins, and I froze with a mouthful of hemlock bulging in my cheeks. I couldn't swallow. I couldn't do it!

I gagged, jumping up to the sink to spit the flowers from my tingling tongue and teeth—*spat, spat, spat*—sobbing behind clenched eyes, and shaking until all traces of the poison had washed out of my mouth.

I threw the jar into the sink, the glass shattering into millions of glittering pieces. "I want the pain to stop!" I burst into a wail. "Josef," I cried, when I heard a noise at the door.

I clamped both hands over my mouth. Maybe the Reich decided to come for me early? Maybe it was the Otts? My heart beat rapidly, waiting for another sign.

The doorknob jittered a moment before it started to twist, and I watched in horror as a streak of moonlight was cast upon my floor, the door pushing the bookcase out of the way. I thought I'd locked it. I swear I'd locked it!

A gray figure of a man stepped into the house and stood in the parlor. I reached for a glass jar—my only weapon. I raised my hand up, throwing my arm all the way back, when I realized it was Tomas.

"Anna?"

"Tomas?" I clutched my chest. "What are you doing?"

"I saw the house was dark and I got worried," he said, taking me by the shoulders to look at me, but his eyes wandered throughout the house. "Where's your mother? Where's Dasa?"

"Gone," I said. "They left weeks ago to find the south tunnel."

"Why?" he asked.

"Because they thought I'd been arrested and they fled." I hung my head, still trying to recover from the scare of his visit while he lit a candle on the table. "I need to breathe for a second," I said, and I fell into one of the kitchen chairs, hand to my forehead. He watched me from the other chair.

"Dasa's girls, you took them someplace safe? They're all right?"

"Yes," he said, and I exhaled in relief, "but that's not the only reason I'm here." He reached into his pocket and pulled something out of it. "I came to deliver this."

He handed me a small booklet. "My documents!" I said, snatching them away. "I never dreamt it would be you who'd deliver them. I've been waiting weeks for these." I read the inside details. "Anna Hager from Berlin." I kissed his cheek. "Thank you, Tomas. Thank you!"

"The wife of a deceased German soldier, Joseph Hager, died in forty-two," he said.

"Joseph," I said. "Almost seems real."

Tomas placed a hand on my shoulder. "Radek told me what you're planning. Are you sure about this?" he asked, and I nodded, sniffling and wiping my cheeks. "Because there is no going back. Once you impersonate a German with phony papers…" He pulled something else out of his pocket. This time a letter. I caught sight of the writing on the envelope and recognized it right away as Josef's, even in the hazy candlelight.

I gazed at it with an open mouth. "Did you see him?"

"It was passed to me in secret," he said. "I know you've been waiting a long time."

I ripped open the envelope, pulling the letter out, thinking even in darkness there could be hope. He must be writing to tell me he'd heard about Ema—from who I didn't know, maybe Radek from the tunnel—and he was going to help me find her, that he loved me and that he'd fight for us.

I held the letter over the candlelight.

My darling, I read, and I burst into joyful tears, glancing up at Tomas. "It's Josef. It's really him…" I went back to the letter, holding it just right over the flame.

> *I heard what happened to our daughter, and of your plans. The danger that lurks behind every corner and building outside of Tabor is even greater than you can imagine. I will work with my contacts to find where they took her. Until then, do not leave. The Germans know more than you, they will outsmart you. You will not survive. Trust me. This is not the place for a woman like you, beautiful, delicate, and loving. Wait at home and I will send word of my progress.*
>
> *Your loving husband, Josef.*

The letter slipped from my hands, floating to the floor face up.

Tomas had been smiling, and instantly looked concerned. "What is it?" He reached for the letter, and I stood from my chair.

"He wants me to stay here," I said, and my body had a physical reaction to his words, shaking and jittering and feeling nauseous. "He says I'm too delicate and to wait for him."

I held onto the back of the chair to steady my legs, and a swell of anger took over. I grabbed one of my jars, squeezing it violently in my hand, letting out a shrill scream that bolted Tomas from his chair.

"Anna!" He scooped me in his arms and hugged me as I cried.

"Why is this happening to us, Tomas? Why?"

He pulled away. "You remember the story, Anna? The one your mother used to tell us growing up about the Huns, the ones who took the best meat."

"What does that have to do with—"

"The Huns didn't care about the ones they stole from," Tomas said. "They ravaged kingdoms and took the best meat for themselves until finally entire groups of people disappeared, and those that remained wondered where they'd gone over cups of warm tea and iced cakes in the shade, remembering the people of Bohemia like fables from the nursery."

"What are you saying?" I asked, wiping my nose.

"We're disappearing, Anna," he said. "I think you should listen to your husband. Stay here and wait for his word. Josef is one of the best, revered in the tunnels and above. And if he wishes you to stay…"

"Now you want me to stay too?" The lump in my throat grew and grew, competing with the stab of pain in my head.

He patted my back as if he knew I'd obey my husband, and we sat quietly for many minutes not saying another word about Josef's letter, but it was all I thought about. And I was alone. Truly, in this big house without a husband, child, or sibling.

The morning sunlight broke through the front window. "Tomas," I said, taking his hand, and we both stood. "Remember me." We embraced like brother and sister, and as if it was our last time.

"What are you going to do?" he asked, but I opened the door and showed him outside. "You'll listen to your husband, won't you, Anna?"

"Goodbye cousin," I said, and after I shut the door, I closed my eyes and listened to the kitchen clock tick, its hands inching closer to the time of my health appointment.

Chapter Thirteen

D own the cellar steps and in the darkest corner of the room was an old cigar box netted in cobwebs. I pulled it from its hiding place, wedged between wooden shelves and the brick wall. The only other person who knew of its existence was dead.

"Dearest Anna," my father said to me. "I need to confess a secret."

He'd pulled me into the cellar while Josef and Matka were outside, interrupting me while I was washing dishes. I dried my hands on my apron. "What secret?" I asked, and my stomach sank with his drawn face, thinking he was about to tell me some bad news.

He handed me a cigar box. "Shh..." he whispered. "Open it." He motioned with his chin, but I was hesitant because my father didn't smoke and neither did I. "Go on." We heard the thud of footsteps above in the kitchen. "Before someone catches us."

I opened the box, but instead of finding cigars, I found a fistful of reichsmarks. "Oh no," I breathed. "What have you done?" I thumbed through the notes. It had been so long since I'd handled that kind of money. "There must be hundreds here." I held them to my nose, inhaling deeply.

He shot a look upstairs before whispering again, "I need to know you'll be all right. You, your mother, and Dasa."

"But that's why we moved here," I said. "Josef said that—"

"I don't care what Josef said. This is a father protecting his daughters, his wife. Your mother will be upset with me, believing I've dug my own grave. She'll tell me to go to the woods for stealing this, which you know is worse than just telling me to go to hell. Dasa would be too nervous holding this kind of secret. But you…" he said. "You, I can trust."

"But why?" I asked. "Is something about to happen? Is there something you're not telling me?"

He looked over my face, pausing. "I've been around for a long time. The Germans will plunder and ravish Bohemia for its resources, more than they've already done. Prague was just the start. Next, they will plunder the people. Our Jewish friends are feeling this now. How much more can they take? The laws put on them will be put on us one day, mark my words."

"Josef thinks—"

"I'm telling you what I know," he said. "I wasn't thinking when I agreed to move here. I should have insisted we leave Europe. It's too late now." He looked down, and his conflicted face led me to believe he was thinking of what if—what if we'd fled? "I've done things, Anna," he said. "I've done things that will get me arrested. I will not die for nothing."

I closed my eyes with his words, and he took the money out of my hand and set it back into the box, closing the lid.

"There will be days you'll want to use this money. Then there will be the day you need to use it—the day your life depends on it. Choose wisely."

"Are you going somewhere?" I asked, even though I didn't want him to answer.

"We're all going somewhere," he said. *"Eventually."*

The notes felt cold in my palm, old, preserved from being in the dank cellar for so long. He must have stolen it from someone wealthy. Mr. and Mrs. Ott came to mind. I sorted and stacked according to the denomination as fast as I could and tucked it all into my handbag. There was enough for a train ticket and a few days to live like a German. I slid the box back in between the wall and the shelf—it was an instant reaction, hiding it from Josef, Matka, and Dasa for years.

I had no time for a proper bath, but scrubbed my hair and arms in the sink with herbs and what little soap we had left. I slipped on Dasa's dress while my skin was still damp, taking only a little bit of time to make sure my hair was styled right and to powder my neck before rushing around, locking up every window as if that would keep the Germans out.

My hand curled around the doorknob, ready to leave. Matka would command me to pray, saying it was bad luck if I didn't. The kitchen clock struck the top of the hour with nine heart-stopping chimes. I'd already missed my appointment, well past two hours late. *They could come for me at any time.* I clasped my hands together and prayed. "Let me find her. Let me bring her home, please…" But my heart raced the longer I stayed in the house knowing the time, and I ditched the prayer to open the door. A car crept up my road.

"Oh no." I covered my mouth, feeling the last seconds of freedom pass before me, only it was Mrs. Lange. "My God…" I held my head, collecting myself as she pulled up to my house near the garden where I'd stored my market vegetables.

She watched me through the windshield with a suspicious eye before turning off the engine. Then, to add to the intrigue, she didn't get out of the car right away and continued watching me from over the steering wheel.

"Mrs. Lange—" I took a few steps toward her after she got out of the car and started loading my carrots into the boot. "What are you doing?" I grabbed her wrist, not concerned at all with how it looked, and to my surprise, she was overcome with emotion.

"I thought you'd left," she said. "It's been weeks since—"

"Why does that matter?" I still had her wrist.

She turned, glancing over her shoulder to where the neighbors were watching. "Let go of me. They'll see," she whispered.

I let go of her wrist to tuck a lock of hair behind my ear, pretending all was well, and waited for her to finish loading the carrots only Germans were allowed to sell.

"You've missed several market days, leaving your stand bare and vacant. People are asking questions, like why I'm not running it. It's only fitting that I officially take it over." She reached for another crate, and while she was bent over, she asked for my herb jars, which made me gasp. "I have to run a proper stand," she said. "I have your car. It makes sense. You know I'm right."

We stared at each other, yet I was powerless to stop her.

I wasn't about to give her the jars in the house after praying at the door; Matka would have told me it was bad luck to go back inside. I gave her the ones from the potting shed, more than she could sell at the market, and told her that was all. What she couldn't fit in the boot, she loaded onto the back seat. I waited, unable to watch as she sorted through my things, looking at my neighbors, waving, smiling, pretending it was an ordinary day, but thinking about the time and how I needed to get going.

"I hate that you had to see me do this…" Mrs. Lange shut the car boot, pausing, looking over my dress and noticing my washed hair, then examining my face, which was a mix of angst and hope. "Anna?"

Without a word, I walked over to the passenger-side door and got into the car.

She poked her head through the car window. "What are you doing in my car?" Her face was as tense as her shoulders and neck.

"My car," I said, and after a moment, she took a deep breath, hanging her head, chin to breastbone.

"I know this is hard, Anna, but—"

"Drive me to the train station," I said, looking straight out the windshield. "Then you'll never hear from me again." I held my handbag and my breath. My eyes shifted to hers.

"All right," she said, and I closed my eyes briefly, relieved. She got into the driver's seat, but before she started up the car, she placed her hand on mine. "I thought you'd left for Dresden."

I caught sight of her watch. "What time is it?" I asked, even though I'd already seen the clock in the house.

"Just past nine," she said, as I fidgeted. "Why?"

I flicked my chin to the road. "Let's go. Now."

She didn't ask any more questions and started up the car and drove away. She waved a hallo to one of my neighbors while I looked straight ahead, waiting for her to drive faster. A girl cut across the road with her bicycle and Mrs. Lange braked to let her pass. "I'll take care of your house, Anna," she said as the engine glugged. "While you're gone."

My mouth hung open. What she meant was that she was taking my house.

"Is that all right?" she asked, and I realized she wanted my blessing. "If I don't take your house, someone else will…"

I turned to her in the stopped car, not sure what to say— this was much more than my stand and my herb jars— when a menacing black car drove past us on the road, miniature Nazi flags flapping near the headlamps. Mrs. Lange craned her neck around, watching it drive toward my house and pull into my garden. She whipped back around and sat firmly in her seat. "Anna." She adjusted the rear-view mirror, her hand shaking.

"Yes," I said, sinking down as we puttered in place, clutching my handbag, hoping she wouldn't have second thoughts about helping me. "Yes, yes, yes."

"Yes, what?" she asked, still looking through the mirror.

"My house. Yes. You can have it. Have everything!" I closed my eyes. "Please, drive away." My eyes popped open when she didn't move. "Please, Mrs. Lange. Drive away!"

She returned her hands to the steering wheel, stepping on the accelerator.

Neither of us said a word the entire rest of the way. She let me out a few streets away from the station where there weren't too many people. Messerschmitts buzzed overhead, headed east, and we listened to their engines slice through the air above the car.

"Mrs. Lange," I said, and I felt my throat ball up. "My mother and Dasa…"

Her eyes sagged when I said their names, and I didn't want to cry, not with what I was about to do, they'd catch me before I even boarded the train—a crying German. "You won't turn them away, will you? When they come back."

I wondered if she knew what had happened to them, or only that they were gone. Her look made me believe she knew something.

She placed her hand on mine in my lap, and I took that to mean she wouldn't. "Do you have a plan?" she asked, and I nodded even though I didn't have anything planned beyond finding the nursery and pretending I wanted to be a nurse. "There's only one person in Germany I'd trust, if you need help. You remember Hans Schmitt, don't you?"

Hans Schmitt came to the theater often when he was in Prague. He was our biggest fan and owned a local theater of his own in Berlin. Josef and I had even visited his theater while on holiday in Germany before the occupation. "Yes, I remember."

"I haven't spoken to him in many years, but he loved the theater and he loved us. It's important to remember the ones who loved us."

I opened the door, but before I could take a step out, she spoke up again.

"Did you know I have a daughter too, Anna?"

I sat back in my seat. Mrs. Lange had never mentioned a daughter before, not in Prague at the theater, and certainly not in Tabor. I shook my head.

"Some people called her dim-witted, a child even after she'd grown up," she said. "I called her my baby girl."

It suddenly occurred to me why Mrs. Lange was so nice to me and Ema, and in a flash, I saw her differently, as if she'd just lifted a mask from her face. I reached for her hand.

"The Reich took her many years ago," she said. "I don't know where she is now. We used to be allowed to visit, but those stopped one day without a word. Every day my husband and I pretend to be supporters of the Party is another day we stay alive, do you understand? I hope you don't think less of me for telling you this now, but—"

"What's her name?" I asked.

Mrs. Lange smiled breathlessly, clamping her hand over her mouth. "Tatiana," she said, and a stream of tears gushed from her eyes. "She was born on a Monday..." She sniffed and swallowed before catching enough breath to thank me for asking, her cry now a series of hiccups. "You will need this watch," she said, slipping off her wristwatch, "It's

German made, and this..." She unclasped her swastika pendant to fasten it around my neck.

"Thank you for helping me," I said.

Our fingers entwined with a squeeze and we looked at each other for, presumably, the last time. "Be safe, Anna."

I walked across the street at a quickened pace, like any traveler late for a train, and feeling confident in the way anyone would with a pocketful of reichsmarks and German documents, but I knew this was the first real test of many—officially presenting myself as Anna Hager—and if I was caught, they'd make an example out of me, a warning to the remaining Czechs.

The station was crowded, and initially I thought that would work in my favor, only everyone had a case or a rucksack or a briefcase with them, while I had a handbag. I stood in line, eyeing the German police on patrol with my handbag brushing against my hip, feeling the bulge of the reichsmarks stuffed inside.

"Next!" a voice shouted, and I stepped up to the ticket counter, smiling at the attendant before pulling a few notes from my handbag. It had been so long since I'd traveled by train, and I thought that it showed, but she handed me my ticket and a few coins for change before waving to the person behind me, making me an official German traveler.

I walked on to the platforms, feeling even more confident after fooling the attendant.

"You!" I heard behind me, though it couldn't have been

for me. "You!" I heard again, and I turned around, and God, I wish I hadn't.

A German policeman motioned for me, curling his finger. Passengers parted, wanting to get as far away from me as possible. I gulped. "Yes?" He took two steps toward me, and that plummeting feeling that usually follows the realization that one's been caught, rose into my throat.

He handed me a train ticket. "You dropped this," he said, and I stared at his hand with the ticket in it.

"Oh," I said, hand to my chest where my heart was screaming. "Thank you." I smiled nervously. "I wouldn't get very far without my ticket, would I?" I told myself to stop talking, that I was digging a hole. I sighed, taking the ticket.

He walked back to his post, and I scolded myself for not trusting my acting. He wasn't concerned with me at all. *Test two.*

I boarded my train a few minutes later and found my seat. My journey had started, and the relief I felt washed over me in the form of an exhausted sleep against the window once we departed, only for me to wake a short time later to a giggling child running up the aisle.

I sat bolt upright, making sense of my surroundings before collapsing back into my seat, breathless from the scare.

His mother apologized to me before turning to the boy. "Don't bother the good German," she said, but he didn't care about me and only wanted a chocolate bar. She talked to her seatmate while digging into her handbag, accidentally spilling the contents.

She stood. "Could you hold this?" she asked, at the same time pushing her newspaper at me.

"Yes, of course," I said, and the boy continued to chew his chocolate bar and his mother chatted with the other woman as she cleaned up her seat. It was a German paper. An invasion had happened on the coast of France, and the Germans were pushing back with great determination, but I'd never heard words like "hope" and "plan" before when reading about the war in a paper.

A finger poked the paper, and I folded down the corner. A girl, a sweet little blonde girl not more than five, gazed up at me. "Hallo," I said, smiling.

She blinked slowly, and I felt like she wanted to tell me something, but before she could, her mother yanked her by the arm. "In your seat!" the mother snapped, and the girl cried out but not with words.

The mother pointed to the space beside her brother as he devoured the chocolate bar, but she didn't seem to understand. The mother turned to her seatmate. "We've been following the Johanna Haarer guide for German mothers, but it doesn't seem to be working."

We passed through a small village on the border, rolling through the train station, which was a single platform and a ticket window. The once-green grass was now straw-colored and sparse. Windows were shuttered while children played barefoot in the streets, and I wondered where the adults were. Empty shops hung signs that read "all out" in broken windows.

"The glorious Czech villages," I heard someone say, followed by a snicker.

The mother burst out in a laugh, and I pulled the shade down over my window. She continued talking to her seatmate, and I overheard her say something about how the girl was adopted. My ears perked.

"I want my mommy," the little girl said clearly—in Polish.

The mother immediately boxed her ears, and I sat up.

"What are you doing?" I cried.

She glared. "Mind your own business!" She snatched the newspaper away and turned to her seatmate, and the girl was still crying and the boy ate his chocolate bar. "The gall of some women…"

I sank down low in my seat, thinking she was a stolen child, and wondering about her real mother and if the girl remembered her. I started to cry myself with her wails. I peeked through my fingers, and the girl did the same, and my heart nearly broke in two.

The attendant walked down the aisle announcing tax collection for entering Germany. I dug into my handbag, scrambling to find a few coins underneath Ema's doll, when I looked up at the little girl, pausing. She was still eyeing me, and I knew I should give her the doll, and the longer I thought about it, the more she sat up as if she knew I was thinking of her, and I couldn't bear it any longer. I saw Ema in the little girl. Having it in my handbag was more of a liability in Germany without a child in my arms, I told myself. It was suspicious.

"Pardon me," I said, and I reached out for the mother, who was shocked at first by my touch. "I'm sorry. I don't know what came over me to question you." I pulled Ema's doll from my handbag. "Can I..." I held the doll out, waiting for the mother's blessing.

"You *should* be sorry," the mother said, then she turned to the little girl and commanded her to sit up and receive her gift.

The girl scampered over to me, wiping her tears heavy-handedly from her eyes. "Here you go," I said, and a smile lifted her face, if ever so brief. I wanted to say something in Polish, one of the handful of Polish words I knew, but I'd be taking a great risk if I did. I reluctantly sat back and away, and when the train pulled into Dresden, I couldn't jump off fast enough.

I bought a city map and followed the winding streets to the address Mrs. Lange had given me, along the Elbe River and under fluttering Nazi Party banners hanging from lampposts, to an unmarked building. I expected a large home, or at least a building that looked occupied and alive, but it seemed to be a shuttered museum. My stomach sank. I looked at the address again. It never occurred to me the address could be wrong.

I asked a passerby where Edelhaus was, but nobody seemed to know. "Please," I said, showing the address to a woman walking her dog. "Have a look. It's a nursery. But the address must be wrong."

I glanced over the nearby buildings, coming back to the museum. I heard a burst of laughter, followed by squeals that peaked and ebbed from children chasing each other behind a stone wall.

"Do you hear that?" I asked, but the woman shook her head.

I walked away in a mesmerized state, leaving her with my piece of paper, trying to decide if this was indeed the place. A tall iron gate connecting the building to the stone wall allowed for a peek where I saw little blonde heads in the museum's garden as the sun set behind the trees.

I gasped, hand to my lips, running toward them.

Chapter Fourteen

The gate rattled and clanked as I breathlessly clawed at the iron bars, before collecting myself in fear of drawing attention, dropping my arms and appearing calm, though my pulse was pumping. There were so many children, oh so many, and I looked for Ema's blonde bunches among the others, but every girl had braids. A piercing whistle called the children inside, then they were gone, and the gardens were empty.

I adjusted the skirt of my dress and flattened my embroidered collar. *Ask about employment and be insistent.* I made my way toward the front door, running my hands over my hair as a last touch before skipping up the stairs with confidence, as any good German woman might do, but I caught a whiff of sour sweat coming from my armpits. I was nervous, and I couldn't afford to be nervous.

I held my arms close and pulled the door open.

Instead of a front office, I found myself looking down a long gray corridor that divided the building in two, with another long corridor running lengthwise at the end. There was no reception because there was nobody inside, only an open doorway that led to a kitchen.

I poked my head in, seeing a cook dressed in white with an even whiter headwrap, holding a steaming pot of water over the sink. "You there," she said, dumping the water out. "What do you want?" A cloud of steam rose into her face.

"Pardon me," I said, "I'm—"

"Hold on!" she piped, and I had to wait for her to finish dumping the pot of hot water out. She wiped her hands on her apron when she was done. "Now, what do you want?"

"I'm looking for Edelhaus. Is this the place?"

A woman stormed through the front door behind me, walking impatiently down the corridor with her blonde curls bouncing off her fox stole. She knocked viciously on one of the closed doors. "Hallo, hallo, hallo…" she said, before disappearing inside after someone had answered.

The cook cleared her throat. "This is the place," she said, and I tried not to let the relief show in my eyes, but I felt it fluttering in my stomach and took a deep breath. She looked me up and down, examining me from my shoes to my dress to the top of my head. "You must be from administration."

I adjusted my handbag even though it didn't need adjusting. "I'm here to see about employment."

"That's what I meant." She stared at me for a moment, then went back to her pot. "Come back tomorrow," she barked, carrying the pot over to the cooktop.

"Tomorrow?" I questioned, and a kitchen aide walked in from the back, this one wearing a blue kerchief over her head. She looked pleased to see me in the same room initially, then sat down with a flump, uncaring.

"Paula," the cook called back, "appointments for the nurse position are tomorrow?"

Nurse position? I blinked.

The aide pulled her sweaty kerchief from her head and fluffed a lump of dark hair to life.

"Sit up!" the cook said, and she jolted upright in her chair.

"Sorry, Cook," she said. "It's tomorrow. Nine o'clock, is what I heard."

The cook reached for a pan, going about her business as I stood. "You heard her, no?" Her brow furrowed as if she expected me to leave now that I had my answer.

"Tomorrow," I said. "Yes." I was stunned by my timing, especially after such an incredibly hard journey making it to this point. As Matka would say, luck was on my side.

I smiled, not wanting to leave, yet not knowing what I could possibly say to stay, now that I had my answer.

"Leave!" the cook said, and I reluctantly scooted into the corridor, feeling my forehead in an attempt to linger, when a nurse in a poufy white dress emerged at the far end, leading children from one side of the building to the other. I threw my back against the wall, and she ordered them to be quiet.

"Don't touch the walls," the nurse said. "A good German wouldn't want to leave an oily fingerprint. We keep our hands to ourselves."

The children marched straight with arms crisscrossed

over their chests, unaware I was watching them near the front door.

The cook came up from behind with her pot. "I thought you left," she said.

I turned halfway around as the children marched on, and in the brief second I took my eyes off them, I thought I might have missed her.

"I'm—" *Ema!* I saw her at the back of the line, just behind a boy. My instant reaction was to run to her, pick her up and carry her away, but I swallowed my instincts, and my throat felt it, immediately lumping up. "I'm going now," I said, leaving out the front doors and scampering down the stairs to the pavement.

Near the bushes, I covered my mouth and had a joyful cry.

"Thank you, God," I said. "Thank you."

I slept at a cheap hotel a few streets away, which offered a dry piece of toast to eat for breakfast. Thoughts of Ema, and how to steal her back, were like a wheel in my head. Constantly spinning, spinning, spinning in thought. If I could get her alone, get her outside the stone wall, anything was possible with German documents and a handbag full of reichsmarks.

I dropped to my knees and prayed before I left the hotel room. I thought of Matka, her words of wisdom, and Dasa. I felt the vast distance between us in that moment, with me inside Germany and the rest of my family scattered to the wind and the woods. I clasped my hands together.

"Dear God, I haven't been to church in so long, but I've always prayed. Always. I've never asked for much, not when Josef left, or when my father died. Our lives have become like sand in our hands, sliding through our fingers into the unknown." I looked to the ceiling. "Let this be where it ends—where the story ends. Let me bring Ema home."

I set out for Edelhaus a whole twenty minutes early in hopes of getting more glimpses of Ema. I walked up the pavement, feeling impatient, nervous, but also excited, only I wasn't the first one there. My armpits sweated. Another woman had beaten me to the front door, wearing a cream dress and socks with white sandals. Her wheat-colored hair was done up in a loose bun, just like the Brown Sisters, and when she turned around, I was struck by her muted beauty.

"Hallo," she said.

I gripped my handbag. "Hallo."

I'm Anna Hager, I reminded myself. *Anna Hager, the good German from Berlin.* I lifted my eyes, feeling very much like a curtain had been pulled back. *Anna. Hager.*

We stood in silence, sneakily eyeing each other as we pretended to search the air. "You're here for the nurse position?" I finally asked, and she nodded once.

"Me too," I said.

We searched more of the air. A burst of noise came from the gardens, one I'd describe as playful children, and my heart raced, thinking Ema was near. I walked over to the iron gate, only the woman followed, and we watched the children together where they'd been let out to play.

"Children of the Reich," she breathed.

"Beautiful," I breathed back, looking for Ema's blonde bunches, but remembering they'd put every girl in braids.

Another whistle. This one from the front steps of the nursery. A hard woman, lean and long, with a brown dress and a black belt. She waved for us to enter.

"You two are here for employment?" she asked, and we both said yes. "I see."

We walked down the gray corridor I'd been in yesterday, only this time I noticed the ceiling, which was incredibly high and painted to look like the Nazi Party flag. The other girl was looking too, and when the woman stopped walking, we nearly tripped over ourselves from staring. She pointed into her office, and we sat down across from her at a large desk with nothing but a pad of paper on it. Hitler's portrait hung on the wall behind her, his eyes almost following me, looking down over her shoulder.

"I'm Frau Brack," she said. "I'm in charge of Edelhaus." She licked a finger and flipped through her pad. "Now, I must have missed the memorandum that said administration was sending two candidates. Which one is Herta?"

"That's me," the other girl said, pointing to her chest. "Herta."

Frau Brack studied Herta with a pleasing smile. "Yes… You look very good. Very good." She flipped the last page over in her notebook, looking up. "Now, who are you?" She leaned back in her squeaky leather chair.

I cleared my throat. "I'm Anna," I said, "Hager, from Berlin." I pressed my lips together, thinking she might want to see my documents, and reached into my handbag. "I have my documents, Frau Brack, if you'd like to see."

As I handed them to her over the desk, Herta had reached for her documents too, and we watched Frau Brack inspect them both, squaring them side by side, with her nose moving up and down like a finger. I held my breath and my smile, trying to look even more confident than before with a puffed chest, but inside I was reeling.

"Yes, looks all in order," she said, and I felt an immediate release when she handed our documents back.

"Now, Fräulein Hager," she said. "Where is your swastika?" She looked at Herta. "You too," she said, and we each reached for our necks, pulling our pendants from our collars.

"We take our commitment very seriously at Edelhaus…" She went on to talk about the nursery and how special the children were, the Reich's finest specimens. "When I have a mother in my office, she must see our commitment to Germany in every crack and crevice of this building. And on your necks. Do you understand?" Her brow furrowed, yet all I thought about was how I was going to get her to like me the most.

"Yes, Frau—"

"Yes, Frau Brack!" I said, cutting Herta off, and there was a pause with Herta and I looking at each other. "I won't let the Führer down…"

But Herta talked over me, saying much the same, and suddenly we were competing for Frau Brack's attention and the position, our voices rising over each other's. Frau Brack sat back in her chair, hands in a steeple position, listening carefully. I ended with something I remembered hearing from the mother on the train. "I believe in Johanna Haarer's guide when it comes to nursing and mothering," I said, and Herta's head whipped around. Her mouth hung open as I continued talking about how special Aryan children were, how important.

"I believe that too!" Herta said, and Frau Brack smiled, appearing to enjoy us trying to prove our superiority over each other, but when Herta mentioned how her one true gift to the country would be to someday have a child for the nation, Frau Brack appeared to have made up her mind. "I had a friend in the Bund Deutscher Mädel who told me all about the *program*," Herta said, trailing in a whisper.

Frau Brack turned to me. "Thank you, Anna, but I believe we've found our newest nurse."

Herta smiled, inching up tall in her seat, while I stayed put, not sure what to do, even though I was told to leave. "That means you weren't chosen," Frau Brack said.

"But…" I looked at Herta, and I'm not sure why I expected her to help because she looked glad to see I'd been dismissed. I burst into tears instinctively and cried into my hands, turning hysterical, sucking air through my teeth and heaving with breathy cries. A nurse came in to see if she could be of assistance, but she was told everything was all right as I sobbed. "I love the Führer," I cried, palms digging into my eyes, and the louder I got and the more hysterical I sounded, the more I realized how perfect my performance was. "I only want to serve…"

The nurse and Frau Brack talked between themselves, then I felt a pat on the back.

I looked up from my hands, eyes puffy and wet.

"I can see the survival of our race means a lot to you, Anna," Frau Brack said, folding her hands. "I do have a housekeeping position available, if you would like to entertain the idea. It's not a nurse position, but equally important to make sure the facility is the cleanest and purest environment for our youth." She looked at my handbag and Herta's too. "These are both boarded positions. I trust you can have your things sent over?"

"Now?" I asked.

"We work extremely fast here," Frau Brack said. "It's a vast estate and if I didn't act decisively, I'd never have enough nurses to care for the infants or enough clean floors for the Reich's children to walk upon." She winked. "I can tell a good German when I see one."

I stood, gripping my dress at the thighs, nodding incessantly. "Yes," I said, swallowing my tears. "I accept the position. Whatever I can do to serve the Reich, and the Führer." I turned to Hitler's portrait on the wall and blew kisses from my fingertips. "Thousand Year Reich," I breathed, and I got a very satisfied nod from Frau Brack.

She searched her chest for the whistle she had hanging from her neck. *Peep!* The kitchen aide I saw yesterday ran into the room, and in with her blew an odorous cloud of overcooked broccoli. "Yes, Frau Brack?" She glanced at me once.

"Fräulein Hager will be joining housekeeping," Frau

Brack said. "Will you see she gets settled in—" She cleared her throat. "Margot's old room?"

"Margot?" the kitchen aide questioned, but then nodded. "Yes, Frau Brack."

I fought a smile—a job well done, another test I'd passed. I followed the kitchen aide into the corridor and toward the stairs. "My name's Paula, Fräulein Hager," she said, turning as we walked.

"Please, call me Anna." At the end of the corridor, we shook hands.

"You'll report to the cook, just like me. She manages the interior." She pointed to a portrait of two Aryan children in traditional clothing near the staircase. "Those are our first adopted children."

I followed her up the stairs, under Nazi Party banners rippling from the disturbance in the air. She put a finger to her lips once we'd made it to the top. "This is where the babies are," she whispered, before pointing to the cots behind a glass viewing area. I imitated her, pressing a finger to my lips, and a nurse with a long, snow-white braid locked eyes with me through the glass, tracking me the entire length of the corridor.

Paula stopped at what appeared to be a closet door. "This is your room." She motioned for me to go inside first, and when I peeked in, I realized it *was* a closet, only exceptionally large, fitted with a single bed against the wall, a chest of drawers, and a stock shelf loaded with cleaning supplies. "You'll be sleeping with your supplies, but I assure you it's quite comfortable." She pointed to the back. "There's a window, a toilet, and a bathtub beyond the supply racks. Do you have any family that will be visiting?" she asked. "Any brothers, or sisters…" She smiled, and I felt a pang, thinking of Dasa.

"No."

She showed me to the window. Beyond the garden I'd seen the children playing in earlier, were two long buildings with lots of frosted windows and a courtyard. The grounds didn't appear to end there, but it was difficult to see through all the trees.

"That building there is the children's dormitory," she said, "and the other one is where the nurses sleep. Do you like your sleeping quarters?" She smiled strangely, as if she expected me to be mortified.

"I'm grateful," I said, glancing over the room. I'd never seen so many cleaning products in my life. I sniffed the air. "Is that chlorine?"

She laughed. "Yes, and the other housekeepers sleep in similar circumstances. I sleep in the pantry, in the back behind the storage. Frau Brack likes it that way." She opened one of the drawers. "Shoes are under the bed, and uniforms are in here—" She reached into the drawer, pulling out a sky-blue ribbon. "This is Margot's," she whispered to herself.

"Margot?" I questioned.

"Don't say her name out loud." Her eyes darted to the door, following the soft pad of nurses walking the corridor. "I shouldn't have said it, and I shouldn't have repeated it in Frau Brack's office either."

"Oh?" I said. "I'm sorry, I didn't—"

"Come down to the kitchen once you're settled." Paula

slipped the ribbon into her pocket, giving me a parting smile. "Welcome to Edelhaus."

"Thank you," I said, but she'd already closed the door. A pounding headache followed amidst the fog of chemicals, but also excitement. I was so close to Ema, and closer than ever to getting her back.

I needed to reach out to her without alerting the other children or the staff—tell her I was there—then get her alone and escape. I pulled one of the dresses from the drawer. It was a button-up thing with a cloth belt—there wasn't much to it—and a forgotten needle hidden in the seam that pricked my finger when I threw it on.

Knock! Knock!

I sucked my finger. "Slipping on my uniform now," I said, thinking it was Paula again. All I wanted to do was get outside and find my daughter. I pulled Margot's work shoes out from under the bed without checking the size, squeezing each foot in, and answering the door with a hop just as there was another knock.

"Yes?" I opened the door to find the cook, and she looked angry, staring at me with a frown in her eyebrows rather than on her mouth.

I pulled my finger from my lips.

"Why aren't you dressed yet?" She barged into my room, hands on her hips. "I've been waiting for you in the kitchen."

The only thing I could tell her was that I'd gotten pricked by a pin, which she didn't care about. She pushed a piece of paper at me. "Here are your duties, and every day the list will change. The Reich's children must live in a clean place." She grabbed my hand to look at my nails, which I'd scrubbed. "That means you must be clean too. Don't give the nurses something to talk about. Bathe yourself daily." She took a bar of goat milk soap from the shelf. "Here," she said, and it was the loveliest soap I'd ever smelled in my life, a scent somewhere between the nape of a baby's neck and springtime under a blossoming tree.

She turned on her way out. "Have you visited security yet?"

"Security?" I put my hand on my chest. I'd thought I was safe after Frau Brack had seen my documents.

"He'll have questions for you—Herr Neider." She paused from my questioning look. "To verify your family tree," she said, and my stomach sank. "Down the corridor, down the stairs, second door to the left, next to the furnace."

She looked me up and down, waiting for a reply, when Frau Brack breezed in next, dismissing her with a twirl of her finger.

"Security? No need to see him now," Frau Brack said. "Herr Neider has informed me he'll come find you." She held out her hand. "He has asked for your documents, however, Fraulein Hager. I know I've already seen them, but he has his own policies to follow."

I turned around after pulling them from my handbag and caught her eyeing me from behind. She smiled widely, slipping my documents into her pocket and giving them a pat.

"Good day, Fräulein," she said, before walking away.

"Family tree," I said to myself, closing my eyes. *God,*

documents. A cold sweat washed over me with my documents headed to security. I didn't have much time. I folded up the duty list before rolling up the reichsmarks and stuffing them between my breasts for the escape, then gathered my cleaning supplies.

I wheeled my mop bucket down the corridor, filled with warm sudsy water from my bathtub, and pulled back the iron gate on the lift. A set of doors closed down below, and I froze with the lift open and the bucket between my legs, hearing a nurse ordering children up the stairs.

I couldn't breathe.

The nurse passed by swiftly, never glancing up, followed by four boys and a long line of girls. One by one they walked past me and my mop bucket, arms crisscrossed against their chests, dutiful, following orders.

Then I saw Ema last in line, and I thought I'd snap in two.

She was older, I could see it in her face now that I was close up. She'd grown a thumb's length in the weeks she'd been gone, and her braids were tight and long. My eyes instantly welled, and I bent down on both knees, meeting her at eye level to make it easier for her to look at me, but I was too afraid to even breathe her name with the others so close by.

My throat throbbed, and my head pounded even more than before, knowing that the seconds I had to make a move were disappearing faster than my thoughts. I stuck my hand out just as she looked up, fingers reaching for hers.

"Ema," I mouthed, but she pulled coldly away.

Chapter Fifteen

I fell backward into the wall, watching her walk away, then scrambled to stand before anyone saw, scooting into the lift to hide and have a silent cry. She'd looked at me as if I was a stranger. *Maybe I expected too much,* I thought. Ema had been under the Reich's instruction for weeks. I could only imagine what kind of lies they'd told her.

I managed to push the button to go down, the gears grinding and shuddering the lift walls. *That's it.* I'd expected too much, though the realization didn't keep my heart from aching with disappointment.

I pulled back the gate when the lift stopped, straightening, trying my best to shake her cold look from my mind and focus on what I knew. She was here. I was here. It was only a matter of time before I could escape with my daughter.

I felt for my heart, taking a slow breath through my nose, which helped.

My plan was to find a crack—work through the duty list

as a means to explore the buildings, get outside and find a secret way out, and all the while avoiding security. I pulled the list from my pocket, listening to muffled nurses' shoes pass through the corridor.

Hours passed, and I managed to clean my way through most of the rooms on the ground floor. I dusted a Nazi flag hanging on a pole near the front door, thinking of my next step as I ran the rag down the thick fabric. I had a good excuse to go outside now with my dirty mop water.

Frau Brack walked from her office down the corridor. *Clack, clack, clack…* "Herr Neider," I heard her say, and my heart almost stopped. I desperately looked for a dark room I could duck into, but my mop bucket was too loud and they'd hear me. I wheeled it into the kitchen, my only choice, for what little cover it could provide, but I wasn't at all prepared for the scent of warm bread hovering in the air. It nearly knocked me off my feet and sent me into the clouds.

Ema will be eating fresh bread today, I thought, closing my eyes briefly, and if there was one comfort of her being in this place, it was that she was well fed.

"Haven't you smelled bread before?" Paula eyed me from across the room, having a chuckle before pulling two big loaves out from the oven. I stood with my back against the door, without asking for permission to close it in the first place, holding my breath.

The cook barked at me to open it back up, and I reluctantly put my hand on the knob as Frau Brack and Neider chatted behind it, walking toward the main entrance, which was just enough of a delay on my part that by the time I opened the door, they'd already made it outside.

I exhaled a mouthful of air. They were gone, and my heart thumped and thumped and thumped.

"I've been smelling chlorine, so the bread took me by surprise," I said, finally giving her an answer. I wheeled my mop bucket closer.

Paula had been nice to me when I arrived, and I thought she might be a good person to strike up a conversation with, and possibly get some information out of. I pulled my duty list from my pocket. "Could you help me? I have a few questions…" Though the only question I had was about the gates, the locks, and the perimeter of the estate.

Paula wiped her hands on her apron before taking a look.

"I'm not sure where to go," I said, pointing to the items on the list. "Are all of these duties inside this building?"

"Looks like you have to mop the pantry, and it's there." She pointed to the pantry door. "But outside, let's see, nothing in the dormitories, or the gymnasium, and doesn't look like you have anything beyond the courtyard or the trees where the women—"

"Fräulein!" the cook shouted, and Paula immediately walked back over to her bread with her head down. The cook turned to me. "Clean the pantry."

I folded the list back up. "Yes, Cook," I said, and I wheeled my mop bucket over to the pantry to clean it, opening the door and squeezing inside.

I pulled the light string and my jaw dropped. Sacks of flour, sacks of sugar, and canisters of beans—every bean imaginable and in every color—along with baskets of fresh vegetables and colorful fruit. I hadn't seen so much food since before the war—from floor to ceiling and ceiling to floor—and I was alone with it and no eyes to watch over me. My mouth watered. Iced biscuits, still warm from the oven, sat on trays near the door, tempting me, along with cream horns, pretzels dipped in ganache, and butter braids.

In the back, behind the storage boxes, I saw what must have been the legs of Paula's bed. She didn't have a window, as far as I could tell. "But all this food," I said aloud. The pantry went all the way back, much bigger than a pantry should be with the number of children I had seen walking the corridors.

I mopped vigorously after taking many minutes to gawk, then Paula poked her head in, first looking at the tray of sweets as if making sure they were all still there. "Everything all right in here?"

"Yes," I said, but I wondered if I'd broken a rule. "Am I taking too long?"

"You have been in here a long time," she said, closing the door behind her. "Actually, the cook wanted me to see about you, but I can tell you're doing just fine, Fräulein."

"Please, call me Anna," I said, and she winced.

"Yes, you told me that. I'm sorry, Anna. I tell people to call me Paula all the time, but the nurses just grunt at me, and the cook mostly yells." She took a deep breath through her mouth. "And then Frau Brack yells at me too, and I don't like the yelling and I wish…"

I nodded continuously, listening to the rambling words

tumbling from her mouth, butting in only after she mentioned the pastries she'd made that morning.

"Is all of this food for the children?" I pointed to the biscuits and the other sweet treats laid out on trays.

"No—" She caught herself. "That's a question for the cook. I'm not allowed to talk about it." She whispered even though we were still in the pantry, alone. "Don't ask too many questions. Rumors get started that way. Understand?"

"I wasn't trying to be intrusive."

"I know," she said. "Don't worry, I won't tell anyone."

We stared at each other for a moment with her smiling, and me thinking how odd the exchange had been. I gripped my mop handle.

"I'd better go," I finally said, and she watched me leave, wheeling my bucket out of the pantry into the corridor.

I listened for Neider; all seemed clear. Nurses padded from one end of the corridor to the other on their way upstairs to the nursery. Margot's name passed in whispers followed by talk about the new girls.

I saw my chance to go outside to dump my dirty mop water, and wheeled my bucket around the side of the building to the garden where I'd seen the children play.

The grounds were beautifully manicured with purple and yellow flowers growing neatly in clusters with an alpine scene painted on the exterior the building, something that was only visible to the children, with swirls of white edelweiss and blue enzian blooming beneath snow-capped mountains.

A painting like that in Tabor would have cost a fortune,

and I thought about the derelict gardens the poor Czech children were allowed to play in back at home, with swings hanging from broken chains, and glass littering the pavements, making it impossible to run around in their bare feet without getting cut.

The door to the children's dormitory swung open with a burst of children running outside, cheering and leaping and bounding over the playground equipment. I reached for my chest after a gasp, and I felt myself smiling. The boys ran for the slides, and the girls for the swings. Ema ran out in the middle of the pack, her little arms pumping, trying to outrun another girl for the swings, but she wasn't fast enough. She reached for a ball instead, and I stood, watching her look at me and panicking inside.

I pulled my list from my pocket, hoping she'd make her way over, my eyes shifting, looking up and down at the other buildings, and to each side. A lone nurse on duty walked the garden, blowing her whistle at the boys.

Ema bounced her ball once and way too hard, sending it rolling in my direction. I picked it up when it bumped into my ankle.

"Hallo," I said, and my eyes welled with tears. I could barely get the word out.

"They're watching." She reached for the ball, but I held onto it.

"Tie your shoe," I said, and she did, and that bought us a few more seconds. "I'm working on a plan, sweet girl. Tell nobody I'm here, not even the other children. We must play a game. Understand? Like we did back in Tabor. I have money…"

She had tied her shoe, and the nurse blew her whistle. "They said I'm German, and that you'd stolen me from my real mother. Is that true?"

My heart and soul shattered in an instant. "I'm your real mother," I said, and my tears started to fall. "Don't believe their lies. I love you, Ema. I love you. I've been looking for you this whole time. I'll figure out a way to get you out of here…" I scanned the garden and the windows and the doors, wiping tears from my cheeks and covering them with a smile and a fake laugh. "You must go now. It will look suspicious if you stay."

The nurse looked over, and Ema ran off with her ball to play with some other children while I clutched my broken heart, watching for a mere moment, my eyes trailing, trailing, until they got caught in the duty nurse's gaze, who'd never looked away.

I stumbled backward into my bucket, feeling exposed and fraudulent and thinking she could tell. I frantically poured cleaning fluid on a rag to the point of dripping and slapped it on a window to clean it, even though it wasn't on my list, but a man was watching me on the other side.

Neider!

He crossed his arms, examining me with a sinister-sweet smile as the fluid dribbled from the rag down my arm to my elbow, before pointing sharply to the door.

I wheeled my bucket around the building to the door I'd walked out from, pausing to quell my pounding heart and fan air at my eyes where I still had tears.

He pulled open the door. "Fräulein Hager," he said.

I reached for my neck. "Yes?"

He held out his hand for a shake, which surprised me, and his palm felt cool and fragile. "Klaus Neider," he said. "Head of security." He smiled, but his lips were as thin as his mustache, which made his teeth look small and pearly like a child's. "Can we have a chat in my office?"

"Oh," I said. "Ahh..." I glanced down at my mop and bucket, stalling, trying to recall Anna Hager from her faraway place. "Of course." I smoothed my sweating palms over my work dress. "Can I put my cleaning equipment away?"

"Yes, that's quite all right." He spoke with ease and made it sound like we would indeed be having a social chat. "You know where my office is?"

I remembered what the cook had told me in my room. "Down the corridor, down the stairs, second door on the left next to the furnace."

"Very good," he said, "but it's the second set of stairs. I'm in the basement."

"Yes, Herr Neider."

He questioned my watering eyes from when I saw Ema. "It's the chlorine," I said, and he accepted this excuse, turning his head slowly and walking away.

I wheeled my bucket down the corridor to the service lift, worrying he'd figured out my documents were forged and that I wasn't who I pretended to be. The crank and grind of the gears didn't help. But if he had, why'd he act so casual? *Maybe he's going to ask me about my family tree?* I blew air from my mouth as the lift stopped. *That's it. God.* He would have had me arrested if it wasn't. Now I was thinking of only one thing. *Who am I?*

The only German I knew inside Germany was the Berlin theater owner Hans Schmitt, who I'd met several times. Mrs. Lange had even mentioned him, reminding me to remember who our friends were. I decided he was who I had to attach my lineage to, and hopefully, before Neider found out I was lying, Ema and I would have escaped.

I wheeled the mop bucket into my room, turning swiftly to leave. The nurses glared at me through the glass. One noted the time. *Breathe,* I told myself, hurrying down the stairs.

I found the furnace and pulled my shoulders back at his door, breathing one long breath in through my mouth in the corridor before knocking. *Calm down! I'm Anna Hager. Anna. Hager.*

"Hallo, Fräulein." Neider motioned for me to come inside. "Have a seat."

The swatch of natural light shining through the narrow basement window disappeared with the snap of his closed door behind me. He adjusted his desk lamp, illuminating his papers and reports, and an ashtray with a burning cigarette. "Please." He pointed through a ribbon of smoke to a chair on the other side of his desk. "Before I forget," he said, putting aside Herta's documents and lifting mine from a pile. "You can have these back."

"Thank you." I held them in my lap, trying not to show

the intense relief I felt at having my documents back in my hands, and waited for his interrogation to start.

I shifted in my seat.

He pulled a pencil from his desk drawer, licking the lead. "Now! Can I have your tree? Family tree, that is." He smiled. "I know you are from Berlin, but who are your relatives?"

A knock on the door saved me from a fumbling answer, even though I had already decided on Hans Schmitt's family. It was Herta, and she looked surprised to see me sitting inside, then a little relieved.

He pointed his cigarette to the chair next to me, commanding her to sit, and she did exactly as she was told, like a good German. He handed Herta her documents.

"Now, Fräulein Hager, your relatives are—"

"Schmitt." I cleared my throat. "Hans Schmitt is my father," I said, and he scribbled on the paper. "My grandfather is also named Hans Schmitt, followed by his father. All very respected, I assure you…" I spouted off all the intricacies I remembered from when Josef and I visited Hans Schmitt in Berlin. How he served in the Imperial German Army during the first war, a decorated hero, and his father before him.

He looked up. "And yet your surname is Hager?"

"I was married at the start of the war." I felt the smooth skin where my wedding band had been for so many years and thought of Josef. "A young soldier." I closed my eyes briefly, recalling the raw pain of when my husband left me, like any good actress would do. "He died in battle."

"Where?" He poised his pencil, ready to write, but this

was a detail I hadn't thought about at all, and blurted the first thing that came to my mind.

"The Eastern Front," I said.

"I see." He smashed his cigarette in the ashtray, and for the first time since Herta sat down, I smelled the light and powdery scent of the nursery coming from her smock and hair. Neider must have noticed too because he sniffed the air after he waved the last cloud of cigarette smoke away.

He asked Herta for her family tree next, and she gave him a detailed account that seemed to please him. Then he addressed us both. "Has Frau Brack informed you two of our larger policies and procedures here at Edelhaus?"

"Policies and procedures?" I questioned.

Neider tapped his pencil on his desk, explaining the estate rules much like a teacher would explain classroom procedures—what time lights needed to be out, what time we could leave our rooms in the morning—not before six, to avoid waking the children—and how we should check with Frau Brack before leaving the estate. "The outbuildings have lights, and we have dogs patrolling the perimeter," he said, and a little piece of me shattered inside. "Wouldn't want you to get bitten."

Dogs?

"A security detail is also in place as an added measure—to keep everyone safe. Guards, you can call them." He ended with a smile that exposed his pearly baby teeth. "Any questions?"

I felt deathly ill after hearing all this news, and flushed, which I was sure was noticeable, a physical reaction no amount of acting could control. How was I going to escape with Ema now? I tried not to fidget. I tried not to let it show, but my entire body ached with thoughts of dogs ripping Ema in half while the guards shot me in the back.

"Are you all right, Fräulein Hager?" he asked, searching my face. "Do you have a question?"

I closed my gaping mouth, thinking up the one question a good German with nothing to hide would ask. "What time's dinner?"

Herta scooted her chair back, standing up stiffly. "If that is all, Herr Neider, may I leave? The babies…"

"That is all," Neider said, and while he wrote a few more things down on his paper, I moved to follow Herta. "For now," he added. "I will find you when I require more of you." His eyes lifted from his paper to my legs as I walked out. "Halt!"

I froze, and he reached for my leg where he pinched a ball of lint from my dress hem. I felt his cold intentional touch on the back of my knee.

"You can leave now," he said, but I couldn't move. He looked up, and I found myself staring quite shockingly into his eyes while feeling the chill of where he'd touched me. "Back to your duties, Fräulein."

"Yes, Herr Neider," I finally said, and I hurried out of his office and back up to the ground floor.

Paula spied me in the corridor from the kitchen, waving me over. "I just remembered you didn't get lunch." She cut into a fresh loaf of dark bread. The smell was tangy and tart and overwhelming, causing my stomach to growl. "You must be starving, and dinner isn't for a while yet."

"Sorry," I said, knowing she heard my stomach. "Not

very ladylike to have a growling stomach." Neider's heels clipped down the corridor, and I instinctively reached behind me for the door.

"No need to apologize," she said. "I was part of housekeeping before I moved into the kitchen. I know how hard it is to clean. Makes you hungry. Close the door." She smiled, and I shut the door moments before Neider passed by, clipping off to somewhere unknown.

"That's it," I said. "The hard work has made me hungry."

Paula placed a thick slice of bread in front of me on the table. I hung my head over the plate, gazing at the bread's crust, the warm rye permeating my nostrils, while she rinsed off some berries in the sink. "Butter is on the table," she said.

I hadn't seen real butter in years, much less tasted it, and while her back was turned, I shoved the bread into my mouth along with a glop of butter, licking every finger as I chewed.

She turned back around, presenting me with a bowl of berries, and I sat up, hiding my buttery fingers under the tablecloth. The fruit looked like a work of art, red raspberries, pink strawberries, and the blackest blackberries dusted with confectionery sugar.

I swallowed. "All this for me?"

She giggled. "Nothing but the best food here at Edelhaus, and to our benefit. The Reich's children need the best."

I dug into the berries as politely as I could, but it was near impossible not to double scoop. The burst of the blackberry and the tang of the strawberry was almost too good to put into words. I swallowed, closing my eyes, enjoying the taste for a moment, before the tangled thoughts of dogs and security guards eclipsed the contented feeling of having a full stomach.

Paula watched me eat, which was only mildly annoying, but then the cook came in barking for her to get back to work. "Get those pastries to the women, now!"

"Yes, Cook!" Paula bolted from her seat.

I watched them load trays of delectables onto rolling carts from over my bowl of berries. "And you," the cook said to me, on her way out with the carts. "Get back to work. And if you're done, then get to your quarters. Frau Brack doesn't like the staff loitering in the kitchen."

I stood from my chair, but they had left and now my stomach hurt more than it did when I was starving. "Ugh…" I moaned since nobody could hear me. The first bite was a memory, and the last one in my mouth was now a mushy burden, and I worried I might retch. I couldn't spit it out in the kitchen sink in case someone walked in, so I ran into the pantry to spit it out in Paula's toilet. After I flushed, worry that someone would see me spitting was replaced with worry about someone finding me in the pantry alone with all the food.

I wiped my mouth roughly, opening the pantry door to leave, only to gasp at the sight of Neider standing near my chair. I closed the door as quickly as I'd opened it, though softer than a feather, and watched him from the crack.

He studied the seat where I'd eaten, and then oddly picked up the empty bowl of berries I'd left on the table, taking a sniff. He set it down when Frau Brack appeared in the doorway.

"Herr Neider," she said, and I wasn't sure, I couldn't be sure, but I thought I heard my name pass between them as they talked. I pressed my ear to the crack. "Fräulein Hager?" she questioned, responding to something he asked, and my stomach sank. Then they both walked in opposite directions with no warning at all.

They *were* talking about me. I slipped out of the pantry and disappeared upstairs in my quiet shoes. A hand grabbed me from behind.

"Ack!" I fell breathlessly up the stairs, clutching my chest. "Frau Brack."

Her eyes popped from their sockets, looking absolutely shocked by my reaction. "My goodness, Fräulein," she said, reaching for her collar.

"Sorry, Frau Brack." I stood up, swallowing endlessly and clenching the sides of my skirt. "I didn't see you."

"Evidently," she said, and after a short pause with both of us staring at each other, she smiled. "I just heard that you met with security."

I blinked. "Yes." I felt my dress fabric crunching in my fists. "Herr Neider."

Her eyes rolled up my arms to my neck and face. "You have a wonderful complexion, Anna. Has anyone ever told you that?" She left before I could answer, leaving me confused and feeling for my chest.

"God," I said, followed by a few deep breaths. I needed to hold myself together, keep my wits about me. Otherwise, I was going to cause suspicion.

I reached for the handrail. *I am still here*, I reminded myself. But now daytime had dwindled into evening and I hadn't formulated a plan to escape. I wouldn't be able to leave with Ema today. But tomorrow...

I still had tomorrow.

Chapter Sixteen

T he morning came early after a night of listening to a baby wail and wail and wail. I kept waiting for a nurse to come in and check on the poor thing, but nobody came. My duty list had been slid under my door. At the top was a reminder to use the goat milk soap, then go down for breakfast.

I threw on a work dress after bathing, and got pricked again by another needle, only this time I noticed the seam had been picked, leaving tiny open pockets near the buttonholes. I was surprised the Germans allowed their staff to wear dresses that needed mending.

The estate grounds looked different in the morning light from my window. I noticed a pathway near the playground that disappeared into some shrubbery and trees, headed directly to the stone wall, as if there was an opening or a gate. It was hard to tell. I needed to find a way to see Ema again, get outside and stay outside, and also get a better look at that path.

I read through my cleaning duties in the lift. After breakfast, I was to dust the lightroom. *Lightroom?*

The lift opened on the ground floor to the smell of coffee. *Real coffee.* I held onto the doorway in the kitchen. *How do they get real coffee?*

My eyes fluttered from the aroma when breathing it in. Paula looked up from a tray of toast cut-outs and jam. "Good morning," she said, and I wheeled my cleaning cart into the kitchen, parking it against the wall. I wanted to know when breakfast was for the children and where they ate.

The cook brushed past me with a tray of baked goods she loaded onto a rolling cart full of steaming bowls of milky-white porridge with strawberries, food I imagined was for the children. I resisted asking her for fear of sounding suspicious and saved my questions for Paula who might accidentally tell me more than she should. "Get your breakfast then get going," the cook said to me.

"Yes, Cook." I sat at the small table I had sat at yesterday, staring at the soft cheese and rosehip jam that had been set out, preoccupied with thoughts of where the cook was taking the porridge. I looked up when I felt her watching from the doorway.

"Now!" the cook barked, and I jolted in my chair.

Paula set a plate of toast in front of me, and I hastily smeared the jam onto my cheesy toast while the cook was still watching, but when I bit into it, the flavors exploded into my mouth. I closed my eyes, trying to recover from the tangy rush and puckering my lips.

"Very good. Tastes like my mother's," I said, chewing,

and the cook accepted my lie, pushing her cartful of breakfast food into the corridor. I swallowed, glad to have something in my stomach, even if it had taken me by surprise. "Where do the children eat?" I asked Paula delicately, as if it were an afterthought.

She looked at me strangely, hand in a mixing bowl.

"It might be on my list." I smiled.

"Oh." She shook her head. "Sorry. They eat in the cafeteria, just outside those doors." She pointed with her head to a side door in the corridor that led to the gardens.

I pulled the duty list from my pocket, unraveling it flat on the table. I needed an excuse to be near the playground, but that excuse wouldn't come until after lunch when I was supposed to empty the rubbish bins in the garden.

"Did you sleep well?" Paula asked, and I looked up from my list. "The babies keep you up?" she added, giggling, and I was surprised she knew, as if it was normal to leave a baby screaming through the night.

"Yes," I said. "How'd you know?"

She set her mixing bowl off to the side to sit down, pouring herself a cup of steaming black coffee. "The nurses follow Johanna Haarer's guide to mothering—*The German Mother and Her First Child*."

That was the guide I had mentioned during my appointment, though I didn't know who Johanna Haarer was. "What does that mean?"

"You don't know who she is?" Her mouth hung open as if she couldn't believe I didn't know. "The Reich's child-rearing expert. A child who is picked up in the night is spoiled," she said, scooping a glop of the jam onto her toast round. "That's what Johanna Haarer says, and that's what everyone believes." She took a bite of the toast—a fine chomp followed by the slow curl of her lips. "Don't they?" she asked, mouth full.

"Oh, yes," I said, nodding, but inside I was horrified—a crying child needs its mother, probably to be fed or because of a wet nappy, not because it's spoiled. "How silly of me."

Paula sipped her hot coffee, and dangerous thoughts of how they treated the other children, how they treated Ema, bubbled up inside of me like a kettle about to steam. If they were willing to let a baby cry, what were they doing to the older children?

German bombers roared over Edelhaus, rattling the windows they were so low. My eyes followed the engine noise, and it reminded me how vulnerable to bombings I was in the city.

"Where's the shelter?"

She scoffed. "Why would we need a shelter?" she asked, but then leaned in and followed with a whisper: "Are you implying the Luftwaffe might fail?" She blinked, waiting for a reply, and I had an overwhelming feeling I wasn't supposed to talk about air raids.

"No, that's not what I'm implying."

"Then what are you implying?"

"We talk about shelters in Berlin in closed circles," I said, thinking up a lie. "I didn't know Dresden was different. I'm just concerned about the beautiful Reich's children. I want to make sure they're safe before me."

"I understand now." She glanced once at the open door that led into the corridor. "I won't tell anyone what you said." She paused, unblinking yet smiling, and I understood she was doing me a favor by keeping our conversation a secret, and I was thankful because I certainly didn't want anyone to think I thought the Reich was weak, even if I was only enquiring about a shelter. "What's next on your list?"

"Oh… ahh…" I ran my finger down the list. "The lightroom. I don't know where that is."

She'd shoved an entire piece of toast into her mouth. "That way," she said, pointing into the air. "Outside, on the right, just after the vegetable patch and before the trees." She chuckled after swallowing and wiping jam off her lips. "You can't miss the vegetable patch."

"Oh?" I said, pleasantly surprised by this news of walking outside so soon, when I thought the lightroom was in the main building. I sat up straighter.

She sketched out a rough map of the estate grounds on the back of my list, marking the dormitories, the lightroom, the playground, and the vegetable patch, complete with paths that connected them all, but stopped short from drawing the hidden pathway I could see from my window. She started to draw what lay behind the trees at the far end of the estate but dropped the pencil. "Dear me," she said, looking up, trying to cover what she'd drawn with her hand before reclaiming the pencil from the floor and scribbling it out. She smiled. "There."

She got up to refill her coffee, and I folded up my list, about to leave, when Neider slunk into the kitchen without a sound and slid into Paula's seat.

"Hallo, Fräulein," he said, and my stomach dropped

even lower than it already had with the sound of his slippery voice. "How are you this morning?"

"I'm well," I said. "Thank you for—"

"And what battle was it?" he asked.

I looked at him, confused. "Battle?"

"Your husband," he said, piling toast rounds on his plate. "You said he fought on the Eastern Front. I was merely wondering what battle he was in."

"You're married?" Paula's head swung toward us, nearly spilling her coffee. "You didn't mention a husband. Frau Brack has strict rules about married women here at Edelhaus."

"I *was* married." I frowned. "He died. In battle." I paused, remembering the only battle I could think of. "Stalingrad. Still doesn't feel real," I said to cover up my hesitation earlier. "That he's gone."

Paula's mouth hung open, and it was clear she regretted asking me. "I'm so sorry," she said, and she turned back toward her coffee, stirring in some sugar and staring out the door.

"Stalingrad," Neider repeated. "Thank you, Fräulein Hager." He patted my hand on the table, his smooth, slender fingers lingering. Gooseflesh bumped up my arm. "Or, should I say Frau Hager?"

"Either is fine." I pushed away from the table with my plate before wheeling my cleaning cart toward the corridor.

"Fräulein Hager," Neider said, and I stood perfectly still in the doorway. "Good day."

"Good day." I gave my cart a push, walking a few feet

into the corridor before taking a moment to think, standing against the wall.

My God! I took a couple of breaths, trying to relax, but how could I when it was clear he was still investigating me? The front doors flew open with a bang and I stood straight, watching the woman with the fox stole, who I had seen on the day I arrived, storm through the corridor. "Frau Brack," she called, heels clicking down the tiled floor to Frau Brack's office door where she knocked endlessly on the wood. "It's Greta Strohm."

I needed to pass by with my cart, but felt odd doing so while she was knocking, so I waited, fiddling with my cleaning supplies. Frau Brack walked in from outside, scrabbling with her keys to open the door. "Frau Strohm, good morning," she said. "I wasn't expecting you for another five minutes."

Paula walked out of the kitchen with a tray of iced cakes. "I thought you left."

I fumbled with my list. "Just checking my list once more."

"You won't miss it," she said.

"Miss what?"

"What I said earlier," she whispered. "The vegetable patch."

I gave her a strange look. I'd never known someone to whisper about a vegetable patch. "What do you mean?"

Paula walked toward a side door that opened to the gardens. "You'll see…" she said, and she walked outside into the bright sunshine with her tray of iced cakes.

"This way, Frau Strohm," Frau Brack said, and the

woman walked gallantly into her office. With both of them gone, I wheeled my cart down the corridor as softly as I could, hearing bits and pieces of their conversation through the cracked door and over my cart's squealing wheels. Frau Strohm wanted a baby to adopt, but Edelhaus had rules and they needed to meet with her husband first. I saw the woman through the door crack, sitting in the chair with her legs crossed tightly. I tensed when my squealing wheels interrupted them.

Frau Strohm spied me through the door, then Frau Brack's dark eyes too.

"Fräulein Hager," Frau Brack said, head poking through the doorway. "If you please."

"Sorry," I said, but she'd already shut the door, and I rolled on at a snail's pace out the side door. I saw Paula at a distance, cutting through the courtyard toward the trees where I couldn't see. I followed the winding path to the lightroom, looking ahead. *Lightroom, lightroom...* Past the nurses' dormitory there was the gymnasium, all very ordinary, but the next building didn't look like a building at all; it was a cinderblock hut with no windows for any light. I looked at my list again and the map Paula had sketched out, then back to the building and its flat roof.

While I considered Paula's directions, I also noted how far away the children's dormitory was on the other side of the playground, and listened for the dogs. The pathway off to the side was more hidden than I thought, covered with an overgrowth of leafy bushes and weeping tree limbs. I rolled my cart forward, walking slowly, watching, learning, taking in every sight of the estate grounds, when I stumbled upon the vegetable patch Paula had mentioned at the far end of the playground. But this wasn't just a patch, this was a sprawling vegetable garden bulging with beans and tomatoes hanging fruitfully from green vines.

I let go of the cart.

I'd never seen so much food in one garden before, and every vegetable appeared to be ripened to perfection. I gasped. "And herbs," I said, and for the first time in so long, I caught myself smiling from stumbling upon something so familiar. I bent down to inspect, envious of how hearty the plants were. "Marjoram, parsley and… and…" I touched them all, smelling their aromas and getting lost in a memory of me and Ema in our own garden, her giggling laugh when she played with a wiggly worm, the sound of her hand when she dug into her seed bag. The way I'd brush the hair from her eyes in the sun.

"Lost?" a man said behind me, and I shot up.

"No," I blurted.

He smoothed back a swatch of dark-blond hair from his forehead. A young man, maybe early twenties. "Are you sure?" He pulled twine from his pocket and a stake from his garden trolley. "You *look* lost." He smiled, measuring out a yard of twine and tying a knot around a tomato plant, but it was the wrong kind of knot for a plant, and I resisted the urge to tell him. He pounded the stake into the ground, shaking the plant, and all those luscious tomatoes.

"I'm on the way to the lightroom," I said. "Do you know where it is?"

"Lightroom?" he questioned, brow furrowing. "Let me see." He let go of his knot and motioned for my list. I waited patiently as he read through all my duties, looking up at the buildings and ticking them with his finger. "I think it's in there." He handed me the list back, pointing to the building without any windows.

"But there're no windows," I said. "And it's the lightroom?"

He smiled before offering me his hand for a shake. "Name's Kurt." He pulled his hand back to wipe the dirt off on his trousers, then offered it again.

"Anna," I said, but despite his effort to clean his dirty palm, I felt the grit of his garden between our hands, and I missed my home. I watched him push the stake into the ground. "I had a herb garden back home."

"You did?" He seemed genuinely interested. "What kind of herbs?"

Frau Brack and that woman, Greta Strohm, had walked outside and were strolling the gardens, heading toward the far trees where I'd seen Paula disappear. They slowed down when they saw me with Kurt, and it was obvious they were trying to hear what we were saying. I reached for my cart, grasping blindly for it behind me.

"I'm sorry," I said, and I latched onto the handle. "I need to be going. The lightroom?" Frau Brack and Greta walked on as I pointed to the building Kurt had directed me to and rolled my cart away.

I stood in front of the windowless building, staring at a sign hung on the doorknob saying not to enter. I debated whether or not to try the door since it was on my duty list, looking over both shoulders, noticing an ivy-covered fence off to the right, and hearing the birds chirp in the trees. I felt somewhat secluded, unable to see the main building and nobody able to see me, but the fence was too high to escape, Ema would never make it over. A burst of noise came from the playground, and I abandoned the lightroom for a look at the children, peeping through the thorny rosebushes and pretending to take a sniff of one of the blooms.

I took a smiling breath. *Ema.* I played with the rose under my nose, eyes set on my daughter jumping and running, when the nurse blew her whistle. For a moment I thought she couldn't have blown it at me, but then she waved. I let go of the rose, standing straight, eyes lifting over the rosebush. I pointed to my chest where my heart was racing.

"Yes, yes, come here!" she said, but now she was motioning frantically. She'd crossed her legs as I approached and by the time I made it up to her, she was hopping, alternating her weight from one foot to another. "I have to go to the lavatory for a while." She squealed as if she was about to wet herself if she stayed any longer. "Would you mind watching the children?" She pulled her whistle over her head, flinging it toward me before I could park my cart, and waddled off.

"Of... of course," I managed to say, but she was already gone and I was holding her whistle in my hand. It had happened so quickly, I didn't have a moment to prepare, and then there I was, alone with all the stolen children. They were extremely observant, noticing the nurse walking away before subtly and silently migrating over to me, dropping all their bouncy balls and abandoning the swings.

"You're pretty," a little girl said, and she tugged on my

hand. Her eyes looked like the sky in the morning. A boy with chubby cheeks came up next. He took inching steps, though his eyes said he wanted to leap into my arms.

Ema stood on the outside of the circle, nervously rubbing her hands, looking up at the buildings and toward the direction the nurse had gone. I bent to my knees.

"My name is Anna," I said, in German. "Can you say 'Anna'?"

Some shook their heads, others stared, and the ones that did speak German said it softly.

"It's all right," I said. Only God knew what countries the Reich had taken these children from. The circle had tightened around me now, the children each vying to hold my hand. Ema scooted through the pack, getting closer as if she was thinking of reaching for my hand too, and I longed to touch her, and wished she'd just reach out. Another girl stroked my hair from behind, while another leaned heavily into my side, almost claiming me and warning the others to stay away.

I could see the hidden pathway very clearly from where I was, and it beckoned to me from behind the trees, the leaves fluttering on long, outstretched tree branches. A gust of wind came out of nowhere and kicked up all the leaves, exposing the stone wall. It was low enough to jump over. It was low enough to escape.

I sweated, knowing I only had a few minutes. I needed a plan. Dasa would have had the children wrapped around her finger in an instant, her attention always wandering like theirs, looking for the next exciting thing. What would she do? What would—

I picked up one of the bouncy balls. "Game?" I bounced it once. "Game…"

They didn't seem to understand the game I wanted to play. So, I took a big leaping step, hoping they'd understand a game of follow. "Follow," I heard in German at the same time I heard it uttered in Czech, deep between the children as if a whisper.

One of the girls shushed the boy who must have said it, and he looked regretful, cowering with his shoulders to his ears. I stepped toward him, and he looked even more afraid, and the children turned silent. "It's all right." I smiled. "Follow," I said slowly in German, and all the children copied me.

We skipped, and hopped, and stood in place. Children laughed and giggled, but my mind was only on one thing and my heart thrummed, thinking of bolting for the path. I kept glancing over, moving closer to the trees, looking for the nurse, thinking any moment she'd be walking around the corner.

Children tugged on my arms, each wanting a piece of me. I needed a commotion; I needed the children to run about so Ema and I could escape.

I blew my whistle, and all the children froze in place.

"Hide?" I questioned with a smile.

A little girl clapped. "Hide! Hide!" she said, and no matter what language the other children spoke, they seemed to understand I wanted to play a game of hide. One of the boys covered his eyes, counting in broken German, while the other children ran off to hide, whooping and howling.

I took Ema's hand, dashing off to the pathway, but she dragged her feet, and when we got to the trees, her legs locked up. "Ema—" I scooped her up and she wiggled and squirmed as I broke for the stone wall, through the trees and leafy bushes. "We must hurry…" My chest felt like it was going to explode, every nerve in my body electrifying. I only had a moment, a few seconds more. I tried lifting her over the wall, grunting, straining to push her over, but she fought me with scratching hands.

"Ema!" I said, dropping her, my face fraught, stretched in all different directions, with my pulse in my ears. "Why are you fighting me? We have to go!" I tried to pick her back up, but this time she pushed me forcefully with both hands to my chest.

"Ema—"

Chapter Seventeen

M y mouth hung open, at a loss for words. "Why, sweet girl?" I pleaded. "Why?"

Ema took me by the shoulders, which shocked me even more, and whispered, "The dogs, the guards… They'll kill us!" She ran back toward the playground, leaving me hidden in the trees as a dog barked viciously from somewhere nearby.

I collapsed on the path, stunned, with my back against the wall and the outside world just beyond it, not knowing where to go or what to do and blaming myself for not planning a better escape. They told the children about the dogs and the guards to make sure they wouldn't run away. Of course, they'd told them.

The nurse had come back, calling for the children to come out of their hiding spots while asking about the housekeeper in the same breath. "Hallo?" she called through the bushes.

I jumped to my feet, wiping my eyes and blowing the

whistle she gave me in short bursts as if nothing at all was the matter. "Hallo!" I said, emerging from the brush, scaring her.

The initial look of fright pinched on her face changed to one of anger when she glanced back to where I'd been. "What are you doing back *here*?" She put her hands on her hips.

"We were playing a hiding game. The children seemed to enjoy it. I hope you don't mind. Beautiful those ones, the children of the Reich. Very smart. Courteous. Good Germans." I walked past her to the playground where the children had gathered as if I'd been at Edelhaus for years and had a command all of my own.

The nurse followed me, and when I turned around to give her back the whistle, her face had softened. "Yes," she breathed. "They are beautiful. Aren't they?"

I smiled. "Mmm." I turned to the children, who'd tightened in a circle around me. "I hope to see you again soon." Their little faces looked up at me, some calling for help behind their silent eyes. Ema's was the worst, and I could tell she was fighting hard to keep from sobbing, twiddling her thumbs and scanning the buildings, the windows, and the gardens.

"You must have quite a duty list, and I kept you from it," the nurse said, her voice turning into a whisper. "Thanks for helping, but don't let Frau Brack see you standing idle." She commanded the children to follow her into the main building, and they lined up behind her, arms crisscrossed against their chests, marching on. Ema glanced at me when the others couldn't see—one last look from her sagging eyes.

I turned away when the tears came, my mind swirling with thought after thought after thought. A window closed up high in the nursery, and I felt exposed and suspicious, standing in the playground all by myself with windows all around.

I pushed my cart back inside the main building to collect myself, even though I still had duties to do in the lightroom. Another housekeeper passed by with her mop, and I pulled my list from my pocket, pretending to look it over in the corridor where it was cool and barren and lonely, with tears dripping silently from my eyes.

"Fräulein Hager." Neider appeared out of nowhere behind me, and I clutched my chest with a gasp, scrunching the list in my fist. He laughed, reaching out to touch my shoulder, but it was more of a grab. "I didn't mean to frighten you," he said, taking a step as if he was about to walk away, but instead pointed his finger at me. "Stalingrad?"

"What?" I asked.

"Stalingrad," he said, again. "The battle where your husband died?"

"Yes—" The word got caught in my throat. "Yes. That's right. I told you in the kitchen."

"Mmm." This information seemed to please him, only his brow furrowed after studying me. "Are you crying?"

"Oh…" I fanned myself excessively. "The chlorine. It's so strong. My eyes…"

"I see." He turned on his heel, walking away and

humming a childish tune, looking out the windows and up and down the walls, stopping to fix a Nazi Party banner that was already as straight as can be, before clipping off somewhere down the long corridor.

I felt my forehead, feeling the distant hour of reckoning drawing nearer, with the seconds I had left at Edelhaus disappearing like sand sliding effortlessly through my fingers. Frau Brack poked her head out of her office, spotting me.

"Fräulein Hager," she said, and I straightened. "In my office." She ducked back inside only to poke her head out once more. "Now!"

"Yes, Frau Brack," I said, and I wheeled my cart down to her office.

"Come in," she said from behind her desk, and I stepped inside, shutting the door behind me. "Have a seat." She paused, pinching her lips, and my stomach dropped, thinking she'd caught me talking to Ema from her window —worse, she'd caught me trying to escape. The reckoning was here.

"Yes?" I felt the reichsmarks between my breasts, sticking to my skin. I scratched my neck.

She smiled. "You're beautiful."

"What?" I tensed up.

"You don't understand." She stood from her swivel chair. "Have a look at the Führer," she said. "Will you?" She gazed upon Hitler's portrait behind her desk as if she were looking at her lover. "Some of us have a calling..." Her voice trailed with an emotional sigh.

"A calling for what?" I asked.

She looked down over her shoulder. "To serve the Reich most nobly." She held her chest with one hand.

"Frau Brack, I don't—"

She whirled around, slapping flat hands on her desk. "Do you love the Führer?" she shouted, and I jerked in place. Music instruction had begun in the classroom next door, and the military-like rhythmic sound of children singing "Long live the Führer" echoed down the corridor and thrummed through the walls. "Well, do you?" she demanded, leaning forward with her left eye twitching.

"Yes," I said, but I was sure she could see the fright in my face. "What is this about? I love the Führer. I do…" I said, but I'd say anything to make her believe it and give me another day.

Her face fell, eyes like hoods. "Come with me," she said. "Will you?" Frau Brack escorted me out of her office to the gardens, walking through the vegetable patch toward the trees at the opposite end of the estate. "Did you join the Bund Deutscher Mädel as an adult? It is voluntary, but I can't imagine a beautiful woman like yourself not being part of the BDM."

Herta watched us outside the gymnasium, her hands full of white towels, her arms drooping lower and lower the closer Frau Brack and I got to the trees. "I'm sure you were as fine a specimen back then as you are now," she said, but I was still watching Herta. "Anna?"

"Yes, Frau Brack," I said, and she led me up a path through the trees where we came upon a guesthouse, but why would a guesthouse be here on the estate grounds? I looked up at the flower boxes, brimming with fuchsia.

Laughter floated through the open windows—women, a lot of women.

Frau Brack rested her hand on my back where I was warm, leading me toward them. I'd never seen grass so green before, and the flowers, each one bursting open, not one withered petal or leaf. And the trees—they'd been pruned and manicured to go with the rest of the scene. A painting, though it was real life.

Paula walked out of the guesthouse's front doors holding an empty tray, the same tray I had seen her carrying earlier that had been laden with cakes. She stumbled over her own feet upon seeing us.

"This," Frau Brack said, throwing her arms out, "is a place for the women of the Reich to do what they do best." She stood in place with her arms suspended in the air, waiting for me to say something, as a beautiful German woman with long blonde braids passed by holding a vanilla ice cream cone, choosing one out of many cushioned lounge chairs to sit and eat in the shade.

Frau Brack turned slowly to look at me, and I swallowed hard.

"What—what do they do best?"

"Having children for the Führer," she said, arms dropping, but I couldn't look away from the woman and her ice cream. "Come now," she said, pushing me awkwardly toward the guesthouse with my feet dragging. "It's a German woman's responsibility to supply the purest of children."

"You—" I gulped. "Want me to have a baby?" I looked

at her, my breath shallow, when she nodded. "But, but...
with whom?"

"There are plenty of good German families ready and
willing to adopt!"

I gasped.

"Take your time, Anna," she said. "You don't have to
decide now. Herta has already expressed interest in the
program, but I saw you and Kurt talking earlier."

"Kurt the gardener?" I looked over my shoulder toward
the vegetable patch, now hidden on the other side of the
trees, thinking back on the brief—very brief—conversation
I'd had with him about herbs. I gulped again.

"Kurt's not just a gardener," she said through her teeth,
and it was clear she thought I was being judgmental.

"He isn't?"

"He is the son of an SS officer from Berlin. He's here on
assignment. Don't get me wrong, we are happy to have
him. He's just the right age, and so are you, Anna. Think
about it, will you?"

She pushed me to walk inside.

I folded my arms, not wanting to touch anything. It was
a beautiful guesthouse, something that belonged in the
Alps, with vaulted ceilings and hand-carved railings.

Frau Brack smiled. "Look at this foyer." Women in white
dressing gowns watched us from the floor above. "This is
just one of many relaxing spots you'd be able to enjoy while
you're pregnant. And after the delivery, you'll get two
weeks to nurse and rest, but most of the infants are
delivered to their adopted parents right away, no need for

the child to be in our nursery with our babies." She pointed to the expansive buffet table which had mid-morning treats displayed on lacy doilies. "Doesn't Paula do an excellent job preparing the pastries for the Führer's women? There is a separate kitchen and pantry here, but we are happy to help."

A woman wearing a satiny robe walked over from the window where she'd been resting, lifting a flaky pastry glistening with sugar from one of the trays. She held it up over her mouth, catching it with her searching tongue. The tiniest bulge protruded from her stomach.

I held my face in my hands.

Frau Brach patted my back, thinking I was crying with joy and was very pleased. "You are overcome with love for the Führer. This is understandable." She handed me a handkerchief she'd pulled from her pocket, and we walked back to the main building of Edelhaus, through the trees and the vegetable patch where Kurt was snipping herbs. He smoothed back the hair that had fallen over his eyes, giving me a smile, a slick of sweat on his chest where his shirt was unbuttoned.

"I will talk to Kurt," Frau Brack whispered to me as we passed. "If he agrees, then I will have a clean dress brought to you, something sophisticated. Something beautiful." She opened the door for me, waving me inside first, where Neider was waiting for us, a tan folder in his hand.

"Frau Brack." Neider smiled mischievously, tapping his foot before handing her the folder. I saw Herta's name written on the front. "She is all clear." His eyes shifted to me. "Just a few more facts to check out, and I'll be completely done with both new employees."

"That won't be necessary," Frau Brack said, smiling pleasantly. "From what you've told me everything has been verified thus far. And just look at her," she said, and he indeed looked at me, but he also took a deep breath through his nose as if he was trying to smell me. "She has agreed to the program, Herr Neider. No need to waste your resources. Her family tree will be verified by the program's administration once we get confirmation from her donor. Especially considering you have other pressing matters to attend to, like pending adoptions and parent profiles."

"The program?" he questioned. "Is that right?"

"Yes," Frau Brack said before turning to me, wrapping her arms around Herta's folder. "You have agreed, haven't you?"

I blinked, looking at the folder, and understanding that agreeing would mean an end to Neider's investigation. I managed a shaky nod, thinking that would be the end of it and Neider would walk away, but he reached up and tucked a lock of hair behind my ear, catching me off guard with his fingers sliding down the nape of my neck, making me shiver. "You are a beautiful woman," he said.

"Yes," Frau Brack said. "She is."

She led me into her office, leaving Neider standing in the corridor by himself, feeling his mustache with his thumb and finger and looking at my legs. "Now, something you must know," she said, closing the door behind us, but kept her hand on the knob. "This program is secret. I don't want to hear you mention it outside of my office. Even in the corridors or with Paula, since she saw you. It's not to be talked about in open spaces. Understand?"

"I understand."

"Good." She opened the door back up, and I was glad to see Neider had left. "Have a nice day, Anna," she said, closing the door behind me.

I stood in the cool corridor feeling lightheaded, and it wasn't from the chlorine. *What did I just agree to?* I wanted to drop to my knees and immediately pray for help. The music room door opened and Ema's nurse walked out with a string of children following her, all with their arms crisscrossed, footsteps muffling down the tiled corridor. Ema was the last child, and instead of looking through me, she smiled faintly. So faintly, nobody else would have seen it except for her mother.

My eyes and cheeks felt heavy with emotion, her smile reminding me not all was lost. I whipped around, watching her walk away, thanking God for that moment. I still had my daughter, and now, after agreeing to the program, I had more time.

Paula waved me into the kitchen where I sat down at the small table near the wall. She handed me a crust of wheaty bread and a slice of cold cheese on a porcelain plate. "Are you hungry?" she asked, but she'd already plated and served me. A decanter of red wine came next.

"This isn't necessary," I said, and she sat down opposite me, head cradled in her hands, smiling. "You're going to do it?"

"Do what?" I asked.

"I know you can't talk about it." She leaned in, whispering. "Frau Brack can't hear us if we whisper. You're joining the program?"

I took a bite of the bread, chewing slowly, and the excitement in her eyes grew to the point where I thought she might burst open.

I dipped my eyes for a yes, and she clapped once, startling me.

"That's great news! Think of all the food you'll get to eat. I know, because I prepare a lot of it. Oh, and the boys…" She inhaled, pressing her lips together and filling up her chest only to blow it out in one exhausted breath. "I feel like we can be friends now. Be real girlfriends."

She watched me as I chewed the bread, and then something happened I didn't anticipate. Her excitement faded, and she looked conflicted with memory. "Is something wrong?"

Paula's eyes snapped back to mine. "No. I mean, yes." She sighed. "Forget I said anything. It was the past."

"What is it?" I patted her hand. "You can tell me. We're friends now." As soon as I said the words, I thought how juvenile I sounded and insincere, but to my surprise, she patted my hand back.

"All right," she said, and she leaned in. "It's a sore subject with me, to tell you the truth." She took a deep breath. "But the last time I made friends with one of the staff, things didn't end well. I know the nurses still talk about it, talk about me, but it wasn't my fault. How was I supposed to know?" Paula cupped her mouth. "It was Margot," she whispered. "I know I told you not to mention her name, but you should probably know—" Her eyes darted to the exit.

"Know what?"

The cook stormed in, barking for Paula to help her get ready for lunch, and she scooted from her seat.

"Paula," I said, but she shook her head at me, finger to her lips.

I ate the rest of my bread and cheese—which was just bland enough for me to stomach—glancing occasionally at Paula and the cook as they worked. I'd moved beyond thinking about Margot and thought about the dogs and the guards, and how I'd find out more information, and report it back to Ema.

I had to reassure her if I expected her to leave with me. I knew that now. And until I was able to find out more, we were stuck.

I finished the rest of my duties in the main building before attempting to dust the lightroom again. I wheeled my cart outside. Kurt was nowhere in sight, which I was glad about. I made my way to the windowless building, tucking my list into my pocket and reaching for the knob, when Herta flew out of the door with a closed fist to her mouth. She looked surprised to see me, then ashamed, trying to hide her emotions by turning her face toward the ivy-covered fence.

I left my cart to see if I could help her. "Herta," I whispered, and she flicked her hand in my direction, but it wasn't clear if she wanted to talk or was shooing me away. "Are you all right?"

She turned around, and a peculiar look had taken over

her face. A forced look. "Yes. Why wouldn't I be?" she asked, but I saw tears in her eyes and knew she was lying.

I looked to the ivy to keep from staring at her watering eyes. "Look at this," I said, reaching for a vine. "It will strangle a tree." I ripped a vine away from the fence, exposing the city pavement on the other side, and she grabbed my arm.

"What are you doing?" She looked behind us, over both shoulders. "It's there to keep peeping eyes out," she hissed. "Don't remove it."

I took my arm back, curling my hands into themselves from having done something wrong. "I'm sorry."

"I didn't mean to snap at you," she said.

"It's all right. Makes sense. To keep peeping eyes out." I looked the fence up and down. It was a curtain—a natural curtain—though I hadn't noticed it before. A shield. "Ivy is a weed where I come from. I've always pulled it."

She leaned in to get a glimpse of the pavement. "The guards didn't see you. That is good. I won't tell anyone. You didn't know."

"Of course, I didn't know."

"I feel safe knowing we are protected, don't you?" she asked. "Edelhaus isn't beloved by all."

"It isn't?"

"I know you know about the guesthouse." She pointed with her head toward the trees. "Pre-marital sex, even for the good of the nation, is unthinkable to the older generation. Even in a crisis."

I looked at my shoes, and I wasn't sure why I was embarrassed.

"Congratulations," she said. "You're beautiful. I'm sure you'll produce a fine baby."

"You're not upset?" I asked, knowing I'd taken her place.

"There will be a time for me," she said. "Now, I must get going. And you'd better clean the lightroom before the other nurses come." She picked a duster from my cart, handing it to me as she walked away.

It was dark inside the lightroom from the lack of windows, and I waited for my eyes to adjust. The smell of dust was overwhelming, but it wasn't dust, it was something else, something heavy, something electrical. I felt the wall for a light switch, flipping it on.

Five small chairs had been set up under a portrait of Hitler and two strange stand-alone lights with thick cords that were plugged into the wall. An umbrella of metal protected each one, something I assumed would only amplify the intensity of the light, which would explain the warmth in the room. I dusted the lights.

A nurse and five little girls walked in. I smiled at the nurse, apologizing for being in her way while cleaning, and she handed me a pair of goggles.

"What are these for?"

"If you must stay and clean, you'll need protection."

She fitted her goggles to her eyes before turning to the children. "Sit and take off your clothes, but do leave your shoes on," she said to them, and after the girls took off their dresses, they began to remove their underwear.

"What's going on?" I blurted, and the nurse glared. She handed each of the little naked babies a towel to place over their eyes. "I'm sorry…" I said, trying to be respectful like a good German and not cause alarm, but I was shaking at what I was witnessing. "Why are the children taking their clothes off," I said, now whispering, "in front of each other?"

She squinted. "No need to be concerned, Fräulein. This is the lightroom," she said as if I should have understood, and when it was clear I had no idea, she rolled her eyes. "For the UV therapy treatments. To make their hair lighter."

She turned to the children, clapping once, and they sat with the towels tied over their eyes, scooting in close, touching arm to arm, centering themselves with the nurse's help under the big lamps hanging over them.

"Oh…" I said, but I covered my mouth, feeling nauseous and about to retch.

"All right, children," she said. "Lights on!"

I rushed outside just as she turned the lights on, hearing a jolting wave of electrical current pumping into the lights and feeling the burst of instant warmth that came with it.

I stumbled toward the ivy-covered wall, swallowing and swallowing to keep my breakfast down.

Chapter Eighteen

That night I lay in my bed with the curtains open, watching shadows shape and shift on the wall, but I couldn't get the children's little naked bodies out of my mind. Every new and horrible truth about the Germans surprised me, and I wasn't sure why. I should have known they'd go to whatever lengths possible to make sure the children stayed fair and Aryan-looking.

My fists clenched under the sheets. I'd never make it out of Edelhaus with my daughter if I didn't stay focused. I needed to concentrate. I needed to stop thinking about it!

A baby yelped from the nursery and I sat bolt upright. Another night of screaming, another night of the nurses following Johanna Haarer's guide for German mothers. *Damn the Germans. Damn these women!* I knew that cry. It was not one of selfishness, or one of being spoiled, but one of hunger. It would only get worse. I had a new understanding of what happened at Edelhaus, one I wouldn't be able to blot out with a pressed pillow over my ears.

I jumped out of bed to change back into a work dress. I needed to get away from the sound, for my own sake. I snuck out of my room, but I made the fatal error of looking through the nursery's glass window during that quiet second between the baby's wails. All was shadowy, except for the cots, with a little hand reaching into the air, shaking with screams.

I couldn't breathe, knowing my hands were tied—I'd be fired if I was caught in the nursery. I dashed away, down the stairs into the garden, and stood under the stars with my eyes closed.

A nighttime breeze blew my hair behind my shoulders, bringing with it the faint scent of freshly seeded topsoil coming from the vegetable patch. I opened my eyes, breathing easier. Only a gardener could smell tilled soil in the air. I padded over, thinking I'd find comfort among the vegetables, but I found it with the herbs.

Even with only the moonlight, I could see the plants were well maintained, more so than I originally thought. Bountiful lavender had been pruned back, as had the roses, each bud blossoming at the same time—a sign of dedication and love.

I rubbed the lavender in between my hands, back and forth, back and forth, pausing to smell it on my palms, the tang and sweetness of what summers used to be before the war, and was carried away. So far away, I didn't hear Kurt walking through the garden to collect his tools.

I dropped the lavender. I thought about hiding behind

the herbs, but that would look suspicious if he found me crouched in the dark. I stepped into a beam of moonlight. "Hallo," I said.

He took a surprised step backward.

"I… I couldn't sleep," I said. "I didn't want to scare you."

"You did scare me. I'm usually the only one out here."

We stood in the dark staring at each other, and I wondered if he knew what Frau Brack wanted us to do together.

"Your lavender," I said, smelling my palms again. "I've never been able to get mine so fragrant. What's your secret?"

He collected a few tools from the ground and set them in a box.

"I'm sorry," I said. "I'm intruding, aren't I?"

"No," he said. "You aren't, and if I couldn't sleep this is where I'd be too. You're interested in what I'm growing?"

I nodded, and he asked me to follow him to the edge of the vegetable patch where he pulled a torch from his pocket. "Look at this. Can you guess what it is?" He pointed his light to a green plant he'd been growing in a special blue pot.

I touched the leaves, examining their triangular shape. I looked up. "Is it a vegetable?" I asked, and he shrugged. I smelled black pepper and felt a slight burn just from touching it.

"It's a new kind of pepper. I invented it."

I laughed. "How do you invent a pepper?"

He shrugged again, but smiled in the torch's light—he

knew, but wasn't going to tell me. "It's a special kind of plant. I'll grind up the leaves later and use it in a cream for muscle aches."

"You're interested in herbs for medicine?" I asked.

"I am." He inspected his plant, gazing at it, getting lost in his thoughts, before checking the soil level and touching the leaves. "And don't ask me why, but the vegetables I plant at night seem to thrive. That's why I'm out here so late."

I held in a laugh—if only he knew what I thought about the moonlight and planting at night. He seemed nice, even if he was a German, which I didn't expect.

He looked up from where he'd crouched. "Frau Brack isn't interested in the process, she's only interested in the end result—how big the tomatoes are, how red."

"It's the process I love the most—"

A dog's bark from inside the estate turned into a mad frenzy of growls and snarls. I backed up. "Are they inside the fence, or outside?" I almost grabbed a hold of his sleeve.

He swatted the air. "That's Biscuit," he said, and I blinked. "And it's just one dog, an old dog who'd rather sleep. The foreman's personal pet. He's trained him to bark as if he's in a fight. We used to have dogs all over the estate, but the war has taken its toll on Edelhaus."

My legs felt weak and I looked for something to hold onto that wasn't Kurt's arm or a plant. *Neider lied about the dogs, a necessary lie to keep the children from escaping.* I sighed heavily, and Kurt looked at me strangely. "I'm afraid of dogs," I said.

"No need to worry." Kurt pointed to another plant.

"Look at this here…" he said, and I was surprised how it had happened so easily, so effortlessly—he'd spilled one of Edelhaus's secrets.

Kurt cast the torch over his array of plants that seemed to go on and on and on. "I had a small garden when I was a boy, but my mother said good Germans buy their produce from the grocer, so I was never allowed to build and grow the garden I wanted. I think my mother didn't want the neighbors to think we *needed* to grow our own food." He waved the air upward, sniffing. "Do you smell the floral scent in the air?"

"I do," I said, looking around, trying to place it, but it wasn't lavender or jasmine, the two scents I knew best. Then he illuminated a flowering purple plant with his torch.

"Steep the petals in hot water like tea, and it will put you right to sleep…" He encouraged me to inspect it, and I went in for a look, but what caught my eye was the plant next to it, green and spindly like a weed. His torch flickered, and I reached behind to pull the planter out as he hit his torch to stay on.

"What's this—" I stopped myself from saying the name aloud, staring at the plant in the dimly lit garden, its white flowerets. *Hemlock.* Nobody would grow this on purpose— it was poison. Unless I was wrong. No, it had to be hemlock. Kurt had fixed his light and pointed it brightly on the ground near my feet. I shoved the pot back into its hiding spot, standing sharply.

"What's what?" He glanced in the direction of the hemlock.

"Oh, nothing. This is quite the garden you have."

Kurt stared at me for a moment before turning off his torch. "You'd better get back before a nurse sees you." He reached for his garden trolley.

"Am I not allowed out here?" I asked.

He looked over his shoulder, pausing. "I don't know, are you? Just be careful, Anna," he said. "Do what you're supposed to do. People who don't end up getting rumors started about them, like the last person who held your position."

"Margot?" I asked, but he'd turned to gather up his things, twine and some tools that lay on the paving stones in a smattering of dark dirt. He was about to walk away, and I had only a few seconds left to repeat the question without looking suspicious. "What happened to her? I've heard nurses whisper her name in the corridors, and Paula told me not to say her name out loud."

"And yet you've asked about her twice just now." He turned his garden trolley around and wheeled it past me. "It was nice talking to you. It's been a while since I talked to someone," he said. "Goodnight."

He left me standing in the garden, feeling like the nurses were watching me from all corners in the shadows. I regretted bringing up Margot's name now. Whatever the mystery, it didn't involve me, and I vowed to not speak of her again.

I made haste to the main building in case I was being watched, each step I took sounding louder than it should, even though I was practically tiptoeing. I walked up the stairs. First thing in the morning I'd tell Frau Brack I'd been in the garden at night, so she could hear it from me first. My heart sped up, thinking someone had already seen me and planned to tell Frau Brack before I could.

I walked down the corridor to my room, but it was quiet. Eerily quiet. I froze. Something felt off. Something felt wrong. My stomach sank when I heard singing. Not just any kind of singing. A mother's voice. Soothing and comforting, followed by Polish words of love for her baby.

I peeked through the nursery glass.

In the shadows near the window, with the grayest glimmer of moonlight resting on her face, sat Herta in a rocking chair, breastfeeding a baby.

She stopped rocking, and I dropped to the floor, hands clamped over my mouth. I made a break for my room when I thought it was safe, crawling on the floor and slipping inside.

Herta, the good German I thought she'd been this whole time, was like me—another mother come to steal her child back!

It couldn't have been easy for her to sneak into the nursery—and the risk—my God, the risk! Now I worried she was going to get caught by a nosey nurse, or an unsuspecting staff member in the corridor.

I heard the nursery door crack open, and I hopped into my bed with a pull of the blankets to hide as if she'd come into my room, but I only heard her footsteps lightly padding down the corridor.

My head pounded, throbbed; the image of her rocking her baby was like a silhouette eclipsed in my mind: the baby kneading his hand against her breast, one of her hands patting his bottom, and that voice—like a puffy cloud, lulling him to sleep.

I found myself feeling nervously for the buttonholes on my work dress, feeling for the tiny pockets Margot had made in the stitching, and clutching them fiercely.

The following morning, I avoided Herta at all costs, striding past the nursery and down the corridor to the lift before the cook had a chance to slip my duty list under the door. I had one goal before breakfast: to find Frau Brack and talk to her. I smoothed my hair into a bun, tucking loose strands behind my ears as the lift cranked down to the ground floor. The door opened at the same time I yanked the gate back, charging for Frau Brack's office, but I bumped into her instead as she waited for the lift, knocking her back a step.

"I'm sorry!" My hands flew to my cheeks, but she was the one who looked astonished and hurt.

"Fräulein Hager," she gasped. "What are you doing?" She held a set of files close to her chest.

"I'm… I'm sorry."

"Yes, as you said." Her mouth pinched. "I was on my way to see you."

"Oh?" I said, and she squinted.

"Come into my office."

We walked the short distance to her office. Paula watched from the kitchen, eyes shifting as if she knew something I didn't. Frau Brack closed the door behind me, pointing to an empty seat at her desk. I held my chin up, smiling slightly, remembering I was Anna Hager from Berlin. Blonde, good German Anna Hager.

"I heard you left your room last night." Her lips pursed. "Where'd you go?"

"I did leave my room," I said, and I think she was surprised I'd admitted it. "I couldn't sleep so I thought a walk in the gardens would help, only I stumbled upon Kurt in the vegetable patch." I smiled, and her face fell. "We had a nice chat then I went back up to my room."

"You talked to him?" she asked. "And it was pleasant?"

"It was."

She set her files off to the side. "This is good."

I put on my best concerned face. "Was I not supposed to leave my room? The way you questioned me... I certainly don't want to break a rule."

She swatted her hand in the air. "It's all right." She smiled. "To answer your question, no, there isn't a policy. But we've had some dealings in the past here at Edelhaus that have been disconcerting, all with new employees, and some of the nurses can't help but talk and start rumors. Oh, I don't want to bore you..." Frau Brack looked at her hands, pausing. "I like that you are talking to him. He will be a hard one to turn, though. He's never been agreeable in the past—" her voice turned into a rasp "—and he comes from a pristine Aryan bloodline."

"He's been asked before?"

"Yes, he has."

I was relieved to hear he'd turned the other women down, and took a breath. She moved to the window and played with her swastika pendant, looking over the gardens. "You've heard about the invasion?" She glanced briefly over her shoulder. "Americans have invaded, and although the news in the paper has been favorable, no doubt there will be a tremendous loss of life. In short order, there will be even more German families wanting to adopt. You're so beautiful. A true German beauty. If anyone could make Kurt reconsider, it has to be you."

A knock on her door ended our conversation. "Frau Brack! Frau Brack!" *Knock, knock, knock.* "It's Greta."

She opened the door swiftly. "Frau Strohm. How lovely."

The woman rushed into the room, looking flustered until she saw me. "Oh. I didn't know you had company." A thread of hair had come loose from her bun and she smoothed it back.

She shook my hand after Frau Brack introduced us.

"Frau Strohm is one of our charitable givers here at Edelhaus," Frau Brack said, "and she came in today to fill out adoption paperwork."

"That's wonderful," I said, but inside my gut twisted, thinking of yet another child stolen by the Reich, another child who would grow up not knowing their real mother.

"Yes. It is wonderful," Greta said. "I've been trying to get a child for weeks."

She looked at Frau Brack, and there was a moment of awkwardness and I wasn't sure if I should smile or not.

Frau Brack ushered me out. "Yes, well, that's all, Anna," she said, and I gladly made my way to the door. "One more thing, if you want to make Kurt's acquaintance again, you are more than welcome."

I craned my neck. "What?" I asked.

"Talk to him any time," she said, "even during your shift." She glanced briefly at Greta, who'd sat down with her legs crossed tightly at the knee. "Off you go." She clapped for me to leave before shutting the door.

I stood with my back against the wall, glad I had cleared the issue about leaving my room.

Paula waved me over from the kitchen where I smelled cinnamon and apple and fresh coffee.

"For you." She pushed the most delectable-looking pastry at me on the table.

"Paula, this isn't—"

"You're refusing?" Her entire face scrunched up like a dry sponge.

I couldn't tell her my stomach wasn't used to such glorious food. "I was trying to be polite." I smiled, moving the plate firmly in front of me, and she waited for me to take a bite. I forked the corner of the doughy pastry, dark and gooey with cinnamon.

"You're joining the program. It's my duty to make sure you eat well. I baked them myself this morning."

"How early did you wake up?" I asked, taking a bite.

"Early." She yawned, watching me eat with droopy eyes, only to pop up bright and alert, focused on my neck. "You're not wearing a swastika," she said, and my hand immediately went to my neck. "Did Frau Brack notice?" Her brow furrowed. "Did Greta Strohm notice?"

I shook my head, still feeling my neck.

"She's the main contributor here, be glad she didn't see your bare neck!" The cook had walked into the kitchen, barking at Paula to help her with a tray. "You'd better go and put it on. You don't want the nurses to find out. There's an adoption today and they'll say you ruined it."

"Ruin the adoption?" I asked.

"Go," she whispered, and I hurried upstairs, worried about my missing necklace and making a good impression, and also hoping nobody else would notice, when two nurses passed me on the stairs.

"Good morning," one said, and I played with my dress collar to cover my neck.

"Good morning," I said back.

I heard whispering between them after they walked on, probably questioning why I was running. I slowed down the last few steps, opening my door and thinking about where to look for my necklace—where it might be—but yelped from seeing that nurse with a snow-white braid standing in my room with her hands deep in my chest of drawers, her eyes cold and blue and studying.

She pulled her hands out.

It was acceptable for a nurse to be in the cleaning closet looking for cleaning fluids, but they were on the shelves, not in my drawers. "Is there something I can help you find?"

She clasped her hands behind her back, smiling, looking bashful, but in a devious way. A clearing of her throat followed, and she pointed to the cleaning fluids on my shelves. "I was looking for something to get a stain out of the rug." She sashayed over to the shelves, looking over the bottles, picking some up and setting others down, mumbling to herself about what would and wouldn't work, but left without choosing one.

I found the swastika necklace hiding in my sheets and clasped it around my neck. Once in the lift, and the door had closed, I slumped against the wall and rested my pounding head against the crank of the gears, whispering to myself in Czech about the Nazi bitches. It was the only place in all of Edelhaus nobody could burst in on me. I was especially glad that I'd hidden the reichsmarks in my undergarments, as she most certainly would have found them in my handbag if she was willing to search my drawers.

The lift opened, and I stood bolt straight, pulling the gate back, and entering the ground floor once again as Anna Hager, the good German.

In the kitchen, a bowl of porridge sprinkled with brown sugar had been added to my breakfast. "No list of duties for you until after lunch," the cook said in passing.

I sat down, looking up at her. "Why?"

"Don't look so alarmed," she said, laughing, and her belly jiggled. "Frau Brack said you should have a stroll in the gardens this morning. Take a book with you from the library." She smiled, and I didn't know it was possible for the cook to smile. "Perhaps venture over to the vegetable patch?"

"Oh," I said, and she handed me a duty sheet for the afternoon with only a few items on it. "I see."

Paula's eyes twinkled behind her, then together they left with a rack of breakfast foods for the children. I stuffed the list in my dress pocket and ate the porridge, thinking about what I needed to accomplish that day with Ema. Only Neider entered the kitchen shortly after and stood near my table, disturbing me.

"Fräulein Hager," he said, fingers tapping.

"Good morning," I said, but instead of walking away, he watched me, his eyes moving from my neck to my lips where I'd licked off some porridge. I reached for my napkin.

"Have you bathed?" he asked, but not in an accusatory way. He was imagining me in the bath—I could tell by the smirk on his face. "All the staff must bathe regularly." He took a deep breath, eyes rolling to the ceiling before settling back on me. "Smells like you used the goat milk soap."

I didn't want to answer, but as he stared at me with his snakeskin smile, I realized it was the only way to get him to leave. "Yes," I said, and he turned on his heel, clipping away, leaving me itchy and warm under my collar from the encounter. I hated him. I hated his mustache and I hated the Germans.

I did as I was told and sat outside with a book from the library. There was no sight of Kurt in the vegetable patch or the children, and I thought they must still be eating their breakfast.

I opened to the first page of my book, bending the cover back and giving it a crack like Matka would have. Of all the books I could have grabbed, it was *Mein Kampf*.

I pretended to read, scanning over the pages, but in fact I was examining the coming and goings of the nurses and the housekeepers and checking for guards. Biscuit the dog barked from somewhere, a harrowing, deep bark that could have only come from a big dog, making me wonder if that was an illusion too, and that he was small. I couldn't wait to tell Ema—tell her we didn't have to worry about the dogs.

The cafeteria door swung open, and the children ran out to the playground. A burst of noise followed, yelps and giggles, as they reached for a bouncy ball or a rope to jump. I looked for Ema among all the blonde heads, book in my lap, scanning anxiously as they bolted out the door, but she was nowhere in sight.

I sat up, still looking, trying to ignore the twist of worry stirring in my gut, but when her nurse walked out as if she was the last one, I bolted to my feet.

A boy I recognized from yesterday watched me a few steps away, a film of milk on his mouth, his eyes wide, and a ball under one arm. "Have you seen..." I could barely talk, and he probably didn't even know German. "Have you seen Ema? The little girl—"

The nurse walked up to me, untangling her whistle from her swastika necklace. "Hallo, again," she said, but my heart moved to my throat, pounding, throbbing with the debilitating thought that Ema was gone, adopted. I looked at the closed cafeteria door, then to the nurse's sunshine-bright face.

"Have you..." I gulped. "Is this all of the..." My eyes skirted once more over the children playing in the playground, over their milky mouths and golden hair.

She blew her whistle, and my eyes welled with tears.

Chapter Nineteen

The children froze when the nurse's whistle echoed through the garden, then the cafeteria door swung wide open with a loud squeal and everyone looked. *Ema!* She was only late to the playground. A hand from inside the cafeteria patted my daughter on the backside and she trotted out the door to the playground, none the wiser. I felt like I might collapse and clutched at my swastika necklace instead of my chest.

The nurse blew her whistle once more, even though the children were already standing stoically. "Remember, share your toys," she told them, and some of the children nodded as if they understood. Others followed with a delayed nod. Then she blew her whistle again, but this time it was more of a toot, and they went back to playing.

She turned to me. "I'm sorry, you were asking me something?"

"Oh, ahh…" I said, still a bit shaken from thinking Ema

had been adopted. "What time is it?" I tapped my wristwatch as if it was slow.

"A few minutes after nine," she said.

The little boy was still staring at me, the bouncy ball under his arm. "Go play." I shooed him away, and the nurse and I sat down on the bench together.

She sighed loudly. "Thank you for watching the children yesterday. There seems to be fewer and fewer of the nurses, and it isn't easy breaking away, even for a lavatory break."

I smiled. "I understand. And you can ask me any time. I'm sure Frau Brack wouldn't mind if you needed me again." I looked to the main building, eyeing Frau Brack who stood in her window, watching me. I waved, and she hesitantly waved back. "See. She is very accommodating. She gave me the morning off because I'm such a good worker." I lied about being a good worker but held my head up, and she seemed to swallow every one of my words as fact—Matka would have called her a muttonhead Nazi bitch.

She held out her hand for a shake. "Clara."

"Anna."

Not long after, a boy skinned his knee and she blew her whistle as he cried on the ground. She shouted that he needed to stand up, but after he stood up, he ran over to me with his arms out, which drew a concerned look from Clara.

She demanded he let go with a commanding clap, but he clung to my skirt. She turned to me, and all the pleasantries she'd greeted me with just moments before had vanished. "You're ruining his training by coddling him!"

My mouth hung open. I couldn't tell her he was holding

onto me because of how I treated him yesterday, and I felt responsible and didn't want him to get in trouble. She put her hands on her hips.

"We follow the Haarer guide for German mothers. Don't you know what that means?"

I stood up from the bench, appearing rather insulted. "Yes, of course," I said, and his arms constricted even more. I managed to pry him from me, holding my composure and looking unapologetically German—stern and cold—when I only wanted to scoop him up and kiss his tears away.

I looked into his eyes. "You're a brave boy," I said, and I could tell he had no idea what I was saying. "Strong German boys get skinned knees, but they dismiss the pain as weakness leaving the bones. Do you understand?"

I nodded, and he modeled me, nodding his head dramatically up and down, just like Ema did at his age, which I guessed was four.

Clara looked pleased with my handling of the situation, but the children had now gathered around us, each looking as if they wanted a sliver of the love I'd shown the boy with his embrace.

"It's quite all right," I said. "I love children. Good German children of the Reich." I turned to the children, staring up at me with their wide eyes, and clapped myself. "Listen to your nurse," I said, sternly. "Play respectfully, and show the Führer how much you love him by being good Germans today."

Clara's attention wandered across the playground to the garden area where a little girl refused to share her toy. She waved her hands in the air to get the girl's attention before blowing her whistle and stomping over to where she was. I braced for what was to come next, hands to my mouth, when Clara's arms flew up and boxed the girl's ears. The other children stared, bouncy balls gripped in their hands, watching without emotion as Clara dragged the child to the corner of the main building for a slap across the face and a lash across the knees and bottom.

Ema stood next to me, her breath in a pant. I turned her by the shoulders but then backed away, hands off, in case Frau Brack was still watching from her window. I handed her a bouncy ball, and we held it between us. "The dogs aren't real. It's a story they made up to scare you." I glanced at Clara, who was still busy scolding the little girl. "It's one dog, an old dog." She blinked, and I thought about asking her if she'd been in the lightroom, but my eyes started to fill with tears just imagining her answer, and I resisted.

"Are you sure?" she whispered.

"I am. He's been trained to bark and scare you. That's all."

Her chest caved with breathy, dry sobs that she tried hiding. "But there's—"

"I'll find out about the guards." I wanted to kiss and hug her, touch my forehead to hers and feel her breath on my face, but I didn't dare. Clara's sharp voice cut through the air. She was still yelling at the girl, but I felt the seconds I had with Ema slipping away. I tugged on the ball between us, making sure Ema focused on me and not the little girl's screams as Clara spanked her. "Ema, we're going to *play a game*." Her face straightened when I said our secret phrase; she was paying much more attention to me now than when

I had said it on my first day. "Tell nobody who I am. You must act like we're strangers. Never let them know. Not even the other children," I said.

With her firm nod, I knew she understood.

"I love you," I whispered before letting go of the ball. "Off!" I commanded in my strictest German voice, and she ran off to play. I threw a pointed finger in the air as a final gesture, watching her trot off, the tips of her blonde braids stiff against her shoulders, and her skirt ruffling against the backs of her knees.

I closed my eyes. *I did it. She knows I haven't given up. She knows I'm still her mother.* Clara marched back, fixing her whistle hanging from her neck. I looked to the vegetable patch, checking for Kurt. *I need to find out about the guards.*

"If it isn't one thing it's another," Clara said, acting completely exhausted from the beating she gave the little girl, who was now sobbing her heart out while being forced to jump rope with some other children. "They'll learn soon enough. And if they don't..." She smiled slyly, slapping her palms together for a burning rub.

"Oh, yes," I said, but inside I wanted her to feel what a hand across the face and bottom felt like, and if she'd been in Tabor, I would have dug a shallow hole for her in my garden with Matka. "They'll learn." I smiled.

She felt her chest. "Handing down punishments makes my heart race. I need to calm down." A laugh puffed from her lips. "Anna, would you mind asking Paula for some milk and honey? She makes the best honigmilch. So soothing and comforting. That's what I need."

I sat for a second before realizing she wanted me to get it

for her. I pointed to the main building. "You want me to bring you a cup?"

"Yes… yes, please, and a biscuit."

I got up slowly. "Certainly." I didn't know I was a servant too, but if it meant I could get on her good side, get her to trust me even more, then I'd get her all the cups in Dresden. I smiled. "I'll be right back."

I walked into the kitchen, surprising Paula as she stirred something on the cooktop. "Clara wants a cup of milk and honey," I said, and she stopped stirring to hang her head over her saucepan. "What's wrong?"

"These nurses…" She shook her head. "I should never have shared my honigmilch with them in the first place. They're going to drink up all the milk and eat all the honey if I don't watch it." Her eyes fluttered. "I'm making a cup for one upstairs now."

I looked into her saucepan and saw the foaming milk. "Do you think there's enough for two? What about the small cups?"

"Yes, that should work. Hopefully they won't notice and complain." She removed the hot saucepan from the cooktop to pour milk into two demitasse cups she took down from the shelf. She had exactly enough. "Here's the secret," she said, reaching for a lemon to zest over the cups. "I use lemon instead of cinnamon. Maybe that's the problem. I make it too good." She smiled, wiping her hands on her apron. "Off I go."

"I can take Clara's," I said, and she looked relieved.

"Thank you, Anna. I have so much to do already without accommodating the whims of the nurses."

"Me too." I walked back out to the playground with the cup, careful not to spill a drop. Clara grinned when she saw I'd brought her the milk she asked for. "Here you are," I said.

She sat up, taking a noisy slurp. "So very good, but where's the biscuit?"

"Oh," I said, and I made up a lie that Paula was all out of biscuits, which she believed.

"Another time then," she said.

"Yes, another time."

I *had* become her servant.

She blew her whistle and the children lined up. "Have a good day," she said, and she left with her cup.

I watched the children follow her into the main building. Ema never looked at me, just like I'd asked her to do—pretending we were strangers. With the children gone, I set out for the vegetable patch to look for Kurt, give Frau Brack an eyeful, and hopefully find out more about the guards.

The herbs were especially fragrant and had already been clipped and bundled for the day. Tomatoes had been put in baskets, and long, yellow roses snipped of their thorns lay ready to be taken inside for display. A casual look back into the main building's windows yielded no clues as to who was watching. I bent down to inspect the herbs, finding the hemlock from last night and getting a better look at it.

It was indeed hemlock, just like I'd thought. I pulled the pot closer over the paving stones and felt its small white flowers, which left a slight sting, then stuck my finger into its dark soil where it was damp from a recent watering. A scuff of feet against the stones startled me, and I shoved the pot back into place, standing up.

"Kurt," I said. "Good morning." He looked surprised to see me, and I realized how odd it must have been to see me pop out from behind the plants two times in a row.

He examined my face. "Good morning."

"I hope you don't mind a visit," I said, followed by a smile.

He looked at the main building, holding his gaze for a moment. "No," he said, tossing a garden spade into his toolbox. "Frau Brack sent you here, didn't she?"

I tried to act casual, as if I'd wandered into the garden by accident, but for some reason, I had difficulty putting on an act. I bit my lip. "No…"

I could tell right away he'd seen through my silly little dance. He tended to his garden, tugging on some vines and digging up a plant, while I pretended I wasn't being ignored. I thought of a hundred ways I could ask about the guards, but nothing sounded plausible, natural, especially since he knew I was lying about Frau Brack.

I sat down on his garden bench, hands to my face, breaking character, and giving him the only thing I felt would save me.

Honesty.

"I'm sorry, Kurt. She did ask me to come over here and talk to you. I don't know why I lied just now." I paused, feeling him staring at me, and peeked through my finger gaps. "But I loved talking to you about your vegetable patch last night so much, I just had to agree. And I got the morning off. You understand, don't you?"

He searched my face before nodding.

"You do?" I twisted around on the bench, pointing to the shed behind the bushes. "Will you show me your potting shed? At risk of being overwhelmed with jealousy, I'd love to see it."

He smiled slightly, and I knew I'd made the right decision. He opened the double doors, and I was immediately met with the smell of cut grass and peaty soil. I took a deep breath, thinking of my own potting shed, ramshackle that it was.

Tilling tools hung on wall hooks, with the smaller handheld ones stored in toolboxes, and I really was overwhelmed with jealousy. Jars filled with oil sat on a shelf away from the light, white flowers soaking inside them. "Is this elderflower medicine?" I asked, taking a jar and swirling it around until the flowers floated to the top. "What do you use it for?"

"Everything," he said. "The nurses won't prescribe it. They prefer the doctor's medicines." He arranged the jars, labels out.

"Elderflower," I said to myself, and I pointed to another jar. "And that one?"

Kurt smiled a bit more now, gladly telling me about his jars, all the herbs he'd grown, and what ointments he'd made. Time passed lazily, and I felt comfortable talking about gardening and herbs, as it was something I knew well. I picked up another jar, smelling the lavender through the holes in the lid, and thinking it was time to bring up the guards.

"You're different than the other women Frau Brack sends over," he said, and I looked up.

"What?" I set the jar down, realizing I'd become *too* relaxed.

"You're different." He looked me over as if he suddenly didn't trust me and had grown suspicious. I reached out to touch his arm, tell him I wasn't like the others because I didn't want to join the program, but he'd taken a step to the side. I pulled my fingers back.

"Maybe you should leave," he said.

"Kurt—" His back was to me, and I could tell he was waiting for me to leave as he fiddled with some heavy-looking tools on his workbench. I was mad at myself for not asking about the guards earlier when we talked about herbs. I'd ruined my chance. I reached for the door because I wasn't sure what else to do—I'd never been thrown out of a room before. I frantically tried thinking up something to say, to give me more time to talk.

"You're nice, Anna," he said, and I felt some relief that he'd reignited the conversation. I turned around, but his back was still to me. "Be careful over there. Frau Brack has a way of getting people to do almost anything for her."

I played with my hands behind my back, watching him haul a sack of soil to a table and cut it open with a knife. "For what it's worth, Kurt, I enjoyed my morning off." My hands felt sweaty, which surprised me, and I tiptoed through all the possible things I could say about the guards. Nothing seemed right, but now was my chance.

He looked at me over his shoulder.

"Are we allowed to leave?" I blurted. "The estate, that is.

I suppose I could ask Frau Brack, but she's so busy, and Herr Neider made it seem like I wasn't permitted to go into the square—not without asking, at least. Is that true?"

"You can leave." His brow furrowed. "But you'll be followed."

"Followed?" I reached up, fiddling with my swastika pendant. "Who would follow me? I'm a good employee," I said, waiting for him to tell me who the guards were and where they were, but he only shrugged.

"Most of us are good employees." He scooped some soil from the sack he'd opened and tossed it into a pot. "Do what you're supposed to do, and you'll be—"

Bells clanged and clanged, and I covered my ears with a shriek from the sheer shock of the noise. Kurt looked worried too, alarmed. My heart sped up.

"You'd better go!" Kurt said, and he tapped my shoulder to leave.

I ran back to the main building, throwing open the side door, expecting to see the staff rushing in and out, and lots of commotion, but instead they seemed calm. The bells had stopped clanging, and most of the staff had lined up against the wall in the corridor, shoulder to shoulder, as if there was an inspection.

I stood in the doorway, trying to figure out what was going on, but I had no idea. Paula waved to me from afar, and I was glad to walk over to her. "What's going on?" I asked, and she smiled ear to ear, showing me her gums.

"An adoption! We do a proper send-off when a child leaves for their new home." She pulled her swastika necklace out from under her collar, centering the pendant on her chest, and motioned for me to follow. "You found it. Good! You'd simply ruin things if you didn't have your necklace on."

The nurse with the snow-white braid stood across from me on the other side of the corridor, eyeing me, while Herta stood stiff beside her and paler than normal.

Paula jabbed me with her elbow. "Here they come," she said in a whisper, and Frau Brack strode down the corridor, smiling, hands up as if holding the Nazi flag painted on the ceiling.

"Attention!" she said, and the nurses clapped reservedly.

"What's happening?" I asked Paula, and she pointed with her head toward the lift. The doors opened, and a nurse carrying a baby bundled in her arms walked down the corridor as everyone clapped, and out the front doors to a car that was waiting for them.

Herta covered her mouth, looking incredibly ill and about to get sick right there in the corridor. The nurses filed away upstairs after the baby left, but Herta stayed still, looking miserable. When she finally did walk away, she did so with her hands wrapped around her stomach, and I realized it was her baby that had been adopted, and I felt sick myself.

"Are you all right?" Paula asked.

I muscled up a nod, and she walked back into the kitchen while I remained standing in the corridor, fumbling with the duty list I'd pulled from my pocket. Seeing Herta had shaken me, and if I didn't find a way to straighten myself out of it, I worried someone would notice. I read through the shortened list.

The lightroom. Again?

I retrieved my duster, passing by Frau Brack's office on my way outside, and was surprised to hear Greta was still here. Voices were raised, and it wasn't hard to listen. Greta was upset that she hadn't been approved for an adoption after the hefty amount of money she'd donated. Just before I opened the side door to walk out, I heard Frau Brack tell her any day she'd have a baby. *Any day.* I closed my eyes, praying she wouldn't think about adopting one of the older children—my worst fear was that Ema would be adopted out from under me.

I walked through the gardens to the lightroom, then ducked inside to give the equipment a quick dust before the nurses brought in any children, only to run out of the doors when I was finished, gasping for breath as if I'd been underwater. I held onto the railing outside, closing my eyes. I didn't know how much more I could take of the lightroom.

By evening I found myself back in my sleeping closet as I had the last two nights, only this time was different. The nursery was quiet. *Poor Herta,* I thought. *She must be lying in the dormitory worried sick about her baby and wondering where he's gone.*

I lay in bed for what seemed like an eternity, staring at the ceiling, thinking of the guards and where to look for them. The dogs were no longer a problem. But the guards... God help me.

The guards will kill us.

Chapter Twenty

I threw on the last of my work dresses to discover it was two sizes too large. The cook would have words with me about it, so I dug into my laundry bag for a dirty dress, finding one that wasn't quite as dirty as the others, but one that fit. I buttoned my way to the top, my heart already racing from the day ahead of me. *Find out about the guards — the guards, guards, guards.*

I heard a crackle near the last button that caused me to pause. I pressed the fabric between my fingers. I didn't feel a needle like last time and the thread hadn't been pulled out —in fact the stitching was done with expert precision. I heard the crackle again, and I thought there might be a piece of paper tucked inside. I found a tiny screwdriver in the cleaning supplies to pick it out.

Knock! Knock!

The screwdriver slipped from my hand, landing on the floor. "You're late!" the cook barked from the other side of the door. "And it's laundry day."

"Coming!" I had to forget about the dress. I reached for the list that had been shoved under my door, hoping the lightroom wasn't on it. *Not again, please not again.* I moved my finger down the list. *The lightroom.* I sighed, closing my eyes.

I slung the laundry bag over my shoulder, then started off for the lift with a cleaning basket hooked on my arm. There was a flurry of activity in the nursery, more than usual, with nurses rushing around and closing all the curtains. Distracted by this, I almost ran into the cook at the end of the corridor.

"Get downstairs with that." She put her hands on her hips. "Frau Strohm is here early this morning to collect."

"Why Frau Strohm?" I asked, but the cook walked away, not answering.

Paula came out of the kitchen as I reached the front door, grunting and dragging her own laundry bag and pointing to the street where a truck was parked.

We handed our bags to the driver. "The cook said something about Frau Strohm."

Paula pointed to the lettering on the side of the truck. "Strohm's Laundry Service," she said. "She gives Frau Brack the best deal."

Best deal.

It appeared Greta Strohm would do anything for a baby —she'd definitely start looking at the older children if she didn't get a baby soon. I followed Paula into the kitchen, as was expected of me, even though I knew my stomach couldn't handle one of her rich breakfasts.

Frau Brack's frantic voice echoed from the nursery down

the stairs into the corridor. Paula pushed a lemon pastry and a tall glass of frothy milk at me, both of us following the noise with our eyes.

"What's going on in the nursery?" I asked.

Paula leaned in, whispering. "One of the nurses is gone."

"Gone?" I sipped the milk. "What do you mean, gone?"

"I don't know…" she said, but she did know. I could tell in the way her gaze trailed to the floor.

I placed my hand on hers. "We're friends, remember?" I held my breath.

"You're right, we're friends," she said, and I set the milk down. "The last thing Frau Brack wants is for the particulars of Edelhaus to get into the wrong hands. So, when a nurse leaves, it causes all sorts of tension. Some leave out the front door. Some go missing, vanish into thin air. Then some leave like Margot—" She pressed her fingers to her lips.

"What about Margot?" I asked, even though I'd vowed not to bring her up again, but I wondered if she'd tried to leave and the guards had caught her—and I'd do anything to find out more about the guards. My heart sped up. "Paula—"

"Forget I mentioned her name," she rasped.

"No," I said. "Tell me. Please."

She looked at both the open doors before continuing. "If I tell you, do you promise not to bring her up again?" she asked, and I nodded. She leaned over the table, her voice but a whisper. "There was a rumor Margot was a spy."

"What?" I sat up in my seat.

"The staff are extremely sensitive about the subject. To speak her name can be dangerous, especially if the wrong person hears."

"What kind of spy?" I asked.

"Shh!" Paula said, waving her hands. "That's the end of it. You promised." Neider's shoes clipped down the corridor. He was coming, and Paula looked visibly shaken. "I... I need to go."

"Wait," I said, and she did. "Who's the nurse that left?"

"Herta," she whispered.

I covered my mouth. Herta must have left to find her baby, which meant she didn't leave out the front doors, she'd snuck out! "But what about the guards?"

"We haven't had guards for months," Paula said, before bolting from her seat and disappearing into her pantry bedroom.

I threw my hands on the table, bracing the edge with a grip of steel. *My God.* The guards were a story, just like the dogs. Neider clipped his way toward the kitchen, pausing in the doorway. My hands went into my lap, sitting still with my heart thrumming in my ribcage. *No guards!* Ema. I needed to find Ema—tell her the news!

He clipped off, and I jumped from my chair to go outside, walking fast, faster than I should. *Breathe.* I slowed down, but my heart was exploding.

I took the day's duty list from my pocket, pretending I had somewhere to be other than waiting for the children to come out of the cafeteria, but my knees bobbed up and down with nerves while sitting on the bench. I looked extremely suspicious, especially since I'd been in the exact same spot yesterday. I needed to carry on like a housekeeper and come back to talk to Ema once she was already outside. After I had a few moments to clear my head, I could plan the escape, a better escape than my first one, now that I knew there were no dogs *and* no guards. I tucked my list away, deciding I should clean the lightroom, since it allowed for me to be away from the main building and close to the cafeteria.

I pulled open the door with my cleaning basket hooked on my arm, and in that brief second where I was still trying to make sense of what was going on, with thoughts of Ema and the guards dizzying in my head, I walked in on five children lying naked on the floor, lit up by overhead lights with blindfolds over their eyes.

Ema!

The door slipped from my hand, crashing closed, and in a single breath I withered and shrank in the doorway. A nurse immediately scolded me for coming into the lightroom during treatments, trying to slip a pair of goggles over my head while commanding the children to stay still.

They fidgeted in place from the interruption, making small noises, but it was Ema who squirmed. She reached up to suck her thumb and was swiftly yelled at, sending a shudder over her body.

I rushed out the door, clutching my chest and breathing heavily as a horse, where I collapsed on the ground with my head feeling light and pounding. My whole body shook with a chill, but it was warm in the sunlight.

I pulled my collar from my neck where I felt choked and retched violently in the bushes. "You're a devil," I cried in Czech. "*Ďábel! Ďábel!*"

I wiped my lips with the back of my hand after finding the strength to stand, only to freeze. Kurt had been watching me from his potting shed and was close enough to hear. Neither of us moved, waiting for the other to speak.

"Good morning," he finally said, scooping up some dirt with his shovel, "Fräulein."

My mouth opened, but no words came out, and I could barely breathe with my chest painfully squeezing.

"Good…" I managed to say before he dug his shovel into the dirt again, and I saw my chance to leave, scampering away to the main building.

I watched him from the window, nervously biting my nails and waiting to see what he was going to do. Would he go to Neider first or straight to Frau Brack's office? But there was no movement from the vegetable patch or the gardens.

I held my head. I should have lied to him. *Milk makes me retch, and I'm not sure why I drank some at breakfast.* That was it—that was the script I should have followed—though I knew it didn't explain the Czech words that had spewed from my mouth.

I was still nauseous from what I had seen in the lightroom, even though I watched the nurses escort the children back into their dormitory, and could see it was over. I fell against the window, closing my eyes. It was quite possible he hadn't heard. Wasn't it?

I needed to go about my day, lie in wait for Ema, and

make my move when the time was right. If I waited to see what Kurt was going to do, I was already caught and we were dead. This was my daughter's last day of Edelhaus, I told myself.

I unfolded my duty list. The library was next.

I dusted the bookshelves, listening to the din of the day and thinking about when I should leave, and *how* I would leave tonight. If I could just figure out a way to sneak Ema away from her nurse.

The hemlock.

I closed my eyes briefly. *Why didn't I think of this before?*

I turned around, bursting at the seams with this plan, but only the books were there to celebrate with me. I'd already made friends with Ema's nurse, and she'd made it clear she expected me to bring her more honigmilch in the future, only I'd soak a sprig of hemlock in it, and she'd be too sick to notice Ema was gone, possibly even dead, especially if I snatched her away at midnight.

Kurt walked out of his potting shed into the vegetable patch to water his plants, and I took notice, standing straighter. I hated myself for reacting the way I did out in the open, but God, I hadn't been prepared to see Ema's little naked body under the lights. I needed to get some of Kurt's hemlock. If he asked me about being sick, I'd tell him the milk story.

I walked up to him as he knelt beside one of his plants, pulling twine from his pocket. I cleared my throat, but he paid no attention to me, cutting some twine and tying a knot.

"Kurt?"

He looked over his shoulder, glancing briefly.

"Good morning," I said.

He tied up his plant, securing its stem in the pot. "Here." He handed me a ripe tomato he'd pulled from a nearby plant. "For you."

"For me?"

He laughed at my confused face. "Do you think it's poisoned?"

"Poisoned?" I squeezed the tomato, feeling its plumpness and its warm, thick skin from the sun. Had I been in Tabor, that tomato would have already been in my mouth with juices running down my arm. "Certainly not." I set it down.

He stood up, dusting his pants free of dirt and looking at me strangely, which made me look at him strangely. He glanced at Frau Brack's window. "Why are you here?"

I waited for him to mention what he saw and heard near the lightroom, but the longer we stood staring at each other, the more I thought maybe he didn't hear me. "I needed some air," I said, then followed up with an excuse to explain the retching. "Breakfast wasn't sitting well."

"Are you better now?"

"Yes." I felt the leaves on one of his vegetable plants but looked for the hemlock.

"Come, I have something to show you. Remember that pepper plant I showed you? Look at it now…" He led me to the pepper plant he'd been growing, and it looked like it had grown a foot overnight; there was even a pepper starting to grow. "Look at the green color…" he said, but I eyed the hemlock growing an arm's reach away and found it difficult to look at anything else. He pulled the pepper pot across the paving stones into the sunlight. "Can you believe the shine?" He looked up over his shoulder, his hands on the pot.

I gazed at the hemlock.

"Anna?"

"Yes?" I shook the look from my face. "Sorry. I was admiring your garden. You're good at what you do." I motioned to his bountiful vegetables and plants. "Some people think it's easy work, but growing a proper garden takes patience."

He stood up, swiping his hands together. "You're good at what you do too," he said.

"Cleaning is easy."

"No, it isn't. Not this place." His face fell upon seeing Frau Brack walking toward us. "Frau Brack. Right on time," he said, and he snatched up some of his gardening tools to leave.

"There you are!" Frau Brack said, walking up. She looked delighted to find us together. "Sorry to interrupt, but I have a task for you."

Kurt walked away with his tools, leaving me to answer.

"Yes, Frau Brack, what is it?"

"I need both of you," she shouted to Kurt, and he turned around after pausing with his back to us. "I need these items picked up from the pharmacy. I'd have the nurses do it, but they're pressed today as it is." She handed me a list of medications. "Can you two handle it?"

"Of course," I said.

"Very good, very good." She stood with her hands clasped before leaving, giving us both a big smile.

Kurt tossed his tools into a bucket, a puff of garden dust rising into the air. We had little choice but to obey, and I didn't have an excuse to get out of it, at least not one that wouldn't raise an eyebrow. Kurt stared at his tools, pulling off his gloves finger by finger, and I thought he was still irritated by her visit, but when he looked back up, he had a different expression.

I felt around for the hemlock with my foot.

"I'm going to change," he said. "Meet you back here?"

"I'll change too," I said, and when he turned to walk away, and couldn't see, I snapped off a piece of hemlock.

I hid the hemlock in my basket with a pinch of grass, setting it high on one of my cleaning shelves before changing out of my work clothes for Dasa's dress. I took the pins from my hair, letting it hang loosely near my neck as a last touch before heading back outside.

I followed Kurt behind the potting shed to an iron gate he opened with keys he pulled from his pocket. A car was parked outside, which surprised me since I thought we'd walk, but I was even more surprised to find out it was his car. "Something wrong?" he asked, and I looked up after watching him twiddle with the keys.

"I didn't know you had a car."

I waited for him to open my door, but he got in and

started up the engine, unlocking my door from the inside as exhaust fumes pooled from the tailpipe. "Sorry," he said as I got in. "I should have opened the door for you."

He revved the engine a few times while adjusting his rear-view mirror, then sped off. I held onto the top of my head. "Whoa!" I squealed, and we both laughed following a shift of gears.

We drove through the streets with the windows down, and it had been so long since I'd felt a nice breeze on my face. I had found my daughter. I had infiltrated Edelhaus. I would escape with her in a matter of hours, and I felt excited and relieved at the same time. I closed my eyes, feeling the soft seat against my thighs, swaying with the motion of the car as the wind fingered my hair in a rare moment of relaxation. All I had to do was wait for the night to fall, and we'd be gone, just like Herta.

"It's not you," Kurt said, and my eyes popped open.

"What's not me?" I asked.

"Why I was upset earlier. It's not because of you." He looked out the windshield, eyes set on the road as he talked.

"It's Frau Brack?" I questioned, though I knew.

"She's asked me eight times to join the program." He glanced in my direction. "Eight."

"Why don't you want to join?"

"Isn't it enough that I don't?"

He parked along the curb near a tattered Nazi Party banner hanging from a streetlamp, a stark contrast to the banners in Tabor where each one looked new. We waited for a squealing tram to roll by.

"I don't want to join the program either," I said.

He twisted in his seat, and it was then I saw how green his eyes looked in the daylight, rather than blue. Crystal, beautiful, and I never thought I'd see anything beautiful in a German. "Why? The others will do anything to get into the program, prove their worth, their heritage. Anything," he said, and I could tell he was genuinely interested as to why I didn't want to join.

I blinked a few times. He almost made me want to tell him the truth. I opened the door, one foot out. "Isn't it enough that I don't?"

The streets looked drab and gray, something I hadn't noticed when I first arrived in Dresden. People walked the pavements solemnly, starved not with hunger but in other ways, and I couldn't help but think they had written this story themselves.

"Have you heard about the Americans?" he asked. "They've been fighting us hard. Took back most of France. Pushed us out of Paris, Lyon, even Luxembourg, is what I heard."

"I heard about it," I said, but I was surprised to hear Kurt talk about how devastating the invasion had actually been. It did explain some of what I saw in Dresden.

We made it to the pharmacy and collected the medicine. I closed the sack up after looking inside.

"Let's have a sit at a café," he said.

"Won't Frau Brack wonder where we went?"

"She wants us to spend time together. Remember? Why disappoint her?" He smiled.

We walked to a café and took seats inside where it was cozy and busy with mostly men. At first it was strange to be inside a café, and even stranger to experience it with a man who wasn't my husband, especially after we ordered tea like we were on a date. I felt the soft fabric of Dasa's dress atop my skin and adjusted the skirt over my legs.

The waiter placed a white napkin and spoon on the table for Kurt, and they struck up a conversation as if they knew each other, at least informally. The waiter's eyes fell to me before he walked off with his tray, giving me a noticeable look.

I reached for my embroidered collar, making sure it was straight and wondering if he could tell I was Czech. "Do you come to this café often?"

"Sometimes." Kurt watched the waiter over his cup as he drank his tea, tracking him as he went about his business behind the counter.

"Is something wrong?" I twisted in my seat to have a look.

"No," he said, setting his cup down. "Enjoy your tea."

The windows rattled from German fighters flying overhead. One after the other, five I thought I'd counted. People turned, trying to get a look at the Luftwaffe out the window where autumn leaves tumbled over the pavements, but the buildings blocked the view. Kurt never turned to look.

"Do you think we'll get bombed?" I whispered, feeling comfortable enough with him now to ask, and I was surprised he said we might.

He took a sip of his tea. "Go ahead and ask me what you really want to know."

"What do I want to know?"

"Ask me why I'm not serving in the Wehrmacht." He paused, cup to his lips, as if he expected me to be suspicious, but I wasn't until he mentioned it.

A German woman would ask why, but a Czech woman would never question a man so blatantly. I held my chin up, doing my best imitation of Frau Brack as if she was the one asking. "*Why* aren't you in the Wehrmacht?"

"I'm just not." He smiled, and I laughed over my tea, breaking my connection with Frau Brack.

"Then why did you want me to ask?"

"I thought it was on your mind, so you might as well speak of it."

"I'm more interested in the peppers you invented. How'd you do it?" I asked. "Peppers pollinate themselves." I sipped my tea and Kurt told me how he had cross-pollinated two peppers by accident. He talked with his hands, waving them about with passion. I was enthralled, and somewhere between him telling me about the bees and when the peppers would ripen, I wished we'd met under different circumstances.

"What about you?" he asked, and I set my cup down.

"What about me?"

"I heard you were married before." He folded his arms, sitting back in his chair.

"Who told you?" I asked, and he gave me a look as if I should have known. *Paula*. "He died. In battle."

"That's what I heard," he said, but his tone made me feel he knew I was lying, which startled me. I looked away. "He was…"

"You were in love?" he asked.

"We were," I said, but now I was talking about my Josef and not the German one Anna Hager had been married to, telling him about our early days in Berlin when I really meant Prague. "He said we'd be together forever. I didn't want him to join." I stopped short of the truth, then came up with a comparable lie to explain how I felt cheated, abandoned. "But he insisted, and if he'd listened to me, taken my advice, I'd still have a husband. He wanted the battle. He felt he could make a difference." I felt sad talking about Josef as if he was dead. I played with my hands in my lap, feeling my bare wedding finger. "I'm…" I shook my head. "I'm sorry for rambling on about him."

"Don't blame him for wanting to fight for his country," Kurt said. "Each of us must follow our passion. Sometimes war brings that out in us, and sometimes it leads you in a different way than your family expects. You can be sure he was doing what he thought was right at the time. Right for you. He wanted you to be proud."

I felt a lump in my throat with his words and worried I might cry with a heavy pool of tears filling my eyes. "Don't cry," he said, and when he touched my hand on the table, all the tears in the world spilled over my cheeks.

"I'm sorry," I said, blotting the tears gently away. "I've spent years being resentful, only now, the way you've just explained it…" The waiter poured us more tea. "Thank you. You don't know—"

"I'm taking my break now." The waiter talked right over me to Kurt, who nodded and tracked him walking away.

"Should we be leaving?" I looked over my shoulder to the waiter as he left, then back to Kurt, but he was still tracking the waiter, all the way to a hallway in the back where no patrons were allowed. "Was I too loud?" I asked, worried I'd made a spectacle. I wiped the last of my tears with his napkin, mortified that I'd not only broken character, but also looked like I didn't belong among the well-trained, reserved Germans with tears streaming down my face.

"Wait here." Kurt patted my hand. "I'll be right back."

I watched him get up. "Where are you going? Kurt—" I started to say, but he walked away and down the hallway, following the waiter.

I sat alone at our table, feeling out of place and watching the door, expecting something to happen, but the café carried on normally with the din of clinking cups, porcelain to porcelain, and laughter and waiters carrying carafes of steaming tea. I thought my nerves had gotten to me, that talking about Josef had made me feel more vulnerable than I was, but minutes had passed and Kurt still wasn't back.

The café doors opened and a whoosh of autumn air blew in a few fallen leaves. People looked for a seat, but they were becoming scarce and eyes moved to me, sitting at a table for two when I was single. Another waiter, someone new on shift, reached for Kurt's empty chair, and I spoke out. "That seat is taken," I said, and he looked at me with the chair in his hands, ready to lift it away.

"No. It isn't."

"It is being used," I said, reaching for it this time, and he winced.

"He's not coming back."

"What?" The waiter took the chair away, and I whipped around, staring down the long and dark hallway where Kurt had disappeared.

Chapter Twenty-One

I jolted to a stand, drawing a sharp look from the couple sitting at a nearby table. Continuing to stand would only draw suspicion, so I gathered my sack of medicine and went in search of Kurt. I paused before passing the sign that said *No patrons allowed*, then decided I must go even if I was questioned.

"Kurt—" I rounded the corner into the darkened hallway.

"What are you doing here?" He emerged from the shadows, looking just as surprised to find me as I did when he left.

"Me?" I'd reached for my chest. "The waiter said you left."

"I told you to wait." He tried to push me back into the café, but I resisted, looking him over where a glimmer of café light had revealed his sweaty face and slobbering lips.

"What happened to you?" Instead of answering, he hurried to fix his disheveled hair. "Kurt—"

The waiter he'd left with walked up behind him, passing by us with a touch of his arms. They exchanged smiles—warm, lingering smiles.

I gulped, and Kurt took me by the shoulders, my mind scrambling at what I'd uncovered, what I'd seen and wasn't supposed to. "Umm…" The sack scrunched in my hands. "Ahh…"

"Anna?" he said, trying to catch my gaze, searching, searching—but he wasn't asking me a question.

"Yes?" I finally said.

"I need you to stop fidgeting," he said, and I exhaled loudly.

"All right," I said.

"And now I need you to walk away," he said, and I nodded feverishly, but couldn't move. "Now, Anna. Outside."

He nudged me, and I followed him out to the car, not a word between us, even after we drove away, but I wasn't sure what to say.

"Everything all right?" he asked as he drove, though I knew what he was really asking. He wanted to know if I'd keep his secret.

"Yes," I said.

"It is?" he asked, and when he took his eyes off the road to look at me, I felt I understood him more than anyone ever had. He was hated by the Reich just as much as a Czech, maybe even more, and in many ways that put us on the same side.

We pulled up to Edelhaus a minute later, Kurt getting

out first. He reached for my hand in passing once we were inside the gate. "Thank you…" he said.

I smiled, saying goodbye with my eyes, and he disappeared into his potting shed.

I entered the building, firmly holding the sack of medicine in my fist and walking down the long corridor with the Nazi flag painted on the ceiling. I felt the roll of reichsmarks between my breasts. *By this time tomorrow, we'll be long gone from here.*

I knocked on Frau Brack's office door to deliver the sack of medicine even though it was open. "Frau Brack—"

She turned around with a baby bundled in her arms, while Greta Strohm looked on. "Oh, I'm sorry," I said, and I stepped backward, but Frau Brack called me in.

"Do come in, Anna," she said. "Look who was brought to us today." Greta had a smile on her face too, taut red lips, and misty eyes. "See…" Frau Brack pulled back the yellow baby blanket.

"Oh, yes," I said, taking a peek. "A beautiful—"

"Baby boy," she said, and my stomach dropped the moment I saw his eyes—my sister's eyes.

Adam. Dasa's baby. I reached out for him as quickly as I pulled away, covering my mouth.

"Isn't he lovely?" Frau Brack asked, and I managed a shaky nod, but inside it felt like a bomb had exploded. I searched for the wall behind me to hold onto but found the door. "And he's been kissed with a heart-shaped birthmark behind his ear." She looked at Frau Strohm. "This isn't a problem, is it?"

"No, not a problem," Frau Strohm said. "The Reich would have caught any imperfections."

They both turned to me as I stood flush against the door, squeezing the knob behind my back.

"Aww, you must be overwhelmed, gazing into the eyes of such a beautiful babe," Frau Brack said. "A true Aryan tot." She pointed to the chair. "Have a seat."

"That's it," I said, "I'm overwhelmed. I didn't expect him to be so beautiful." Greta watched me suspiciously as I sat, taking deep breaths through my mouth.

"Anna's joining our program," Frau Brack whispered to Greta as I scrunched the stomach of my dress.

"Is that so?" Their whispers passed over the top of my nephew as if I wasn't there, talking about the brightness of his skin and his blond locks. His little hand reached into the air, cooing and babbling.

I looked up when Greta asked where the baby came from. "Near Munich," Frau Brack said. "Poor mother. Her husband died in the war, and she couldn't keep him. She wanted him to have the best life possible. He's good Aryan stock."

Greta Strohm believed her story, and I realized the German parents were being lied to. They had no idea they were being given Aryan-looking babies from occupied lands.

Warm tea rose up my throat, and I stood. "I should get going. I didn't mean to interrupt." I made my way to the door, but I still had the sack, hot and crackling in my clenched fist. I turned back to leave it on Frau Brack's desk, keeping my head down for fear she'd see the horror twitching on my face.

"Anna," Greta said, and I stopped cold in the doorway with my back to her. "Did all your laundry make it into the bag today?" she asked, and I was annoyed she'd ask me such a frivolous question when all I wanted to do was run to my room. "We take our laundry very seriously at Strohm's Laundry and I feel like there was a garment missing. I didn't want to think it was our fault."

I opened my mouth to answer but shook my head instead.

"Very well," she said, and I hurriedly walked upstairs to my room where I slid to the floor in a puddle of silent tears.

I cried for my sister, then Adam, and then for… My throat balled up and I couldn't swallow without a punch of pain. How were we going to escape now? I dug my palms into my throbbing eyes. It was one thing escaping with one child, but two? I'd never make it out of Germany with a baby. *I can take him to Berlin*, I thought, *beg Hans Schmitt for help*. No, Herr Schmitt would be the first place Neider would look.

A round of applause rattled the wall when Adam made his entrance into the nursery, but it was the knock at my door that made me jump. "Yes?" I wiped my eyes, straightening from the floor as swiftly as I could, knowing they could walk right in.

"Anna?" Frau Brack said. "When you're finished getting dressed, would you meet me in the nursery?"

I hesitated. "Yes."

I threw off Dasa's dress for Margot's worn one, working

my way down the buttons, sniffling. My eyes were puffy and pink and my cheeks were warm and splotchy from crying. I dumped chlorine into a small bucket as a way to cover it up. *Glug, glug, glug...*

"Anna?"

"Coming!" I carried the bucket into the corridor and was surprised to see Greta Strohm talking with Frau Brack just outside the nursery window.

"There she is," Frau Brack said, and she waved me forward. "Come here, dear." Her nose pruned when she smelled the cleaner.

"It's strong," I said, waving the air under my nose.

She looked concerned. "And your eyes are watering."

"I'll be all right," I said. "The Reich's children deserve a clean place to live."

She seemed pleased but asked me to set the chlorine aside on the floor, which I did. The nurses crowded around poor baby Adam; even the white-haired nurse I'd caught in my room was all aglow, gazing into his eyes.

"Did you find the garment, Anna?" Greta asked, and I looked at her, confused.

"What garment?" My attention was scattered, especially with the nurses touching Adam on the other side of the glass.

"From the laundry," she said, "I asked you about it downstairs. I believe a work dress was missing from your laundry bag."

"A dress?" My hand went to my chest, feeling the buttons under my palm, where I felt the crinkling piece of paper hidden in the stitched seam. "This dress?" My mind and stomach spun. "You want this one?"

"Well, I don't know, is that the one that was missing?" she asked. I hadn't seen Greta Strohm angry, but my best guess was that she was getting close.

I dropped my hand, shaking my head to start over. "Sorry, Frau Strohm—"

"Call me Greta."

"You're right, Greta. There was a dress missing. This is it. I'd dirtied my other dresses and my only clean one was too large. I pulled this from the laundry bag because even though it had been worn, it wasn't crusted with salts from scrubbing the floor." I smiled. "It will be in the next load."

She nodded hesitantly, eyes set on mine, and the tension was undeniable between us as I realized something wasn't right.

Frau Brack took me by the shoulders, scooting me toward the window. "Look at this baby, Anna," she said, and all three of us stared at poor Adam, naked as the day he was born, getting poked and prodded by the Reich's nurses, who were checking every limb and hair on his body. I felt Greta's gaze shift to me, and my neck heated up around my collar.

"I really must get to my duties," I said, pulling away from Frau Brack's hands. "I'm behind as it is."

"Very well, Anna," Frau Brack said, but Greta folded her arms.

Instead of walking down the corridor, I walked back into my room, closing the door, then frantically blocking it with a pull of the dresser drawers. I shimmied out of my dress, feeling the buttonhole and the piece of paper inside, hearing it crackle. I reached for the tool I'd tried to use earlier. Chills shot up my spine and across my shoulders, picking, picking, before I managed to yank the last stitch away from the fabric, finding another needle.

And a note.

I paused, hearing the nurses with Adam, and thinking about Greta Strohm standing in the corridor with Frau Brack. I unfolded it carefully.

Two boys, Prague. Last name Svoboda. 16 June.

I clamped my hand over my mouth, eyes fluttering. The rumor was true! Margot was a spy. I breathed heavily, half disbelieving and half reeling in shock. All the tiny pockets made sense now. Margot was slipping Greta Strohm notes. I read the message again.

These are children, I thought. *My God. Records of the stolen.*

I'd found her needles. But the thread? *Where did Margot hide it?* She would have been smart enough to hide it someplace where the nurses wouldn't find it, maybe she'd even unraveled it from the spool.

I scanned the shelves, the chest of drawers, and landed on my bed. I threw back the sheets, and searched the heavily threaded mattress seam, inching my fingers along the edge, and caught a thin piece of thread in the lining, pulling it back, and noticing it wrapped all the way around the mattress. An entire spool's worth.

I bit off enough thread to sew the note back into place. Satisfied, I looked myself over in the mirror, pressing the button to my chest and hearing the note crackle in its pocket. I slid the needle into the seam near the button where nobody would find it.

I didn't know what I was going to do with this information just yet. I had to think. I had to digest it. My heart thumped.

I gathered up my cleaning supplies and walked back into the corridor, only instead of finding Greta Strohm talking to Frau Brack, it was Ema's nurse, Clara. They whispered into each other's ears as I wheeled my cart toward them, then Frau Brack dismissed her and she left down the stairs.

"Anna," she said, and I stopped with my cart. "There is something I need to ask you. We are down a nurse and Clara has recommended you as a replacement. She said you have a natural way with them."

"She recommended me?" I asked, surprised.

Frau Brack nodded. "I know what you are thinking."

"You do?"

"This is only temporary, as I'm hoping you will move to the guesthouse just as soon as Kurt agrees to be your donor. Come with me and meet some of the nurses."

I let go of the cleaning cart and followed her into the nursery.

I saw Adam being fussed over, nurses reaching for talc and another preparing the metal scale as he cried, waiting to be weighed. The other infants were snug in blankets, wrapped up like packages. Quiet. Dutiful. The nurse I'd caught snooping in my room called Frau Brack over to the corner, and by the look on her face I knew she was not pleased I had been permitted to walk among the babies.

I wandered over to Adam's cot where his arms were outstretched and legs too from being left uncovered. I reached for his trembling hand as he wailed, and he opened his eyes from my familiar touch, searching, searching…

And I closed mine.

Dasa had been in labor for a day. She walked back and forth and back and forth, making tracks in the rugs, holding her lower back with one hand while fanning her face with the other. The sunlight from the window cast through her birthing gown, silhouetting her round belly and bulging breasts. "It wasn't like this with my others," Dasa said, moaning and baring her teeth. "It's a boy. I know it. This birth is going to kill me!" She held her shaking hands out in front of her. "Look."

"Don't say that!" Matka clapped once from the kitchen, where she'd opened all the cabinets to induce labor. "It's bad luck. I've opened the cabinets. Things should start progressing now." She walked toward Dasa, rolling her sleeves up and pulling her hair back for a long night.

"Everything is bad luck," Dasa cried. "Having a baby in secret is bad luck. Doesn't matter how many cabinets you open, Matka. This labor was destined to be hard."

I touched Dasa's shoulder, and her eyes rolled toward mine, already exhausted. "Everything will be all right. This is like your other births. No different."

"But what if it's not?" she asked. "What if—"

"I'll raise all of your children as my own," I said, and her head flopped forward, crying as I rubbed her back. "All right? You have my word."

She took several short puffs of air, nodding, and closing her eyes. "Thank you, sister." She moaned from another contraction, only this one sounded gut-wrenching and trailed in a ragged whimper. "It's time," she said, nodding. "Now's the time." Her face pruned up in a cry as she reached out for my hand, lips pinched, holding the pain in. "Anna…"

"I've got you." I helped her into her bedroom where we'd prepared it for birth. Fresh towels had been laid out. Scissors, cloth, and clamps for later. Matka had lugged in a bucket of sloshing hot water that would be cold by the time we needed it.

Dasa was unhappy to see that the bed hadn't been positioned as she liked. "I need the wall to push against," she said, and I could tell by the wobble in her voice that another contraction was coming. "I need the bed moved, Anna…" She looked at me. "Please—" Her voice was shrill this time.

I rushed to the side of the bed, waving for Matka to help.

Matka pushed her sleeves up again. "This doesn't make sense," she said, and Dasa yelled.

"Don't tell me how to give birth!" Her lips hung from her face, the pain controlling every morsel of her body as she whimpered and shook.

"All right, all right…" Matka said, and together, with Dasa lying on the mattress, we pulled the bed out enough to wedge ourselves between the headboard and the wall.

"Don't upset her," I whispered to Matka. "How to give birth is the only thing Dasa has ever been sure of."

"I'm trying not to," Matka gritted.

We put our backs to the headboard, and pushed, sliding the bed across the wooden floor to the other side of the room, so Dasa could have a wall to push her feet against.

"You'd be better off squatting," Matka said.

"Matka!" I snapped, and Dasa growled from the bedsheets.

"Don't tell me what to do, Matka," she said.

"Fine," Matka said, and after she'd stewed for a moment, she took Dasa's hand. "Let's pray," she said. "Anna, take her other hand."

Dasa breathed through her mouth in quick spurts. "Make up your mind, Matka—" she breathed some more "—are we in God's hands or are we at the mercy of luck and superstition?"

"Shh!" Matka said, but Dasa moaned, squeezing both our hands from another contraction before we could pray.

"It's coming!" Dasa said, huffing and sweating as Matka swiped the hair from her eyes.

I squeezed in between the wall and the bed, throwing back Dasa's birthing gown and spreading her legs apart. "I see the baby's head." I looked up, hoping I could remember how to deliver a baby. It had been a few years since I delivered Dasa's last child, but we'd had a midwife with us. This baby would be delivered in secret, and if there was a problem, we'd have nowhere to go, nobody to ask for help.

"Dasa, time to push," I said, and she pushed, and pushed, and pushed for many minutes, taking only small breaks in between, then the baby's head slowly began to move. "He's coming!" I reached for his shoulders, and gently pulled. "One more," I said, and Dasa bore down with grit, but it wasn't enough and I worried he might be stuck. Matka tried to get a glimpse of the baby between my hands, as if she knew something was wrong, which alerted Dasa.

"What's wrong?" Dasa squirmed, trying to get up with the baby stuck between her legs. "Anna?" she said, but I was too busy to answer. "Anna!"

"Nothing's wrong. Now, one more push," I said, looking at

the baby's wrinkled face half out of my sister's body. "You're safe with me, little one," I said to the baby, then shouted a command to Dasa. "Go!"

Dasa took two short breaths before pushing hard one last time, and the baby squeezed out of Dasa's pelvis into my hands, followed by a very healthy cord slithering out behind him like a sausage in a casing.

"It's a boy, Dasa," I said, gasping, and she burst into tears, crying for her husband as Matka hugged her.

The baby yelped with a lungful of air, and I looked into his eyes, wiping his nose and mouth with a rag. "I told you," I said to him. "You're safe with me." I wrapped him up.

"Your son, sister," I said, handing him to her.

Dasa noticed the birthmark behind his ear while cradling him in her arms, and called him her heart.

Adam stopped crying, and we gazed at each other in the nursery and I almost burst into tears, realizing he remembered me. Out of all the nurseries he could have been brought to, he was brought to mine. Matka would call it luck, but I thanked God. "I'm not leaving you," I mouthed. Somehow, I'd find a way to sneak him out too. There was no other choice.

An eerie chill prickled my spine, and I turned around only to see what I'd already felt—Frau Brack and the nurses staring at us. A nurse marched toward me, yanking my hand away from Adam's, and he immediately cried. "You're spoiling him," she said, then turned to Frau Brack. "She isn't the nurse for us."

"We don't have any other candidates," Frau Brack said, and the nurse didn't have anything to say after that, only passing glares as the other nurses brought Adam over to yet another scale.

"Anna," Frau Brack said. "This is Ursula. She's the head nurse here."

I smiled, giving her a nod, which I think only made her more upset because her eyes turned to slits. "Yes, we've met," I said, but I didn't mention that I'd caught her in my room and going through my drawers. Little did she know that I was wearing the only thing worth finding.

Ursula folded her arms. No words.

Frau Brack took a deep breath. "Be glad you have the help, Ursula. For now. Anna has agreed to join the program," she said, and Ursula's face changed. I couldn't tell if she was upset or surprised, with her white eyebrows furrowing into her eyes.

"Oh? That does change things," she said. "In that case, I will be glad."

Ursula walked over to a shelf, clicking her shoes against the tile floor when all the other nurses' shoes were muffled, and took a white nurse's dress and apron from the shelf. "Clean uniforms every day." She held out her hand with the uniform hanging from her closed fist, but I hesitated to take it.

Frau Brack's smile fell instantly. "You have decided, haven't you?" she asked, and I looked at Adam in the far corner of the room being pulled and yanked and measured by the nurses. They were like ants on a crumb of bread, and he was powerless and vulnerable. I was his only hope.

"Yes," I said, and I took the nurse uniform. "I'll have a change, then I'll be in." I turned to leave. "Will I have different sleeping arrangements?" I held onto the nursery doorknob, hoping she'd say no. I didn't want to move in with the other nurses—it would be even more difficult to escape. I held my breath.

"You're all settled, so I don't see the need right now," Frau Brack said. "But when I hire a new housekeeper, you'll have to move."

"Yes, Frau Brack," I said, exhaling.

Chapter Twenty-Two

I walked back into the nursery after changing into the stiff white nurse's outfit, only Ursula stood in the doorway and refused to let me in. "You need to be trained before I can allow you back in here," she said, and another nurse handed her a thick book, which she shoved at me. "Here. Learn it. Then come back."

"The German Mother and Her First Child," I read off the cover. "I know this guide, by Johanna Haarer," I said, but she still wouldn't budge.

"Be off," she said, and I heard Adam crying, which kept me from moving.

"Go visit the older children. See if Clara needs help. Then after you've had a read of the guide—a healthy read—come back."

"Fine," I said, but the offer to see my daughter was the only thing that could have taken me away from Dasa's baby. I left, passing by the library on the ground floor where

Neider rounded the corner. We both stopped. I should have noticed his distinct clip of shoes.

"Herr Neider," I said.

"Fräulein Hager."

We stood a foot away from each other, staring at each other in the empty corridor. I moved to the right and he moved to his left, blocking me while scanning my nurse's uniform. I pushed the guidebook into my chest, crossing my arms, before taking a big step to my left.

He snickered, enjoying the cat-and-mouse game he'd started, before letting me pass, though he craned his neck to watch me walk away. Paula had just carried an empty tray in from the guesthouse. "Paula!" I padded over, taking the opportunity to talk to her and get Neider's eyes off my back.

Her mouth hung open, looking at my nurse outfit. "Promoted?"

I smiled big. "Isn't it wonderful!" I said, and out of the corner of my eye, I saw Neider walk into the library.

She adjusted the tray in her hands, still looking me over. "It is wonderful—"

My smile fell. "I have to go," I said, and I abandoned Paula in the corridor to walk outside to Ema's dormitory. I collected myself at the door, not knowing what I'd find, or what horrible truth would be uncovered about the children, having never been in the children's dormitory before, but I found Ema sitting on the floor with the other children in a circle, about to be read to as if she was in nursery school.

Clara looked surprised to see me. "Anna!" she said, sitting up straight in her chair. "I wasn't expecting you."

I crept over, pretending I didn't want to interrupt, but had to. "I wanted to thank you for recommending me." I tapped the guidebook. "And I was told to give this a study and see if you needed help."

She smiled. "Excellent," she said, then a little girl in the back said a word that sounded Czech, and Clara pointed a finger in the air, gritting her teeth. "Who said that?" All the children stiffened, and there was a quiet, frightened pause among us all.

I coughed. "Sounded like a stomach growl to me," I said. "What are you going to read?"

"Oh..." She looked at her book, and I sighed, relieved at having diverted her attention. "I was going to read this book of German fairy tales." She pointed to the cover. "But since you're here, maybe you can do it?" She stood up, whispering, "I have to take a lavatory break."

"I'm happy to help," I said, and she offered me her chair to take her place, complete with a footrest.

I waited until she'd left the dormitory before sitting down. Ema watched me carefully, eyes wide, probably wondering what I had planned and if we were about to escape. "Hallo," I said, but only a few answered me in German. The others remained quiet. "Do you remember me from the other day?" I asked, and most of them nodded.

The little boy I had talked to on the playground with the skinned knee popped up, wrapping his arms tightly around me and burying his head. My instant reaction was to hold him, which didn't sit well with some of the others.

"He's not supposed to do that," one of the girls said.

"And you're spoiling him." She pointed, addressing the others. "She's spoiling him!"

My mouth hung open, having never been spoken to like that by a child, but also knowing I had to tread lightly. I didn't want her to tell on me, and by the look in her fire-blue eyes and furrowing blonde eyebrows, I thought she would.

"I know the rules." I scoffed. "And you're not being a very good German right now." I looked at the other children. "Who knows a song?" One boy raised his hand. "Sing a song and I'll be back."

He stood up from the floor and led a song for them to sing, while I dragged the boy I'd met on the playground to the corner of the room where nobody could see, and gave him a hug.

"What's your name?" I asked in Czech.

"My name used to be Jan. Now it's Hans," he said, and I closed my eyes briefly. This boy *was* Czech. They were renaming them to sound German. Of course, they were renaming them.

"Listen to me," I said as the other children finished their song. "You must learn German. Tell nobody I spoke Czech to you." I gave him another hug. "Our secret. Now go back to the others."

And he ran off, and the other children had no idea what kind of punishment he'd received.

"All right," I said, picking up the book of fairy tales. "Where was I..." I cracked the book open, skimming the pages, but found stories about a Jewish man using candy to seduce a young German girl, and another about a terrible Jewess—not the good Czech stories I was used to.

A girl stood up next after waiting too long for me to choose. "Can we go outside now?"

"Outside?" I repeated, and the other children started standing up and heading toward the door. "Yes." I closed the book on a tale about the Jewish wolf in the woods. "You can go outside."

The children raced for the door, but poor little Jan looked like he wanted another hug, when I wanted to talk to Ema. "It's all right. Go on outside," I said, and my heart broke for him, and I wondered how the hell I could save them all. He slowly walked away, and Ema inched closer to my skirts, waiting patiently, then threw herself into my arms just as soon as he'd left.

"Mama," she cried. "When are we going to leave?"

I bent to my knees, wiping her face. "I have news." I smiled. "There are no guards," I said, and I was relieved to finally have had the chance to tell her.

She gasped, her glistening eyes growing wider.

"I'm working on a plan. Be ready." Seeing her beautiful face, and hearing her fraught voice made me want to cry, and I sniffed back the tears. "I love you." I kissed her cheeks before pressing my forehead to hers, where I closed my eyes. "I love—"

Clara burst through the doors, and I bolted to my feet, taking Ema's hand behind my back as she tried feverishly to wipe her tears away with her sleeve.

"Thank you—" Clara's eyes settled on Ema crying

behind my back. "What is this?" She marched over. "Are you crying?" She pointed at my daughter. "Is she crying?"

While Ema shook her head, every bad deed the Germans had done to us rose to the surface, pounding in my heart and curling in my hands, and I knew that if she laid one hand on my child, I would kill her right there and wouldn't wait, strangling her first then bashing her skull in with the footrest.

I smiled. "She is crying," I said, and by the time Clara's mouth had dropped, I'd already thought up a story she'd believe. "I told the girl I met the Führer, and she was overcome with emotion, as she should be, wanting to meet him herself."

Clara looked shocked. "You met the Führer?"

"Yes," I said, holding my chin up. "I did." I turned to Ema, bending down to her level. "Go on outside and play, all right?" And she ran off, gladly, as I went on about that one glorious time I met Hitler at a military parade in '41. "He even touched my hand."

She cocked her hip, lips smooth, and looked abnormally girlish. "Now that's luck."

"That's what my mother said." I smiled again.

Clara waved for me to follow her outside, but then opened the door for me to go first. "Where are you from?" she asked.

"Berlin," I said.

"Me too," she said, "perhaps we know some of the same people?"

I laughed. "Berlin is a huge city." I kept laughing,

thinking how stupid she was—a muttonhead Nazi bitch—
which drew a strange look from her. I swallowed. Now was
the perfect opening to bring up the honigmilch. "What time
is lights out for the children?"

"Eight," she said, with an exhausted gasp. "Why?"

"Oh, I was just thinking about how lovely it would be
for some nighttime milk and honey, the way Paula makes it.
I could visit, bring you a warm cup," I said, and she
touched my arm.

"That sounds wonderful! Yes, please." She blew her
whistle, startling me. "Hold on," she said, and she marched
over to a girl and boy playing jump rope, hands on her hips,
about to scold them for jumping wrong.

I didn't even have time to celebrate that she'd agreed to
our date, before she was on her way back. Kurt looked up
from his garden and we both waved, which wetted her
wagging tongue.

"You think he has an eye for you?" she asked.

"Perhaps," I said, looking away, and she laughed.
"What's so amusing?"

"He doesn't like the women here, if you know what I
mean. So many have thrown themselves at his feet."

"No, I'm afraid I don't know what you mean," I said,
but I wasn't sure if that was her opinion or if rumors had
spread. "I've spent some time with him."

"You have?" She took me by the shirt sleeve and led me
to the bench. "Tell me more. Have you kissed?"

I tapped her hand. "Oh, Clara, a lady never tells." I sat
back. "He is attractive, isn't he? Nice to look at."

She looked over her shoulder, watching Kurt as he worked in the sun. "He is. Though I'm not sure why he's here and not serving the country."

"He is serving the country," I said. "The children of the Reich deserve the best food, do they not?"

"Yes," she said. "I see what you mean." She blew her whistle again. "Inside!" she growled at the children, then turned to me with the sweetest voice. "Have a good day," she said, and the children followed her into the dormitory. Ema trotted up last, arms folded, looking at me once.

I smiled. *Tonight.* I watched Clara walk away, thinking she only had a few hours left of her despicable life, and normally that would have made me sick to my stomach, but I was completely at peace with the idea of killing a devil.

I sat down on the bench with the book in my hands when Ursula's face appeared in the window. *The German Mother and Her First Child.* I took a breath before opening it up and having a flip through the pages in the empty garden, giving her a good look at me reading. I had an idea what I'd find—don't spoil children, let them cry—but that was because of what I'd experienced sleeping next to the nursery. What I read was even more heartbreaking, and I started to wonder if any German mother loved her child. The book referred to babies as selfish and controlling, and warned mothers about giving in to a child's wants—no unnecessary affection. Matka would have shaken her head at this, calling the author and all German mothers who followed such advice bitches and perfect for our garden, and she'd be right.

I'd had enough of the guide and went back inside to the nursery to be close to Adam. The nurses stared at me as I walked in, some with hands in cots, others weighing babies on a scale as they screamed. "What's she doing back so soon?" I heard.

Ursula walked up to me, not a word, folding her arms around her book—a ledger she held to her chest.

"Why were you searching my chest of drawers?" I asked.

I wasn't sure why I decided to confront her right then or there, but a good German wouldn't stand for such intrusions. I pulled my shoulders back like she had done.

"You were new," she said. "New girls need to be watched."

"Mmm," I said.

"But today is a new day, and I don't want to fight," she said. "I was being sincere earlier when I said I'd be glad. We're a nurse down. You're here." She smiled thinly. "I'm glad."

"Good," I said. "I—"

"Now, let's get to work," she said. "The shelves need a good dust and the floor is never clean enough. Mop that, will you?" She pointed to the floor and from wall to wall.

"You want me to clean the nursery?" I asked, peeking into Adam's cot while he slept, making sure he was safe and to see what the nurses had done to him since I was gone, but it looked like they'd only swaddled him up tightly like a package. Ursula moved to pull my gaze from him.

"Yes." Her arms tightened around her ledger. "But not now. That will need to be done at lights out. Right now, I need you to sit and monitor for a spell while we have our dinner." Nurses took off their aprons and began tidying up the supplies, leaving the babies in their cots, wrapped up snugly in their swaddling blankets. "Now, since you're well versed in the guide, you know not to touch a crying baby. They've been fed and changed. There is no need for unnecessary affection."

My insides twisted. "I understand."

She pushed a box toward me with swabs and bandages and clean nappies stuffed inside. "Unpack this box and sort the items on that shelf." She pointed. "I'll be back in twenty minutes so you can take your break," she said, and she left with her ledger tucked close to her chest, clicking her heels once and leaving with the other nurses trailing behind her.

The nursery turned quiet with just me and the sleeping babies. I unpacked the box, careful not to wake the infants, and taking inventory myself on what baby items I needed to escape with. I couldn't bring too many things, enough for a few days. A bottle, dehydrated milk, nappies. I thought my best chance of survival was to rent a room on the other side of the city. Neider would think I'd left Dresden, which was exactly why I needed to stay—a German widow with children. This was the story I'd tell, and then I'd think about what to do after that.

A whoosh of air fluttered my hair from the nursery doors opening behind me, and I turned around, thinking Ursula was back. "Hallo—"

Neider.

"Fräulein Hager." He took guarded steps, clasping his hands behind his back. "How are you this…" He glanced at the clock. "Late afternoon, is it?"

I studied him, not sure where he was going with his questions, especially since I'd just seen him in the corridor not that long ago. He laughed after smiling. "I can see you're doing fine."

"Shh," I said, finger to my mouth, and he patronized me, putting his finger to his lips.

"Yes, yes. The babies," he said. "Shh, indeed." But the babies hadn't woken up from his voice and I wondered why, when now I needed them to cry.

"A nurse," he said, circling me. "That is quite the promotion." He walked clear around me, slowly looking me up and down.

"It's what I applied for," I said, "but with Herta gone—"

"Yes, with Herta gone you are the logical choice," he said. "I've heard this from Frau Brack."

I went back to unpacking the box, hoping he'd leave, but he continued to watch me, his eyes heavy in the quiet nursery, and breathing from his mouth. I reached for a blanket, looking back unexpectedly, catching him bent over and studying my hind end.

He stood bolt straight. "Yes, well, didn't mean to disturb you," he said, and he took a few steps toward the door, casually, while peeking into the cots. "I regret to inform you that your father, Hans Schmitt, has been arrested."

The blankets fell from the shelf, tumbling one after the other onto the floor. "What?"

"This worries you, no?"

I put my hand to my mouth while Neider studied my reaction. "What did he do?" I asked. "And how do you know?"

"How do I know, indeed," he said. "You see, Frau Brack doesn't control my investigations. I can investigate anyone I want. I'm sure this will have no bearing on your employment. Frau Brack likes you very much." He walked toward the door, his hands behind his back, clipping his heels, and that sound did wake the babies, several of them squirming with shuddering cries. "Just thought you should know."

"What else can you tell me? Is he all right?" I merely wanted to know what he knew. "Herr Neider, I beg you…"

"I can tell you more in a few days after I take a trip up there."

"You're going to Berlin?" I asked.

"Does that worry you?"

"Why would it worry me?" I asked, but he turned on his heel and left me in a room of quivering infants that wanted to be touched, and fed, and loved. The nurses had come back and were not pleased with the state of the babies.

Ursula ordered me out. "Your first test and you failed," she said. "I suggest you read more of the guidebook." She shoved the book at me, and I left, finding Clara in the corridor.

"Anna," she said, hearing the babies. "Everything all right?"

I forced a smile, holding onto the guidebook, and trying hard to shake off Neider and his news. "Everything is fine.

I'm looking forward to Paula's milk and honey tonight," I said, and she grimaced.

"Sorry," she said. "I have to reschedule. I just found out I have another assignment this evening. Ursula is taking over for me in the children's dormitory."

"Ursula?" I crumbled into a million pieces inside.

"You're disappointed," she said, trying to look sad herself. "I promise we'll have that honigmilch very soon." She went into the nursery and I didn't know what to do other than run into my room and hide.

I wanted to scream—I felt it in my chest, clenching with the slow tick of time. I opened my window for some air when I felt the walls closing in on me, and Kurt motioned to me from the vegetable patch, which took me by surprise.

"Me?" I thumbed my chest, and he nodded and laughed, then motioned again for me to come down.

I couldn't get outside fast enough.

Kurt pulled out a planter, sliding it across the paving stones. "Look at this." He pointed.

"Are those…" I questioned. "Is that…"

He laughed. "The peppers."

"Kurt, they're gigantic!" I bent down and touched the peppers, feeling their waxy skins. "What are you feeding them?"

He waved me into the potting shed, where it was warm with electric light, and showed me the fertilizers he'd been using. I hadn't expected to be here another night. I hadn't expected to be back in this potting shed. "It's my own blend," he said, explaining what he'd fed them, but my mind had wandered and I looked lazily at the ground. "Is something wrong?"

There was no use hiding it. I was upset after hearing from Clara. "I'll be fine."

"Pot this and you'll feel better." He pushed a small pot across the table, followed by a basil plant that needed to be planted.

"You promise?" I asked.

"Yes."

There was nothing I could do but wait another day. I reached for the basil, and he reached for the thyme.

I smelled my palms after rubbing the leaf in my hands. "I think basil might be my favorite herb."

"What other herbs did you grow?" he asked, and he arranged his herb jars and listened to me talk about the fennel I used to grow, and how I'd hang the stalks upside down.

"Upside down?" he asked. "Why would you do that?"

I talked with my hands. "I'd use a paper sack, and that's how I harvested the seeds for tea."

"Wait a minute," he said, and he reached for a notebook and pencil. "Say that again." He took notes about what I'd grown and how, and it felt good to talk plainly without worry or threat.

"You remind me of my sister," he said.

"I do? Tell me about her."

"She's an actress."

"Oh, I'm not acting," I said.

"I know you aren't," he said, and I looked up with my hands in the dirt. A cricket croaked in the potting shed, and a car sped by not that far away, but otherwise, the air was deathly quiet and still. "Not now, with me, anyway."

My God, he knows. He did hear me speaking Czech. And maybe he saw me with Ema too. I stared at him, swallowing a million times, though realizing he'd kept my secret just like I was keeping his.

"Is there something you want to ask?"

"Why are you growing hemlock?" I asked.

"Why did you take some of it?"

I pulled my hands from the pot and shook off the dirt. "I should go," I said, and he grabbed my arm just hard enough to keep me from walking away.

"Anna—" he said, but I'd wiggled from his grip. "There are spies here. Be careful. I heard you speaking Czech," he said, and I closed my eyes, hands on the doorframe. "I might not be the only one."

I nodded, my back to him, and his hand slipped from my arm. I wanted to tell him more, but I knew not to.

I crept upstairs to my room where a note had been placed on my door instructing me to mop the nursery.

Don't wake the babies!

Another test. I saw right through Ursula's plans. There was no way I could mop the nursery without waking them up. But I was thankful for the invitation into the nursery—a reason to be inside.

I yawned, feeling the weight of the day. *Tomorrow* would be the day. I'd be rested. *Adam will be rested*, I thought, to make the delay seem like a blessing, but I knew each day I spent at Edelhaus was another day closer to being caught.

I slipped into the nursery, setting my bucket and mop

near the wall, and tiptoed over to Adam's cot. His back arched when I picked him up. Between his neck and his chin I smelled the sweetness I remembered. "You're safe, little one," I whispered in his ear in Czech. "You're safe." And I laid him on my chest where he fell asleep, and I rocked him under the window with the moonlight on my face.

Chapter Twenty-Three

I jolted awake in the rocker as the sun rose. Adam barely moved, sleeping peacefully on my chest, but I was in a panic, knowing the nurses would be in at any minute. I placed him gently back in the cot, trying to hurry, and backed my way out. I wheeled my bucket to the door as the babies started to stir, and I thought if I could just get into my room, if I could just get out of the nursery before anyone saw me…

I reached for the doorknob at the same time I heard the dreaded crank of the lift at the end of the corridor. My stomach dropped, next hearing the tap of footsteps, knowing it had to be Ursula.

I clenched the mop handle, bracing for her to walk in and see me still in the nursery, my heart pounding, but she'd walked past and paused at my bedroom door. All was quiet, and I held my breath. Then she walked away, and I peeked through the nursery glass, exhaling with relief and expecting to see her backside, but it was the cook's!

There wasn't a duty list for her to deliver anymore. *Spies*, just like Kurt had warned.

I snuck back into my room and flopped onto my bed, but by this time the babies had woken up and they screamed their hungry morning cries. I pressed my pillow over my head. It was my fault. They'd heard each other stirring and the ballooning noise from one baby had woken them all.

The babies were still bawling when the nurses marched down the corridor for work, throwing on the lights and being loud themselves, which brought on more cries. I rubbed my face to fully wake up, then pulled down my basket to look at the hemlock, make sure it was still there. *Today's the day.* I held my head.

A booming knock at my door threw me against the cleaning shelves. "Wake up!" Ursula demanded.

I tucked the basket away and opened the door. "Good morning," I said, followed by a pause. "Ursula."

She smiled, arms wrapped around her ledger. "Did you clean the nursery?"

"Yes," I said, though of course I didn't, but wondered how she could tell. The nursery was already so clean as it was.

She turned to leave, but then looked over her shoulder. "Your shift starts in thirty minutes. I suggest you have breakfast." She rolled her eyes over my nurse uniform. "Did you sleep in your uniform?"

I scoffed, smoothing the fabric against my thighs. "No. I'm up early, just like you. But I did wear this yesterday. Will I be getting another?"

She'd walked out, but came back with a clean uniform and told me to bathe.

I washed my face and limbs with the goat milk soap and pinned up my hair before heading to the kitchen to receive my breakfast from Paula, who was waiting eagerly for me at the table.

"How was your first day as a nurse?" she asked.

I sat down in my chair, yawning.

"Don't let Ursula see you yawning." She poured me a cup of frothy honigmilch. "Drink up. Wake up. There's sugar in here. Shh! Don't tell anyone. Otherwise, every nurse in the building will be coming in and asking for some. The sugar will perk you up." She sat down again, but this time whispered. "How are things going with Kurt?"

I sat up. "Fine. Why?" I whispered back.

"There's talk…" she said, eyes darting toward the cook who'd just walked in and was tying up her apron. "That nobody can turn Kurt. That there must be something wrong with him. Some of the nurses have mentioned sending an inquiry to Neider."

"What do you mean, something wrong with him?"

"Look at you, Anna. You're as beautiful as they come. If Kurt isn't willing to get into bed with you, then…"

"Then what?" I asked.

She blew air from her mouth, looking slightly frustrated from having to say the words. "They think…" She patted her forehead where she'd perspired, before whispering even softer. "They think he might be a homosexual."

My face was one of shock. Rumors *had* spread about him. "That's a serious charge, Paula. He only needs to be persuaded. Many of the traditional German families feel pre-marital sex is immoral," I said, repeating what Herta had told me. "He's one of them—an old family. That's all."

Paula sat back. "I'm only telling you what the talk is." The cook yelled for her to help, and Paula sat bolt upright. "I have to go…"

"Wait!" I said, and she stayed in her seat a moment longer. "If you must know, we kissed, and I can tell you he is definitely attracted to me," I lied, hoping she'd spread this to the nurses if Clara hadn't already.

She smiled. "That is good news!" The cook yelled again, but it was for Paula to bring me my breakfast.

I expected a piece of her tangy dark bread with creamy cheese and jam, but instead she gave me a slice of dry white bread. She winced when I examined it, which I was sure she mistook for disgust, when in fact I was pleased—it would be easy on my stomach.

"Sorry. You've heard about the invasion?"

I looked up, nodding.

"Food for the staff will be different from now on. Hopefully not for very long. But I was told the children's food may change too." She rubbed her head. "It happened so suddenly. Our food."

I ate the bread and sipped my milk, watching the clock and adding up the seconds it would take me to wander out to the gardens, find Kurt, warn him about the nurses, and get up to the nursery on time. But there wasn't enough time. I closed my eyes. I'd have to find a way this afternoon. Paula topped off my cup with more sugary warm milk when the cook wasn't looking. "Not sure how long this will last," she whispered. "Better drink what you can."

I took my cup of honigmilch upstairs. Ursula watched me through the glass before opening the door, lips pursed, holding her ledger and marking things down. "Where's your swastika?" she asked, and I set down my cup of sugary milk to pull my pendant out from under my dress.

"Good." She reached for my cup of honigmilch and drank it herself, going back to her ledger.

"That's mine—"

She glared. "Yes?"

"Nothing." I smiled and waited for her to tell me what to do, when another nurse mentioned an adoption.

"Has the baptism been arranged?" Ursula asked, and the other nurse assured her it had been.

"Baptism?" I questioned, and she glanced at me over her ledger.

"All the babies are baptized in the name of the Party before they leave Edelhaus." She looked into Adam's cot. "Today it is this baby."

I grabbed forcefully onto Adam's cot. "This one?"

She looked at me strangely, pencil pressed against a page in her ledger, while I felt dizzy from a spinning room. "Yes," she said, and she wrote a few things down before taking a sip of the milk I'd brought. "What's wrong with you?"

I could hardly get the words out. "I feel nauseous," I said, then felt I should explain to avoid suspicion. "My breakfast…"

She pointed to a chair. "Sit down over there and collect

yourself. I don't want a dizzy nurse working in my nursery."

I looked into Adam's cot after having a short sit and held his little hand.

"Frau Strohm will be here at nine for the baptism, then we'll prepare the baby, get him fed, and I'll deliver him myself."

"Frau Strohm?" I asked.

"That's right. She's been waiting for so long too. Finally got approval." She went on, mumbling under her breath about why it had taken so long, and that it had something to do with her husband being away for extended periods of time in Berlin. "It is a good day. She'll be an excellent parent. Good German family."

I turned away, trying to figure out what this meant, feeling my forehead.

"Are you settled?" Ursula asked, and I dropped my hand. "Looks like you are."

I turned around. "Yes."

She pointed her pencil at the other nurses. "See if they need help preparing the library for the baptism."

"Yes, Ursula," I said, clicking my heels once, and I helped the others carry flags and banners to the library for hanging. The nurses practiced the procession, deciding where to stand and where the chairs should be set up. A special Nazi Party flag half the size of the wall was brought in and hung especially for Adam over a cot with wheels.

"It's about time to start," Frau Brack said. "Anna, would you alert Ursula?"

Greta Strohm walked in through the front doors of

Edelhaus alone, clicking down the corridor, which alarmed Frau Brack, who met her outside the library doors and questioned her about where her husband was.

I walked back up to the nursery to tell Ursula that it was time to start, but I was now thinking of the discussion between Frau Brack and Greta Strohm. Where *was* her husband? Ursula marked a few things down in her ledger, calling Adam by his new German name as she wrote, before picking him up.

"You'll have to stay here," she said to me, making her way to the door. "And keep the babies quiet."

I paced once I was alone, thinking about Adam being baptized under a Nazi flag, then talking myself down and knowing it didn't really matter. Dasa would never have to know. I'd never tell her. I looked to the ceiling, closing my eyes. *But the adoption.* I had to think of what to do. Ursula would be back soon and they'd be packing him up for delivery. I had to think. *Think. Think. Think—*

The note.

I gasped, taking a heaving breath, wondering if it would really work. I raced back into my room, pulling Margot's dress from the laundry bag and ripping out the seam. I unfolded the note. "It's the only way," I said, but then second-guessed myself. Maybe I'd read the signs all wrong. Maybe she wasn't working with Margot, but was trying to expose her?

My head pained instantly—Ema's life depended on whether I was right, and Adam's too. I heard clapping from the library and babies crying on the other side of the wall.

The baptism was over. I raced back, looking frantically for a pencil, and found Ursula's.

The lift opened at the end of the corridor, followed by the nurses' muffled steps as I scribbled out a message on the backside of Margot's note. *I know your secret.* I set the pencil down just as Ursula threw open the nursery door to a room full of crying babies.

I straightened, hands hidden behind my back with the note scrunched up in one of my fists. The other nurses spilled into the nursery behind her, all in a tizzy, wondering what I had done to upset the babies, because of course, it was my fault. They were good little German babies, after all, who'd been trained.

"I left for the stairs," I said. "I had to see the baptism. The beautiful baptism," I said, and Ursula seemed to understand this, and instead of getting mad at me like I'd expected, she asked me to help prepare Adam's bag.

The other nurses chatted and laughed about how I reminded them of Margot, and I was surprised to hear them talk about her so plainly, when Paula nearly fainted every time she whispered her name. "What a little traitor she was," the nurse said, then turned to me. "Margot had a way of keeping the babies up. She'd come into the nursery to mop the floor and they'd cry and cry and cry. So glad she was arrested."

"What?" I questioned, and they looked surprised I didn't know.

"You didn't hear?" she asked, and I shook my head.

"She wasn't who she said she was. Neider had her arrested."

"Oh?" I said, but inside I felt like I'd been punched in the gut with the news that Neider had been the one who'd uncovered her secrets. "I didn't know why she left."

Cans of dehydrated milk and a bag of sugar were added to the baby bag, along with a few clothes and a copy of Johanna Haarer's guide for German mothers. I heard Ursula tell someone that she would stay at Greta's estate until she felt the baby was settled, and that Frau Strohm understood the importance of a good, strict upbringing.

The nurses rushed downstairs once he was ready to leave, and it was then that I asked Ursula for one last hold of the darling Aryan child.

"Only so you can look into his eyes properly, not to show affection," she said.

"I understand," I said, and when her back was turned, while she was adjusting her apron and smoothing her braids, getting ready for the baby's send-off down the long corridor of claps, I wiggled my hand up into his blankets and stuffed the note in.

She turned around, and I smiled with a hold of my breath.

"All right, give him back," she said, taking him from my arms. The bells clanged and clanged in the courtyard. "It's time to shine."

She walked away, and I exhaled, feeling for my chest.

I had done it.

We filed into the corridor with the bells still ringing, about to send baby Adam off to his adopted home, when I saw Paula standing across from me, looking despondent, gazing at the floor near her shoes.

Frau Brack commanded our attention, and we clapped reservedly as Ursula walked down the corridor with Adam in her arms.

I stood dutifully, as expected, and even though I'd set a plan in motion to get him back, I felt sick watching them leave out the front doors. It was then that seeds of doubt started to take root; I wondered if I'd hidden the note well enough, and what if Ursula found it instead of Greta Strohm? My head throbbed and throbbed, thinking of all that could go wrong as I smiled and waved.

The nurses broke away, and headed back upstairs while I lingered near the window, reaching for the standing flagpole to hold and keep me upright.

Paula walked up next to me to watch Ursula's car drive away. "The last time there was an adoption, a nurse disappeared." She turned to me. "You're not going to disappear, are you?"

"Why would you ask that?"

"Because every time I make a new friend here, they leave," she said. "And every time it seems to happen after an adoption."

"I'm not going to disappear," I said, and I played with my swastika necklace, rubbing the pendant between my fingers and feeling the reichsmarks between my breasts.

Neider walked into Frau Brack's office with a messenger bag over his shoulder. He glanced once at me and Paula, smiling slyly before saying something about a trip, an important background check he was wrapped up in.

"You promise?" Paula asked.

He left Frau Brack's office with his bag, a gleaming smile

on his face as if that trip he'd told her about was indeed the trip to Berlin he'd threatened me with, clicking down the Nazi-flag corridor, straight for us and the doors.

Paula reached for my arm.

"I promise," I said, answering her, catching Neider's shifting gaze as he brushed past us, tipping his hat.

An hour had passed, and I couldn't do anything other than worry. If Ursula had found the note, I'd expect the Gestapo to come marching into Edelhaus any second and drag me away. I wanted to see Ema, scoop her up, but the thought of her seeing me dragged away tore me to pieces. I walked downstairs to the ground floor to see if there'd been any developments, when Ursula marched in with sharp words directed at Frau Brack.

"She's irrational! And she wouldn't let me stay," Ursula said.

Frau Brack tried to comfort her, but she wasn't interested and walked up to the nursery. A moment later, Greta Strohm's car lurched to a stop outside, sending gravel spitting into the air.

Frau Brack ambled up next to me, and we stood in shock by the front door. "What's she doing back?" she asked just before Greta stormed through the doors.

"The baby is fussy," Greta said. "I'd dismissed Ursula, but now I need a nurse for the day. This one will do." She slipped Frau Brack an envelope. "Here's enough money for her wages."

"You… you…" Frau Brack stuttered, not making any sense, alternating her look between the envelope and Greta Strohm's determined eyes. "You want Anna?" she finally asked.

Greta pulled her shoulders back. "Yes," she said, "and I don't have all day. The baby is waiting."

"Go, Anna," Frau Brack said, and I think she was glad she'd pacified Greta Strohm so easily. "I'll tell Ursula not to expect you upstairs."

I followed Greta outside where we climbed into the back seat of her running car. "Hurry, driver," she said, and we sped off through the city and into the country.

"Frau Strohm," I said, and her lips pinched.

"Not a word from you."

We made it to her home, a big estate near the village of Rabenau. She dismissed her housekeeper and sat down on the divan near a window where it was still warm from the afternoon sun.

"Now," she said, folding her hands together. "Who are you?"

"Who are you?" I asked back, and she smiled after a pause.

"Is that what it has come to? A game?" She laughed. "You don't want to play games with me." She stood up to pace her carpets, rubbing her swastika pendant between her fingers. Adam cried from the nursery and I moved toward him, but she grabbed me by the arm near the elbow.

"I know about the children," I said, glaring. "And I know you do too."

"How?" Adam cried again, and I tried to push her aside

to get to him in the other room, but she wouldn't let go. "How do you know?"

I looked up while we struggled, knowing I had to tell her my secret in order to find out more about hers. "Because he's my sister's child," I said, bursting into tears. "The Reich stole him from her."

She'd stumbled backward. "Go to him," she said up against the wall, and I ran down the hallway into the nursery, picking him up and holding him close.

"Adam," I said, pressing my forehead to his. I smelled his breath. I smelled his skin. "You're safe, little one…"

He'd stopped crying, and Greta watched me from the doorway after making up a bottle for me to feed him with. He reached for my chin and grabbed for my lips as he drank in my arms. Afterward, I just held him.

"I can tell you're being truthful with me. This baby knows his aunt. Where are you from?"

I hesitated, but ultimately told her about Tabor and how far I'd traveled, and it felt odd to be Anna from Tabor again, but also freeing. "This baby isn't the reason I came to Edelhaus in the first instance," I said, and she looked surprised. "My daughter was taken. I tracked her to the nursery and was about to escape with her when Adam arrived. It was by accident I found Margot's note and made the connection."

"Do you know what happened to Margot?" she asked, standing straight.

"I know she was caught," I said.

She took a deep breath. "Neider never did understand how Margot was getting information out of Edelhaus. After

Margot was caught, and I had nobody inside to work with, I thought the best thing I could do was adopt as many children as I could with the hopes of returning them to their parents. There's a small resistance network working on the Lebensborn program here in Dresden. The women in the guesthouse are only part of a much larger program to repopulate the world. Thousands of children from occupied lands have been stolen. They are reissuing birth certificates, which I'm sure you know by now. Margot was passing me names and dates of the children for our records, hoping one day to find the main ledger."

"Ursula's ledger?" I questioned, and her jaw dropped.

"Yes," she said, walking closer as I held Adam. "Have you seen it?"

I nodded.

"Anna," she said as the baby cooed. "Do you think you can get it from her? Steal it and pass it to me?"

"I… I don't know. It's never out of her sight."

"Anna," she said, eyes wide. "There are thousands of parents who want their children back. After the war, do you think the Reich is going to help them? And with the Americans plowing their way through France, I suspect that time is nearing. You could be the one who saves them all."

I looked away, out the window, focusing on some leaves that had blown across the garden. I had plans to leave that night with Ema and Adam, and she was asking me to stay.

"Anna, I need that ledger. Anna?"

"I'm escaping with my daughter tonight," I said, and she scoffed.

"And what? Come here and rescue Adam too? Neider

will alert the Gestapo and they'll track you down and hang you before you can leave the city."

I paced her carpets with Adam, patting his bottom through the blanket, holding him snugly.

"Anna," she said. "I can help you."

"How?" I asked.

"What do you want?"

"I want my daughter safe," I said, "and my sister's baby."

"That's the answer," she said. "Don't you see?" She put her hands up, referring to the room, the toys, the soft and fluffy blankets.

"What's the answer? I don't understand."

"I'll adopt your daughter," she said, and now it was my jaw that dropped. "Frau Brack has approved me for a girl, it was part of the agreement—I paid her directly."

"How?" I asked. "I heard she made it difficult for you to bypass some of the restrictions, and with your husband not here…"

"She promised. I already paid. I'm to choose the girl today and adopt her tomorrow. She'll be telephoning any moment to find out my choice." I looked at her blankly, and she took me by the shoulders. "Don't you see, Anna?" she said. "Your daughter and the baby will be safe here. Nobody will think they're yours if I adopt them. Find the ledger and drop it in the laundry, then disappear. There's a special pick-up tomorrow, kitchen rags and things. I'll make sure it gets to where it needs to be. After the war, I'll bring the children home. I promise I will." She paused a second before her voice took a stern turn. "Anna. You will not survive in Nazi Germany with two Czech children, tugging one by the hand and holding another on your hip. For your sake and the children's, disappear on your own and leave them here."

I paced nervously, praying for direction, praying I'd make the right decision. "I don't know..." I patted my warming forehead before clutching my stomach. A squadron of Messerschmitts flew over Greta Strohm's estate, sending a rippling shiver up my spine with the rattling of her windows.

Greta searched the ceiling, following the sound of the planes. "That's another thing, Anna," she said as the planes whirred past. "Dresden will be a pile of rubble by the time the Allies are through with it. Out here the children will be safe from the bombings."

My eyes welled with tears, and the lump in my throat throbbed with such pain, I thought I'd like to cut it open and let it drain. "And what about your husband? I heard someone say he was important."

"I haven't seen him in years. He wanted a wife for a promotion, and I needed a husband for the money. He won't be a problem." She touched my arm. "Trust me, Anna."

The phone rang in her parlor, and we both looked.

"That's Frau Brack," she said. "Anna, we are on the same side. Surely, in your heart you know this is the right choice. As for Ursula, you'll have to find a way." She stepped toward me, looking pointedly into my eyes. "Tell me, which one is your daughter?"

Ring, ring, ring, ring...

"Anna," she said, and I slid to the floor with the baby in my arms, listening to my heart thump and thump. "What's her name?" she asked. "Anna—"

I closed my eyes. "Ema," I finally said, and a bumping cry erupted from my throat, leaving me shaking. "She's five. Last in the line, shoulder-length blonde braids. Sucks her thumb when the nurse isn't looking—"

Greta raced down the hallway to answer the phone while Adam tugged on my hair.

Chapter Twenty-Four

Greta Strohm's driver drove me back to Edelhaus just before dinnertime. I walked into the cafeteria unannounced, determined to see Ema and tell her the plan before it was too late and she'd gone to bed. Clara looked pleased to see me, popping out of her chair and waving me over.

She pointed to one of the many empty chairs available near the children. "Have a seat."

I rubbed my hands nervously, scanning the sparse row of blonde heads scooping boiled potatoes into their mouths, looking for Ema, looking for her braids. The children glanced up from their spoons one by one, until I got to the last child, a boy, and my heart sank. "Looks like you're missing a few children," I said, but hoped Ema was hiding somewhere.

"Some went to wash up already," she said.

I immediately wanted to cry at having missed her and did my best to hide it behind a smile, but the more I tried to hide it, the more my lip quivered. Not that Clara would realize something was wrong with me, because she was always thinking about herself.

She touched my arm suddenly. "Would you like to meet for that honigmilch? I'm free tonight, after the children go to bed."

I rested my throbbing head in my hands at the table, and she cleared her throat after waiting for an answer.

"Did you hear me?" she asked.

"Honigmilch?" Clara had no idea how close she'd come to being poisoned. No idea. Part of me wanted to tell her. "I have a headache," I said.

"That's all right," she said, eyes twinkling. "You can still bring me some."

I pulled my hand away from my forehead, watching her get up to retie her sagging apron and smooth the fabric against her thighs. A sharp blow of her whistle jolted the children in their seats before they too rose to scrape their plates of sour cream and dill. I wondered where Ema had sat, which chair was hers. Which scraped plate she'd eaten from. Ema hated sour cream.

Clara followed the children out, shouting over her shoulder when Paula arrived to clear the stacked plates. "Paula! Perfect. Bring me some honigmilch, will you?" She clapped for the last child to hurry up out the door. "Extra honey!" The door closed with a bang, and Paula slumped forward.

I rubbed my forehead. I'd have to catch Ema tomorrow before the adoption. Somehow, I'd have to find a way. Paula placed the scraped plates on her cart, mumbling and grumbling about how every nurse in Edelhaus was going to drink up all the milk. "No more honigmilch for them," she said, then she looked at me. "Except for you. And me. Our secret, though." I pressed my palms to my eyes, and she stacked the last of the plates on her cart. "Did you hear me?"

I stood from my seat. "Yes, Paula. I heard you," I said, and I walked out, leaving her with the dirty dishes and a blank and confused look on her face. I made my way to my room, walking up the stairs and feeling the trudge of every heavy step in my feet, and in my body. I paused at the top, looking at the painting of Hitler and his dark eyes.

The last nurse on the floor walked past, heading downstairs. "Don't wake the babies!" she said, then noticing my trance, looked up at Hitler too. "Our Führer," she breathed. "You're lucky to have him watching over you all day and every night in this corridor."

"Lucky?" I said, as if it was a distant word.

"I wish I had that kind of luck." She padded down the stairs, and I went to my room.

I lay in my bed, desperately thinking of Josef. I thought about what he'd say, knowing I had just arranged Ema's adoption. "I had to," I whispered into the air, followed by a gush of tears. I hoped Greta Strohm would explain the situation to Ema once they were at her estate. She'd be reunited with Adam, at least, and that was one comfort. *But the send-off.* I wiped my eyes, thinking of watching my baby girl being led out of Edelhaus, with her watching me standing still as it happened.

"Give me a sign, God," I said. "Give me a sign that this

will work." I rolled over, burying my head in my sheets, imagining Dasa and Matka in my room with me, talking to them.

Matka wiped her hands on her apron, smoothing it flat. "I've dug a fine hole in the garden for that bitch in the nursery." She looked at Dasa standing beside her. "What was her name? Ursula? The Germans name their children horrible names. Nobody good has ever been named Ursula."

Dasa scoffed. "Plenty of decent women are named Ursula, Matka." She leaned over, looking at my face in the bed as I looked up at her. "You made the right decision. My baby boy is safe because of you. Now you will do this for Ema too."

I sat up, wiping tears from my eyes. "If that's so, then why does it hurt so much?"

Matka folded her arms. "Motherhood, Anna," she said. "It is not for the weak. Trust yourself." She kicked my bed. "Now stand up. We need to prepare."

I stood up in the dark and they examined me. "You have gained weight," Matka said. "This will be good for when you escape. And you have the money your father gave you?"

I put a hand to my chest, feeling the wad of reichsmarks that had been there since I left Tabor. "Yes, Matka," I said.

"Good."

Matka looked over my room, examining the cleaning fluids and checking for dust on the chest of drawers. "Germans giving my daughter a bedroom in a cleaning closet..." Matka mumbled. "It will be their coffin. I swear it! Just as soon as you get that ledger."

"How?" I asked. "Ursula has it in her hands all day, and

probably all night. I wouldn't put it past her to sleep with it." I closed my eyes.

Dasa turned to the cleaning shelves, looking over the cleaning buckets and bottles before standing on her tiptoes and reaching for my basket. She handed it to me. "The hemlock," she said. "Give it all to Ursula and steal her ledger."

I put my hand to my mouth. "The hemlock."

Matka smiled, putting her arm around Dasa. "Yes," Matka said. "Kill the bitch with the hemlock. Put it in her honigmilch. Shouldn't be hard, she stole your last cup right out of your hands." They both folded their arms, watching me gasp and turn toward the window. "Everything happens for a reason."

I had the right idea with the hemlock, just the wrong person. It was meant for Ursula this whole time. I closed my eyes with the breeze flitting through my hair from the open window when I heard Josef's voice behind me.

"My darling," he said, and I nearly crumbled to the floor, gripping the window ledge.

"Josef," I said, and he reached for me, bringing me to a stand so he could hold me. "Forgive me. I blamed you all these years…"

"Forgive me, my darling," he said, and there was nothing more to say. No more conversations to dwell on. Dasa and Matka faded into the cold background, and Josef too.

My eyes popped open, sitting bolt upright in bed, and I realized I'd had my first dream since arriving at Edelhaus. I looked toward the hemlock on my top shelf.

I hoped it was my last.

The next morning, I waited for news of Ema's adoption while the nurses stayed busy feeding the infants and complaining about the lack of cots. "One baby gets adopted only for another to take its place," one nurse said. Ursula casually glanced up from her ledger.

I was too nervous to eat breakfast and already lightheaded, looking through the nursery glass to the corridor, waiting, waiting, waiting for the clang of courtyard bells signaling an adoption send-off, but they never came. I had no excuse to be outside near the playground. My only chance to talk to Ema would have to take place in the corridor. By nine o'clock I started to wonder if something had gone wrong, and excused myself for the toilet, but instead snuck downstairs where it was quiet. I'd practiced what it would be like to see Ema and tell her about the plan and not to worry.

Laundry bags had collected near the entrance for the special pick-up. One from the kitchen, and one from the dormitory. Paula was in the kitchen with the cook, a normal day, and as if nothing had been planned. I raced back up to the nursery, fearing Ursula would know I'd lied to her, but halfway up the stairs I heard my name swirling down the staircase.

"Anna," Frau Brack said. "There you are! Let's talk in my office."

I forced a smile. "Yes, Frau Brack." I followed her into her office, sitting down dutifully as she studied me from her desk with a statuesque look hardened on her face.

"I'm going to be frank," she said, clasping her hands together.

I heard the clip of Neider's heels walking down the corridor. My eyes shifted to the door. *My God, he's back from Berlin.* I gulped.

"Have you persuaded Kurt to be your donor yet?"

I reached for my chest. "Donor?" I repeated, still staring at the door, expecting Neider to barge in any moment with his files.

She got up to shut her door just as a housekeeper passed by in the corridor—it wasn't Neider after all—and I slumped forward, blowing air forcefully from my mouth. "Anna." She clasped her hands together again, looking rather annoyed with a cock of her neck. "I said, have you—"

"I'm sorry, Frau Brack. I heard you," I said, and I got up from my chair to walk to the window, hiding the relief on my face and the breathy gasps that accompanied a rib-cracking beating heart. "I ahh…" Kurt tended to his plants at a distance in the garden. "You said you were going to ask him. Has he said anything?"

"No, he hasn't," she said, and now there was no mistaking it; she was annoyed with me, and quite possibly with the entire situation of waiting for Kurt to agree. "Rumors are floating around—you may have heard them— that he isn't…" She coughed. "Able to be a donor."

"We kissed," I blurted, surprised *that* rumor hadn't made it to her ears.

"You have?" Her entire face lifted. "This is wonderful news!" She watched Kurt through the window with me. "I need an answer today, you see? It is important."

"Why?" I asked, but then corrected myself when she

took a step backward. "I mean… now?" I didn't want to miss Ema. Even with the clang of bells as a warning, I could get stuck outside, and I had to tell my daughter the plan, I had to. God knows what she'd think if I didn't get to her in time. "We have talked about it. I didn't know getting his acceptance was an urgent matter."

"It is," she said. "Security has taken an interest in the rumor—" She smiled, catching herself. "Never mind that. Will you talk to him now?" she asked, and I closed my eyes briefly.

"Yes, Frau Brack." She watched me from her window as I made my way to the garden.

Kurt straightened as I approached, looking once at my hands and noticing them shaking and curling in front of me. "Smile," I said. "Now, invite me into your potting shed." His eyes flicked over my shoulder to Frau Brack in the window, then he nodded.

"What's going on?" He closed the door.

"They know about you," I said. "The other nurses have started to talk and the rumors have reached Frau Brack. And Neider."

He didn't say anything. I thought he'd ask me what they knew or try to deny it, since we only had a quiet understanding, but after a long pause, he let out a sigh and rubbed his neck.

"I suppose I knew one day…" he said, looking up. "There's only so many women I can say no to."

"Say yes to me," I said, and he looked surprised. I stopped short from telling him I would be gone soon enough, and that he didn't have to worry. "What we do with our alone time is between us," I said to reassure him. "Besides, the war might be over soon, and in the meantime, nobody will doubt your intentions about the program."

"Thank you, Anna, thank you," he said, and I headed for the door, but he stopped me. "What do I owe you?"

"I want your pepper plant," I said, and he laughed. "I'm serious. I'm very jealous." I smiled. "I'll go tell Frau Brack and you'll be safe."

"But first," he said, "let's make it official, shall we?" We walked into the garden where we held hands over the tomatoes, showing all who walked by that we were indeed joining the program together, and that Kurt had no issues with women, while I waited for the damn bells to ring. There was no sign of the children in the dormitory, and no one playing on the playground.

Frau Brack moved away from the window. "She's gone," I said, and we broke away. I headed back to the main building.

"And…" Frau Brack said from her office door.

"He said yes," I said as I passed.

"Well done, Anna." She kissed her swastika pendant.

I raced back up the stairs to the nursery, glad the bells didn't catch me while I was outside. I took a deep breath and patted my perspiring forehead before walking back in.

The nurses had moved beyond breakfast and were now looking forward to lunch. More laundry had been set out in the corridor, waiting for the truck, but still, there was no sign of Greta Strohm, news of an adoption, or the slightest ringing of bells. I started to think the adoption wouldn't happen at all, and the torturous thought of Frau Strohm having second thoughts spun viciously in my brain, making my hands shake even more.

I rearranged some items on the shelf, glass canisters of talc and swabs of cotton, trying not to think about it, but it was all I thought about, with the clock ticking and ticking. And Ursula. And the ledger, and Adam. Now my insides shook from all the uncertainty. I skipped lunch, and with dinner approaching I thought all was lost. Frau Strohm had my nephew, and Ema and I were still trapped inside Edelhaus.

"Anna," Ursula said from her ledger, and I jumped. "Will you open the window in the corridor? It feels stuffy in here." She pointed with her pencil, and I did as I was told, walking out of the nursery to open the window, where I took a breath of the fresh air.

An evening grayness swept over the streets and pavements. A car was parked outside with its motor running. I listened carefully from above to see if I could hear voices. It looked a lot like Greta Strohm's car, but the bells hadn't rung. Then I saw her fox stole when she got out of the back seat.

I gasped audibly.

It was happening. I turned around, looking to the other nurses for signs of getting ready for the send-off, but everyone was busy with a baby, unconcerned with the passing time. I looked back out the window, searching, searching, before falling limp against the sill, seeing Frau Brack lead Ema out the front doors carrying a small blue suitcase that matched her coat.

"Oh no." My heart felt ripped from my chest. There

wasn't a send-off after all, just a quiet delivery, and I wasn't ready for that to be the last time I saw her. And she didn't know the plan. She'd think I'd abandoned her.

I watched Greta Strohm shake my daughter's hand, then touch her blonde braids like I had always done with her bunches, smoothing them with her palm. I put my hand on the glass, about to be sick, when Ursula stepped into the corridor.

My palms sweated and I felt dizzy. I swallowed and swallowed. Ursula peeked out the window, and we both watched Ema climb into the back seat of Greta Strohm's car. "So, she gets another child," Ursula said, and I collapsed.

Ursula caught me in her arms before tossing me like a rag to the floor. "What is wrong with you?" she asked, waving her ledger in my face. "Did you eat breakfast?" I shook my head. "Lunch?"

"No," I managed to say after standing.

"Go get something from the kitchen," she said. "I'm going to have to talk to Frau Brack about this. Eating is a priority for proper health."

"I'll go eat," I said, and the other nurses immediately started whispering to each other as I left.

I walked uneasily down the corridor, feeling Ema's absence from the estate in my heart, thinking she believed I'd abandoned her, that I'd let her down, but by the time I made it downstairs, I thought and felt differently. I was glad she was gone—she was safe. And that was what I'd wanted all along, for her to be out and safe. I felt the relief deeply, even if my heart ached to see her face and talk to her one last time. *Greta will tell her,* I thought. *Once she sees Adam, she'll know. She'll know.* And that was the thought I carried with me into the kitchen—it was the only way I'd survive.

I looked for the honey.

Paula was busy as usual preparing for the next meal service, hauling a pot of water to the ovens for a boil. The cook gathered up dirty tea towels and stuffed them into a laundry bag. "Laundry is delayed," she barked in the air.

"Yes, Cook," Paula said.

"Why is the laundry delayed?" I felt my pulse quickening.

"Everything is delayed now," Paula said. "Why does it matter?"

I looked up from my watch, pausing to think up a lie. "There are nappies from the nursery that need to be washed. What time do you think it'll be here?"

"Anytime," she said.

"An hour?" I asked, and she nodded. I had time.

Paula reached for a bowl of peeled potatoes and dumped them into her pot. "Potatoes again." She sighed when the cook left. "I'm already sick of this new menu." She pointed to the pantry. "We'll be lucky if we receive honey next week."

I didn't account for the honey to be gone. "Is there honey?" I asked, and to my relief, she said there was. "What about milk?"

Paula smiled. "For you, yes. I told you that. But not another person. There won't be enough for the children if I'm not careful." She slid a canister of powdered milk across the table where she was prepping food. "Be discreet."

"Our secret," I said, and I felt the hemlock through my

apron pocket. The only thing that could spoil my plan would be Neider.

"Herr Neider likes honigmilch too," I said, waiting to see what she'd say, and she scoffed.

"I told you, not another person. Besides, he left for Berlin for one of his investigations, not due back until tomorrow." I closed my eyes briefly. He was still gone. "The honey and the lemons are in the pantry." She put her potatoes on to boil then left for other business. "And make sure you put it all back—and remember, be sparing," she whispered on her way out.

I stirred the milk as it warmed over a medium flame, pulling the hemlock from my pocket and dunking it into the saucepan where it disappeared under a froth of creamy bubbles. A rank odor wafted up in a cloud of steam, and I was immediately reminded of when I'd tried to eat it. Ursula would never drink something that smelled. I added a heaping spoonful of honey and zested the lemon over the froth, which seemed to take care of it.

I picked out the prettiest cup Paula had in her cabinet. The milk bubbled up to the rim, looking delicious. I tossed the limp and soggy hemlock into the rubbish bin and carried the cup into the corridor, mindful to hold it steady so as not to spill a drop, when Clara breezed around the corner.

"Mmm..." she said. "Is that mine?" She reached for the cup, and I almost spilled some, trying to keep it away from her grabby hands.

"Tisk, tisk," I said, smiling. "This isn't yours."

She sulked, walking over to the table to eat an apple from the basket.

I took the lift upstairs and made my way past the nursery window. I held the cup to my nose, smelling the milk one last time before walking through the doors. "I'm back! Just needed a little nourishment," I announced.

Ursula casually looked up from her ledger as I blew gently into the cup to cool the milk down, walking strategically between the cots. I set the cup down close enough for her to reach.

I waited for her to take a sip with my back turned, closing my eyes, only to open them when I heard her sniffing. My heart pounded. "Mmm," I heard her say, followed by the glorious sound of her slurping the poison.

And I waited, making busy work folding blankets, eyeing her with side-glances as she walked over to the window to drink in peace and watch the birds. I saw her look once into the cup after downing the last sip, as if the flutter of suspicion had crept into her thoughts. She set the cup down.

"Anna?" she said, and I faced her.

"Yes?" I played with my fingers.

She felt her teeth with her tongue. "Never mind." She reached for her ledger to write a few things down, while my eyes danced over her, looking for signs of stress. "Why are you looking at me like that?"

"No reason," I said, and I thought I saw her knees buckle. I collected the soiled burping rags and cot sheets and stuffed them into a laundry bag as she unsteadily reached out for the shelf, violently knocking over glass canisters and sending them to the floor.

Crash, crash, smash!

Nurses shrieked, watching her stagger around with half-closed eyes among the shards of sparkly glass. "Get her a chair!" someone said, and the ledger slipped from Ursula's hands onto the floor, while the nurses tended to her every need.

I picked the book up casually, feeling the power of every stolen child's name listed, page after page after page. Ursula's eyes roved from side to side, and I stuffed the ledger into the laundry bag just as her eyes settled on me, a shaking finger trying to point in my direction, saying words, but it was all gibberish.

I backed up with the laundry bag, pulling the string tight. As milk foamed from the corner of her mouth, I thought of all the broken-hearted mothers whose children were stolen and felt no pity for Ursula as she lay dying, only regret it hadn't happened sooner. Matka would have said killing her slowly was the reward, and I accepted it on behalf of every mother the Reich had wronged.

"What's she saying?" a nurse asked, while Ursula gasped for words, still shaking her finger in the air.

"I'll get Frau Brack!" I said, noticing that the laundry truck had pulled up outside. The driver got out and unlatched the back, and while the nurses huddled around Ursula, I bolted from the nursery and ran downstairs with the bag.

The cook handed the kitchen laundry off to Paula near the front doors, followed by housekeeping with bags of their own. I walked outside with her like I normally would, as if nothing was wrong, smiling, with my heart racing and my armpits sweating and holding my breath.

We stood next to the laundry truck as the driver took the bags, heaving them into the back hatch. I kept turning around, looking for signs of Frau Brack, clenching the bag and waiting for my turn, while Paula tried to talk to me about a new biscuit she was making. "They need more sugar, but we're almost out and the cook doesn't like them…" she said, and the driver reached for my bag.

"Thank you," he said, heaving it behind him into a pile, and I almost collapsed again, realizing I had pulled it off. He closed up the hatch and drove away with Ursula's ledger while Paula was still talking about her new biscuits, hands on her hips, and I hadn't even taken a breath yet.

"And that's my new recipe…" She dusted her hands off, staring at me for a second or two, blinking, before walking back inside the building.

And suddenly I was standing alone near the front steps of Edelhaus in a fog of gray exhaust fumes. It had all happened so fast, so easily in the end, just like I'd imagined it last night in my room. I glanced to the upstairs windows where Ursula had been trying to call out my name, and made my way toward my escape. I was almost to the iron gates. I saw the park benches on the other side, and the pavements where I'd disappear. Pace quickening, looking over my shoulder, left and right, huffing and panting, when Neider appeared out of nowhere from the road, blocking my way out and reaching for my wrists.

"Not so fast." He yanked me toward him.

Chapter Twenty-Five

He took me around the side of the building, through a door I'd never seen, and dragged me down into the basement to his office. "I know you lied to me about your family tree." He threw me into a chair. "Turns out Herr Schmitt doesn't have a daughter named Anna. Didn't take long."

I sat up tall. "What are you—"

He slapped me across the face, his ring catching my lip as I yelped. "Now," he said as I felt my mouth for the blood. "It's time to answer some questions."

He pressed me about everything—from my accent, where I learned German, to information about my dead husband, but I refused to answer. "And to think Frau Brack asked you to join the program." He ticked his tongue, shaking his head. "Wait until she finds out you lied. Where are you from? It isn't Poland. Are you a Jew?" His finger danced over my hand, laughing as I flicked it away. "You are teasing me, no?"

I looked off to the side, eyes lazy and bored, and it sent him into a fiery fit, slamming his hand on his desk. "Look at me when I talk to you!" He caught his glass paperweight when it rolled off his stack of papers. "All that talk about a battle your husband died in. *What battle?*" he said, imitating me from one of our earlier meetings. "I knew then something wasn't right. You fooled everyone else, though. Why are you here?" I looked at him, and he smiled. "Yes… Why are you here?" he asked, sitting in his chair but still handling the paperweight. "You want me to know, don't you? You want to gloat. You think you got away with something."

Trampling above, one floor up, caused my hair to stand on end. Neider barely seemed bothered, kicking his legs up on his desk, but I was waiting for someone to burst in, finger pointing, saying I killed a nurse.

"I have all night, Fräulein," he said. "Why are you here?"

I never said a word, even when he mentioned a child, but he must have seen a glimmer in my eye because he shot up from his chair. "That's it!" he said, finger pointing. "You're here for a child?" He smiled when I shook my head.

"No, I'm not…" I kept shaking my head.

He slipped his jacket off and placed it neatly over his chair to keep it from ruffling. "I knew I'd break you." He loosened his tie next, pulling it from his neck. "Doesn't matter now. You'll be gone soon. Everyone goes to the same place." He sighed. "I do believe my questioning is done."

He reached behind my head, grabbing me forcibly by the hair and shoving his nose into the hollow of my neck.

"You've been using the goat milk soap…" he said, sliding his nose up my neck to my chin, smelling me, mouth open, lips wet. "*Ah… Ah… Ah…*"

"Get away!" I screamed, leaping from the chair with fists in the air, though I knew I couldn't fight him off. I waited for him to attack me, then something happened that took us both by surprise and drew our eyes to the ceiling. The menacing drone of RAF bombers.

One after the other they flew over the nursery, shaking the building from all directions in electrifying terror. I reached for his prized paperweight.

"Ack!" I grunted, slamming it into the side of his head, hearing a fine crack between the rumble of the planes. He dropped heavily to the floor like a bag of laundry with blood pooling from his ear, but I was already running into the corridor and looking for a way outside.

I burst into the courtyard, and Kurt caught me between the playground and his roses.

"What are you doing out here?" He gave me a shake as the planes buzzed overhead. "It's a raid!"

I pulled him toward me and talked directly into his ear. "I need your car key," I said, closing my eyes tightly, "but now it's you who needs to walk away."

I let go of him as the air-raid sirens wailed. The lights in the main building and the dormitories flicked off and the grounds turned pitch black. Nobody could see us. Only he knew I was there. He dug into his pocket and handed me the key to his car.

I pulled him toward me again, but this time for a hug, and we embraced.

"Be careful," was the last thing Kurt uttered, and then he was gone, disappearing into the shadows while I ran for the side gate to get into his car.

I sped off at an ungodly rate down the streets of Dresden, crying, tears rolling down my face and into my lap for all I'd lost and gained. Black figures lit up in flashes. *Boom! Boom! Boom!*

I swerved into the curb, crashing into a lamppost. Smoke billowed out from the bonnet. More planes! This time I heard the dreaded whistling from the bombs slicing through the air between the whirr of the sirens. I tried starting the car again, pushing on the accelerator and turning the key as the bombs closed in, with explosions drawing nearer.

I abandoned the car to jump into another one where a man sparked wires together under the steering wheel. "Get out!" he yelled, but I refused, even as he took a swipe at me.

I pulled the reichsmarks from my dress. "I'll pay you!" He immediately grabbed for it, but I held it beyond his reach. "Take me to Rabenau."

He paused. A fire erupted from a bomb-struck building behind him, and he came to his senses. "Hold on!" he said, sparking the engine to life, and we sped off, maneuvering through the throngs of people running for their lives and out of the city.

He let me out in the middle of Rabenau while it was still dark. Businesses were shuttered and nobody walked the streets. I shut the car door. "Thank you," I said, but he didn't stay around to talk and motored off.

I remembered my way from passing through the village

last time and walked down the remote country road to Greta Strohm's home, arriving after the sun had risen. I stood next to her fountain, listening to the water flow in gushes, looking at her front door. Her car was parked nearby, and an October frost dusted the boot. Out here, you'd never know Dresden had been bombed.

I walked up to her front door, straightening myself the best I could, patting back my matted hair, and dusting the dirt from my cheeks. I went to knock, and the horrendous thought of her taking the children someplace else passed through my mind. What if they weren't here?

I held my breath, lips pinched, and rapped three times, sending an echo through the courtyard. A bird chirped from the eaves, and field animals scurried into the bushes. I knocked again, holding my breath, only this time the door opened to a frightened and bewildered Greta Strohm.

"What are—" She clutched her chest through her sleeping gown. "Did anyone see you?" She yanked me inside, then peered through the window curtains.

"Nobody saw," I said.

"I told you not to come here."

"No," I said, shaking my head. "You said to disappear, but you didn't say I couldn't come here."

She argued with me over exactly what she'd said when I blurted, "Neider's dead."

"He's dead?" She blinked and blinked. "Oh, thank God."

I looked over her parlor, seeing a few toys sprawled out. Girl toys, and a baby rattle. "Are my…" I gulped, rubbing my hands nervously. "Children here?"

"They are," she said, and I finally felt myself breathe.

I followed her down the hallway to the nursery. Adam lay in his cot, happily cooing and playing with his feet in the air, while Ema sat in the far corner reading a book on the floor in her nightclothes, her body half-turned with her hair hanging long and loose, shielding her face.

Greta watched me from the doorway as I stepped into the room. "Be easy with her," she said.

"Ema." I patted my cheeks where a few tears had fallen. "Ema, my sweet girl," I said, but she barely moved. I walked closer, bending to my knees as she read her book. I swept a lock of hair behind her ear and she pulled away, shocking me breathless.

I looked her over with my hands curled up into themselves, not sure where to touch her, if she wanted to be touched. "Ema…" She turned the page of her book, and her body too a bit more. "It's me, sweet girl…" I looked to Greta.

"Did you tell her?" I asked, and she nodded. "About why she's here?" Greta nodded again, and I closed my eyes, blowing all the air from my lungs.

"Ema, darling, I tried to tell you about Frau Strohm, but I couldn't find you. It all happened so fast," I said, and I cried as I talked, the lump in my throat painfully growing. "We're safe now. We're together. And the baby…" I touched her back and she shuddered, which threw me into a fit of sobs and moans.

Greta picked me up off the floor and hugged me as I cried. "Give her time," she said. "Give her time. She's been through a lot." Greta wiped the tears from my cheeks. "As have you, Anna. As have you…"

I nodded and sniffed.

"Have patience," she said. "You only know half of what happens at Edelhaus. You may never know fully what Ema saw or experienced, but you can bet it was more than you know." I shook my head, but I knew she was right.

Ema set the book down to play with a doll on the floor, tapping her over the carpet in a pretend walk, murmuring in hushed tones, and ignoring us as we stood watching her. Greta nudged me to try again, and I stepped toward her cautiously.

"Is it all right if I sit down?" I asked, but I didn't wait for a response and sat down gingerly, crisscrossing my legs on the floor like her. "I know you're angry," I said, and her eyes shifted, and the doll froze in her hand on the floor. "It's all right to be angry. I'm angry too, but not at you. I'm angry at the Germans, the nurses, at Frau Brack. Edelhaus. The Reich." I looked up at Greta.

"You're doing fine," she mouthed, motioning with her hand for me to continue.

I took another breath.

"But Ema, I need to tell you a story." As soon as I said the words my voice wobbled and I cried into the open air. "It's about a woman from Prague. Do you remember that story?" She resumed playing with her doll. "You see, the actress, that beautiful actress from Prague, married her prince. And you were right about the devil. He showed up with an iron fist, crushed all her dreams. Until one day she found out she was having a baby…"

And I told Ema the entire story about the woman from Prague. How she had other plans, plans to save her family from the devil when he came after them, but that her prince also had plans of his own. And although each plan was different, they came from a place of good and love.

"Nothing was going to stop the woman from finding her child after she was stolen. She followed the devil all the way to Edelhaus, pretended she was one of them to gain their trust, and then she tricked them, tucking her child away someplace safe while she stayed behind to save the others." Ema's eyes shifted again. "She had a chance to steal the devil's adoption records, so that all the other children at Edelhaus would have a chance to be reunited with their real mamas and papas too…" I wiped my eyes, and Ema looked at me.

"Mama?"

"Yes, sweet girl?" I said, and she threw her arms around my neck.

"Don't let go," she said, and I sobbed into her hair.

"I won't, baby," I said. "I won't."

Chapter Twenty-Six

The war dragged on until spring, and the bombing I'd escaped from was nothing compared to the firebombing that winter—Greta was right, we were safest with her.

Greta had dismissed all her servants, and we'd become our own family, playing a game of secrecy and lies and staying hidden at all times. She was there for Adam's first steps. She was there when I helped Ema through her nightmares, and she was there for me when we heard word about Josef's death through her contacts. He'd been killed along with my cousin and Dasa's husband many months before, during a raid on the Czech Resistance one rainy night, with orders to take no prisoners. They had died like true warrior patriots, facing their enemies. I'd forgiven him and forgiven myself for being angry that he'd left us. In war, we had learned that there was no time for regret. We had to hold onto every moment we were alive and live it with love.

We never heard news about Kurt, or what happened to the rest of the staff at Edelhaus. When the liberating armies stormed the city, the Resistance descended upon the nursery to find it vacant; only the older children were left and living without supervision. But it was my hope that Kurt was able to reinvent himself among the rubble, find himself a country house where he could grow his vegetables and herbs and live in peace. He was born into the Reich, but he'd never been a Nazi.

News about Matka and Dasa never came. Greta told me to remain hopeful. "Many are displaced," she said. "You must also give this time."

A program had been set in motion by the liberators to find the stolen children, but everyone was trying to find someone. Ursula's ledger had records on thousands of children, and those were just the ones that had passed through the doors at Edelhaus.

When it was safe for us to return to Tabor, we said our goodbyes at the train station. We'd heard of reprisals against the Germans—ordinary people, some who were part of the Party, as well as those who were not. Women and children were not spared. I pinned tags to the children's clothes and my dress while standing on the platform. *Czech.*

Greta kissed Ema and Adam, but they were too young to understand and had no idea what she'd really done for us and the risks she'd taken. "Thank you," I said, and we embraced moments before she walked away with a handkerchief to her eyes, too choked up to say anything.

That was the last I saw of Greta Strohm, walking down the platform through a puff of steam.

Ema played with the tag I had pinned to her shirt. "Tell nobody where we've been," I whispered, knowing if anyone found out she'd been in a German nursery, she'd be shunned the rest of her life. "Ever." She let go of the tag, leaving it to hang, and I wondered if the day would ever come when we didn't have something to hide.

I tugged on Ema's hand and we boarded the crowded train with Adam on my hip. Strangers eyed us in our seats as I recited Czech fairy tales to the children, petting Ema's head in my lap and stroking Adam's cheek. Nobody bothered to whisper their thoughts. If someone thought you were German, they pulled you from the train. But it was clear, among the returning half-dead, our clothes said enough without our Czech tags. Our bones said enough.

Nothing could have prepared me for the devastation that was waiting for us, and I thought I'd already seen it all. Entire villages had been reduced to piles of rubble: there were craters instead of buildings and abandoned military vehicles lay burned in the streams and in the middle of farmland. Long lines of homeless families walked the roads for shelter, belongings tied to their backs, and women with babies as thin as string beans—the Germans had indeed picked the best meat for themselves and left us a ruin, just like Tomas had said they would, but there were no victors resting in the shade to talk about it. Only the ghosts who'd remained and the ones who'd returned, and we were still too stunned to talk.

The train pulled into Tabor on a Sunday in June, nearly one year to the date from when the Brown Sister visited Dasa. The Nazi Party banners were gone—burned, torn, I didn't know, but shame shrouded those who had once hung them.

I paid for a ride that brought us to my road, letting us out at the corner where all the neighbors could see.

Anna had come back.

I held Adam tight against my hip, and held Ema's hand, and as we approached the old farmhouse in Tabor that used to be ours, I wondered if it still was. A honeyed breeze blew through the linden trees, warm and sweet, without memory of the war. Not like the soil, the ground, where the memories lay hidden, scars to be unearthed later.

I saw my old car parked out front, and I stopped. "Ema, sweet girl," I said, and she looked up, but I wasn't sure what to say, suddenly overwhelmed with the thought that nobody else had come back. That we were the only ones left, and Mrs. Lange and her husband had settled into our home and made it theirs, instead of returning my possessions after the war like she'd promised.

"No matter what happens," I finally said, "we will always be together." I kissed Adam's cheek, and when I looked at him, I saw Dasa's eyes and I started to cry. "Let's go," I said, and we walked up to the door, but it flew open with a bang and Matka ran out, screaming my name with her arms open to scoop Ema up.

I collapsed to my knees, weeping in my hand with the baby still on my hip, when Dasa and her girls came out next. Dasa kept asking me over and over again if Adam was her baby, as if she couldn't believe it, and when I told her he was, she crumpled into a pool of gut-wrenching moans with her hands outstretched for her son, a baby who'd grown into a boy.

I looked toward the sky, blowing a tearful kiss to my husband. I was broken—we were broken—and what remained of our family was now on their knees in the dirt. But like so many, we'd been left to pick through the fragments of what once was, to somehow, someway, find the strength to live again, and begin a new story.

This one about the Czech survivors—the mothers from Tabor.

Author's Note

Throughout World War II, the Third Reich stole thousands of Aryan-looking children from occupied countries, gave them new identities, and then used them to repopulate their idea of the master race. They lied to the children, told them their parents had stolen them from Germany and that they were victims of the inferiors. Many of these children were taken from orphanages, while many others were simply snatched from their mothers' arms. Some returned to their parents after the war as strangers, having forgotten their native languages and who they were. Most never made it home.

This story is a work of fiction, but the experiences and events in this novel were inspired by survivor interviews and diaries, and also by the reports written by tracing agents after the war. While writing this book, I found out more than I wanted to know about the Lebensborn program. Every time I thought I'd learned every awful truth, another mind-blowing aspect of it would pop up.

Many of the nurseries didn't survive the war, and most were never "officially" on paper to begin with because of unfavorable public opinion.

Because of the Reich's secrets and lies, we may never know the exact number of children who were stolen, but it is upwards of 200,000. Many were sent to nurseries and adopted, others who didn't pass the Reich's rigid tests or refused to Germanize (a lot of the older kids knew their roots and refused to be indoctrinated) were sent to camps and executed. Some of the stolen children, now in their eighties, recently sued Germany for their pain and suffering —but lost their legal case.

I stumbled upon the kidnapping campaign while doing research for *The Girls from the Beach*. My thoughts went straight to the mothers. I don't know one mother who wouldn't go to the ends of the earth to find her child, though during the war this would have been extremely difficult for many reasons. But what if one of them was able to go all the way and break into one of the nurseries? Would she be able to steal her child back?

This was the story I wanted to write.

Thank you for choosing to read *A Child for the Reich*. If you enjoyed this story and fell in love with my heroine mothers, Anna, Dasa, and Matka, please consider leaving a review with Amazon, or with the retailer you bought this book from. I also invite you to check out my other books, *The Girls from the Beach*, *The Girl from Vichy*, and *The Girl I Left Behind*.

Acknowledgments

I'd like to thank Charlotte Ledger at HarperCollins UK and the fantastic team at One More Chapter for giving this novel a home. Thank you to my agent Kate Nash, because without her this book would still be on my hard drive. I'd also like to thank Paula Butterfield for always reading my first drafts and providing the best feedback. Thank you, Carmen Radtke, for helping me with the name Edelhaus, which wasn't as easy as you might think. Every writer needs a tribe, and I have the most supportive writing tribe ever: Aimee Brown, Sandy Barker, Fiona Leitch, Nina Kaye, Terry Lynn Thomas, Olivia Lara, and Casey King. Thank you to my family, and especially my husband Matt and my two kids, Zane and Drew, for their endless support. Last but not least, thank you to the readers out there who have bought and enjoyed my books.

ONE MORE CHAPTER

One More Chapter is an award-winning global division of HarperCollins.

Sign up to our newsletter to get our latest eBook deals and stay up to date with our weekly Book Club!
<u>Subscribe here.</u>

Meet the team at
<u>www.onemorechapter.com</u>

Follow us!

@OneMoreChapter_

@OneMoreChapter

@onemorechapterhc

Do you write unputdownable fiction?
We love to hear from new voices.
Find out how to submit your novel at
<u>www.onemorechapter.com/submissions</u>

doubt and the others saw. I cleared my throat again. "People associated with the nursery program will be at Fischer's party," I said. "I'm going to find out where the nursery is and apply for employment. Pretend I'm one of them." I shifted in my dress.

"And after the party, even if you are successful and find the information you need, how will you enter Germany?" he asked. "You'll need more than a nice dress to get past the checkpoints. The documents you showed me say you're Czech."

"Can you get me a German Kennkarte?" I reached for him but stopped short from touching his sleeve. "If anyone can get me fake documents, it has to be the Czech Resistance." I pulled my documents back out of my handbag. "Use my photo—"

"It's not cheap," he said as I pushed my documents at him, but he wouldn't take them. "Do you have money?"

I felt my wedding band, cool and small and sliding around in my undergarments.

"Money is one thing we can't help you with—" He looked when someone called his name and I thought he might leave.

"Wait!" I reached down the front of my dress for my wedding band. "Here."

Radek examined my wedding band, pressing it between his calloused fingers in the dim light before looking back up. "You are sure?"

"Yes," I said, and he finally took my documents from me, which was a great relief.

"I told you earlier that I knew your husband," he said.